Beyond the Arch

Beyond the Arch

David Evered

Matador
9 Priory Business Park,
Wistow Road, Kibworth Beauchamp,
Leicestershire. LE8 0RX
Tel: 0116 279 2299
Email: books@troubador.co.uk
Web: www.troubador.co.uk/matador
Twitter: @matadorbooks

ISBN 978 1788039 406

British Library Cataloguing in Publication Data.
A catalogue record for this book is available from the British Library.

Printed and bound in Great Britain by 4edge Limited
Typeset in 11pt Adobe Garamond Pro by Troubador Publishing Ltd, Leicester, UK

Matador is an imprint of Troubador Publishing Ltd

For the people of Tyneside – with affection

About the Author

David Evered's professional career was in academic medicine and research. He has been a consultant physician in Newcastle Upon Tyne, the Deputy Head of the UK Medical Research Council, a Special Adviser to the International Agency for Research on Cancer (WHO – Lyon) and a Trustee of Macmillan Cancer Support. He has lived in Newcastle, London and France and is now retired. He and his wife live in rural West Berkshire. This is his first work of fiction.

All experience is an arch wherethro'
Gleams that untravell'd world whose margin fades
Forever and forever when I move.

Alfred Tennyson – Ulysses

In order to arrive at what you do not know
You must go by a way which is the way of ignorance.
In order to possess what you do not possess
You must go by the way of dispossession.
In order to arrive at what you are not
You must go through the way in which you are not.

T S Eliot – East Coker

1

Ann's parting injunction as he had left for work that morning could not have been clearer. Under no circumstances should he be late for the dinner party she had arranged. Peter reached the street and glanced at his watch. He was now irretrievably late. He hesitated, wondering if he should return to his office and call but decided that this would only delay him further. He sat anxiously on the edge of his seat in the bus, impotently willing it forward, as it edged through the evening traffic. Waiting on the rear platform as it reached his stop, he looked once more at his watch. Already twenty minutes late, he suddenly remembered Ann had asked him to drop into the off-licence on his way home. What the hell was it – sherry, gin or wine or was it more tonic that was needed? It would be best to cover all bases by stocking up on the lot. He smiled inwardly for a moment at the thought of Ann trying to maintain the party with inadequate supplies of alcohol, particularly with Andrew present.

He opened the door as quietly as was consistent with avoiding the accusation that he was creeping in. As he had anticipated, Ann was in the hallway to meet him. 'Wherever have you been?' she muttered. 'They've been here almost half an hour. It's not a good start to a dinner party.'

'I'm sorry, I was just leaving when a client with pressing marital problems came in'. Peter was a solicitor. 'It took some time to sort things out. She was extremely distressed, custody problems.'

'You could have phoned – it's always possible to phone.'

'I know, but I was so involved and only realised how late it was after I'd left. I felt it would be better to hurry home after getting the drinks you asked me to buy rather than spend time looking for a call box. You know how often they're out of action.' He reflected that minor decisions which seemed eminently reasonable at the time frequently sounded less than adequate when recounted later.

'I am sure you could have made time. You'd better come through or they'll be wondering what we're doing out here.'

'Ah, the prodigal or is it the reprobate?' asked Andrew.

'Probably both, but this prodigal is not returning empty-handed,' said Peter as he held his purchases up. He looked around at the four guests. He knew Andrew and Sue Hepscott well. They lived in the flat below. Andrew was a lecturer in economics at the local tertiary college and Sue was a primary school teacher who worked four days a week and devoted the remaining day to voluntary work in a hospice shop. Peter enjoyed their company although there was a certain antipathy between Andrew and Ann which sprang from widely differing political and social views. He had known them for a year or so before he and Ann had married. Andrew, in particular, was given to advancing challenging and, at times, anarchic views. Ann was prone to remark that he reminded her of his old friend from Cambridge, Michael Rattray, a serious handicap. Sue shared her husband's radical political views but was more tolerant and less outspoken. She was generally happy to exchange simple domestic trivia on social occasions. The other two guests were Adrian and Blanche Rogan, an accountant and his wife, whom they had met playing tennis at the local club. They had found them consistently even-tempered and amiable and they had been invited to establish closer social contact.

Peter greeted the four and tried to excuse his late arrival in a sentence. It was evident that his absence had provided a focus for discussion during the preceding thirty minutes. He seated himself on the settee next to Blanche and found he was being pressed for more details of the problem which had detained him than he was prepared to divulge. He disliked discussing the law socially except in the most general terms and then would do so only under duress. She was unusually persistent and it became clear that their earlier conversation, in his absence, had offered endless opportunities for speculation. The questioning became progressively more probing and the others started to listen with a level of attention which he found disconcerting. He tried to explain the legal problems relating to custody disputes in simple and comprehensible terms, although they were complicated in this instance as the principal residences of the now separated parents were in separate jurisdictions. He was just finishing his account when Ann opined that this was not a suitable topic for a dinner party and announced that the meal was ready. Peter was relieved when Andrew insisted he had only been discussing his work under pressure from the others and that he should be permitted to leave the cares of his work behind him. His relief, however, was lessened by the recognition that support from this quarter was not necessarily to his credit in domestic disagreements.

The party moved to the dining room while Peter collected discarded glasses and placed them in the kitchen before returning with two bottles of wine. Ann was completing the seating arrangements, male and female alternately and no husband sitting next to his wife. The conversation drifted easily, if haphazardly, from one topic to another. The assassination of Martin Luther King, the terrorist attacks by the Baader-Meinhof gang, student unrest in Paris and David Bowie's film "2001 – A space odyssey" were all touched on and discarded.

The dinner was almost over when they were interrupted by the telephone. Peter left to answer it. He was about to return ten minutes later as the others were entering the lounge for coffee. Ann had come out as she heard the call finish. 'You were a long time. Why didn't you ask whomever it was to call back tomorrow?'

'It wasn't the sort of call I could cut short. It was Jenny. Your father's been admitted to hospital and they're not too sure what it is. They think it's some sort of a heart attack and that's on top of his chest problems.'

'Oh, my God.' Ann sat down. 'How bad is it? Should we go?'

'The hospital apparently said that there's no immediate cause for concern but he's quite ill and they cannot be certain how things will progress over the next few days. It occurred to me while we were talking that it would be a good idea if we both went up there tomorrow as it's Saturday. I told Jenny we would go.'

Anne hesitated for a moment. 'Yes, we should. Could you manage that?'

'I can get John to deal with any urgent problems over the weekend.'

'Go in and explain to the others but don't let them feel that they have to go. I just need a little time to collect myself before I join them again.'

He went through to the lounge. 'It was Ann's sister, Jenny, who has just phoned.' he said. 'Their father's had a heart attack. It seems to be fairly serious, particularly as he has chronic chest problems but we really don't know much more at present.'

'I'm so sorry,' said Adrian. 'Where is he in hospital?' he asked Ann as she followed Peter back into the lounge.

'In Newcastle.'

'Is it Upon Tyne or Under Lyme?' asked Sue.

'Oh, it's Upon Tyne.'

'I didn't know your parents lived there,' said Andrew. 'I don't remember you talking much about them. In fact, you've kept them very dark. Now Peter, over there, we know about his parents. He has very proper parents – standard issue of two who live in Surbiton or Cheam or along one of the more salubrious suburban lines that run out of Waterloo.'

'My family have always lived in the north-east and one doesn't talk much about parents, I guess, because we all have them.'

'I suppose I might have guessed where you came from

– you once told me your maiden name was Robson and historically they were border raiders, were they not?'

Ann smiled. 'Yes, that's right.'

'Did you collect Peter on a border raid?'

'Oh no, he required a well-thought out strategy and a prolonged attack.'

'Are you going up there?'

'Yes, Peter suggested we should go tomorrow and as we have a bank holiday on Monday we shan't have to hurry unduly to get back. He says he can stay until Tuesday morning as he has no major commitments that day.'

'I'm so sorry,' said Sue. 'Would you like us to go?'

'No, no, I should prefer you to stay – it would be a distraction. It's a long time since I was last in the north-east.'

'I've never been to that part of the country,' said Adrian 'but I'm told that the countryside is magnificent.'

'I've not been home for a long time. The last time was eight years ago, immediately after I'd graduated. If I'm honest, I have to admit I was glad to get away.'

'Why was that?' He paused before continuing. 'Look, I'm sorry, I'm probing and you would probably prefer not to talk about it just now.'

'No, it's alright.' She hesitated. 'It's always been something I've felt uneasy about and perhaps a bit guilty as well. I always felt that the north-east would restrict and limit my horizons and ambitions. That's why I left and came south, first to university and then, after I graduated, I stayed. The job opportunities were here. My lasting memories of the city, or at least of the part where we lived, were of a rather cheerless world. My father was an amazing man but he lost his job as shipbuilding declined and joined so many others in their fifties for whom unemployment unavoidably became a way of life. It was mainly very drab and grey but there was a bright and unreal (and sometimes surreal) night life dominated by a tinsel clubland, but that was never for us. The world of "you've never had it so good" never seemed to quite make it to Tyneside. People were always trying to be seen to be enjoying themselves with loud and sometimes drunken conviviality. You're right, the countryside is magnificent, but for most of the time it was almost as remote to us as London. It really didn't impinge on our lives in the city. Our only experience of the countryside and the coast was on our annual fortnight's summer holiday.'

Peter walked over and put his arm around Ann. 'I've only been there once,' he added. 'That was after Ann had left but before we'd met. It has some wonderful and very grand early nineteenth century architecture.'

'How did you meet then?'

'Oh, Ann was working for a television company, as she still is, and living in a flat close to the one I shared with a friend. We met at a party.'

Andrew had been silent for some time but said quietly, 'You know, I taught in Newcastle for three years. I saw it rather more positively but, I acknowledge, that was with the eyes of an outsider. I never thought it was sad. It seemed to be very much a place of people, of warm, active, vibrant and occasionally violent people with a pride in their own traditions, songs, brown ale, football and their almost, at times, incomprehensible language. But Geordieland has a socially stable, independently-minded and loyal community which has grown up there. It's sad that too many of the local people, or at least its most vigorous members, leave. Ann has left as she found her prospects too limited and sadly those who leave rarely return or discuss their home. As for the incomers: "You're being moved to Newcastle? Where's that? My God, anywhere but there" the clipped middle-class accents proclaim in voices in which both astonishment and pity can be heard.'

'There's something in that,' concluded Ann. 'But perhaps we should have this conversation another time.'

'I suppose that rather illustrates my point,' Andrew said emphatically. He was nudged by Sue and added in a more conciliatory tone, 'I'm sorry. Of course, you'll want to change the subject in the light of the reasons for your visit tomorrow.'

Peter relaxed in his chair. Andrew sober or semi-sober could be expected to socialise politely; after drinking, such expectations were often hopelessly optimistic. He had managed to terminate one dinner party in a dramatic manner and his presence was generally only acceptable to Ann in the presence of Sue. The whisky glasses were refilled. Peter wondered if he should refill Andrew's but felt that such an omission would be too conspicuous. He was relieved and reassured by Andrew's wink as he poured him only a modest tot.

'No, it's alright,' said Ann. 'I might have added that opportunities for women are more limited in the north. The spirit of Andy Capp still persists.'

Ann rarely spoke of her family or her upbringing even when she and Peter were alone. He knew she had spent her childhood in a small terraced house and that her horizons had been restricted by the steep banks of the Tyne. The sad splendour of the Cheviots and the broad sweep of the coastline had been as inaccessible to her as they had to him as a child in Surrey. Peter had never met Ann's parents, although he had tried to understand the blow it must have been to the family when her father had been made redundant and had joined so many other middle-aged men with little prospect of finding another job.

'So you decided to make a break for freedom,' said Andrew. 'From my experience in the north-east it was brave to take such a step away from the tight bonds of family which are so characteristic of Tyneside.'

'Yes, you could look at it that way but again, if I'm honest, I would have to admit that my motives were largely selfish, as I said earlier.'

'You may be being over hard on yourself. You had the motivation and the drive to grasp the opportunity to manage and take control of your own life.'

'You're right,' said Peter anxious to channel the conversation into other waters. 'Ann did that. None of the rest of us have taken control over our own lives and destinies in such a decisive manner. Most of us remain enclosed and limited by our childhood environment and upbringing and simply don't have the drive or initiative to cast off the shackles which constrain us. I was brought up in an irremediably middle-class environment where I and my peers all moved seamlessly from school to national service to university to a respectable profession, well mostly respectable,' he smiled, 'if you include the law in that category, and then on to marriage. Perhaps society should provide us all with opportunities to develop more freely and we should have the courage to take them.'

'Right, Peter Bowman, that's all very well but how would you develop given free range?' asked Andrew.

'I suppose I rather walked into that challenge! I'm uncertain in the absence of opportunity but possibly society might or should be more accepting of changes in one's occupational, social and emotional life.'

'But why do you think society should offer you opportunities? If you feel your life is incomplete or unchallenging – should you not create your own as Ann has done? We've never had so much freedom and so many opportunities to break out. We were discussing student unrest and the extreme activities of the Baader-Meinhof gang over dinner. This is a time of revolution and change – or at least a time to challenge the certainties of our everyday worlds. There are opportunities if you look around you. I'm not suggesting you become a terrorist but why should students have all the fun? Most of us are simply too content with the trivialities of our lives. Would you, would any of us, have the confidence to manage an ever-changing life and the inevitable emotional and economic uncertainties which would accompany such a change? Could you, or any of us, really adapt to a free-living, free-ranging lifestyle? Would we not all soon hanker after a life of stability and certainty?'

'I think Andrew's got it right,' said Ann. She turned to Sue, 'These men do nothing but dream from the security of their own homes. Peter cannot even say what he might do if the world were his oyster.'

'I find it difficult to imagine why you would want to

change,' said Blanche. 'Solicitor, lecturer, accountant. Aren't you satisfied with the lives you have?'

It looked once more as if Andrew might rise but Peter forestalled him by saying, 'Perhaps you're right, and that is why we sit and talk interminably but never leave the comfort of our centrally-heated caves.'

'I guess you're right,' said Andrew.

'I think we should go at this point,' said Sue, 'particularly if these two are travelling to Newcastle tomorrow.'

* * *

Peter went across to Ann after their guests had left and put his arms around her. 'I think it was quite brave of you to be as open as you were.'

'Well, in a way it was an act of confession. It was something which I should have shared more freely with you before now and it's certainly something that I should have acted on. I do feel guilty. I've been away from Mum and Dad for so long. And I'm nervous about tomorrow. It's a long time since I've been home.'

'I know, but I'm coming too – and I shall be interested to see Newcastle again and to meet your family.'

Later, while they were clearing up, Ann turned to him. 'Thinking about Andrew's challenge, would you really want to head off in another direction?'

'Perhaps. I've always thought that I might go away and write, but this is probably no more than the idle pipe dream of a man trapped in the hinterland between youth and middle age.'

'Surely that is something you could do in the evenings or at weekends?'

'I'm sure that's true, but we are too comfortable now and I'm not certain that I have either the energy or the drive to do that. I also don't know if I have the talent. I, or anyone, would need to be strongly motivated and single-minded to change career at my age. One would probably have to adapt to a reduced standard of living, accept the middle-class astonishment of friends and after all that, very possibly, discover that one did not have the ability to cut the mustard in a parallel life. It's only too easy to have fantasies of a different, more stimulating, more exciting life in another environment and assume that this would ineluctably lead to an expansion of one's mind and a broadening of one's horizons. The reality is almost certainly different and more mundane. Sadly, it's too hard for most of us to relinquish deliberately and consciously our small achievements, our material acquisitions and a lifestyle to which most members of the great British bourgeoisie aspire.'

'Don't use that terrible phrase.'

Peter laughed. 'Sorry – "I only do it to annoy because I know it teases" to misquote the duchess in Alice in Wonderland. Ultimately, I find the thought of a group of men in their mid-thirties kicking over the traces and adopting Bohemian lifestyles unutterably comic. I cannot take my own fantasies very seriously and neither should you. I find it equally difficult to view my current life at work and at home without seeing certain absurdities in our pretensions and vanities. Perhaps we should go to bed as we have to leave early tomorrow, before there is any risk of my starting to believe what I say!'

Ann looked at him for some time. 'There are some times when I really don't understand you.'

'Well, that would make a good line to deliver to some bimbo! My wife simply doesn't understand me!'

'Oh, for God's sake, be serious! I don't know how you can be so flippant at times and yet take so much of your job so seriously.'

'I'll tell you all about it some other time, but now to bed.'

2

'We used to travel a lot by train after the war when I was a kid,' said Peter. 'The first thing I would do in the compartments in the old third-class carriages was to walk round and look at the five pictures above the seats. The only view I can remember now was that one, perhaps because it was there more often than any other.' Peter indicated the view from the Durham viaduct of the cathedral and the blackened massif of the Norman castle on the promontory surrounded on three sides by the river. 'The view's better in the sun,' he said. They took in the sight through relentless rain.

'You might well have known that view better than I did. I'd never even been to Durham until an uncle took me there for a day when I was fifteen.'

They travelled on in silence and shortly they were passing through Gateshead. 'Does this feel like a homecoming?'

'No, too much has changed.'

'What has changed?'

'Almost everything. I have, and just look at the city. I was told that when Queen Victoria passed through on her rail journeys to Balmoral, she always instructed John Brown to lower the blinds so she wouldn't have to see the dirty little houses by the river. Newcastle has changed though,' she added as they crossed the Tyne and gazed at the new pallid concrete structures rising behind the old buildings on the Quayside. Already some of the newer buildings were starting to exhibit stains resulting from inadequate drainage of roofs and the grime produced by the industrial and domestic effluent of a thousand chimneys. Paradoxically, some of the older buildings looked startlingly clean following recent sandblasting.

Peter looked across at Ann, uncertain of her reactions. This journey was opening a window into a hidden part of her life which he had never known except through the occasional light-hearted anecdote. Her confession the previous evening had been uncharacteristic. Previously, probing on his part had always been rebuffed or evaded gently but firmly. He had often felt uneasy that such a major element of her history remained closed to him. The ready acceptance of his offer to accompany her would impart a glimpse of that past.

They pulled into the station. They reserved a room at the Station Hotel and then hired a taxi to take them to Ann's parents' flat. She leaned forward to the driver. 'Will you take us out along Scotswood Road, and then turn up to cross over Elswick Road and along Hartington Road to the Westgate Road?'

'That's an odd way to Cowgate, but still if that's what you want.' The cabbie shrugged his shoulders.

She turned to Peter. 'I'll show you where they lived before they were re-housed – where we all lived when Jenny and I were kids. Good God, look at the flats!' Much of that part of the city was changing out of all recognition. Many of the rows of small brick houses stacked tightly together on the steep northern bank of the Tyne had gone. Tower blocks stood at regular intervals, some decorated by fading coloured panels. They were separated by areas of scrubby turf littered with half bricks, broken glass and the rusting skeletons of abandoned vehicles. 'I don't believe it! Is this really Scotswood Road?'

'Yes. Sometime since you were here then?' asked the driver.

'Eight years.'

'You'll see some changes then.'

'I'll show you where we lived. I just need to get my bearings. It's so changed but it must have been somewhere near here.' The car swung up the hill and crossed Elswick Road, where much of the old industrial era city could be seen, and then into Hartington Road. Ann pointed. 'That was our house and behind is where we played in the back lanes.'

Peter had known from his earlier visit to the city that it must have been in such an area that Ann had grown up and that it represented an ineradicable element of her background. It had been the hard and ambitious edge of her personality which had driven her to leave totally and irrevocably. She had suppressed her Geordie accent and severed all links other than those with her closest family, and even those had become very limited.

They left the small terraces and travelled through a more affluent residential area to reach a new apartment block which had the immutable uniformity and style of a municipal development. Ann's parents' flat was on the third floor. Her mother was short and thin almost to the point of being cadaveric in appearance. Her breathing was clearly audible and she had to purse her lips to exhale. Despite the warmth of the day she was wearing a hand-knitted cardigan which might have been the same one she had been wearing the day that Ann had left many years before.

She looked at her daughter for a few moments. 'You're a grand lass now but it's been a long time.'

Ann choked and said, 'Yes, I know. This is Peter.'

Peter leaned forward and kissed the old woman gently – 'I am sorry we've not met before.'

Ann squeezed her husband's arm. It was clear that he had touched the right note. 'I'm so sorry that I've not been back before but life has always seemed to be so busy.'

'I'm sorry too, but come on in. You'll be wanting a cup of tea. Your Dad's not too good. They say it's his heart and you know he's always had a weak chest. He's in the General Hospital, that's what they call it now, the old Wingrove. We can go up and see him shortly.'

'Where's Jenny?'

'She's out. She'll be back soon.'

'Things have changed, haven't they?'

'In every way. It's been a long time. It's nearly four years since you married, isn't it? I was sorry you got married so quickly. I should have liked to have seen London again. I've only been there twice. The first time was on our honeymoon when we had a weekend in London. We've been in this flat for three years now. It's much warmer than the old house but folks are not so neighbourly as they were.'

'When was the last time you saw London, Mrs Robson?' asked Peter.

'I went when Ann's Dad went up for the cup final. My sister looked after Ann and Jenny for the weekend. That was nearly fifteen years ago and, please, do call me Peg.'

'Perhaps you'll come back sometime and stay with us.'

'Aye, if I'm asked.'

'You will be.'

'Perhaps we should go up to the hospital,' suggested Ann. 'Peter can get us a taxi.'

'Oh no,' said her mother. 'He would have to go out to a call box and most of the time they're broken. The rain has stopped. The bus will do.'

* * *

They left the bus a hundred yards from the hospital. Peter took Peggy's arm. Ann lingered behind absorbing the contrasting sights of the city in the pale evening sun. The silent, shuttered suburban shops provided a backdrop to the glittering stream of vehicles returning from various Saturday afternoon amusements in the countryside to the west. She appeared spellbound by the sights, sounds and smells; part forgotten, part suppressed and part remembered. Bright new illuminated signs shone out from the older stone buildings contrasting with newer structures brashly rendered in contrasting colours. She stopped to gaze at the large brick building opposite the hospital which exhibited the various phases of its evolution from cinema to dance hall to bingo palace. It was like looking through a kaleidoscope turned through a small angle – sufficient to distort and add colour to the older patterns without destroying their fundamental entity. They approached a building on the hospital site which had neither changed nor improved with time, a relic of the old Poor Law hospital. The haphazard and untidy array of buildings stretching across the site from road to cemetery appeared unwelcoming and cold.

The ward came as no real surprise to Ann. It was depressingly similar to the one which she had visited unwillingly and repeatedly as a child after her grandfather had suffered a stroke. Her mother led them to her father's bed. He was asleep. She could see he had gained a great deal of weight. He lay propped up on four pillows breathing stertorously, a cyanotic tongue protruding from his suffused and plethoric face. They sat around the bed and waited, speaking occasionally in subdued voices.

'What do the doctors say about him?' asked Ann quietly.

'I'm not sure but the sister says that he's not too good.'

'But haven't you spoken to the doctor?'

'Oh no, he always looks much too busy. The sister tells me everything.'

'Well, I think we should talk to the doctor. You never know what might be happening. You come with me, Peter.'

They made their way to the small ward office to ask if they might have a word with the doctor. They found the house physician in the sister's office drinking coffee and were shown into a small room set aside for relatives. They sat facing the young doctor.

'You must be Mr Robson's daughter. He has told me a lot about you.'

'Why is that?' asked Ann quickly and defensively.

'No particular reason, he just likes to talk. He was

obviously a very sociable man. But he is very ill now. He's had chest problems for many years, as you know, and these have begun to affect his heart. He's now in heart failure. He's getting all the treatment we can give him and that makes him somewhat more comfortable but this is doing no more than delaying the progression of the heart failure.'

'But there must be something else you can do. You can't just sit there and do nothing.'

'We're not doing nothing. We're doing all we can and we are making your father comfortable.'

'Perhaps you should have another opinion, a private opinion.'

'We could, of course, if you wished, but I would suggest that no private opinion would be of any greater value than the medical attention which your father already has from Dr Tunstall, the consultant, and the rest of us. Sadly, this is all too common a clinical situation.'

'But neither you nor any consultant can always be right.'

'No, of course not. We're not God, but that's also the reason that we must sometimes acknowledge that the remedy for some conditions is beyond our competence or that of anyone else and beyond the reach of modern medicine.'

'I must do something,' said Ann suddenly, sounding small and helpless. 'Surely I could arrange a private room for him?'

'You could, but frankly I don't think he would appreciate that. He enjoys the company of others in the ward and you would deny him much of that if he were to be on his own. Can I gently suggest that now you're here you give him some of your time and, if you are able to do so, delay your return to London for a few days?'

'I suppose you're right, but I should have liked to do something – well thank you,' she said a little curtly and left to return to the ward.

Peter lingered for a moment to say, 'Thank you for what you are doing. It is appreciated. She's upset. She's not seen her father for a long time.'

'I understand – but I do know from talking to him that he would welcome it if your wife could stay in the north-east for a little longer and visit him each day. I believe there's a lot of catching up to do.'

They returned to the ward and re-joined Ann's mother who was holding her husband's hand. He had just awakened and looked up with considerable pleasure as they approached.

'I'd not known that you were coming back after so long. Peg just told me.' Even short periods of conversation were made difficult by the old man's breathlessness and he was now wheezing audibly. 'Come and tell me about your life. There must be a lot to hear.'

'First tell me how you are, Dad.'

'Getting worse. These hospitals, they're a bloody death trap.' He grinned. 'Don't fret – at my age it's a way of life in a manner of speaking. I want to hear all about you and Peter. As you can see, it's easier for me to listen than talk.'

Ann visibly relaxed, kissed her father and introduced Peter. Then, with a spontaneity that had been absent from her conversation earlier, she described the life she had been leading in London since obtaining her English degree at Royal Holloway College. Peter was surprised at the ease with which she was able to describe her career in simple and direct terms – the appointment as an archivist and researcher at the BBC and then the recent move to London Weekend Television as a production assistant with some public relations responsibilities. Her descriptions of some of the work and her portrayals of some of the celebrities and the over-inflated egos with which she had to deal entertained her parents. It helped establish a rapport with her mother which previously had been absent. It also provided some compensation for her failure to translate her belated filial concern into action which she felt had been frustrated by the young doctor. The small group around the bed was surprisingly animated by contrast with the other family groups dutifully performing the melancholy rites of hospital visiting in almost complete and reverential silence.

They returned to the flat to be greeted by Jenny. Ann's sister was her junior by seven years. She was taller than Ann with long straight fair hair which might have been described as ash blonde but which she referred to as pale mouse. The slim face was decorated by a pair of gold wire-rimmed spectacles which might have portrayed a degree of solemnity but any such impression was totally undermined by the persistent laughter which emanated from her lips. She had once stayed in their London flat for a week. Her improvidence had nearly driven her highly organised older sister to despair but her sense of the comic had struck a chord with Peter. Jenny had been a postgraduate student in English in Newcastle and had submitted her master's thesis a few weeks earlier. Her future career was uncertain.

Peter and Ann arranged to have dinner that evening with

Jenny at a small Italian restaurant close to their hotel but Peg had resisted all pressure to join them. The atmosphere was restrained. Ann clearly felt unhappy and guilty at only returning to the family when her father was so ill. It had not been possible to expiate the guilt by purchasing better medical care for her father and she was concerned that she had been deterred too easily from doing so by a young doctor imbued with what she saw as immature idealism. She had desisted from pressing the point further as she had sensed intuitively, and correctly, that Peter was in sympathy with the doctor's views. Anxious to atone for her failures, she determined to pursue the possibilities further the following day in Peter's absence. She resolved to spend a large part of the Bank Holiday Monday alone with her parents and to spend the remainder of the week in the north-east. She suggested to Peter that he might hire a car and explore the Northumberland coastline on the following day as the weather was now set fair. Peter offered some nominal resistance to this suggestion but was speedily overruled. Privately he was pleased to have a day for leisure and reflection. It was decided that he should return to London on the Tuesday and that Ann would stay in the flat for the remainder of the week to see more of her father. Jenny had an interview with a publishing house in London a fortnight later for a possible job now that her postgraduate course had finished and she would accompany her sister back to London.

3

Peter was awake early on the Bank Holiday Monday. After driving Ann to her parents' flat, he headed for the Great North Road with a sense of release. He drove fast and with some abandon across the wide upland fields with distant views of the Cheviots and as he did so the sun emerged from light cloud cover. Half an hour later, the massive towers and outer bailey of Alnwick Castle came into sight. He crossed the Aln and, turning the car towards the coast, drove more slowly to the fishing village of Craster and parked by the quayside. On leaving the car, he was immediately overwhelmed by the smell of kippers emanating from the smokehouse. He walked north along the coastal path towards the jagged, upraised fingers of the ruins of Dunstanburgh Castle on its promontory overlooking the North Sea. Standing in the heart of the old fortress in the mid-morning sun, he quietly absorbed his surroundings, refreshing the memories of his previous visit. He rotated slowly through three hundred and sixty degrees taking in the great southern curtain wall terminating at its western end in the monumental drums of the gatehouse, the square northern Lilburn Tower and the gentle slope of the soft moss-interwoven grass of the main ward leading to the cliff edge. He made his way slowly down, stopping close to the seaward point of the lime-stained dolerite cliff which marks the point where the Whin Sill meets the North Sea. He looked down into the rumbling churn below funnelling the spray high into the air. The ever-changing patterns of the plumes of water and surf held his gaze for several minutes and then, stepping back a few paces, he lay on the grass in the sun and re-ran the film clip of the previous forty-eight hours in his mind. The office seemed a hemisphere away. A number of thoughts disquieted him. Ann's sensitivities and vulnerabilities had been exposed to him more starkly than ever before. Previously these had been hidden by her protective and often impenetrable shell. Some had been brought to light through the conversation at the dinner party which, despite his flippancy, he had found unsettling and challenging. More had become apparent as they had reached Newcastle and she had reacted to the half-remembered environment of her childhood and family. A mixture of affection and guilt had engendered a wish to assert herself at the hospital through positive action, a wish which had been frustrated by the young doctor. Finally, as he reflected, his eyes closed and he drifted off to sleep in the sun.

He awoke after ten minutes or so and glancing round saw a woman about twenty yards away walking very slowly towards the cliff edge. There was something about her progress which perturbed him. He got to his feet soundlessly. She stopped close to the edge and stood, neck extended and eyes closed with her face bathed in the sunlight. She was young with fair hair and wearing a white summer dress which contrasted with her deeply tanned face, shoulders and arms. He found it impossible to decipher the expression on her face. She swayed gently in the sun and Peter, unsure of her intentions, walked quietly along the grass track to within about six feet of her, looking uncertainly between the figure and the sea repetitively striking the rocks below. She slowly opened her eyes and turned her head to look directly at him. He started to look away, embarrassed and concerned that his proximity might be misinterpreted. He turned back again a moment later, disconcerted, when he heard the sound of soft laughter. She took a pace or two towards him. 'That was kind of you but I can assure you that nothing could have been further from my thoughts.'

'Oh, I never imagined anything.'

She turned to face him and said with an unsettling directness, 'Oh, I think you did. I think you were confronted by a dilemma. You weren't sure as to whether you might be making an embarrassing and un-British fuss about nothing but finally decided that you would never forgive yourself if I had leapt off and you had done nothing to try and prevent me doing so. Isn't that right?'

'Near enough, I guess. I'm sorry.'

'Now you're apologising for making a fuss about nothing. That's not necessary. Now I shall drop the subject and you'll probably be grateful for that.'

Peter blushed and started to mumble further apologies while backing away feeling embarrassed and somewhat foolish. She held out a detaining hand which did not quite touch his arm. He raised his head and found that she was scrutinising his face. He stared for a moment too long before looking away and knew that courtesy demanded that he should stay and talk for a few moments. He looked back at her once more as he heard further light laughter.

'Now I've discomfited you again. I'm really quite safe. My name is Sally Dunham. What's yours?'

'Mine's Peter Bowman.'

'Why don't we sit in the sun and then you can tell me what Peter Bowman is doing in Northumberland?' They walked slowly back up the grassy slope to the centre of the ward and sat facing south as the sun reached its zenith. Peter was sitting slightly behind Sally and was grateful for the opportunity to examine unobserved his companion in profile. She was a little older, perhaps his own age, than he had first imagined. Her easy movements, soft slim figure and clothes all belied her age. They rested back against the stones allowing the sun to caress their faces. 'Have you visited Northumberland before or do you live locally?' Sally asked.

'No, I live in London but I have visited Dunstanburgh before and with a free day I wanted to see if my memories of the place were accurate.'

'And are they'?

'Yes, and the sun was shining on my last visit too. Do you live in the area?'

'No, I also live in London and I've never been here before. Perhaps it's a place which should always be remembered in the sunlight, like the memories of youth.'

'Now you're laughing at me again.'

'Perhaps a little. Memories are much more important to some than to others. But this view is memorable. Are you staying for long?'

'No, I'm going home tomorrow. My wife's family live in Newcastle and her father is very ill.' Then he added, 'She's been away for many years and wanted to be alone with her family today. I'd never met her parents before we came north yesterday. But what are you doing here? Are you on holiday?'

'I'm partly on holiday and partly collecting information for a project.'

'What project is that?'

'Oh, I'm a freelance journalist. I write features for various magazines and occasionally for the Sunday papers. They include travel articles mainly on Europe, opinion pieces and some on literary themes.'

'I thought your name was vaguely familiar, but haven't you written a novel as well?'

'Yes, but most of the time I prefer to suppress that particular memory and rather hope others will have done so as well. It was not well-received by the critics or, as they say in a euphemism much beloved by the book trade, it "didn't work". I'm surprised you even know of it – most people don't! But I think that's enough about me.'

'No,' said Peter abruptly and then he paused. 'I'm sorry. I didn't intend for that word to come out quite so emphatically, but I might never again have another opportunity to ask someone like you a question like this. How do you go about writing a novel?'

Sally turned laughing and looked at him. 'You're apologising again but tell me, what's your job?'

'I'm a solicitor. It's a profession where all that we do is done within a well-defined legal framework. Creative writing must be very different.'

'Yes, of course it is. It draws on many elements – imagination, fantasy, personal experience, prejudice, emotion and these must then be integrated to construct a coherent whole. I'm quite unable to describe how I did this and I suspect there are as many different ways of doing so as there are authors. I really can't give you any guidance since I can't even communicate the ways in which I prepared to create fiction. Some of it, probably most of it, was simply flying by the seat of my pants. In any event, as an unsuccessful novelist, I'm certainly not the most satisfactory source of knowledge.' She paused and looked at him directly. 'I sense that the question was important to you. Is there a particular reason why you ask?'

Peter hesitated before responding. 'Yes. The night before we came away we had some friends over for dinner and spent some time reflecting on the routine and conventionality that most of us impose on our lives – or allow to be imposed on our lives. We speculated why so often at an early stage of our adult lives we opt for or simply accept long-term stability and certainty. I was challenged and asked what I would do if I were to throw off all my bourgeois inhibitions and constraints and redirect my life. I chickened out and didn't answer that question, but if I had been more open I should have said that I should like to write.'

'I'm not laughing now, but why did you say "should like to"?'

'Perhaps I held back because if I'd said that I was going to write a novel this would have sounded pretentious and possibly opened me up to ridicule. You see, bourgeois inhibitions again. Certainly, the thought of writing a novel is daunting.'

'I can well see that you might feel inhibited by the thought of making a casual announcement that you were about to write a book, an intention that would perhaps be treated with the same level of seriousness as a statement between dessert and cheese that you were off to swim the Channel or planning to become an astronaut.' They laughed. 'I personally solved this problem by telling all my journalist friends that I was going to write a book and then going away to a cottage in the south-west of France for six months and writing alone without distractions. This was easier for me since my job is centred around the written word and some of my colleagues had already written works of fiction with mixed success. I knew my pride would not allow me to return until I had at least produced a manuscript.' He looked away, uncertain of his ability to undertake so large a task. Sensing his diffidence, she added, 'You'll only know if it is within your capabilities if you sit down and try. There is nothing which concentrates the mind quite so effectively as sitting down in front of a typewriter with a ream of pristine paper. It's challenging even to get to that point.'

'I guess that's true. If I'm honest, I must admit that my life is too comfortable at present and being a lawyer and a man I've not yet got beyond pen and paper.'

'I'm not so sure that anybody's life is that comfortable. Your dinner party conversation and your reaction to it suggest that you and some of your friends are very possibly not as satisfied with life as you claim. Now I must be making you feel very uncomfortable – again.'

'Yes,' he laughed, 'you've succeeded in doing that. I'm not sure I'm any wiser but possibly a little better informed and more insightful than I was. Thank you for listening to me. It's often easier to rehearse thoughts with a stranger than with those to whom one is close.' He hesitated before asking, 'Would you be prepared to walk back to Craster with me and have a drink and a sandwich in the pub so that we can talk for a little longer?'

'I've left my car in Embleton,' she said pointing towards the small village to the north of the castle, 'but if you can drive me back there afterwards then I should enjoy that.'

They began to walk down the track to re-join the coastal path when Sally suddenly took off her shoes and started to run. Peter gazed after her in some surprise before following and did not catch up with her until she had reached a gate on the path where she had stopped to regain her breath. 'It's the effect of the sun, the warmth and the grass under my feet,' she said. 'Sometimes I just feel like running. But now I shall adopt a more regular pace.' They continued more slowly, eyes part-closed against the early afternoon sun, and as they walked Peter was able to learn more about her. She was single and unattached, and after three years at Oxford had worked as a journalist. Her mother had been French and her father a diplomat and, as a consequence, she had travelled a great deal, first as a child and later in the course of her work. Neither parent was now living nor had she any immediate family. Her mother had returned to her native land after her father had died and Sally had been left her house in France. This, together with some private sources of income, had made it possible for her to leave salaried employment and pursue a career as a freelance journalist and spend the summer months in rural France.

They reached the village and sat companionably on a rough bench outside the small pub looking over the kipper smokehouse. She told Peter she had been planning to drive further north up the coast that afternoon. Impetuously he offered his services as a chauffeur and guide despite his scant knowledge of the area and was quietly pleased that these offers were accepted. He was uncertain about his motives in inviting her to spend the afternoon with him. His interest had been aroused by her freshness, candour and perceptiveness. He had been disturbed more than he had cared to admit by the challenges posed by the dinner party conversation. These had highlighted the extent to which his orthodox career and conventional and comfortable marriage, despite occasional frictions, were bound by routine. This chance encounter had offered him an opportunity to act out of character and the discovery that she was a writer had given him vicarious access to a sphere of activity of which he knew little. He felt some disloyalty to Ann in enjoying Sally's company for several hours of the day when her father was ill and knew he would have felt some relief if she had declined his offer, which irrationally he thought would have diminished any feeling of guilt. He assured himself that he was not driven by any specific sexual interest, although he was aware that she was an attractive and desirable companion.

They drove north to Bamburgh and sat on the soft sand at the foot of the castle and later, stimulated by Sally, they walked and then ran, shoes in hand, along the cool firm sand at the water's edge. They talked much and as they did so Peter began to wonder if he did have the courage and initiative to break free from his life and construct a new world, entirely dependent on his own endeavours and enterprise.

He drove Sally slowly back to her car and turned to face her as she was about to leave. 'Can I see you again in London?'

'I don't think that we should make arrangements like that.'

Peter looked at her. 'I have enjoyed today.'

'I too, but I suspect that you might not be planning to tell your wife about this encounter.'

'No, I suppose not.' Peter was surprised by the directness of the comment and his readiness to admit this so freely. He knew that it would be difficult to explain the day to Ann, particularly the unsolicited offer to act as a driver and guide for the afternoon, without sounding apologetic and defensive. It was more than likely that Ann would misinterpret the meeting. On the other hand, a failure to refer to the meeting would suggest complicity in an affair which did not exist.

'You should not make arrangements or assignations,' she said with a grin, 'on the basis of occasions like today which are purely serendipitous and not entirely real. Therein lies their pleasure and charm.' She leant forward and kissed him quickly and firmly on the lips and then sitting back laughing she said, 'We shall only meet again if it is in our stars – farewell middle-class man!'

She slipped out of the car and into her own and was gone. Peter restarted the engine and set off to follow her but thought better of it and drove slowly back to the city in the evening gold.

4

It was a Friday evening three weeks later back in London. Peter had not mentioned his encounter at Dunstanburgh. Jenny had travelled to London with her sister and was still with them. After an inconclusive first interview she had been invited for a further one the following Monday. Ann's father's condition had stabilised and he remained in that grey and uncertain clinical no-man's-land, neither well enough to leave hospital nor yet sufficiently ill to cause immediate concern to his family or medical attendants. They were to be joined by Peter's parents for dinner that evening.

Ann was preparing dinner when Jenny wandered into the kitchen to help, which she was doing in a desultory manner. Ann was not entirely prepared for the discussion which was to follow. She had often found Jenny's direct and uninhibited conversational style a challenge to her more conventional attitudes, imprinted through her nonconformist and, initially, pre-war upbringing.

'Ann, did you sleep with Peter before you were married?'

'No, of course not.'

'Why do you say "of course not" and why are you blushing?'

'Don't be ridiculous and I'm not.'

'Was Peter a virgin?'

'Yes.'

'How do you know?'

'Because he told me.'

'Oh, did you ask him? What a wonderful conversation to have had: "Peter, have you had experience with women or are you pure and virginal?"' Jenny mimicked her sister with an easy and disconcerting skill.

'Oh, do shut up or go away or even better do both.'

'No, seriously, Ann – I really do want your advice. There's this guy who was on my course, Simon, and I'm reasonably serious about him. We sleep together.' She giggled. 'Actually, we don't do a lot of sleeping when we're in bed, and don't look like that – I'm on the pill. The trouble is I'm quite fond of him. He's fun socially and in bed but he's now suggesting that we live together and I'm just not sure that I really want to make that sort of commitment.'

'Well, do you want to? Do you love him?'

'Frankly, I'm not sure. I really don't know how to answer that question.'

'Then I should be pretty confident that you don't, but that's a question you'll have to answer for yourself sooner or later.'

'I guess so. I'd be happy to continue as we are for a time but I suspect it will come to an end if I say no to him.'

To Ann's relief, the dialogue was terminated by the arrival of Peter's parents. They lived in a solid red-brick double-fronted house in Wimbledon which was discreetly shielded from the road by a high privet hedge. The house was surrounded by a meticulously kept lawn and flower beds laid out with an obsessive regard for geometry. Peter could readily visualise the horticultural transformation which would have taken place, as spring gave way to summer, with the planting of regimented rows of annuals which would now be regularly dead-headed before the beds were cleared for winter. His father, Geoffrey, was a retired accountant. He was a slim grey-haired man who walked with a slight limp, the consequence of a car accident many years previously. Molly Bowman was a tall woman whom he might have described as handsome if he had been more certain of the implications of that particular adjective when applied to a woman. Good-natured and voluble, her conversation was generally quite inconsequential and she could leap with the agility of a mountain goat from topic to topic. Her husband affected not to notice her non-sequiturs and frequently appeared to be conversing quite independently of his wife. Peter had long suspected that his parents had perfected the art of conducting lengthy conversations without the inconvenience of a thought passing through the mind of either of them.

They had just concluded dinner when the discussion was interrupted by the doorbell. Peter opened the door to find Andrew outside clearly drunk.

'Andrew, what are you doing here?' he asked lamely and without enthusiasm.

'Wanted to talk,' said Andrew somewhat incoherently and, before Peter could protest or stop him, he made his way to the lounge. Peter followed and found his father on his feet waiting to be introduced. Peter completed the formalities as Andrew sank heavily into a chair. Before he could say anything further his father, with the predictability of a character in a melodrama, suggested that Peter should get Andrew a drink. He accepted the inevitable as Andrew asked for a whisky.

Peter took the burden of conversation on himself in an attempt to avoid any verbal outrages. Mundane and neutral topics were introduced with unusual speed by Peter and by Ann who had also recognised the need for verbal diversion. All might have been well if Molly Bowman had not at that moment discovered that Andrew was a lecturer and chosen to make one of her more banal interventions.

'I think it's wonderful that you have chosen such a worthwhile profession.' This was the sort of patronising remark which, at best, would make Peter feel uncomfortable and, at worst, could evoke the most vigorous expression of views from Andrew. No more than an honest and simple appreciation of traditional standards, it could have been accepted with some non-committal response. However, Andrew was not in the mood to show much forbearance in his present state.

'Crap,' he said indistinctly.

'I beg your pardon!' said Molly.

'Crap.' This time it was repeated with sufficient clarity and volume for the word and the sentiment which belied it to be evident to everyone in the room. Jenny giggled.

'Really, I don't think there is any need for that sort of language,' began Geoffrey in mild reproof.

'Come on, Andrew, it's time for you to be getting back to your flat,' said Peter. 'I'll walk you down there.'

Andrew showed no inclination to move. 'I said crap and I meant crap. Is my profession worthwhile? Is yours or yours?' he asked looking first at Geoffrey and then at Peter who knew from experience that a drunken rant was likely to follow. He made a further but unsuccessful attempt to encourage him to leave.

Andrew was now sitting forward on the edge of his chair facing Peter but also challenging the others. 'I spend my days trying to teach recalcitrant A level students, most of whom are not remotely interested in the subject and don't give a fuck. I do it because I'm not qualified to do anything else and it's a living. Look at us all – we're all too comfortable, physically and financially. We see ourselves as the salt of the earth. We are all incarcerated in our petty middle-class suburban culture – characterised by the Jaguar in the drive and the flowered hat to wear to a Tory garden party. We've all been born, schooled, learned to work, to fuck, to marry, to procreate and to die in this culture, adapting and fine-tuning the peripheries of life rather than attempting to take life by the scruff of the neck and make it different. We're all smug and self-satisfied.' Peter made another attempt to suggest that they should withdraw to the flat below but this was rebuffed and, short of manhandling him, he could see no way of quickly bringing this diatribe to an end.

Andrew drew breath and resumed, ignoring the interruption, looking directly at Peter. 'Can you not remember those nights when we were much younger when we raged at the injustices of the world? The massacre at Sharpeville and the war in Vietnam? We had passions and missions. I cannot recall that we wept, but we felt for people and causes and life – perhaps transiently and superficially but we did feel. We were certain we could instigate action and change. We believed in a music of reason and perhaps of revolution. Our words and thoughts matured us but now our spirits and pusillanimity betray us. Our protests are now purely verbal; elegant and articulate maybe, but our emotions have been emasculated. They are now protests which appeal only to reason and these are nothing without substance or conviction.'

Peter managed to intrude. 'Come on, Andrew, you're being pompous and melodramatic – I think you've said enough.'

'I've scarcely started. Perhaps our jobs do have some value, but have you recently compared your achievements to your aspirations? I don't believe that you've audited your performance in life. You've grown old and forgotten your youth. I speak as if your youth is past but you're only in your mid-thirties. I wonder now that you had a youth. You have migrated seamlessly from your nappies to a three-piece suit.'

Andrew rose slowly and unsteadily and then, in a slow and portentous voice, he intoned, 'I am your God, omnipresent and omniscient but sadly not omnipotent. I may have failed, as you have, to weep for some of my lost causes but I can at least weep for the silence. The music of reason and passion has died.' He concluded by raising his hands in a pontifical manner.

There was a momentary pause. Peter rose to his feet and put out a hand to lead Andrew gently away.

Andrew turned and slipped. He tried to save himself by grasping at the heavy glass top of the coffee table and the audience watched as he fell to the floor followed by coffee cups, whisky glasses and After Eight mints. Jenny and Peter moved forward and helped him to his feet as he turned and announced his departure for bed. Peter walked him down the stairs to the flat below to guard against further accidents and handed him over to Sue who, disturbed by the noises from above, was already at the door of their flat.

'I am sorry,' she said. 'I heard a lot of noise upstairs. I do hope he was not too disruptive to your evening.'

'Don't worry about it. He just needs to get to bed.'

Peter returned upstairs. 'I can't think what you are laughing at, Jenny,' Ann was saying irritably. 'Come and help clear up this mess. Thank God nothing's broken – but look at that coffee stain.' She glared at the stain on the fashionably hirsute off-white rug. 'Why did you let him in, Peter? You should have seen that he was drunk.'

'It's difficult to bar the door to a neighbour,' he said peaceably.

'That was quite disgraceful – he was quite drunk…'

'Really shouldn't use such language…'

'Trouble is, these chaps are too young to have been in the war – that would have instilled some discipline.'

'Yes – we were taught self-control then…'

'You say he's a lecturer, presumably economics or sociology or something leftie …'

'Well, as a matter of fact…'

'Oh bugger – this stain will never come out…'

'Really, Ann – your language.'

'Can't think what he was trying to say…'

'Oh, straight out of one of those socialist pamphlets…'

'Probably teaches economics…'

'I guess there are reds at the LSE…'

'Just too blind to see it…'

'Well, I thought that was magnificent, futile but magnificent,' and Jenny started to mimic Andrew's pontifical voice.

'Don't be so immature, Jenny. It was just a load of pompous rubbish. A lot of it due to jealousy.'

'He must be touched – what does he mean by "I am your God"? – it's so irreverent.'

'Peter, can't you say something?' Ann looked at him with exasperation. 'Come and help clear this mess up.'

'Yes, we should get it cleared up.'

'I think it's time we were going,' said Geoffrey. 'That's quite enough excitement for us for one evening.'

'I know,' said Peter. 'I am sorry about what's happened – but he really is a very genuine and caring person generally.'

'Surely, you're not going to make excuses for him after that disgraceful display?'

'No, not excuses – just explaining.'

'Oh, what's the difference?'

'Quite a lot.'

Finally the evening was over. Peter's parents had left; Jenny had gone to bed and Ann had withdrawn declaring that she felt a migraine coming on. Peter was about to follow when the doorbell rang again. He was just heading towards the front door when Ann appeared from their bedroom.

'If that's Andrew, I don't want to see him and don't let him in.'

'No, of course not – go back to bed.'

Peter opened the door to find Sue standing outside. 'Have you seen Andrew recently?'

'No, not for some time now.'

'I know that when he was with you earlier he made something of a fuss. It was kind of you to steer him back. I generally manoeuvre him quietly into bed when he gets like that. It doesn't happen very often and he just wakes up with a sore head in the morning. But this time I heard the crash above and realised that there had been some sort of an accident so, stupidly, I had words with him and he shouted and went out again. That was over an hour ago and I wondered if he had come back to you.'

'No. We haven't seen him since I handed him over to you at your door.'

'I'm worried, Peter.'

'Where else could he have gone?'

'I really don't know. That's what's worrying me.'

'Could he be just wandering around somewhere?'

'I suppose so – but he wasn't in a state to wander very far or do very much else.'

'I'll come and help you look,' said Peter. He went back to the bedroom to explain the situation to Ann, overriding her objections that Andrew had already caused enough trouble for one evening. He set out for the street accompanied by Sue and Jenny who had been disturbed by the noise and elected to join them in the search.

Sue searched the streets methodically close to the flat returning every quarter of an hour to see if Andrew had returned. She was uncertain where he might have gone and was unable to give the others any guidance to help in their quest. Peter, by common consent, had agreed to search the Common but soon realised that this was an almost impossible task, even with the aid of a flashlight. He had no way of knowing if Andrew was walking, sitting or lying and it was impracticable to search the Common systematically alone. Footpaths and bridleways crossed it at irregular intervals and the trees and bushes threw monstrous shadows across the stunted and irregular tufts of grass from distant lights on the adjacent streets. Even at that time there were others abroad singly and in pairs, and Peter's attempts to identify individuals with his flashlight were generating hostility from nocturnal walkers and accusations of voyeurism from those engaged in more intimate activities. Jenny, meanwhile, was searching the nearby shopping area which was still brightly lit from the window displays. They had agreed to return to the flat after forty-five minutes to see if Andrew had returned. They had had no success and were standing in the entrance to the flats when Andrew came around the corner walking slowly but steadily with his head down. Sue saw him first and waved and called his name. He came slowly up the opposite pavement seemingly unaware of their presence even though he was so near home. A taxi drove along the road and as it drew close to Andrew he turned and started to cross with his head still bowed. The scene slowed momentarily in Peter's mind as Sue screamed and Jenny gasped, 'Oh, God no!' and then the sounds succeeded each other at ever-decreasing intervals – the strident note of the horn, the discordant scream of the tyres, the lifeless thud of metal striking flesh and for a moment absolute silence – and then there was movement again.

They all ran forward simultaneously as windows from the flats illuminated and the taxi-driver emerged white-faced and walked back slowly to the small group surrounding Andrew. Reluctantly, Peter knelt and felt uncertainly for a pulse, first for Andrew's wrist and then inside his shirt. 'He's alright – he's breathing alright' and as if in confirmation Andrew turned his head and moaned gently.

'Thank God – but look at his leg.'

'There's a lot of blood.'

'Go and call for an ambulance, Jenny.'

'Is he alright? Stepped straight out and didn't look.'

'Perhaps we should move him off the road.'

'I never had a chance to stop.'

'I don't think we should move him.'

'Has someone sent for an ambulance?'

'You saw how he just stepped out.'

'Shouldn't we call the police?'

'Look, he's moving again.'

'Andrew, darling, can you hear me?'

'He's going to get very cold there.'

'I'm so sorry, Andrew.'

'No – I'm sure he should stay where he is. We can cover him up.'

'Isn't that leg broken? It's at a very strange angle.'

Despite the lateness of the hour, a small crowd gathered around Sue and Peter as they looked up anxiously and helplessly.

'Surely, there's a doctor who lives at the end house.'

'It's alright. I'm here.' The spectators parted to admit the doctor with a coat pulled over his pyjamas. He passed his hands expertly over Andrew. 'There's not a lot I can do here,' he said. 'His pulse is good, he's breathing alright and there's no obvious chest injury. Nasty compound fracture of that right leg; it should at least be splinted before he's moved. We just need to wait for the ambulance, but no great danger by the look of it.' He leaned forward and sniffed. 'Had a drink or three, hasn't he?'

Sue looked at Peter. 'Thank God it's not too bad. I should never have said anything this evening and this would never have happened.'

'You couldn't know that this was going to happen.'

'Did that doctor say that he'd been drinking?' asked the cabbie.

'It's alright, we know that it wasn't your fault.'

'You oughtn't to let him out in that state, lady.'

'Leave it,' said Peter.

This unhappy dialogue was interrupted by the return of the doctor who gently manipulated the leg to splint it and then helped to transfer him into the ambulance. Peter sent Jenny back to the flat and joined Sue and Andrew for the short journey to the hospital.

* * *

'I suppose it was to be expected.'

'Possibly – though it was an unlikely sequence of events which brought Andrew and that taxi together. Poor old Andrew!'

'I shouldn't waste too much sympathy on him.'

'Come on, that's too harsh, Ann. The poor bugger's got

to cool his heels in hospital for at least three weeks now. It was a difficult compound fracture and the doctor said that it's going to need surgery and internal fixation.'

'Well, no more than he deserved.'

'Don't get so bloody puritanical! Anyhow let's go to bed for the little that remains of the night. It's nearly five o'clock and getting light and I'm dog-tired.'

'I can't think why you went on that wild-goose chase – and Jenny too.'

'There was little else that I could do to help and Sue was beside herself. Now let's get to bed.'

'Well, it's been a fine night and Andrew has been the cause of all the trouble! First that ludicrous scene and being so rude in front of your parents, and then falling like that, quite apart from the mess he's made of the rug. Finally, he's had us in and out of bed all night.'

'Oh, leave it, Ann, for God's sake, and get to bed.'

'I don't know how you can talk so calmly about going to bed.'

'Ann, I'm far from calm, but what else can we do? And for God's sake, try and be a little more tolerant of people's frailties. Not everyone can meet your impossibly high standards.'

'How can I? That's a fine thing to say after all the trouble that man has caused. Why can't he be a little more tolerant and allow us some domestic privacy to live our lives the way we want to live them, or do we have to be tolerant whatever people do?'

'Don't be silly – all I'm suggesting is that you just show a little understanding.'

46

'So I'm at fault for not being sufficiently understanding. You're just too soft and wishy-washy, Peter,' Ann almost shouted.

Peter sat on one side of the bed and Ann on the other gazing down at the carpet. 'Look,' he said finally and much more quietly. 'It's very late and we aren't getting anywhere. We're not going to solve anything tonight and there is nothing for us personally to solve anyhow. I'm going to bed.' He walked round the bed and took Ann's arm gently but she shook him off.

'You go to bed if you want to, but I couldn't sleep and I think that there is something for us to solve personally. I shall probably go into the spare room.'

'You can't, Jenny's in there.'

'Well, there are two beds in there.'

'Oh, don't be silly.'

'Stop calling me silly and leave me alone!'

Peter tried to put his arms around his wife but she remained angry and aggressive. She got up and announced that she was going to make some tea. Peter followed her but finally, defeated by her coldness and passivity, made his way to bed. She followed after a short time. He was conscious of her rigid posture, facing away and lying tensely on the further edge of the bed.

5

Ten days later Peter and Ann were alone in the flat. Jenny had returned to Newcastle to await the outcome of her interviews. Ann, uncomfortable (but only a little uncomfortable) about the hard line she had taken the previous week over the episode with Andrew, became the self-appointed sympathiser, guide and supporter of Sue. Her position was made more secure by Sue's frequent apologies for Andrew's behaviour. She organised expeditions for essential shopping, insisted that Sue join them for meals in the evenings and arranged for mutual friends to accompany her to the hospital at visiting times. Sue, who might have been expected to find much of this irksome, accepted the role of recipient of these good works with unusual passivity. She said little of her visits to Andrew beyond transmitting the apparently uncomplicated details of his medical progress. Ann went to the hospital with Sue on one or two occasions but elected to sit and read in the visitors' waiting room. The single visit she had made to Andrew had not been a success. She reported that he had been neither penitent nor unrepentant over the episode in the flat. It had simply not been mentioned and they speculated whether this was because he considered it singularly unimportant or that his memory of that evening was uncertain. In either case, Ann felt that Sue had been at fault in failing to reprove her husband and insisting that he apologise.

Peter had few opportunities to speak privately to Sue that week and his enquiries about Andrew's progress were answered with little detail. He suggested diffidently that he might visit Andrew the following day, a proposal greeted with rather more enthusiasm than he had expected. It was arranged that he should meet Sue and Ann at the hospital the following evening after work and then accompany them back to the flat. Sue suggested he should have some time alone with Andrew at the start of the visiting hour while she and Ann remained in the waiting area.

'So, you've been permitted to visit the sick or perhaps you are just confirming that the sinning Andrew Hepscott is suffering due punishment meted out by a just God,' Andrew said as Peter sat down at the bedside. He then said rather more contritely, 'I really am very sorry for all the disturbance that I caused and I gather that I made a bit of a mess.'

'Oh, not too bad.'

'I did try to apologise to Ann but I didn't find it easy. I couldn't find the right words, so I desisted after a short time. Perhaps she'll be happy that retribution came and commendably quickly.'

'I don't think she looks at it like that.'

'Perhaps not, but I'm grateful for the support that she is giving Sue.'

'That's no problem.'

'And how are you?' he said laughing. 'Back securely in your rut once more?'

'I guess so.'

'I can remember some of the things that I said that night; most of it was pompous and pretentious rubbish.'

Peter laughed. 'Those were precisely the words Ann used.'

'Well, she was largely right. You should congratulate her on her perspicacity and me on my insight now that I am no longer in my cups.'

'I'm not certain whether you are laughing at yourself or at Ann!'

'Probably both,' he paused and looked directly at Peter. 'But it wasn't all pompous nonsense. Somewhere in there was a nugget of truth struggling to escape through my inebriated lips.'

'You're being pompous again!'

'Yes, perhaps. But there's a dilemma here; to deliver truths simply often results in them being dismissed as trite or naive or, if stated in a way that you refer to as pompous, they can be disregarded as pretentious.'

'Now you're laughing at me – and perhaps at yourself.'

'And you're trying to dismiss all that I've said because it makes you feel uncomfortable. Truth often is uncomfortable.'

'Now you are trying to make me rise. Andrew, you are absolutely bloody incorrigible. This is all part of a front. You have accepted your own position as a part of the great British middle-class but you neither feel entirely at home there nor do you have the drive and initiative to enable you to get out. Your trendy, lefty talk is simply part of an act to portray yourself as something you're not. You preach at the rest of us but it's all a matter of "do as I say and not as I do"

– or in your case fail to do. You are simply no different from the rest of us.'

'Don't be so perceptive, you bugger. You're deflating me and I shall develop complications.'

'What complications could you possibly develop? I understand that the various bits of your leg have been secured in place with high tensile steel screws. It's also in traction and encased in a plaster which seems to have the consistency of armoured plate.'

'You are not even allowing me to wallow in what little sympathy I'm receiving.'

'Why should you?'

'I know – retribution again.'

The remainder of the visiting period passed and Peter was joined by Sue for the final few minutes. They left and joined Ann who had remained in the room reserved for visitors. Peter stood aside for them to leave and then paused to allow another woman to enter. He didn't pay much attention to the figure passing in the doorway and was startled when she stopped and said very quietly, 'Well, well – and we never did arrange to meet in London!' The gently mocking voice made him look down.

'Sally – I never expected to bump into you again. What are you doing here?'

'Visiting, as I assume you are but I think you'll have to go – your presence is required.'

Ann had stepped back to see what was delaying Peter. 'Oh, Ann, this is er' (old friend, new acquaintance, Peter wondered) 'Sally Dunham.'

'Oh, it's nice to meet you but you must excuse us.

We must see our friend home. Her husband has had an accident.'

'Yes, of course. I must be getting on too. Bye, Peter.'

'Goodbye, Sally.'

'And who was that?' asked Ann as they walked over to the car.

'Just someone I met briefly socially. It was a strange coincidence meeting her again like that.'

They drove home and, after the meal, Peter walked Sue down the stairs back to her flat.

'Well, who was that woman?' Ann asked again when he returned.

'Who was who?'

'You know perfectly well. The woman you bumped into at the hospital.'

'She's a woman called Sally Dunham and she's a journalist.'

'Where did you meet her? '

Peter hesitated. 'It must have been at a drinks party or at some reception,' he said uncertainly.

'I have no recollection of meeting her.'

'You must have been talking to other people at the time or it may even have been a work-related affair which didn't involve you.'

'Whose party was it? – you never mentioned it.'

'I really don't remember and it never seemed sufficiently important to mention.'

'Well, it seemed to be a very intimate exchange.'

'Ann, you're imagining things. It was scarcely intimate. It was a narrow doorway and we exchanged two sentences commenting on the coincidence of meeting in such a place.'

'Well, it seems a very odd sort of coincidence to me.'

Peter shrugged his shoulders in acquiescence. The coincidence was certainly remarkable but the opportunity to explain the circumstances, if not the detail, of the previous meeting had now been irretrievably lost. He was ashamed at his duplicity but reflected that the possibility of ever reporting that first meeting in a plausible manner had always been remote. This new and totally fortuitous encounter suggested a number of interesting and disturbing possibilities central to each of which was further acquaintance. The highlights of that day on the Northumbrian coast remained clearly imprinted on Peter's memory but, like a photographic vignette, the peripheral events had become diffused and indistinct. His recollections would have remained permanently thus, or more probably would have become even less distinct, if the encounter that evening had not thrown them all into sharp relief once more. Any further association could only be contrived. Peter knew this could be no more than a fantasy that would fade with time.

* * *

The doorbell rang late that evening. It was 11.30pm. Ann and Peter looked at each other as it rang continuously and stridently. Peter crossed the room and went to the front door. Ann heard it being opened but still the bell rang.

'What is it, has the bell stuck?' asked Ann.

Peter looked out. Sue was standing outside leaning

against the bell. She was holding her head in both her hands. 'For God's sake, what is it, Sue?' He went forward and gently pulled her fully upright. In the sudden silence she gasped and sobbed and then leant against him. Peter put his arms around her as the sobs continued irregularly and with frightening force.

'What's going on?' Ann asked from close behind.

'I don't know. Help me to bring her inside.' Slowly the three moved into the lounge as Sue continued to cling to Peter. 'What's happened, Sue?' He whispered urgently into her ear, 'What is it?'

Slowly between her sobs she said, 'They rang, they just rang from the hospital. It's Andrew – something dreadful has happened – not long after we left.'

'But what, Sue – he seemed so well?'

'I know, but they explained. They said it could all happen quite suddenly and out of the blue. A clot of blood from his legs went to his lungs and it's all over.' They gazed at Sue in disbelief.

'Surely, that can't be right? He was his normal provocative self when we left.'

'Oh, Sue, love.' Ann went across and put her arms around the sobbing figure. Peter left the room and instinctually went to the kitchen to make some tea. He returned and poured mugs for each of them. They sat rigidly, silently, privately apart.

Sue started to talk again, flatly and almost inaudibly. 'They explained it all. They said it can happen to people who are otherwise quite well. It happens to people who are in bed with illnesses or after accidents, especially after operations on their legs. They lie quite still in bed and the blood clots in their legs. Then suddenly it just goes to their lungs and sometimes, if it's a big clot, there is nothing they can do about it. I just sat in the flat. I couldn't believe it. I couldn't move and all this because I didn't help him when I should have known that he needed it.'

'He broke his leg in an accident. You weren't responsible for that.'

'I think I was.'

'No, Peter's right. It was an accident. I can't believe it either.'

'Neither can I. It's not real. He was his normal self. I can't go back to that flat again.'

'No, of course not, you must spend the night here.'

'I don't want to sleep.'

'Perhaps you should try. Peter will ring the doctor.'

The presence of the doctor, who provided a sedative and reinforced the suggestion that she stay the night in the flat, offered some relief. She was the partner of the doctor who had helped on the night of the accident and she confirmed that there were occasions when such tragedies occurred and that they could not be predicted.

6

The immediate drama was over. The three surviving witnesses to each stage of its development and its unexpected and sad end retreated into behaviours which were personal, private and automatic. The passage of time appeared suspended during the days that followed and quotidian activities were performed reflexly and unthinkingly. The personal devastation for Sue contrasted strikingly with the relative public insignificance of such everyday events as had culminated in Andrew's death. The polished professional sympathy she encountered did nothing to allay her grief or assuage her sense of guilt as she was supported through the rituals and observances demanded by law and prescribed by convention. The days between the death and the cremation assumed an air of unreality. She was suddenly lost, remote and incapable of making decisions and would only return to her flat when accompanied by Ann who would stay the night with her. She agreed passively to all suggestions for the cremation and the management of Andrew's affairs. Ann automatically re-adopted the role of mentor, guide and friend. She accompanied Sue to the hospital to complete the melancholy task of collecting Andrew's personal effects, presented impersonally in a polythene bag incongruously labelled "hospital property". She was standing close to Sue when they learned that there was to be an autopsy and an inquest as he had died indirectly as a result of an accident.

Peter was cast without a role other than as a witness to the accident and, through Ann as an intermediary, an informal legal adviser. A verdict of accidental death was returned and neither blame nor opprobrium was attached to the cab driver. Peter continued to go to work each day but, apart from the time spent with his clients, he was unable to settle to work systematically. He spent much of the following week leaving his office at quiet times and wandering aimlessly around the streets. He found himself excluded from the mutually dependent roles which Sue and his wife had adopted. He reflected endlessly on the sequence of events, major and minor, which had ultimately led to Andrew's death. It seemed that the words and sentiments he had expressed in that drunken oration had acquired an additional dimension. He found he could no longer simply dismiss them as pompous, whimsical or jejune. For Peter, death and distance had invested those judgements with a force and significance which had not been there originally. He was conscious of the irrationality of his reaction. The practical reasons for disregarding such challenging statements were overwhelming. Nevertheless, he remained unsettled by the apparently unceasing routine and uniformity of his life. It seemed very likely that when the anti-climactic days following the inquest and cremation were over, Peter and Ann would be little touched by the event in the longer term. Each would slowly drift back into the regular routine of their lives.

Three days after the cremation, Peter and Ann were having a meal with Sue in her flat. It had been arranged that Ann would spend a further two nights there. Later that evening as Peter was returning to their flat he heard the telephone ringing as he climbed the stairs. He hurried in to find Jenny on the line, distraught and unhappy. Her father had deteriorated during the previous day and the hospital had suggested it would be wise to send for Ann if she wished to see her father once more.

Ann looked tired and distressed when Peter relayed the message but was dissuaded from trying to catch the overnight sleeper. He accompanied her in a taxi to King's Cross the next morning and promised to follow at the weekend. The day was warm and, knowing he had no fixed appointments for that morning, he decided to walk to his office in Westminster. He set off along the Euston Road but soon turned off to escape the noise and fumes of the traffic. He ambled generally southwards and westwards through the quieter streets and squares of Bloomsbury. He took no notice of his precise route so it was with a shock that he came to a tall red brick building which he recognized as the hospital where Andrew had died. He walked on a little further south, perturbed and unhappy, and finally reached a garden square where he sat on a bench in the sun. The warm, humid day closed in on him as he re-ran the events of the previous six weeks in his mind. He was shortly joined by another man on the bench and, without thinking, he moved a little further along although there was more than adequate space between them.

'It's alright, my friend,' said the newcomer. 'People who

dress like this don't always have lice and I've had a shower today.'

Peter looked at the figure to his right. It was a man in his late twenties, with a goatee beard and long hair gathered in a ponytail. He was dressed in a faded T-shirt, denims and trainers with a silver ankh hung around his neck on a fine leather thong.

'I'm sorry,' Peter said awkwardly and looked away, unwilling to engage further in conversation.

'It's alright – but you look real down.'

It was not possible for Peter to totally avoid the question implicit in that statement. 'I just wanted to sit somewhere quietly and think through some problems,' he said.

'Oh, you think away. I won't overtax my brain by thinking, I'll just sit.'

Peter resolved to sit for a further five minutes and then walk on, but he was disturbed after a minute or so by a sharp monotone whistle from his companion. Looking up, he saw that his companion was beckoning to a young woman who was crossing the grass towards them. She was of less than medium height with pitch black hair, just short of shoulder length, wearing a coat of a startling shade of purple. She stood directly in front of his neighbour on the bench.

'Were you summoning me?' she asked.

'Yes, I thought it would be great if we all got to know one another.'

She shrugged her shoulders. 'I'm in no hurry today.' She sat between them.

'I'm Stefan,' he announced, 'five foot ten when I stand,

which I rarely do, and I weigh one hundred and fifty-six pounds.'

'I'm Cass and Irish, my height and weight like my parentage are a mystery but I am permanently optimistic and my personality belies my full name. I work at the V & A – the pre-Raphaelites.'

He turned towards Peter. 'Ah, she enjoys the mysterious pleasures of medievalism and mysticism. I work with eternal hope but for modest rewards in a music shop.' He turned back to Cass. 'This is my friend,' he said waving his hand towards Peter at the end of the bench.

'Good to meet you,' said Cass, 'but who are you?' she added looking at Peter. 'This man clearly has no manners and appears to be unable to introduce his friends in a courteous manner.'

'Would have introduced him properly but the guy who introduced him to me spoke so indistinctly that I never caught his name properly.'

'Oh er – it's Peter, er Peter Bowman.'

'Pete – this is Cass. Cass meet Pete, one of my oldest friends. He's looking very sad today.'

She stood up, turned round and kissed him on the cheek saying, 'If Stefan is your friend then I shall also be your friend,' and once more sat between them.

'That's fine,' said Stefan, 'but you haven't said good morning properly to me.'

'Sorry, Stefan.' She leant across and embraced him.

'That's much better – now the day can really start. Where are you lunching today, old boy?' he asked looking at Peter, 'the Café Royal?'

'Oh no, no,' said Peter confused. 'I must go to my office.'

'No, you must call and say that you've been delayed or, better still, tell them that you've met with a fatal accident and that they should leave you in peace for a few days – or at least until you've been cremated.'

'No,' said Peter firmly, alarmed by the surreal turn of the conversation. 'I must be off.'

'No, don't go. We're only just getting to know one another,' said Cass gently putting an arm around him. Peter looked around nervously expecting their companions or others to close in on him. The pedestrian traffic continued to criss-cross the square quite unaware of his discomfiture. 'This bum doesn't know where the Café Royal is, but we could go and have a beer and a sandwich. I should be sad if you left us now. A little company might distract you.'

'I really have to go to work now.'

'What do you do?'

'I'm a solicitor.'

'Give up soliciting for the day. Join us.'

He was conscious that he might be being set up but curiosity overwhelmed him and he agreed to go along with them. He insisted, however, that he should telephone his office to offer some pretext for his unexplained absence. He dialled the number from a call box while the others stood holding the door open. As soon as the connection was made he pressed the coin home but, as he did so, Stefan quickly took the receiver from him and placed his hand over the mouthpiece as Peter expostulated and tried to retrieve the instrument.

Stefan turned away and said quickly into the mouthpiece, 'Hold on, do not drop ze instrument, ve haf ze international call for you.' He pushed Peter gently out of the call box making a sharp clicking noise into the receiver before continuing. 'This is an intercontinental call from Eastern Anatolia, routed through Istanbul, Southern Belgrade and Oberhellandam.' Then changing the timbre of his voice he intoned, 'We have your partner Peter in isolation in Eastern Anatolia. He has bubonic plague, fortunately only a mild case, and will be back at work in a few days after treatment with the new wonder drug – Godamycin.' The receiver was replaced as Peter looked on with resignation. His plea to recall the office was ignored and with Cass and Stefan each taking an arm he was led back across the square to a pub.

'Your round,' said Cass firmly pushing Stefan towards the bar. She led Peter to a table in the corner of the saloon. Uncertain, bewildered and acutely embarrassed, Peter looked at her. 'Well?' she said.

'Did you really not know Stefan before this morning?' he asked after searching for something to say. He felt rather stupid, like the butt of a practical joke who is not sure of the nature of the joke and concerned that he might be the victim of a deception.

'No, of course not; but how would one get to know anyone if we all just walked on and avoided chance encounters?'

'Weren't you concerned that you might be being picked up by undesirable characters?'

'Now you're talking like a lawyer,' she said. 'If I hadn't liked the look of him, then I would have just walked on. Risk-taking is part of life. Anyhow, the risk was trivial. Although I didn't know him personally, I recognised him and I know who he is. He works in a little music shop off Fleet Street and he's making a name for himself as a violinist. I read an article once saying that his parents named him Stefan after Stephane Grappelli in the hope that he would become a violinist – an experiment in nominative determinism which seems to have been successful even if they managed to spell the name incorrectly. Now we can spend the day together. You haven't told us why you are so low.'

'Mainly because a friend of mine died recently in rather sad circumstances after visiting our flat.' Peter recounted the tale.

'But you couldn't be held responsible for such a tragic sequence of events.'

'No, but I find myself unable to dismiss the things he said that evening as the ramblings of a man who had just had too much to drink. Quite irrationally, they seem to be of much greater significance because of subsequent events.'

'But what did he say that has so discombobulated you?'

'He provoked me – in fact he provoked all of us but perhaps me more than the others. He questioned our middle-class pretensions and preoccupations and challenged us all to break free of our bourgeois shackles and pursue our dreams and fantasies.'

'And do you have dreams and fantasies?'

'Yes.'

'Are they decent or are they salacious?'

Peter laughed. 'No, they're not in the least improper. I have an aspiration to write fiction – but have absolutely no idea whether I have the necessary talent or commitment.'

'Well, you must spend the day with us now and free your mind for a few hours.'

'Oh no, I must get back to the office.'

Stefan had brought drinks back to the table and looked directly at Peter. 'Will you be in trouble with Miss Prism when you get back to work?'

'Miss who?'

'The cock-freezing receptionist at your office.'

Peter smiled at this description of their Sloaney receptionist – the daughter of a disgraced Tory MP. 'I shall simply tell her that it was an old friend playing a practical joke.'

'Why?'

'Why not?' said Cass. 'He is becoming an old friend.'

'Yes – me and sweetie Petey here are about to be the oldest of friends.'

'I'll just get us all another drink and then push off,' said Peter rising when he had finished his first.

'You can't do that.'

'Why not?'

'Because it's Cassandra's round, of course.'

'That's it,' she said pushing him back into his seat. 'You can't go yet. I don't have to be anywhere until 4.30 and that is a long time away.'

Peter sat back and tried to relax. The inconsequential discussion flowed back and forth haphazardly as he attempted unsuccessfully to detect any links in the topics as they merged into one another. Any attempt to buy further drinks was firmly rebuffed by the statement that it was

Stefan's round or Cass's round. Finally, resigned and partly drunk, he started to join in the game shouting out randomly 'Stefan's round' or 'Cass's round' with what he regarded as a magnificent degree of impartiality. The noise he was making began to draw looks of disapproval as the pub filled with dark-suited men gathering in small clusters around the bar. The clock was approaching 1.30 when Cass got up and, taking his arm, led them out onto the pavement where she hailed a taxi.

'Where are we going?' asked Peter.

'To the zoo, of course. Where else would we go to play games in the afternoon?' They reached the turnstiles as the sun came out and then both turned to Peter. 'Your round,' they said simultaneously. Stefan invited them to talk to the animals and in turn each approached a cage to 'converse' with the animals within. Peter found that he was repeatedly led to the more silent creatures in the zoo and after being instructed to speak to the giraffes in sign language, he retired petulantly to a bench with an ice cream.

* * *

He didn't know how long he had been asleep when he awoke with a jolt as a young child started playing round his legs. He looked at his watch and saw that it was approaching 5pm. His erstwhile companions were nowhere to be seen. He felt anxiously for his wallet and found that it was still in place. He stood and shook himself and as he did so a slip of paper fell to the ground. He picked it up and looked at it. 'Flat 8, 23 Bedford Street. Your oldest and your newest friends. See you there sometime. S & C.' He looked at it for a moment and then crumpled it up and threw it into a bin. Immediately regretting the action, he retrieved it and flattening it out placed it in an inner compartment in his wallet.

Still feeling light-headed from the alcohol he had consumed, he took a taxi to his office, arriving as most of the staff were leaving for the evening. He apologised for the earlier call and went and sat in his office where he reflected on the surreal events of the day. Half an hour later Ann telephoned from Newcastle. Her father's condition had not changed through the day. He told her that he was in the office later than usual and would not be home until late. The prospect of an evening alone seemed particularly uninviting so, half an hour later, he called his old Cambridge friend, Michael, and invited himself for a meal in his flat.

7

Michael, like Peter, was a lawyer. He had a strong social conscience and radical views. He worked in a legal aid centre in Islington. His early life had been spent in Liverpool where his father had worked in the docks and been a trade union official. They had met as freshmen at Cambridge. Both had elected to do National Service before university and thus were a couple of years older than many of their contemporaries. They were also two of a small number of law students in their college which was largely dominated by scientists. Both had found adapting to university life a challenge. In Peter's case this resulted from a degree of innate shyness. Michael's uncertainties arose from finding himself in an environment so remote from that of his upbringing. Peter had been drawn to Michael by his intellectual ability and by his preparedness to challenge lecturers and tutors on points of law with a fluency and cogency that he himself was unable to command. This was matched by the ease with which he would enliven small social occasions, although he was less comfortable at larger or formal events. He had graduated with a first.

Michael lived alone surrounded by books in a small flat

in Hammersmith and he frequently worked at home to a background of classical music. He greeted Peter at the door, informing him that he would order a takeaway to have with the bottle of wine he already had chilled. Looking at Peter's slightly dishevelled state he said, 'Methinks you have already had a few or maybe more than a few. Is this really the sober solicitor that I've known for so long? In other words, what the hell have you been up to?'

Peter looked at him and collapsed into a chair. 'I really don't know where to begin. It has been a strange and disconcerting few weeks and I've simply no idea about what went on today. It might be simplest to start with today and then go back to the beginning.'

'OK, as you wish. This sounds as if this might be a long tale. I suggest we order our takeaways and I shall fortify myself with a glass of wine before you start. It's water only for you. I wouldn't wish to be held responsible for returning you to your home half cut, or fully cut if that's a phrase that would be understood. I know I'm not the flavour of the month or even an occasional flavour of the day with your dearly beloved. I might require a signed affidavit from you before you leave that I'm in no way responsible for your present condition.'

'You're right. I'll settle for a glass of water and maybe have a glass of wine when the food arrives.'

They settled comfortably and Peter recounted the events of the day. At the end of his account he said, 'I simply don't know what to make of it. Was it real, unreal or surreal? I felt at times that I had wandered inadvertently into a parallel universe. Why did Stefan and Cass pick each other up and, more bizarrely, why did they pick up someone like me? At times I thought it was an elaborate scam but it turned out not to be that. We wandered, talked, laughed and, once I had relaxed, I enjoyed the sense of freedom and abandon which came over me. We talked earnestly and passionately of things which I know absolutely nothing about – the pre-Raphaelites and the merits of various violin sonatas. I really don't have a clue what it was all about.'

'Well, I'm quite confident I can't enlighten you other than to say welcome to the wacky hippy world of the sixties! But how did you, a conscientious 8.30am to 5.30pm solicitor, come to be walking halfway across London from a point nowhere near your home to your office in the first place? That's quite out of character.'

'True.' Peter described the chain of circumstances which had followed from Andrew's tirade in the flat to the accident, its sad sequel and his random wanderings which had brought him to the hospital where Andrew had died. He explained why he was alone that evening as Ann was in Newcastle having, to an extent, reconnected with her parents as a consequence of her father's illness.

'I see. I had never realised that Ann is also another authentic working class kid made good,' said Michael with a wry smile. 'But I sense that there is more behind this than you are letting on.'

The pizzas arrived at this point and Peter accepted the offer of a glass of wine. He glanced across at Michael. 'May I ask you a question?'

'I guess you're going to, whatever I say – so go ahead!'

'Are you happy and fulfilled in your work and life?'

Michael looked somewhat taken aback and paused before speaking. 'Peter, I really wasn't ready for an existential question of that profundity. Anyhow, that's at least two questions and I'm not sure that either have simple or straightforward answers. I'm beginning to feel as I did at Cambridge when put on the spot in a tutorial.' He paused before continuing, 'Possibly the only escape route from that spot is through a detached and academic response. Both questions need some thought if I'm to answer them adequately or even inadequately. I sense this is important to you and I hope you'll share the reasons why, but before saying anything I need to add a disclaimer. Nobody can be wholly objective about themselves and nobody can be expected to reveal all that they feel. I also ask you to remember that what holds good for me may very well not hold good for you. We've been friends for a long time and I probably know you better than anyone outside your own family.' He gave a slightly mischievous smile and added, 'It may be much easier for me to open up, coming from a Catholic working class family in Liverpool, than it is for you with the inhibitions imposed on you by your upbringing. I was brought up to bare my soul weekly at confession!'

'Alright, I accept the health warning – go on.'

'It was partly delivered to give me time to think! I can only start by begging the question. I'm not certain how one would even start to define happiness. I can accept that there are events, occasions, meetings and friendships which make one happy – just as some occurrences might make one sad or angry. But happiness in life must be much more than simply a positive response to episodic events which one finds pleasurable. This is where I have difficulty and I believe I'm not alone in that. I understand that philosophers have tried to define the state of happiness without being able to reach a satisfactory or universally acceptable definition. In the absence of an acceptable definition or standard against which to measure my sense of happiness, I have to say that I just cannot answer the first part of your question. I am, in general, contented with life which is a somewhat neutral view of happiness. It implies that the progress of my life is relatively undisturbed by disagreeable occurrences and that the ratio of pleasurable activities and events significantly outweighs the distasteful ones. Thus, I prefer to say that I am contented although that makes me sound like a cow quietly chewing the cud. None of this is to say that changes in my life might not enhance my state of contentment – and I can think of possible developments in my life which might do just that.'

He paused before continuing. 'Fulfilment as a concept seems to me to raise similar questions although it's perhaps somewhat easier to define. The degree to which I or anyone might feel fulfilled can to an extent be calibrated against the objectives which we have set for ourselves or others have set for us. This applies in both our working and our personal lives. I'm doing the job which I've wanted to do since childhood. I enjoy the challenges of my day-to-day life. I enjoy it most and feel most fulfilled when I can chalk up successes and less so when I fail. I could, of course, theoretically increase my level of fulfilment by setting less challenging objectives but that would be inconsistent with my approach to life. The best answer I can give you is that I wouldn't wish to be doing anything else.' He paused. 'This monologue has gone on for long enough. I'm sure your question though was not simply an idle one. Are you happy and fulfilled or, at a lower level, simply contented or are you discontented with your life at work or at home or both?'

'I suppose there's an element of both involved.'

'Is this a temporary and premature mid-life crisis or is there something more fundamentally amiss in your life? Is it that you feel discontented and sense that you would be better doing something different and, if so, can you define what that "something different" might be?'

'I really don't know the answers to these questions. If you had asked me several months ago if I was contented with my lot, I should have answered "yes", probably with no more than a moment's hesitation. Now I feel a nagging sense of unease which has been brought into sharp relief by the events of the last two months and the challenges which have been put to me.'

'Peter, I can't resolve your dilemmas for you. I'm happy to listen and share my views of the world, but they are no more than that – my personal views of the world. They are coloured by many things, particularly my Catholic background and upbringing. Even though I've rejected the faith, the culture still plays a major role in the way I think. I was educated and spent my childhood in a very different environment to yours. Even our National Service experiences could not have been more different. While Private Rattray was sweating and often shit-scared in the jungle in the Malayan insurgency, 2nd Lieutenant Bowman was much more safely ensconced in Minden in Germany.

I know you believe that we both had similar difficulties in adapting to Cambridge, but our responses were inevitably different. There are no covert judgements in what I say. Our long friendship has its foundations in much that we share but we are not identical twins from a single egg. I cannot and should not advise you – or even comment.'

'I accept that. I know I'm constrained by my background and my desire to break away is probably unrealistic and fanciful. I'm sure I'm far from being alone in having escapist fantasies and unrealistic ambitions. You're right – our genes, our childhood environments and our experiences shape our behaviours and attitudes more than we probably realise, but religious observance in my family was probably just as pervasive as it was in yours. It was low church and puritanical and the spectre of hellfire was ever present as a threat if we transgressed. This might have been at the other end of the Christian spectrum from your Catholic upbringing but Catholicism also has its puritanical elements. There were things that my brother and I were not allowed to do at home on a Sunday. We were not permitted to play games with dice or playing cards, however innocent, like snap. The outcome of such games was dependent on chance and we were taught that chance was the realm of the devil. Conversely, we were encouraged to believe that resolve, application and commitment were essential for our development and that these attributes were the basis of righteousness. These attitudes dominated my schooldays to an extreme degree. Pupils were not permitted to play certain chords on the chapel organ as they were judged to be ungodly and the singing of Jerusalem was banned. I think it was the line

"Bring me my arrows of desire" that was the problem. It was thought that such words might arouse unhealthy and lustful thoughts in our adolescent minds!'

Michael laughed. 'I can see that you've also had some major barriers to surmount but most adolescent minds are perfectly capable of generating lustful thoughts without going to the trouble of singing Jerusalem! But your response was very general and defensive. Can you not enlighten me further about the specific circumstances or events which have brought on this acute attack of introspection? Or are you simply envious, as one of the pre-war generation, that the baby-boomer generation seem to be having all the fun as fully paid-up members of the permissive society?'

'I'm really not sure about that. It goes back to what I was saying about Andrew's challenges. It raised a question in my mind – do I want to spend the next twenty-five or thirty years locked into my current job and, if not, do I have the courage and talent to succeed as a writer or anything else for that matter?'

'Does Ann know of or empathise with your self-examination?'

'I've only discussed it with her briefly but I suspect she regards such aspirations as insane and she may well be right.'

'May I ask, is all well on the domestic front?'

'Oh yes, we have our ups and downs like all married couples but, yes, the marriage is fine.'

'I hope so – but you must know that fine is often regarded as an acronym – "fucking incapable of normal emotions".' Peter laughed uneasily but did not respond. Michael continued, 'It's far from clear to me where your thoughts and aspirations are leading you and I suspect that they're not entirely clear to you either. Perhaps I can offer another health warning.' He picked a book off his shelves and as he thumbed through the pages he said, 'I'm sure you're not as familiar with the works of Karl Marx as I am and I'm quite certain that it was not required reading at your posh school! He wrote "Men make their own history, but they do not make it under self-selected circumstances, but under circumstances existing already, given and transmitted from the past". He was writing about Louis Bonaparte and while I'm not suggesting that you have imperial ambitions, only you can determine if you have the commitment to create an alternative history for yourself unconstrained by the circumstances of the past. I cannot and will not advise, although I am always here to listen and, after your disclosures this evening, I can scarcely wait for the next instalment!'

'Thank you, you're right. I really don't know where I want my life to go. I guess I'm in the position of Cromwell when he said "I can tell you what I would not have but I cannot what I would". But that's enough of my existential angst for one evening.'

'You're right. It's been good to see you but let's move on to less emotive topics and listen to some music before you go home and sleep off the alcohol which you have ingested today.'

8

The telephone rang insistently early the following morning. Peter woke with a start and felt instinctively for the alarm clock but when he was unable to silence the noise he identified the source and lifted the receiver.

'Peter, I was trying to get you last night. Where were you?' Ann's tense voice came down the line.

'Me? Oh, I went out to have a meal. You remember, I told you on the phone yesterday evening that I would be late home.'

'Yes, I forgot. Dad died at about 7.30 last night.'

'Oh God, I'm sorry. How are you and your Mum coping?'

'She's devastated at one level but she is managing. As you know, she had been prepared for this for some weeks. I think I shall have to stay up here now for at least a week. I can't leave her and Jenny to make all the funeral arrangements on their own. I phoned Francis yesterday when it was clear that Dad was on the way out and he agreed that I could stay away from work on compassionate leave until the middle of next week. He wants me then to meet him in Birmingham. I shall have to go there directly from Newcastle. We're making a documentary programme about the Lunar Society and he wants the whole team to be there. He says it's important that I familiarise myself with the background and immerse myself in some of the history. Could you bring my briefcase to Newcastle when you come? I shall try and arrange the funeral for next Tuesday.'

'What in God's name is or was the Lunar Society?'

'This is really not the time to talk about the Lunar Society,' she said rather irritably, 'or anything other than getting through the next few days.'

'No, I'm sorry. It was just that I was somewhat taken aback by the unusual name. Do you want me to come straightaway?'

'No, and I'm sorry to be so snappy. I'll tell you what little I know after I've been to Birmingham and am home again. That won't be until the end of next week. There's no need to come straightaway, but it would be helpful if you could come on Saturday and then stay until after the funeral's over.'

Peter repositioned himself and saw from the clock that it was only just after six-thirty. They spoke for a few more minutes and agreed to keep in touch by telephone. He sat on the edge of the bed, his head in his hands regretting his intemperance of the previous day. It was clearly not worth trying to go back to sleep again. He walked through to the kitchen to make himself some coffee which he drank slowly and took some paracetamol. Breakfast was not an appealing prospect that morning.

The following days passed slowly. He was still incapable of sustained periods of concentration when alone in his office, responding to the routine business of his clients reflexly and courteously but distantly. He succeeded in keeping up with the inflow of work but it was completed with little interest and even less enthusiasm. At lunchtimes, he would avoid his partners, preferring to eat something in his office or to sit quietly in the corner of a pub lingering over a small glass of wine and a sandwich. On one dry day, he walked home from the office after work, deviating along side streets away from the flow of the anxious, febrile traffic of the homebound city. It was a means of avoiding his own company for too long in the flat. When at home he would spend the evenings aimlessly switching between the television and the record player. One evening he took a pile of scrap paper home from the office and spent several hours filling the pages with maudlin sentiments but he screwed the paper up and then, regretting the gesture, straightened each sheet out. He re-read the sheets once more and finally tore them up before taking the fragments out and burying them deep in the dustbin, apprehensive that the inadequacies of his style and the banality of the content might be seen by others.

The funeral was planned for the following Tuesday. He decided to drive knowing that this activity, although almost devoid of cerebral stimulation, would be a desirable alternative to a crowded and almost certainly delayed journey on the weekend trains. He was awake early on the Saturday and ready to leave before eight. He had told Sue he would be away for a few days. He had visited her on two or three evenings for coffee while he had been on his own. The first visit he had undertaken willingly but subsequent visits were more out of a sense of obligation. He had thought that the company might lift his spirits and fill the time with a greater sense of focus and worth than he was gaining from the daily routine of the office, but he found that Sue was still constrained by a sense of apathy and inertia which would have been difficult to penetrate at any time. Peter, already withdrawn and uncertain, found that his poor conversational initiatives were drawing monosyllabic responses and that the greater part of the evenings were spent in silent reflection. He would willingly have discontinued these visits if Sue had not pressed him to stay longer as he prepared to leave each evening, insisting that he should return the following day.

Peter was glad to escape the city and reach the Great North Road. He settled back in his seat as he accelerated up to and just beyond the legal limit. He switched the radio on and relaxed as he held the wheel in the tips of his fingers, an affectation that created for him a sense of masterful control. The signs listing the distances to various northern cities and one which simply and unambiguously stated that the road led to "The North" were challenges as he envisaged himself controlling the vehicle through the miles and across the pages of the road atlas. His vision was focused on the road as it continuously widened and disappeared beneath the front of the car. The drab changing colours of the road surface, the vibration transmitted through the tyres and the monotone of the wind all contributed to his introspection. The sentimental and simplistic words of the songs emanating from Radio 2 appeared suddenly to be imbued with deeper meanings which matched his mood. The aspirations and ambitions expressed through the trite and vapid lyrics acquired a significance which was enhanced by his altered receptivity. He started to think of alternative paths ahead for himself but with more urgency than previously. He was persuaded that there was an inescapable need to re-evaluate his life and this was starting to add clarity and refinement to his thoughts. He was thirty-five and had acquired, achieved or, perhaps, accidentally stumbled on a solid conventional respectability with an occupation and income beyond the aspirations of many. It would be possible to come to terms with this life and achieve a level of fulfilment through work completed with competence. It might be possible to write in the evenings to satisfy his alter ego. This would be an attractive compromise but one, he felt, which would almost certainly not achieve anything of substance.

The alternative would require him to take time away from home and his practice and deny himself at least some of the material benefits which he had acquired. He would be forfeiting these things to follow a shadow or a chimera, working towards objectives which he could only dimly perceive and which might prove to be wholly illusory. Natural caution and bourgeois inhibitions would counsel against setting out along such a path which would demand skills and competences which were untested and unknown. He could perhaps embark on such a course if he were to leave his firm for a year, leave London and lead the life of a recluse away from familiar haunts. This would be an attractive possibility although he was aware that leaving a line of retreat open behind him suggested a certain lack of commitment and confidence. He started to reflect on the practicalities of such an arrangement and was suddenly brought out of his musings by an awareness that he had scarcely thought of any of this in the context of his marriage.

He could not claim with any justification that he was unhappy in his marriage although it had not really provided the excitement or the level of happiness which, in his naiveté, he had hoped to find in a lasting relationship. It was difficult, indeed impossible, to be sure if that deficiency should be attributed to Ann or himself or the precisely ordered nature of their married state. It was most likely attributable to all three factors in indefinable proportions. Perhaps it was inevitable that the intensity of emotion in a marriage would diminish over time. Any action which would alter their present mode of living and the equilibrium of their marriage would ineluctably exclude Ann from a large area of his life. It was difficult to envisage the alternative of a formal separation. Peter shrank from the thought of ever raising such a topic. In the abstract, he found the notion of establishing an independent existence appealing although he recognised that his own loneliness during the previous week was in part a consequence of their enforced separation and, in part, the aftermath of the events of recent weeks. It would only be possible to consider a separation if each was patently unhappy or if one had formed an attachment to someone else making a rupture of their own relationship imperative. It would be quite another matter to coldly plan a separation simply to relieve a sense of unease and to damage or destroy a marriage to try and fulfil an uncertain dream.

* * *

It was late afternoon when he arrived in Newcastle. As the flat did not have room to accommodate him, he needed to stay in a hotel. Ann and Jenny were sharing the second bedroom. He was disconcerted that Ann would not join him but had chosen to remain in the flat to support her mother and sister. He drove up to Cowgate to join the family as soon as he had checked into the hotel. He greeted them and, over tea, was brought up to date with the details of the funeral arrangements. He had been delegated various tasks, principally those which he could carry out most easily as he had a car. Peg and Graham Robson had been intermittent churchgoers and had attended the Dilston Road Methodist Church close to their old home in Hartington Road. The funeral was to take place there so it was agreed that they would all go to the church the following morning and review the arrangements after the service with the minister. It was also agreed that Peter would take Ann to the station after the funeral so that she could catch a train to Birmingham. He would then drive Jenny back to London as she had a further interview on the following Monday.

The day of the funeral was cool, bright and clear. The undertaker's car arrived to take them to the church shortly before ten-thirty. There were few mourners; no more than fourteen including two distant cousins and Peg's widowed sister. Peter was not familiar with the words of the funeral service and he became progressively more dispirited as the service proceeded. Finally they reached the words of the committal: 'Man that is born of woman hath but a short time to live and is full of misery. He cometh up and is cut down like a flower: he fleeth as it were a shadow and never

continueth in one stay. In the midst of life we are in death.'
He could think of few more depressing words for the family
nor a more abject and inaccurate summary of a life, of
almost any life, but he reflected that they simply mirrored
the attitudes of a religion which has all humanity cast as
sinners in need of redemption as its default mode.

It was a sombre group that gathered in the hall adjacent
to the church after the ceremony for a cup of tea and after a
short time they started to disperse. Ann whispered in Peter's
ear, 'I must go.'

'You're in very good time for your train.'

'I know but I must get away from here. I really can't take
any more reminiscing and the occasional comment on the
length of time that I was away from home. Please, just take
me to the station and then come back and take Mum home
before you and Jenny drive back to London.'

He drove Ann to the station in silence and hugged her
when she got out of the car. 'Will you be alright?'

'I will be when I get away – go back to Mum and take
care of Jenny while she is in London. She was much closer
to Dad than I ever was.'

9

Peter returned to work for the last three days of the week. Jenny had been disinclined to talk during the long drive south and he left her to her own thoughts and memories of her father. As they entered the northern part of the city she said, 'I'm sorry I've been so silent but I feel I've reached a tipping point in my life and I'll be entering a new phase, particularly if I land this job. I'm also sad at what I'm leaving behind. Ann was able to isolate herself from Tyneside but I don't feel I can ever do that. The bonds are too strong. I also want to visit and support Mum and I hope now Ann has returned and re-established contact that she will see her regularly. This is something we must sort out between us.'

Peter left Jenny free to explore London and prepare for her interview. Her presence in the flat was welcome and provided a distraction after the events of the previous few weeks. They relaxed together the first evening and Peter proposed that they might go out on some of the following evenings. He found her frankness and her preparedness to laugh at almost anything refreshing, despite inevitable episodes of melancholy on her part. A couple of evenings later they went to see a film, "If…", an allegorical tale depicting a savage insurrection in an English public school, focused on three non-conformist pupils who rebel against sadistic older boys and staff. It finally ends in a bloody gunfight.

'Could such a thing really happen in a public school?' asked Jenny as they returned to the flat.

'I'd like to think it was highly unlikely.'

'But what are conditions like for younger kids? Can they really be treated so sadistically and exploited in the sorts of ways shown in the film?'

Peter hesitated. 'There was certainly a fair amount of bullying in my school days nearly twenty years ago, not to mention fagging. There's no doubt that life could be made pretty miserable for new arrivals at the school. I don't recall anything as brutal as that shown in some of the scenes and I'm sure things will have changed since I left.'

'But even so, why would anyone want to send their sons to schools where such things happened?'

'It was the established pattern for middle- and upper-class families and I suspect that parents scarcely gave it a thought, even if they were aware of what was going on. If challenged, it would have been excused, if not justified, on the basis of tradition. It was assumed to be character-forming! The film is very much part of the challenges to traditional attitudes which we are seeing all around us now – although in an extreme form.'

'Well, I'm happy that experiences such as that played no part in shaping my character. If I ever have a son I would not want him exposed to such an environment.'

'No – and I'm not sure that I would either. Life really has changed. When I was a kid, boys were simply deposited at boarding school and parents would only see them at the rare exeats, once or twice a term, when we were allowed out on Sundays between morning and evening chapel. Parents were not expected to interact with the school in those days but that has quite changed. This is a depressing subject; let's change it. Tell me about yourself and your romantic life. I understood from Ann that you have a serious boyfriend.'

'No, no longer. Simon was fun and I was fond of him but it was getting very heavy, far too heavy for me. He suggested we should move in together. I didn't feel sufficiently strongly about him to make such a commitment and it would have tied me down just as I have the opportunity to spread my wings. On a scale of one to ten on the Richter scale of romantic entanglement, it only reached about three or four on my side. I think it was at least double that for him. We have split up with the usual assurances that we'll remain friends but I suspect contact will fade over the years and it will remain as a pleasant but relatively insignificant memory.'

'That sounds a little detached.'

'I guess so but that's how I feel and it's realistic.'

'So what do you hope to do now?'

'Is that a question about my love life or about my job prospects?'

Peter laughed. 'I was enquiring about your career aspirations. I wouldn't dream of delving into your romantic dreams. I'm more than ten years older than you and it might be more than I can take!'

'Well, I'm glad that we've got that straight.' She smiled. 'Anyhow, I don't have a love life at present but if you were to press me to reveal any amorous aspirations I would plead the

Fifth Amendment! My interview is for a job as an editorial assistant with a company which publishes fine art books and magazines. I suspect it's the lowest of the low in the company hierarchy. However, it's a small outfit and I understand it will involve some interaction with writers. It will give me the chance to decide if publishing is where I want to spend at least the first part of my working life. But there are so many more opportunities out there which I also hope to explore.'

'So there's no point in asking you where you might see yourself in ten years' time?'

'None whatsoever! The possibilities that life offers are simply too exciting to plan that far ahead. There will be opportunities which I don't even know about at present and I imagine that in ten or twenty years' time there will be jobs out there which don't even exist now.'

'And developing a social life?'

'What will be, will be. I'm different from Ann. She always planned for a life in which she would make her way in a glamorous industry and would cement a secure relationship early in her adult life and she's achieved all of that. She was always held up to me as a role model, but it was never a model which totally appealed to me. That's not a criticism of Ann but it's a life that was never for me! But how about you – did you always want to be a solicitor and get married?'

Peter hesitated. 'I suppose the honest answer is no.'

'Is this a confession? So, when did you decide and why?'

He paused again. 'I'm not quite sure when I decided – or even if I did consciously decide. I was reasonably bright and it was always assumed that I would enter one of the professions or take up some safe job in the city. The law had some interest for me and it seemed like a respectable way of making a reasonable living. It also gave me the opportunity to spend three years at Cambridge and that was perhaps the least worst option. You can see my horizons were neither very broad nor very distant. It all sounds pretty unambitious.'

'Didn't you ever dream of other possibilities? Have you never had a passion to do something which would match your wildest ambitions?'

He hesitated again but simply said, 'Occasionally, but my dreams are never more than passing fantasies and they're probably not very wild by most people's standards. Most of us of the pre-war generation are neither very imaginative nor very adventurous. You baby boomers are the imaginative and emancipated generation. Aspirations in the environment in which I was brought up were almost always judged in terms of respectability and wealth acquisition and little else.'

'That sounds just like Ann.' Jenny giggled. 'What a shame! I should like to see you break free from your shackles and fly. Even better, I should like to see Ann do so.'

'Come on, it's time you and I were off to our beds. Tomorrow's Saturday – there's no rush to get up in the morning.'

'Ann would tell you that there is absolutely no need for that injunction!'

'You're safe. She won't be back till Sunday. I thought that I might ask my friend Michael Rattray to come and share a takeaway with us tomorrow evening. You might enjoy his company – although your sister is not too enthusiastic about him. Sleep well.'

* * *

They were joined by Michael the following evening. 'Tell us what you're doing,' said Peter.

'Oh, my life moves on. The work in the centre all too often takes me from one seemingly intractable case to another resulting in outcomes which are neither satisfactory to me nor, more importantly, to the client. These are the perennial battles with the "insolence of office" which characterises the petty bureaucrats of this world.'

'You're sounding very dispirited.'

'It's been a bad week. It happens at times although I do believe I play a useful role. At the very least those who come to me feel that someone has made an effort to address their wrongs, real or perceived. It's possible, however, that there could be some major change in my life. I'm seeking adoption as a Labour parliamentary candidate. I'm not sure if I'll be successful and, even if I am, it's most likely that I shall be given a first run in an unwinnable seat! An election is, of course, still a little way off.'

'This is a surprise – I knew you were interested in politics but I was not aware that you had active political ambitions. Where would you like to stand if the choice were yours?'

'Of course, the choice will not be mine but Merseyside if it were. It was my home.'

'But do you think that you will be able to change things if you are elected?' asked Jenny.

'Quite possibly not, but I should try. Few of us have the right combination of talent, people skills, native wit, low cunning and opportunity to make substantial changes to the world. A few of us manage to change things in our own small corner but the majority settle for simply being part of the poor bloody infantry of life for which I am well qualified! I guess I'm also saddened by what I see in the wider world around us, the use of violence to advance causes. I long to see radical change but assassination, as we saw of Bobby Kennedy, urban terrorism or the imposition by arms of a western sanctioned regime as we are seeing in Vietnam cannot be the way forward. I'm finding it difficult. I applaud political activism and I've been on a couple of anti-Vietnam War marches but I deplore the violence which can erupt on some of these occasions. Peter knows I served in Malaya during my National Service. I'd been tempted to seek alternative service as a conscientious objector, but my Dad was emphatic that he wouldn't have any bloody conchies around the house! But Malaya was a challenge. I was terrified much of the time, jumping whenever there was a noise in the jungle – and jungles are naturally noisy places. It was also difficult in that I had some sympathy with the communist ideology, although not with their methods, nor with their wish to impose their ideology on the local ethnic majority. We had to do many things which made me uncomfortable like forcing the relocation of many local people and defoliating crops to deprive the insurgents of their support systems. I'm sorry, this is a depressing subject for a Saturday evening. Jenny, you're the youngest amongst us – what do you think?'

'I don't think that I should be asked to carry the burden of being the spokesperson for the twenty-somethings. I imagine there is as wide a range of views amongst those of my age as there is amongst those of yours. I sympathise with much of what you say and I suppose watching that film yesterday also highlighted the possibility of people seeking to achieve their ends through violence, extreme though it was.'

'This is far too gloomy a topic for a Saturday evening. Tell us what your plans are for the future, bonny lass.'

'I'm not sure I have plans. The world is changing ever more rapidly. I think there may have been a step change in attitudes in the half generation which separates us.'

'But you must have some ideas for the next year or perhaps just for the next week?'

'I have an interview in two days' time. If I'm offered the job and if I like the people, I shall take it. I shall be working in an area which interests me so I'll see how it goes. I shall certainly enjoy London. If it doesn't work out – well, I'll simply look for another job. I shall probably do that anyhow within a year or two even if I do enjoy it. There are so many opportunities, both here and abroad, many of them in fields that I know nothing about at present. The world is changing; I'm a free agent and I find uncertainty about my future exciting and motivating.' She laughed. 'My sister would have a fit and certainly disapprove of such an attitude to life!'

'What about a personal life?'

'Are you referring to sex? I am not concerned at present. I'm single, relaxed and unfettered. I'll see who might come into sight over the horizon. I don't want to get into a long-term relationship for many years yet. But what about you, Michael? You're ten years or so older than me and you're single.'

'I'm in much the same position as you. The right person

has not yet come into view or at least not come within touching distance. The time will probably come but I am not into predictions. I don't know when it might happen and indeed it might not happen at all.'

'He's an interesting man,' said Jenny after he had gone. 'Is he always so serious?'

'No, but he does take his life and work seriously. He has come a long way from Liverpool and his upbringing. He has got where he has partly through hard work but principally through pure intelligence. He can be very entertaining when in his lighter moods. You and Ann have also come a long way from your origins. You have a lightness which seems to pervade everything you do and a tendency to laugh at life's absurdities and to lighten some of its darker moments in the same way.'

She laughed. 'I guess you're right. But our childhood wasn't always too serious. It was a tightly knit family and a very supportive one. Ann and I were always encouraged to learn and to go to uni. I think it was very selfless of them to encourage us to do so away from Newcastle. It was a typically close Tyneside family unit.'

* * *

Ann returned the following day. 'That was exhausting, particularly following the days in Newcastle,' she said.

'So what was it all about? What is this Lunar Society? I've never heard of it.'

'Some of it is a mystery. It was an informal gathering of major figures in the Midlands at the end of the eighteenth and early in the nineteenth century. They were all people who contributed to the development of Birmingham industrially or to the sciences and the arts. They included Matthew Boulton, Josiah Wedgwood, Joseph Priestly, James Watt, William Withering, Erasmus Darwin and others and they also drew some from a little further afield like Wright of Derby and Joseph Banks. They're a mystery in that it seems the society never had a constitution or kept minutes nor were there any membership lists.'

'So what's the focus of the series of programmes?'

'It's really about the lives of a remarkably inventive group of men. We spent some time looking at archives which contained correspondence amongst the group and then started to construct bio-dramas of their lives, visiting locations where they had worked and lived. This will provide the framework for the series. It will now go to the researchers to furnish further detail and then to the scriptwriters before we can go back and start filming. It was exhausting travelling around the area visiting relevant sites. It seems they went quite far afield for their meetings. It was just Francis and his production assistant and me.'

'Sounds interesting – but why Lunar?'

'They apparently met on evenings when the moon was full so that they had more light when travelling home. They sometimes referred to themselves as "lunarticks"! But enough of work. What have you and Jenny been up to?'

'She's been entertaining herself while I've been at work. We went to see a film one evening and Michael R came round yesterday.'

'I hope he hasn't been filling her head with his radical views.'

'It was a quiet evening – we talked about world events and various other things. He's hoping to be adopted as a candidate for a seat at the next general election, whenever that might be.'

'Has Jenny been preparing for her interview?'

'I assume so but I've not been here much of the time. She's a grown-up, she has to take responsibility for herself.'

'I'm not always sure that she is so grown up. She needs to face the realities of getting a job and supporting herself in the real world.'

'I'm sure she'll do that but her perception of the real world is very different from yours and mine. She's a free spirit.'

'Being a free spirit doesn't necessarily equate with responsibility and it doesn't earn you a living.'

'No – but she'll have to make her own way and make her own mistakes.'

'I guess so. I've been thinking about Mum. I think I shall have to go up to Newcastle again in the next few weeks, particularly if Jenny is going to start a job in London. I thought we might encourage her to come down and stay sometime in the autumn or possibly over Christmas.'

'Good idea. We could show her the sights while she's here.'

'Thank you. Yes, that is a good idea.'

'It would also be good for her to meet my parents.'

'Yes – I know. I feel guilty about the way that I maintained so little contact with my parents during all those years away. In many ways Jenny has been a much better daughter than I have. She spent most of her vacations at home when she was at uni and then chose to go home for her postgraduate years.'

10

'It seems a long time ago now,' intoned Michael.

'For God's sake, look out!' shouted Peter gripping the edge of his seat.

He had been on his own at the flat and, overcome with an unwelcome sense of solitude, he had called Michael and arranged to meet him for a meal in a small Italian restaurant in Barnes. Ann had left for a long weekend in Newcastle to be followed by a further two days exploring possibilities and preparing briefs for the researchers for the planned series on the Lunar Society. Jenny had been successful in her interviews and was in Newcastle preparing for her move to London. The job would start ten days later in the second week of December. 'Just in time for the office Christmas parties,' she had said cheerfully. She would live in the flat with Peter and Ann until she had found her own accommodation. She planned to look for a flat-share somewhere not too far from the firm's offices in Bloomsbury.

During the course of the meal snow had fallen heavily and the temperature had dropped sharply. The roads had become treacherous and the few cars which had driven along the residential roads beside the Common where they had parked had created a rutted and frozen surface. The car skidded, finally coming to rest at a right angle to the kerb.

Michael looked across at Peter with an air of resignation. 'Turn into the skid, they always say, the omniscient "they", but what do they mean by that? Turn left, right or up the bloody centre? I never understood that instruction and what the hell does it matter? By the time anyone's thought it through it's too late!' He swung the wheel and engaged reverse and as he removed his foot from the clutch the wheels spun ineffectually on the ice. 'Idyllic,' he said as he finally removed his foot from the accelerator and took the car out of gear. He waved a hand at the wintry scene. 'Is this Barnes Common or is this fairyland that I see before me?'

'Oh, shut up,' said Peter good-humouredly although he was beginning to regret the impulse which had led him to telephone Michael. 'I'll get out and push you round while you run the car in reverse but, for God's sake, do go gently on the accelerator and release the clutch slowly this time.'

'As you say, Master.'

Peter got out and stepped cautiously onto the pavement and stood looking at the front of the car. There was a man walking slowly, drunkenly and unsteadily towards him, half singing and half humming Lilli Marlene. He lurched towards Peter and stood by his shoulder for a moment swaying gently. 'That,' he said judiciously, 'if you don't mind my saying so, is a very poor piece of parking.'

'Oh, go home, Dad,' said Peter as he placed both his hands on the nearside front wing and braced his feet against the kerb. He started to push the car as Michael took his foot off the clutch and revved slowly in reverse. The car began to straighten and the rear wheels started to grip in the tracks left by an earlier vehicle. This moment coincided with the point at which Michael could contain his impatience no longer and pressed more firmly on the accelerator pedal. Peter slipped, half recovered and then fell prone in the snow. He reappeared at the passenger door brushing the snow from his coat.

'Is this the Yeti that comes in the night?' asked Michael as Peter climbed in.

'For God's sake, let's get on.'

Michael drove back to his flat in Hammersmith, rather more cautiously, where they settled down with a drink. 'It seems a long time ago now,' Michael repeated.

'A long time since when?'

'Since we were at Cambridge and the short time that we shared a flat when we both first came to London. I enjoyed that evening with you and Jenny a couple of months ago. It seemed almost like old times as we talked about our futures – at least Jenny and I did. You were notably silent.'

'I'm not sure there was much to say. I think you summed it up correctly when you said that most settle for being the poor bloody infantry of life. Though, speaking as a foot soldier, you must not forget how essential they are to the conduct of a war. A masterful strategy is quite useless without the means to implement it. Even a National Service 2nd Lieutenant has sufficient grasp of strategy to work that one out.'

'Yes, but I sensed that there were times that evening when you were on the verge of expressing some discontent with your lot, as you did when we saw each other in the autumn after your surreal Bohemian day.'

'Perhaps, but you shouldn't read too much into that. Everyone must have dreams from time to time of breaking free from the daily round. I guess events over the last few months have rather unsettled me.'

'What events? There's something that's quietly bugging you, isn't there? We don't see each other for a year or so and then three times in three months. You offered some details of the occurrences which had touched you during the previous few weeks at the first of our recent meetings but we then veered off into an inconclusive discussion about happiness and fulfilment. Tell all.'

'All would be going a little too far!' Peter paused before continuing. 'I guess it really started with that dinner party last August. That was the evening when we were called by Jenny to say that her father was seriously ill. It led us into a fairly light-hearted conversation about Tyneside which then moved on and focused on the extent to which people are able to free themselves from the familial, emotional and cultural constraints imposed on them by their parents, peers and upbringing. I guess this mirrors the comment by Marx which you quoted when we met earlier. This brought a number of latent thoughts to the fore as I reflected that I'd pretty much travelled along pre-ordained paths through life – really without questioning it. All this would have just become a distant memory within a day or two if it hadn't been for the subsequent series of wholly unconnected events, some of which I outlined to you. Some were trivial and some more substantial but they kept that discussion at the forefront of my mind. Andrew's death has affected me deeply, more deeply than I had expected. I suppose it's often the case that that such tragedies can, in retrospect, seem to have a particular significance.'

Michael was silent for a few moments. 'This is really not telling me anything other than that you have a nagging sense of unease. Where is all this going to take you?'

'I really don't know. Maybe, probably, nowhere at all. A major change in the direction of my life would involve a leap into the unknown and a major disruption of my life and that of Ann as well. She would probably think I'd taken leave of my senses, as would my parents. It's interesting that they come from entirely different places and yet I'm certain that they would hold exactly the same views. Perhaps I would reflect as Hamlet did, although in somewhat different circumstances, that "conscience does make cowards of us all, and makes us rather bear the ills we have than fly to others that we know not of". I have to admit that my choice is rather less stark. It is not between life and death and I cannot in truth claim that I have too much in the way of ills to bear.'

'I guess the smart money would be on all this going nowhere.'

'I'm sure you're right, although I feel somewhat wimpish in saying that. I can, of course, put together a case articulating reasons why my current role in life is worthwhile. Much of it is designed to help ordinary people navigate through the storms of life. Like you, I see clients at times when they are stressed and often when they are vulnerable.'

'Yes, we are both in the same trade. I'm not sure that I suffer from the same anxieties as you – and I have my political ambitions to spur me on. It remains to be seen if they will amount to anything. Even as an agnostic I do have a missionary streak!'

'I believe I see your Catholic upbringing still lurking somewhere in the background.'

'Perhaps so. As we've been saying, it's almost impossible to throw off the effects of nurture on our lives, but I would reject the suggestion that it has imposed on me the uncertainties and agonies which are so characteristic of the fiction of some Catholic authors.'

'So we talk but continue to walk along our accustomed paths. This, stripped down to its bare essentials, was the basis of Andrew's challenge. I remember once when I was at school I was posed a question by one of the staff. He looked at my face as I struggled and failed to answer and suggested in a wonderful phrase that I was "in an ecstasy of indecision"! That phrase comes close to summing up my position although I'm not sure that it currently constitutes a state of ecstasy. I must be going.' He rose to leave. 'I'll take a bus if they're still running or a taxi if not.'

* * *

During the first full week in December Jenny moved into the flat and started her job with Fine Arts Monthly and Ann returned from her trip to Newcastle and the Midlands. After a few days commuting from Barnes to Bloomsbury, Jenny decided that she would look for a flat-share as soon as possible. It was evident that she was not only motivated by the inconvenience of the journey but also by a wish to live nearer the centre of the city. She decided she would start to look in earnest after the Christmas holiday period. Ann announced her intention of going to Newcastle on the Friday before Christmas so that she could travel back with her mother. The Bowmans, as Peter had predicted, invited the family to join them on Christmas Day. They were to be joined by Peter's older brother, Matthew, and his family who had been living in Frankfurt for the past three years where Matt had a job in the financial sector. Matt and Jilly had two boys aged six and four, Oliver and Piers.

They all met as instructed for a family visit to church on Christmas morning and then walked down the hill to the house. They gathered in the lounge for a glass of champagne before lunch as presents were distributed and the room rapidly became knee deep in discarded wrapping paper. Conversation flowed slowly at first as new connections were made.

'I think it's a pity that we didn't get to know you before today and that we never met your husband. It's so sad that you were unable to come to Peter and Ann's wedding,' said Molly ignorant of the fact that Ann's parents had been actively discouraged from attending by their daughter.

Loyally, Peg responded saying that it would have been a big journey for them and that Graham was already unwell by then.

'Peter tells me that this is the first time you've been to London since you came up for a cup final.' She ploughed on blithely and wholly unaware that she was discomfiting her son and daughter-in-law.

'That was my second visit. We came here on our honeymoon – for just two nights. That was in 1932.'

'So there was quite a long gap before Ann was born?'

'Yes, she was born shortly before the war and Jenny just after it was all over. It took some time for me to fall with Ann.'

Molly looked a little nonplussed at the response. 'What do you mean?'

Ann interjected to explain that "falling" was a northern term for becoming or falling pregnant. Then, planning to divert the conversation towards more general topics, she added, 'We plan to show Mum some of the sights and take her to a show.'

'What are you planning to see?'

'Mum loves music. We thought of Cabaret but a friend said that it might be better to go to see "Fiddler on the Roof." That seemed like a good idea so we've booked for that.'

'That sounds like just the ticket,' said Geoffrey. 'I wouldn't mind seeing it myself. Is young Jenny in on this party as well?'

'Absolutely, if she wishes to come.'

Peter turned to Matt. 'It's a year since I last saw you. What's family life like in Germany? I imagine you've already had some celebrations for St Nicholas.'

'Yes, but these vary widely from region to region and St Nicholas goes by a variety of different names. The celebrations are fairly small scale. Children put a boot outside the door in the hope that it will be filled with sweets or small gifts. The tradition is that he will only leave gifts if the children have been good through the year and he leaves a stick in the boot if they haven't.'

Geoffrey looked at Oliver and Piers. 'Did you get a stick?'

'Of course not, Grandpa,' they chorused. 'We're always good.'

'A likely story,' he said genially.

'Do you speak German fluently now?' asked Ann.

'I regret to say that my German is only average. The principal language in the office is English and, of course, we speak it at home. Jilly is much better than I am as she has to deal with all our everyday affairs – shopping, the services, plumbers, butchers, bakers and probably candlestick makers as well. I suspect if we're there for another year the boys will be the most fluent as they pick it up from playing with other kids from the housing complex. They learn so quickly at that age.'

'It must be great,' said Jenny. 'I should so love to work abroad for a time.'

'So what exactly does your job involve?' asked Jilly. 'Peter told us that you have just started to work for a publishing company.'

'Yes, it publishes fine art books and magazines. I have the job title of editorial assistant.'

'What does that involve?'

'Difficult to say in detail. I've only worked there for just over two weeks and most of the second week was given over to Christmas parties. But I think the answer will be almost anything I'm told to do. I suspect it will involve some copy editing, some liaising with contributors to the magazines, possibly providing a little assistance in developing promotional material and being a general dogsbody. Fine art publishing is a small scale business. I understand that I'll be going out of the office a bit but mainly in the London area which is where most British experts are based. I don't think I'll get anywhere more exciting.'

'Might the Frankfurt Book Fair be a possibility?'

'I suspect that would be for more senior people in the company. I still have so much to learn. It helps that my degree was in English and my thesis was on Christina Rossetti.'

'And how is your life going, Peter?'

He shrugged. 'Plodding on – after all, I am a solicitor.'

'I'm sure it's not as boring as it sounds.'

'I suspect most people would think it is. I spend my day dotting "Is" and crossing "Ts" and generally trying to make sure that everything is as unambiguous and, therefore, as boring as possible. Like most lawyers, I'm forever utilising that awful phrase "for the avoidance of doubt".'

Molly had been out of the room attending to the turkey. 'We haven't seen you, of course, since that terrible night with your neighbour. It was very upsetting and even if he did behave outrageously, what happened afterwards was very sad.' There was a pause while Peter delivered an edited version of the events of that evening and its consequences to his brother. 'How is that sweet wife of his managing?' she finished.

'With great difficulty,' said Ann. 'Peter and I have been trying to be as supportive as possible but she is very low. Peter has seen more of her as I've been away quite a bit in Newcastle and in Birmingham with preparations for a documentary series we are putting together.'

'Sounds interesting,' said Molly. 'You must tell us more over lunch. Geoffrey, come and carve the bird.'

The rituals of a traditional Christmas lunch having been

duly observed, they returned to the lounge for a brandy and a semi-somnolent afternoon while they watched the film "The courage of Lassie" on the television with the boys. Finally, Ann and Peter together with Jenny and Peg returned to their flat.

* * *

The day of Peggy Robson's departure was approaching. She had been delighted to be treated as a tourist viewing the sights of London, and claimed that the visit to the theatre to see "Fiddler on the Roof" had evoked happy memories of a more innocent pre-war world. Ann, Peter and Jenny sat talking together the night before Peg's return after their mother had gone to bed. They had tried to persuade her that it might be a good idea if she were to move to London so they could see more of her and visit her regularly. This proposition had been firmly rejected on the grounds that she had lived in Newcastle all her life and did not plan to up sticks at this stage and that her friends were all there. 'You're all too busy with your lives,' she had said. 'I'm not sure that I would see so much more of you. It has been lovely having Jenny living at home for the last year but now she has a job and the freedom to go anywhere. I don't want to hold her back. Ann took her freedom nine years ago,' she had said rather pointedly, 'so I know what happens when you young people get away and start to make a success of your lives.'

Ann had been stung by the last of these remarks and proposed to Jenny that they should continue to try and persuade their mother to move south although both Jenny and Peter insisted that such an attempt was almost inevitably going to end in failure. Eventually she said, 'Well, Jenny, you and I will have to get up to Newcastle more regularly to see Mum. I think she is being a little selfish in refusing to consider moving south, but I guess we can encourage her to come and stay once or twice a year. It's going to be difficult for me to travel north very often as I'm now so busy in my job and, at times, I have to work in the evenings and at weekends.'

'That last comment is scarcely fair,' said Jenny somewhat angrily. 'In fact, not much of it is fair. I've lived with Mum and Dad as an adult, something that you haven't done. Her friends and contemporaries are important to her and they are there day in and day out at the Social Club. She would be isolated here in London with only occasional visits from us.'

'Well, I think that most of the burden of travelling to Newcastle will fall on you.'

'Why should that be?'

'Simply because I'm so busy.'

'OK, you've established yourself in your career but I just don't know how busy I shall be nor where my career might take me. You seem to think, just because I have an open mind and am ready to explore various possibilities for my future, that my ambitions are somehow less significant than yours. You just left home and didn't come back until Dad was dying.' Jenny was quite angry now.

'I think Jenny has a point,' said Peter.

'It's nothing to do with you.'

'Perhaps not so much but I am simply saying that Jenny

has a point and as you work out how you are to continue to keep in contact, you do need to consider both your needs. The first thing you might do would be to get a telephone installed in her flat and pay for it, although that is no substitute for visits.'

'Yes – I agree with that and yes, we do need to work together,' Ann said in a rather less dictatorial tone. 'We'll all take her back to King's Cross tomorrow and I'll make arrangements for a telephone to be put into the flat.'

11

St Valentine's Day started like any other working day. Peter and Ann left for work shortly before eight as usual. Jenny no longer lived in the flat as she had been offered a room in the house of a colleague from her office. Ann, despite earlier protestations, had made two visits to Newcastle combining these with trips she had been required to make to progress the Lunar Society project. She told Peter that it looked as though there might be possibilities for making further programmes based around some of the individual luminaries of the society. She had returned the previous day and Peter had booked a table for dinner at a restaurant in Barnes Village. She had been very reflective during the meal and attempts to get her to open up were met with an apology and an insistence that she simply had a lot on her mind about work at that time. They returned to the flat and Peter moved to switch the television on for the news.

'I should prefer not to watch the news tonight. Do you think I could have a brandy?'

'Yes, of course.' Peter poured the drink and after a little hesitation poured one for himself.

'Peter, I want to talk – I, we, need to talk.'

'Fine, go ahead.'

'Well, I really don't know how to begin – just give me a moment.' She sat clasping the glass in both hands, as if to administer the sacrament, looking down into the drink. She sat in this position for some time.

'Well, what is it?' Peter asked fighting to keep a note of irritation out of his voice after what seemed an interminable period of silence. She looked up and he saw that she was crying silently. 'I'm sorry,' he said more gently. 'It's just that you said that you wished to talk in such a doom-laden voice and then said nothing. I was trying to imagine what it was all about.'

'Yes, I know,' she sniffed. 'Can you get me a tissue and I'll try and straighten my voice and face and tell you.'

'You've been through a lot during the last few months, providing a shoulder for Sue to cry on and much more with your father's death and taking on responsibility for your mother. It's inevitable that it has all been a bit overwhelming, particularly with all the times you've been away travelling.'

'No, it's not just that. I have another problem.'

'Well?'

'Peter, please don't interrupt me. Let me finish what I have to say. This is going to be difficult enough. I've been thinking a lot about things while I've been away. There is no easy way of saying this. I want to leave you.'

'Ann! What are you saying?'

'Please let me go on. I've been thinking so hard about how I could say this to you. I finally realised that it could not be said in any other way. I know this comes out of the blue. I don't expect you to excuse me but it would help if you could understand a little.'

'But you can't just sit there and say calmly that you are walking out. What is wrong? There must be some reason.'

'Yes, of course there is, but please listen,' she added more gently. 'I'm sorry. I'm far from calm. I really am sorry, I didn't mean to sound so irritable, it isn't easy.' Peter leant forward resting his arms on his knees and gazed unseeingly at the floor. He found it difficult to comprehend and process the words he was hearing. It seemed he had wandered unwittingly onto the set of a play and was simply an observer of a dialogue which had no personal implications for him. 'Peter, I don't know what has gone wrong, or even if anything has gone seriously wrong, but something has changed. You're not the same man that I married. You've altered so much and very likely I've changed too. Our lives seem different, separate and we no longer communicate so easily with one another. You seem to be so remote.'

'But surely that is not a reason for walking out. It must be a reason for trying to improve our marriage, for sitting and talking about what either or both of us sees is wrong and trying to put it right. I see this so often at work where I sometimes feel that couples give up too easily on their marriage.'

'Peter, you may be right and possibly I should have had the courage to try to do that some time ago. But now, I'm sorry, it's too late for that because I have made up my mind and I cannot change it now. Please understand, it has not been easy. I think I want to marry someone else.'

Peter looked up frowning, puzzled and hurt. 'You think that you want to marry someone else,' he echoed foolishly and incredulously, 'but who is it?'

'Please listen, I'm trying to explain. I've become very close to Francis Carvalho, the director of the programmes we're planning. I've known him since he joined the company three years ago but it's only in the last few months that we have become close, very close. I've seen much more of him during the last two or three months and we have developed a very easy and comfortable relationship.'

'Obviously,' he said resentfully.

'No, it's not been like that. He was divorced before I ever knew him but we're in love and just want to be together. I feel rotten telling you like this, particularly on such an evening, but I couldn't go on saying nothing. I feel dreadful doing this to you. I can only say that it just happened. It wasn't planned and I certainly wasn't looking for an outside attachment or an affair. It started to become serious when we were together in Birmingham after Dad's funeral. We had a couple of drinks together that evening and he provided me with some much needed comfort. I was feeling vulnerable after Dad's death and guilty that I had largely written Mum and Dad out of my life for so long. It developed from there. Francis supported me through all that. He provided me with something I felt was missing when I was at home. He made me feel that I was the most important person in his life.'

'But what was missing? I tried to give all the support I could. I was with you all the time through the funeral and our earlier visit to Newcastle.'

'I know – but somehow with Francis it was different. Peter, I really don't want to hurt you but we don't seem to have the relationship that we had. In many ways you were, and still are, all that I dreamed of for a husband but somehow the chemistry has changed; with Francis, it's just been different. It will be better for you in the longer run to be free of me and on your own to make what you will of your life now this has happened.'

'That may be your view but it's no more than a rationalisation, and what right do you have to decide what is best for me?' he said angrily. 'You're only thinking of yourself. Those are simply words designed to exculpate yourself.'

She got up and walked across, kneeling directly in front of him and held his hands. 'I really had not intended this to happen but people do fall in love.'

'I suppose so,' he said flatly, 'but these things don't just happen.'

'It's not your fault – if anyone is to blame it is me.'

'That's not the impression I got from what you've just said.'

'Peter, I really didn't mean it in that way. I have been thinking and worrying about this endlessly. People do change, sometimes in ways which are predictable and sometimes in ways which are not. Those changes may be convergent or they may be divergent. They are generally not planned. We may adapt or we may not. There are so many uncertainties in this life. You have a lot going for you. You'll very likely meet someone who will really appreciate you.'

'And I suppose you've got that all arranged for me as well,' he said bitterly.

'Please don't, it's difficult enough for me as it is.'

'Surely you don't expect me to try to make it easier for you?'

'I suppose not.' She dropped his hands, knelt lower and

started to cry once more. 'Peter, I hope we can still remain friends after this.'

Peter did not respond for some time and was suddenly ashamed. He stood up and said abruptly, 'I'm sorry, Ann, I think I need to go out and take a walk.'

'Please don't do that, don't leave me alone just now. I haven't any right to ask you that, but please don't go out just now.' She lay crouched, head on the carpet and the tears started to flow once more. 'Oh God, I knew this would be awful but I didn't realize quite how bloody terrible it would be!'

Peter sat down again and resumed his position staring blindly at the floor. He knew that he should offer some help, a hand, a voice to comfort and console but was unable to act. The scene remained fixed for seconds or minutes – neither knew for how long. Finally, slowly, stiffly, deliberately and self-consciously, Ann got to her feet and walked silently from the room. She returned a few minutes later carrying a tray with two mugs of tea. The banality and incongruity of the action provoked Peter to laughter. He laughed softly at first and then with an uncontrolled harshness as he recognised the irony of this commonplace response to an emotional crisis.

'For God's sake, stop it! What are you laughing at? Stop it!' She shouted the last two words with such force that the laugh died in an instant.

'I'm sorry, Ann, I couldn't stop myself. The contrast between what you have just had to say and your appearance with the all-purpose British panacea was too much for me.'

'Yes, I suppose so.' She smiled wanly.

They drank the tea sitting as silently and remotely as strangers in a station waiting room.

'I think I'll still go out for a walk,' Peter said more quietly. 'I need space to think things over. Don't wait up for me. I'll sleep in the spare room.'

'You're not going to ...... do anything silly?'

'No, I shan't. Will you be alright on your own?'

'Yes, don't worry about me.'

* * *

Peter left and walked down to the street. The rain which had been falling had stopped and the streets shone wetly under the lights. He walked to the corner and was surprised to see from a clock that it was only 10.20. The whole scene in the flat had been over in twenty-five minutes. A number of couples were emerging from local restaurants holding hands after celebrating Valentine's Day. Initially he had no clear idea where he would walk but headed up the broad expanse of Castelnau towards Hammersmith Bridge. He walked over the bridge, pausing for a few minutes to watch the dark waters of the Thames ebbing and carrying their regular load of debris towards the centre of the city. He walked on to the area around the Broadway and on an impulse pushed open the door of a pub. The noise from within escaped and washed momentarily over the pavement as he made his way in and edged towards the bar. The babel of voices enclosed and isolated him and the nauseous smell of damp clothing almost overwhelmed him. He ordered a brandy and turning uncertainly was unable to find an isolated corner to sit or stand in the crowded bar. He emptied the glass in two quick gulps and, creating a passage for himself through the crowd, walked directly back into the street again. He leant against the outer wall of the pub for a few minutes breathing deeply and then started to walk slowly and aimlessly along King Street looking at the shop windows, the advertisements and the pedestrians walking past in secure encapsulated pairs.

A brief flurry of rain drove him into a shop doorway and he stood there looking out. He heard a soft voice behind him and looked round to see a couple locked in an embrace. Apologising incoherently, he ran out towards the next doorway but was checked by a group of teenage boys with close-cropped hair, tight leather jackets and heavy boots. He moved on and eventually found cover under an arch, where a woman was also sheltering. Peter leant back against the wall to recover his breath. He was unaware that he was being inspected until her voice broke in. 'You look a bit miserable, dearie. Why don't you come with me? I'm sure I could put a smile back on your face for a bit.'

'Oh God,' said Peter as he escaped from under the arch and started to run down the street, a shrill laugh echoing in his ears. He tried to hail a taxi but despaired as all seemed to have been taken in the further outbreak of rain. He finally paused in his flight as he found his passage barred by a policeman.

'Hold it a minute – and where would you be going in such a hurry at this time of night?'

'I was trying to find a cab.'

'It didn't appear to me that you were trying to hail a cab.

Perhaps, sir, you would step into the car here so that my colleague and I can have a word with you.'

He was about to protest but was suddenly overcome with fatigue and stepped into the car at the kerbside. The interior light was switched on. The constable examined him more closely and then said less abruptly, 'You seem pretty upset, sir, and very wet without a coat on.'

'Yes, I know, it must seem odd.' He struggled to regain his composure. 'The fact is I've had a bit of a shock and I went out for a walk to clear my head. When the rain came I sheltered in an archway and then I was approached by someone soliciting and I just ran to get away.'

'And where was that?'

'I'm really not sure – I was just trying to get away. I can't remember and frankly I would prefer not to.'

'Very well. I think we can guess where it was that you were sheltering. Now, I would be grateful if you would identify yourself.'

Peter did so. He declined a lift home and asked to be dropped at a cab rank. He took a taxi to his office and, letting himself in, stood at the window looking at the tall darkened offices around him. The lights of the street lamps and the passing cars reflected off the wet surfaces in an ever-changing kaleidoscope of colour. The cars passed with a sibilant hiss over the wet road while the few pedestrians hurried by, keeping close to the sides of the buildings. Occasionally the bow wave from a car would generate an arc of spray and the walkers would press themselves even more closely but unavailingly against the walls of the buildings for protection while shouting angrily but impotently at the drivers. A figure ran along the opposite pavement swiftly and furtively. Remembering his own frightened run a little earlier, Peter turned away from the window and started to laugh.

Finally, he went across the room and sat at his desk. He had come away from the flat to allow himself time to think but his thoughts were dominated by the instinctive reactions of those who feel themselves betrayed – the reactions of the cuckold. He had resisted the instinct to strike out angrily and blindly. Reason reminded him that he himself had calculatingly contemplated some sort of disruption or even separation in his marriage and he had even considered how this might be contrived. He was ashamed of his instinctive reactions to Ann but knew he was unlikely to admit that thoughts of a radical change, even if only for a limited period, had been in his mind too and that he had not discussed these with her. He reflected that the separation might be liberating but remained uncertain whether he had the resolve to take the necessary steps to reorient his life. The events of the last few months, viewed in retrospect, could be seen as the prologue to a tipping point in his life and the events of this evening might set in train a sequence of changes which would acquire their own momentum – but only if he had the courage to allow them to do so.

Peter left the office and took a cab back to the flat. Ann was awake and looking anxious. He realised that he had been out for well over two hours. He replied gently to her enquiries that he was alright and, pleading tiredness, went directly to bed in their spare room.

12

The following two weeks were occupied with activities which precluded thought. Peter and Ann's separation was scarcely mentioned as each started to adapt to a life independent of the other. They would meet briefly over breakfast and exchange the pleasantries and remote courtesies of those who are compelled to share a table in a dining car on a train. Otherwise they saw little of each other. They made their own separate arrangements for meals in the evening and they slept apart. At the weekends they both spent much of the day out of the flat by tacit agreement. The division of the acquisitions of the marriage was accomplished with the same politeness which now characterised all their exchanges. Neither volunteered information relating to their personal plans and neither sought to interrogate the other. Ann had been insistent that she was not seeking support from Peter and that she was prepared to sign over her share in the flat to him.

Two weeks after Valentine's Day Ann announced that she would be moving out the following day. She would be joining her new partner in his apartment. She suggested that they might have dinner together that evening. The conversation was slow and interrupted by many silences. Peter asked some questions about Ann's future domestic arrangements and listened to the replies politely but with little interest. He tried to imagine Ann naked with another man but the image in his mind had a distant asexual quality and failed to arouse any emotion in him. The tensions and the passion had been dissipated and there was little for them to do but play out their particular roles in this everyday domestic drama and close the scene.

Ann's departure from the flat left an unexpected void in Peter's life. He felt deeply the loss of companionship, missing even the limited contact of the previous two weeks. He would leave the office each day long after his colleagues had departed. The evenings still seemed interminably long and he took to roaming the streets without any clear purpose in mind. He became increasingly depressed with his own company as he continued to wrestle with thoughts about his future. One Saturday, he went to his office and, after dealing with some routine paperwork, did some calculations which showed that he had sufficient resources to live simply, but not too frugally, if he were to take a year away from work. It occurred to him that he might approach his partners to ask if they would be prepared to permit him to take an unpaid sabbatical, although he condemned himself for his timidity in limiting his thinking to the possibility of no more than a year's absence. Late one afternoon, three weeks after Ann's departure, the prospect of another evening in the flat on his own seemed to be even more unappealing than usual. He decided he could no longer tolerate his own company. Prompted by musings on his own aspirations, the thought occurred to him that he would enjoy seeing and talking to Sally Dunham again if he could contrive another meeting. He was not sure how he could find her but started to call the newspaper offices. Finally he reached the features editor of the Daily Express. She confirmed that Sally did make occasional contributions to the paper but was emphatic that they would not reveal the address or contact details of contributors. Feeling frustrated and then, surprised by his own stupidity that he had not thought of this earlier, he looked in the telephone directory. It did occur to him that she might be ex-directory but was encouraged by finding four subscribers with the surname of Dunham and one with the correct initial. He noted down the address of a block of flats near Kensington High Street.

He hesitated for a further ten or fifteen minutes before leaving the office, uncertain what he hoped to achieve. He finally left saying to himself that he could identify the apartment block and then turn tail if his resolve failed. He also thought it possible that she might not be at home or even that there might be another S Dunham in the city and that she was indeed ex-directory. As he travelled to Kensington on the tube in the evening rush hour he thought he would be sorry not to see her again. He recognised that in trying to locate her address he had set in train a process which might develop its own momentum or might lead absolutely nowhere. She had intrigued him.

He emerged from the station in the dusk and slowly started to walk up the High Street. Turning between two of the stores, he located the building on the corner of a street and a garden square. He stood back and examined the dark red brick Victorian Gothic building. The windows set into half-hexagonal bays were mainly dark. Peter hesitated for some minutes before he went across to the entrance and pressed the appropriate bell. He felt apprehensive and was conscious of his heart beat as he waited. He watched the second hand of his watch and, after two minutes with the near certainty that nobody was at home, he pressed again more firmly. He turned away after a further minute and decided he would return to the West End and have dinner or go to a theatre. He was starting to retrace his steps to the station when he was startled by a voice from very close behind him.

'I don't think either of us can attribute this to chance.' He turned and looked at Sally who, looking at his face, suddenly burst into laughter. 'Considering you must have taken a fair amount of time and trouble to hunt me down, you don't look so very pleased to see me.'

'Oh, I'm sorry but I thought that you were out.'

She laughed again. 'It must be unusual to have a visitor, other than one with nefarious intent, who calls expecting one to be out.'

'Oh no, I didn't mean that,' he said hastily. 'I did want you to be in but when there was no reply it all seemed much better.' He paused. 'That really wasn't an improvement, was it? But I'm certainly pleased to see you. I wanted to see you.'

'That sounds very serious and portentous. Perhaps one of us should take the other for a drink in the pub before we are both overtaken by an acute attack of gravity. I'm sure that a quiet drink won't trouble your conscience too much.

121

Wait while I drop my shopping and work stuff in the flat. I shall be with you again in a moment.'

She returned with unusual speed and kissed him on the cheek. 'It was good of you to call. Now, not another word until we are in the pub and I will buy you a drink in recognition of your exceptional services as a chauffeur and guide in Northumberland.'

They sat in a corner and he was very silent. Sally turned to him, 'I assume that your life has moved on over the last few months,' she looked closely at him, 'or perhaps it has been moved on for you? So why is it that you have hunted me down?'

'It didn't quite happen like that. I just didn't want to be on my own this evening. I thought I would try and find your address and come and walk around and then simply go away somewhere. I didn't really expect to be able to find it and then I thought I wouldn't have the courage to ring the bell and, even if I did, I was certain you would be out and that might be for the best. It just seemed that the whole process once it was under way was unstoppable.'

Sally laughed. 'That's the most extraordinary example of negative thinking I've come across for years. And now you're not sure whether you should be feeling pleased or guilty.'

'I suppose so – but that makes me feel stupid.'

'No, not stupid, but tell me, what has been happening to you since last summer? I sense that there may be much to tell.'

'There certainly seems so.'

'That's not a problem. I had no fixed plans for this evening; I was not even planning to wash my hair. Even if

I had, I should have cancelled that! So just go ahead and I shall listen.'

Peter refilled their glasses. 'First of all, Ann has left me – she moved out three weeks ago. She says that she has fallen in love with someone else. I had no inkling of this at all, although in retrospect I can see that we had slipped into a routine. We had, I suppose, drifted apart to a degree. I feel betrayed to some extent but no longer resentful, if that makes any sense. I can understand her reasons and we have parted amicably. I still have a sense of guilt and perhaps also of inadequacy.' He recounted the series of events which had started the evening his parents had come for dinner, how it had been enlivened by Andrew's outburst and then ended disastrously with the accident and its tragic sequel on the night of their chance encounter at the hospital. The narrative was interwoven with accounts of the funeral of his father-in-law and his discussions with Michael. Finally he described the surreal events of the bizarre day which he had spent in the company of Stefan and Cass. 'I seem to have been involved closely but accidentally in a series of events which I don't understand and now everything that Andrew said that evening and my discussions with Michael seem to have a greater depth and meaning. I just feel I need to change my life in some way but am uncertain how and where to start.'

'Well, that is quite a narrative!'

'Is that all?'

'Peter, I'm not quite sure what I can say and I really don't know what it is you want me to say or were hoping that I might offer. I understand your feelings and I sympathise with your uncertainties, but I really cannot determine the ways in which you might change your life – or even advise if you should or should not do so. Only you can make those decisions. I scarcely know you! It's only the equivalent of a snake-oil salesman who would be prepared to hand you an instant remedy off the shelf.'

'I think the main problem is… no, I cannot burden you with my problems and uncertainties.'

She smiled. 'Why not go on? You've gone to considerable trouble to find me. Your problems will not be a burden for me. I cannot carry them for you or alleviate them but I am interested to hear them and be a sounding board, if that's what you're looking for. I shan't offer advice since any solution I could devise to resolve your dilemmas would be considerably more ill-informed and arbitrary than your own.' He looked at her with despondency and disappointment. 'Don't look so crestfallen. I am interested to hear and to talk. I'm a professional spectator and observer of life, hence my profession. But it doesn't follow that I'm uninterested,' she paused and smiled before adding, 'nor am I wholly disinterested. I try to put issues into perspective. One thing I've learnt by trying to examine life dispassionately is that almost all personal decisions are arbitrary and frequently based on wholly inadequate information. They are driven as much by instinct and emotion as by reason and calculation. Observers lose their objectivity if they try and involve themselves in the process of problem-solving for others. I'm also aware that much of our lives is shaped by wholly random events. In this, perhaps, we are mirroring the impact of evolution on the development of our species.'

'I guess you're right.'

'Peter, I'm sure that you will, over time, come to resolve your dilemmas in your own mind and if you are still serious in your intention to write then that is possibly what you will choose to do.' She smiled. 'Perhaps that remark is a little mischievous as it could be looked upon as a stimulus or a challenge. I also feel there's a grave risk of you taking me too seriously and that should be avoided at all costs. Now I'm going to buy you another drink and leave you to muse while I go back to my flat and change. Then we can go out to dinner somewhere, split the costs and talk some more.' Peter nodded his assent. Thirty minutes later they were seated in a restaurant in the High Street.

'I think that this has been growing in me for some time but it was brought to a head by Andrew's outburst and death and then by the events which followed and perhaps also by my first meeting with you.'

'I understand, but remember, it's not just events that mould our lives. The way we choose to analyse them and react to them is also significant and our interpretations and responses reflect our own ambitions, desires and prejudices.'

'I suppose that must be right. For a long time, I've been uneasy and uncertain and, when I compare my ambitions from years ago with my achievements, I'm depressed by the disparity. I'm now starting to feel that if I don't achieve anything of significance in the near future then I can do no more than resign myself to following the life that I'm leading for another thirty years or so.' He paused. 'Perhaps this acute attack of existential angst has been exacerbated because I've had a little too much to drink!'

'Or perhaps you've had just sufficient – in vino veritas!'

'Possibly, but I still feel hesitant and reluctant to say that I'm going to write, that I'm going to detach myself from my present life – no, I don't mean that or perhaps I do. I shouldn't be saying all this to you. I wouldn't have said anything when we first met if you hadn't been a writer or if I had thought that there was any chance that we might meet again. No, that's not entirely true. Perhaps I did want to meet you at least once more. I am sorry for these incoherent and inarticulate ramblings. What should I do?'

'Peter, I repeat, I'm not going to dispense advice. You have to choose your own paths. I sense you've reached a point where neither course will be easy for you. You can continue your present life which I suspect is more valuable and more fulfilling than you assume in your gloomier moments. You would probably become reconciled to living with a failure to attempt to achieve other ambitions. It's a course which accepts the non-fulfilment of some dreams and is one which is accepted by many and probably most of us. It's a pragmatic acceptance of the realities of life. The alternative involves a journey to a destination which you cannot identify with certainty in order to fulfil objectives which have been poorly articulated and are incompletely understood – a journey which may end in disaster or failure or as a triumphant success.'

'That would seem a rather stark choice.'

'And so it is. Fundamentally, such choices expose our preparedness to take risks. As we all pass from childhood to adult life most of us tend to choose courses which minimise risk. Most of us do little more than act out those modest aspirations which are straightforward to realise but which, nevertheless, are reasonably satisfying and we learn to live with a sense of non-fulfilment in relation to those which are more ambitious. That's all part of the game of life.'

'You seem to be telling me that I must choose either – to follow my current life or select an alternative, hazardous and ill-defined route.'

'Peter, I'm not telling you that – I'm not telling you anything. That just seems to me to be a summary of your current dilemma. The choice is important to you but it's your choice. It's also important to recognise that it's part of the game of life. That is not to say that the game is not serious. We not only become more adept at game-playing as we grow older but it also becomes easier to delude ourselves that life is not a game. Life has all the possible components of a sport intermixed – farce, comedy, drama and tragedy.'

'Now you're talking in riddles or is it just me, now that I've definitely had too much to drink?'

'Quite possibly both of us have at this stage in the evening. Perhaps it's time we should go home.' The meal was over but they lingered over coffee. Peter had no desire to go until he was certain that he was sufficiently tired and sedated with alcohol not to feel the oppressive emptiness of the flat.

'May I see you again?'

'You seem to have achieved that very competently on two occasions now without asking permission,' she said smiling, 'but the answer is yes. You have my telephone number now as a result of your sleuthing but don't leave it too long as I shall be going to my cottage in France for the summer at the end of April.'

'Where is your cottage?'

'In the Dordogne but not right beside the river. Have you ever been to the area?'

'No, but it seems to be becoming very popular and fashionable.'

'Perhaps, but I don't do fashionable. I go there to work and, away from the tourist hot spots, it remains an essentially French part of France. There are English cars and tourists but I see very little of my compatriots during the time I'm there.'

'Where exactly is it?'

'The cottage is just outside a very well-preserved mediaeval town called Sarlat. That's where I shall be writing during the summer.'

The conversation drifted slowly away and Peter walked back to Sally's flat where they parted on the pavement. 'Perhaps we shall meet again.'

'Perhaps we shall. As I said, judged by past performance the likelihood of our doing so would now seem to be very high!' She smiled. 'Yes, it would be good to see you again. Go on, it's past your bedtime.'

The emptiness of the flat suddenly seemed unimportant. He slept well that night for the first time for weeks.

13

The last weekend in March was cold but sunny and Peter decided to take himself out of London. On an impulse, he drove to Henley (in Dickens words "the mecca of the rowing man") and set off to walk along the Thames Path in the direction of Marlow. He felt the need for exercise and sufficient time to focus his thinking. He had reached a point where he felt it was essential to make a choice; to continue in this state of indecision would ultimately have a corrosive effect which would pervade all aspects of his life. Stripped down to the essentials, his options were straightforward. One was to continue to follow his chosen career. He knew that he was regarded as competent by his colleagues and sympathetic by his clients. This would be a safe choice, one for which he had been prepared by upbringing and education. He would continue to make a comfortable living with sufficient resources to fill his leisure time in almost any way he chose. He would very probably meet another woman and possibly re-marry. The alternative would be to break free and attempt to fulfil his dream of writing. This would be a riskier but a more interesting choice. The events of the last few months and the final parting from Ann meant that this was an unusually opportune time to make such a break. He could mitigate the risk if his partners were prepared to agree that he might have a sabbatical and grant him leave of absence for a year. He recognised that to set up such an arrangement with an assured escape route would be regarded by some as timorous or even pusillanimous. There would be advantages in burning his bridges comprehensively behind him; a total break with his past would certainly provide a stimulus which would drive him to achieve. The knowledge that an exit was available might diminish his drive and take the edge off his ambitions. He also reflected on the impact that a decision to drop out would have on his parents. They were bound to disapprove and it was highly likely that they would deploy every conceivable argument to discourage him from doing so. They would take the view that he had developed a successful career and that this was a proper return on the monies spent on him over many years at Marlborough and Cambridge. They would certainly consider that he was squandering their investment and his education.

The river glittered in the March sunshine, its surface shimmering in the current, highlighting the turbulence created by the oarsmen. The views across the river, unimpeded by foliage on the trees, revealed the classically styled buildings of Phyllis Court and the Management College, each brightly reflecting the sun as it reached its height and, between them, the Wren masterpiece of Fawley Court could be seen in all its magnificence. He reached Hambledon Lock and Mill and after crossing and re-crossing the river he took the track away from it and walked up the slight incline to the Flower Pot Inn. He bought himself a sandwich and a beer and sat in the garden enjoying the sunshine. He knew that the one person with whom he could discuss his options was Michael but he hesitated to do so. He recalled the various conversations of the last few months and decided that the time for agonising over possibilities was over. The time had come to decide and the decision had to be his and his alone. This was almost certainly a once in a lifetime opportunity that had been handed to him by events largely beyond his control. He knew he should take it. He finished his lunch and with a lighter step walked back down to the river and along the towpath to his car. An hour later, he was back in his flat where he sat down to make a list of the issues that he would have to address before he could abandon his present job and face up to the challenges ahead. The first of these was to discuss the possibility of leave of absence with his partners. The second was to inform his immediate family. He stopped at this stage suddenly realising that, apart from dealing with certain minor everyday practical issues, this was the limit to the key matters which needed to be resolved.

Peter raised the possibility of a year's leave of absence at the weekly partners meeting the following Wednesday, arguing that he needed time to pause and reflect following the breakdown of his marriage. His natural reticence held him back from outlining his particular ambitions to his colleagues. There was a certain amount of resistance and grumbling by two of the older partners who said that it would be an unsatisfactory precedent if others sought to take a year away following a personal crisis. They pointed out that everyone experienced critical periods in their lives. Peter was asked to leave the room while they considered his application. He was invited to re-join them twenty minutes later, to be informed that they would agree to a year's leave of absence which would be unpaid although, as a partner, he would be entitled to a share of the profits for the year. The period would commence not less than three months from the date of that meeting and would be subject to his finding a satisfactory locum to cover his time away. Peter knew that this was the best he could have hoped for and accepted the conditions readily. One of the other younger partners told him subsequently that it had raised the possibility of a sabbatical in the minds of several of them and that they had been more than happy to argue that they should create a precedent.

* * *

'The grace of our Lord Jesus Christ, and the love of God and the fellowship of the Holy Ghost be with us all evermore, Amen.' The rapid monotone concluded the service and the congregation rose with rather more agility and animation than they had shown at any time during the previous fifty minutes. The vicar and the choir filed out, and the worshippers genuflected as a brief intonation could be heard from behind the almost closed vestry door. Peter looked around as handbags, hymn books and shoes were covertly sought and recovered while the Reverend James Andrewes walked rapidly round the exterior of the church to the west porch in time to greet the first of his parishioners as they were leaving. Peter's mother had suggested that he should join them for lunch on Easter Day and insisted that he should attend church with her that morning. Geoffrey by tacit agreement rarely went other than on Christmas Day. They moved from their pew into the nave, progressing slowly towards the porch, exchanging occasional commonplace comments with acquaintances as they did so. Finally they emerged and, having shaken the vicar's hand, walked briskly down the slope back to the family home. Molly grumbled about the weather and the way the frosts which had occurred on one or two nights had disturbed her routine for the garden, although the pelargoniums and begonias which she had bought for the troughs and pots were all secure in the greenhouse, together with some bedding plants which she had grown from seed and laboriously pricked out.

This was the first time that Peter had been home since Ann's departure and Molly was obviously delaying the moment when she might interrogate him about the breakdown of his marriage until Geoffrey was present. It was inevitably going to be the first topic of conversation as he settled down with his parents for a pre-lunch drink.

'What went wrong?' enquired Geoffrey as soon as they were seated. 'You always seemed to be perfectly comfortable together and we were not aware of any problems when we saw you here with Ann's mother and sister at Christmas.'

'Yes, I think in general we were and I wasn't aware of any problems at Christmas. It's difficult to put into words. There was no great schism but I suppose no great passion either. We just seemed to live somewhat separate lives. I'm sure there must be many couples who live in such a way and remain married. I couldn't claim that we were ill-suited but possibly we were not as well suited as we might have been.

It's perhaps unsurprising that Ann fell for someone else, particularly someone whom she saw daily at work. That was the immediate cause of the break-up but it would be unfair to place all the burden of responsibility on Ann.'

'What do you mean – have you also strayed?'

'No,' said Peter emphatically, answering the query which lay behind the euphemistic verb which his father had used. 'We have parted amicably. It came quite out of the blue but now that I've come to terms with the parting I've started to think positively of what the future might hold for me.'

'Surely your future's clear,' his mother intervened. 'This doesn't have any implications for your job and perhaps you'll find a new and loyal wife in time.' Peter noted the emphasis which had been placed on the second of the adjectives. 'But you shouldn't rush into any new liaison.'

Peter smiled at the assumption that this was likely to be the limits of his aspirations for the future and that this was still an era in which a wife, who would be expected to stand by her man, was an essential accessory for any professional. 'I think that's unlikely,' he said 'but I am going to make some changes in my life and I will tell you about them over lunch. They may surprise you.'

They sat down to eat at the kitchen table as there were only three of them. 'Well, tell us all,' said Molly.

'I have been talking to my partners and have raised with them the possibility that I might take a sabbatical. They have agreed that I might take a year.'

'Were they happy with this?'

'I removed myself from the meeting room while they discussed it. I understand that two of the older ones were somewhat hesitant and felt that this was creating a precedent. One of my younger colleagues confided later that they had taken the view that they themselves had never felt the need to take time out. He thought they were probably a little envious that they had never had the opportunity, or thought to raise the possibility. He added that my proposal had also put it in his mind and that of the other younger partners that they might think of following suit at a later date. That has been put on the agenda for discussion at a future partners meeting.'

'But what are you going to live on?'

'I shall be on unpaid leave of absence for a year and have worked out that I can live simply, but reasonably comfortably, for that year on savings. I shall also have a modest income from my share of the partnership profits for the year even though I shan't receive any fee income. Ann has insisted that she doesn't want to make any financial demands on me.'

'And what will you do during this year?'

'I'm going to write.'

'What about? Will this be a book on some aspect of family law – and can you attach yourself to the law faculty in one of the universities to do this?'

'No, I have for many years had a hankering to write fiction and this seemed to be a once in a lifetime opportunity to attempt to do so. Circumstances are such that I can. I may fail, in which case I shall return with my tail between my legs and take up my profession once more.'

'You've never mentioned this before.'

'No, but it has been there at the back of my mind for a

number of years. If I don't take this chance, I know I'll regret it. It seems that fate has delivered this opportunity.'

'How do you know you will be any good at it?'

'I don't. I just know that this is something that I want to do and I shall regret it if I don't give it a try.'

'How will you go about it?'

'I think in the first instance I shall shut up the flat and go away over the summer. I shall be leaving the office at the end of June once I've found a locum. First, I shall have a short holiday and then I'll try to find a place somewhere in the countryside to rent, well away from all distractions. I shall become a hermit and sit there with a pen and several reams of blank paper. I think, if I stay in the flat, routine daily activities may weaken my resolve. I imagine that the most difficult part will be to get started.'

'But what will it be about?'

'The honest answer is I don't know yet. I have several ideas but I need to start seeing them in black and white to get any feel for their credibility.'

'I believe there are creative writing courses that you can attend. Have you considered signing up for one of those?'

'Yes, but I just want to get on and give it a go.'

'Are you really certain that this will not harm your career?'

'No, I'm not, but I'm determined to go ahead with it. I've negotiated my leave of absence. The die is cast.'

'Well, it seems crazy to us but I guess we can only say good luck to you.'

* * *

The next few weeks were taken up with preparations for his departure from the office. His partners had advertised for a locum to fill his place and Peter was asked to sit on the interview panel. He and his colleagues were encouraged that the advertisement had generated a strong field and they quickly agreed that Grace Jenkinson, a young solicitor with three years' experience and excellent academic credentials, should be appointed. She had been working in Birmingham but had planned to move to London for personal reasons. The opportunity to work in the firm for a year suited her well and she would be available to work alongside Peter for the last two weeks of June to ensure a smooth handover. Peter was encouraged and buoyant. Everything seemed to be falling into place.

He decided to call Sally the following week. They agreed to meet once more in the restaurant where they had eaten in March. They settled into their seats, ordered their food and a bottle of wine.

'Well?' said Sally.

'Well, I have made some decisions about my life and, more importantly, taken steps to implement them.'

'Sounds good – are you going to expand on that?'

He smiled. 'Yes, I fear I rather burdened you a few weeks ago with the story of my life since our first, and definitely chance, encounter last summer. I have decided that events have created both a stimulus and an opportunity for me to chance my arm and detach myself from my job for a year. I, we, shall see if I have what it takes to be a writer. If I fail, then I can return to my job and see what else life might hold for me. You'll have spotted that I have left a possible escape route open. I know this could be thought likely to reduce my commitment and that would be a fair judgment, but I can only work hard to ensure that it doesn't.'

Sally raised her glass. 'Good luck – I think that is very brave of you.'

'I suspect my parents think it's foolhardy although they have been polite enough not to say so. If I had simply resigned from the firm, they would surely have said something and I suspect that the words naïve and stupid would have been included in their comments. But you've made similar decisions and taken the same steps.'

'Not exactly. I have always been a writer and initially I was salaried, working for a magazine group. When I went freelance, I already had an established career as a writer and I had contacts which stood me in good stead. The availability of freelance writers with an established track record is helpful to editors in that they can commission articles and features but without the inconvenience of having to pay a regular salary and without the other responsibilities of an employer. There are also risks. Two or three sub-standard submissions and further commissions will dry up like water in the desert. Word gets around fast; journalism is a relatively small world. Touch wood, that has not occurred so far.'

'What are you working on at present?'

'I have three items – fortunately with very different deadlines. The most ambitious is one which I suggested. It's for a series of articles, and perhaps a book, about the infiltration of the French coast and countryside by the British over the course of recent years. This fits well with the location of my cottage in France and my fluency in the language. It also gives me the opportunity to travel to other areas of France where there are reasonable numbers of Brits. I shall have the opportunity to refer to the long history of the interactions, often fractious, between the English and the French. Additionally, it may give me the chance to spin off some articles on aspects of French life for travel magazines and one on a subject that particularly interests me – the number of English language authors who have lived in and been inspired by France (and I include some American writers in that).

'Are there so many?'

'Quite a number and some very influential ones. From way back they include Robert Louis Stevenson and Tobias Smollett. In the last hundred years, Henry James, Scott Fitzgerald, Somerset Maugham, Hemingway, Graham Greene, James Joyce, Henry Miller and Samuel Beckett.'

'That's quite a cast list.'

'Yes, but what's the next step for you?'

'The next steps are purely practical. I have to work through a period of notice and ensure that there's a smooth handover of business to my locum and my partners, particularly if I'm involved in any complex cases. At the start of July I shall take a brief holiday and then I shall go and buy a large quantity of paper and set to work, or I may even take the paper away with me and take the first tentative steps towards becoming a writer. I thought in the first instance I would rent a country cottage for three months, somewhere well away from London so that I can immerse myself in the effort, free from the distractions of everyday life.'

'That sounds like a good plan – if you're a success I

might claim you as my protégé! Will you let me know how you're getting on, even if things are not going well, which is bound to be the case at times?'

'I shall.'

'I'll give you my other address – although with your well-honed detecting skills you could probably discover it for yourself!'

* * *

One evening early in June the telephone rang in Peter's flat. 'Hello, it's Jenny – I was wondering how you are?'

Peter was surprised by the call as he had neither seen nor heard from Jenny since his separation from Ann. 'I'm fine but how about you?'

'I'm also doing well. The job is turning out to be much more interesting than I thought it would. An editorial assistant is normally the lowest form of animal life in the magazine publishing industry but we are such a small outfit that I'm doing things which could be considered way above my pay grade.' She laughed. 'Not that it has led to any increase in my pay, but I'm not complaining. But I really wanted to know how you were managing. I was so sorry you and Ann had parted. She doesn't say very much about it other than that you've been very good and understanding. I'm just sorry that she has deprived me of a brother-in-law. I wondered if you might like to meet up for a drink one evening after work?'

'That sounds like a nice idea.' They arranged to meet immediately after work on the following Friday in a pub in

Islington as, later that evening, Jenny was meeting a friend who had promised to take her to a jazz club and the pub was nearby.

They met as arranged and Peter bought drinks for both of them before settling in a corner of the bar.

'How are you and your Mum and Ann?' asked Peter. 'And have you seen Ann and her new partner, Francis?'

'Yes, to both those questions. Mum is very upset that Ann has left you. I know that you met only a few times but she took quite a shine to you and you were so gentle with her. She has been quite angry with Ann. Otherwise she is managing well. She has a good group of friends and, if I'm honest, I think the strain of looking after Dad over the last two years told on her more that she let on. I'm not saying they were not close, they were. It was a good marriage. But at one level I think his death has been a relief. We are both managing to get up to Newcastle every few weeks. Mum was quite right to resist pressure to move south. Ann seems to be happy. Francis is very different from you, more flamboyant, more loquacious and, I imagine, more given to risk-taking. Ann is also having to adapt to the presence of stepchildren on alternate weekends, two girls aged seven and five who are currently sizing up this new woman in their father's life. I sense that Mum is a bit dubious about Francis. She thinks he's a bit flash! She and I still feel that you're a much better match for Ann than Francis.'

Peter shook his head slowly. 'The water has flowed under that bridge. It's not going to flow back again.'

'I know. But tell me what is happening in your life.'

'I think that I'm going to surprise you!'

'Have you found another woman? That was quick work!'

Peter laughed. 'No, I've not suddenly turned into a rash and impetuous Lothario!' He paused. 'I'm sure you remember that awful evening when Andrew was round and the terrible accident which followed his outburst that evening. There were some things which he said then which got under my skin. You probably also remember those few days when you stayed in the flat before the interview which led to your job. We talked for a time about ambitions and fantasies and you said that you would like to see me break free from my middle-class shackles and fly. Well, I'm about to do that, at least in part. I'm about to become a risk-taker.'

'Really?'

'Yes, in three weeks from now I shall be leaving my job for a year. I've been granted unpaid leave of absence for that time and I'm going to go away and write.'

'But what are you going to write?'

'Fiction.'

'It's often said that all first novels are autobiographical. Are we all going to be in it?'

'No. It sounds odd at this stage to say so but I have not formalised a theme in my mind yet. I'm sure I shall draw on my own experiences and observations and I'm certain that I shall pick and mix to create characters based on aspects of people I know, but I shall work hard to ensure that it is not autobiographical. I'm too private a person for that. I should feel too exposed if it were to be recognisably so. Of course, if it's published that will not prevent people speculating. My family and friends might wonder what I'd been getting up to covertly, particularly if I include steamy sex scenes replete with anatomical detail!'

'I really don't know what to say other than that's amazing! I do hope it works out for you. I'm just beginning to wonder if Ann's new partner is a greater risk-taker than you! Would you mind if I ask from time to time how things are going?'

'Not at all.'

'I'm so glad that you agreed to have a drink – can we do this again?'

'Absolutely.'

They talked on for a time and then Jenny looked up. 'My friend is here to lead me to the jazz club and she's got someone with her.'

Peter looked up as a young woman approached. 'Cass!' he said totally surprised.

'Got it in one and Stefan will be here in a moment when he has bought us drinks.' She leant forward and kissed Jenny on both cheeks and then kissed Peter.

'How do you know Cass?' asked Jenny taken aback by the encounter.

Peter laughed and was greeted by Stefan with a hug when he appeared. Cass introduced Stefan to Jenny. 'Perhaps we all have some explaining to do,' said Peter.

'My explanation is simple,' said Jenny, 'but I should love to hear yours. I suspect it might not be so simple. I'm beginning to think that my earlier judgements about your propensity for risk-taking were seriously mistaken! You may remember,' she said looking at Peter, 'that my thesis was on Christina Rossetti. One of the magazines is doing a series on the Pre-Raphaelite painters and their relationship with

Ruskin. I was assigned to the project and Cass came into the office as a Pre-Raphaelite expert to discuss it. We met and we hit it off and have had a drink after work several times now.'

'You're right, my explanation is not so straightforward. It was early in September, just a few days after Andrew's funeral, that Ann had to go back up to Newcastle. I took her to King's Cross and I just felt very low. I decided to walk to the office. It was a warm day and I was in no hurry so I sat on a bench in a square in Bloomsbury. I fell into conversation with Stefan who was sitting on the same bench and then Cass joined us. It was a strange and almost surreal day but they took me in charge. Oh God! That sounds like being arrested but it wasn't like that. We went for a drink and several more and then we went to the zoo where I fell asleep on another bench in the sun and when I woke up they had gone. They were very kind to a total stranger.'

Jenny's eyes had opened progressively wider and wider through this abridged account of his meeting with Cass and Stefan. 'Peter, I would have said twenty-four hours ago that you were quite the most unlikely person to astonish me and you have managed to do it twice within an hour.' She was laughing and hugged him. 'You are quite my favourite brother-in-law or ex-brother-in-law.'

'That's not too difficult to achieve as I'm the only one in that category.'

'Maybe, but you are still a lovely man and I have to say that my sister is a very silly woman to have left you.'

'That's lovely, but I must also thank Stefan and Cass for looking after me that day. They offered me company in a way that I never knew I wanted, but it was welcome.'

'I'm sorry we had to abandon you at the zoo,' said Stefan, 'but we had to go and you looked so much at ease that we decided it would be kinder to let you sleep on. We left you my address.'

'Yes, I still have it. It's in my wallet.'

'So are you a happier man than you were?'

'Yes, Jenny can tell you all about it.'

'Why don't you come to the jazz club with us and you can both tell Cass about it while I'm playing and attempting to live up to my name?'

Peter hesitated. 'Come on,' said Jenny. 'Be the new Peter! I love the new Peter even more than the old one and even the old one was pretty good.'

'Alright, let's go.'

He relaxed as the three of them cradled their drinks and let the music flow over them in the informal setting of the club. The violin, guitars and bass created an authentic gypsy jazz sound, playing many of the standards: Limehouse Blues, Dinah and a number of Django Reinhardt compositions. As Peter left to go back to Barnes, Jenny whispered in his ear, 'Do let me know how you're getting on. I don't want to lose touch.'

14

Peter wrote to Sally the following day to say that he was planning a short holiday before starting to look for a retreat and commit himself to writing in earnest. He would be coming to France and crossing over the channel on the last Saturday in June and wondered if he might visit. The reply came a week later. It posed no questions and passed no comment. 'Peter, you are welcome to stay for a few days. I have a spare room. If you are driving and leaving on 28th June then I would suggest that you arrive here the following day. The house is quite difficult to find. I shall be sitting on the terrace of La Belle Etoile in La Roque-Gageac taking a tisane at 5pm on 29 June. Take care and remember to drive on the right! Sally.'

The last two weeks of the month were fully occupied with making practical arrangements and ensuring that there would be a seamless handover of his work. He arranged to board a ferry very early on the morning of the last Saturday of June so decided to leave the evening before and stay in a small inn close to Newhaven. His journey out of London in the summer Friday evening exodus was slow but that mattered little. Peter felt light-headed and almost carefree as he reflected on the endless hours that he had agonised over making such a momentous decision. Now that it was made and the venture was underway he felt buoyant and assured that he would succeed.

* * *

The early morning call had been unnecessary and, after a scanty breakfast, Peter covered the short distance to the quayside. He waited in the car in the early morning mist, surrounded by overloaded vehicles filled with anxious and expectant holiday-makers. The cars were taken through the checks and controls, part of the pre-holiday ritual which reaches its climax as the cars are marshalled into position in the bowels of the ferry. He climbed up to the deck and stationed himself at the stern of the boat as it steamed slowly out of the harbour and headed for France. He stood looking back at the receding port along the expanding, perspective-distorting avenue of the wake. After a while he turned and started to scrutinise his fellow passengers. The most striking distinguishing characteristic of those on deck was that they all formed part of an identifiable group. A cluster of hyper-active schoolboys were being shepherded by an anxious, tall, bespectacled, etiolated schoolmaster with short sideburns wearing a tired tweed jacket. This was decorated with a series of enamel badges on the lapels, four ball-point pens in the breast pocket and leather patches on the elbows. There were numerous family groups with anxious fathers enjoining their offspring not to lean too far over the guardrail as they gazed excitedly at the sea below, tentatively holding soft toys out to catch the spray. Mothers were eagerly scanning the duty free price lists in the pamphlets they had been handed as they drove on board. He saw older couples savouring each remembered stage in the journey as if re-watching a favourite and well-loved film. Then as the gulls started to wheel away and leave the stern, passengers dispersed to seek refreshment, duty free shopping and the lounges. He remained on deck and relaxed on one of the benches as the sun warmed. There seemed to be little point in sitting alone amongst the crowd below. He closed his eyes as he anticipated the days ahead.

'Hello, has England gone away now?'

Peter looked round and found that a small girl whom he judged to be about seven years old had climbed onto the bench. She was kneeling and looking over the back of the bench towards the stern. She eyed him with solemnity and patience as she waited for a reply.

'Yes. It's all gone away now.'

'Good,' she smiled, cheeks dimpling and long dark hair falling forward over her face. 'Will France come soon?'

'France will come that way,' he pointed towards the bow, 'but I think it will be a little while before we see it.'

'I think I'll sit down then,' and she turned and sat demurely with her hands on her lap.

'What do they call you?'

'I'm called Tanya and I'm going on holiday to France. Do you know, we got up awfully early this morning at four o'clock. It was still quite dark and there were no other cars on the road and now here we are on the boat and Mummy and Daddy are asleep,' she concluded rather breathlessly.

'And have you any brothers and sisters?'

'No, except William, but he doesn't really count because he's only a baby.' She paused, 'I saw you all alone. Is your Mummy with you or has she gone to sleep too?'

Peter divined correctly that he was being questioned about a wife. 'No, my Mummy's not here; I haven't really got a Mummy to look after me.'

'That's sad. Are you going on holiday all on your own?'

'Well yes, but I'm going to meet someone.'

'Is it a friend or a girlfriend?'

'It's a girl who's a sort of friend.'

'Is she nice?'

Peter hesitated for a moment – was Sally nice? That flat and insipid word seemed wholly inapplicable to Sally. He tried vainly to conjure up a suitable adjective but failed. 'Yes, she's very nice,' he said finally.

'I'd better go and see how Mummy and Daddy and William are.' She jumped down. 'Perhaps I'll come back later.'

'Well, I shall be at the front later to make sure that France doesn't forget to arrive.' She waved and was gone.

The crossing was finally concluded and the passengers disembarked at Dieppe. It was mid-morning and the sun was reaching its zenith as the cars left the quayside, the drivers intent on making their way to their various destinations. The cohort of English cars rapidly dispersed and was absorbed into the French domestic traffic. Peter opened his sunroof and stopped on the edge of the town to arrange his maps on the vacant passenger seat and re-read the note from Sally. He folded the letter, re-buckled his seat belt and set off on the long drive to south-west France.

The temperature and the humidity rose steadily and after crossing the Seine at Rouen he headed for the long straight roads which crossed the central plain. Mirages glistened on the road ahead. The sentinel poplars gave a stroboscopic view of the countryside. Hectares of maize stretched into the distance on either side, erect inflorescent heads contrasting with the lanceolate leaves covering the forming cobs. He drove steadily on through the day as it became uncomfortably hot, stopping only for a brief lunch of cheese, fruit and beer. He finally stopped for the night between Châteauroux and Argenton-sur-Creuse, happy that he had covered some two-thirds of the distance and comfortable in the knowledge that he would be able to complete the journey at a more relaxed pace the following day.

The hotel in which he spent the night was unmistakably French. The small bedroom was above the bar and the sound of the nearby A20 provided a continuous backdrop to his evening. The ill-fitting door and the shutters shook and clattered as the occasional camion rolled down the village street. It was a restless and solitary place to spend the night. He took dinner in the small restaurant below but it was almost impossible to prolong the meal so that it would occupy more than a small fraction of the evening which seemed to stretch interminably ahead. He consumed the food with neither thought nor appreciation. He drank a brandy as he took his coffee and finally headed to bed just before ten.

He awoke early after a night disturbed by the traffic and the resonating chimes of the church clock. He found it impossible to delay his departure beyond eight o'clock. It was evident, with a journey of less than two hundred miles, that he would arrive some hours ahead of the appointed time but the thought of covering most of the distance before the sun reached its height had its attractions. The arable plains slowly yielded to the wooded hills of the Périgord Noir, riven by deep valleys as they fell towards the river. He reached Souillac and turned westward alongside the Dordogne. The road followed the convoluted course of the river as it passed from wall to wall of the gorge, the high limestone cliffs overhanging each bank in turn. Crenellated, turreted châteaux stood on their several vantage points overlooking the one-time border between the Angevin Empire and the kingdom of Burgundy. He stopped in the early afternoon some fifteen kilometres short of his destination at one of the small pebbled beaches in a concavity of the river. He consumed the sandwich which he had purchased earlier and then lay on his back in the sun. The catacombed cliff rising above the southern bank was in deep shade. The summit of the cliff appeared to be moving slowly and languorously below the cirrus scattered haphazardly against the brilliant azure cupola above. Trees clung improbably and horizontally to the cliff face. The powerful and oppressive heat drove Peter into the river where he swam indolently on his back in the fast flowing and weedless stream.

Finally the time had passed and he made ready to leave for the meeting place. He drove slowly knowing that he would still be early for the rendezvous. He continued along the river road to La Roque-Gageac, glancing at his watch from time to time. The restaurant stood close by the road. He was still twenty minutes early so he parked and walked down to the wall overlooking the river. Leaning back, he looked up at the cliff towering above him wondering at the randomly scattered dwellings, half house and half cave, set into the rock and the holm oaks clinging to the cliff. The single row of dwellings was framed by the Château de la Malartrie at one end and the Manoir de Tarde at the other. The late afternoon sun illuminated the houses, throwing their reflections onto the gleaming river. The restaurant shone brightly in the sun, highlighted by rows of pelargoniums and petunias below and red and blue striped sun blinds above. As he stood there enjoying the scene, a figure descended from the restaurant by the outside steps. Peter started forward but she was already running across the road towards him.

'Hi,' she kissed him on the cheek. 'I guessed you might be early so I thought I'd come early too and wait here for you.' She led him back across the road. 'First, we shall have a drink and then I'll take you to the house. It must have been a very long and extremely hot journey.'

'It was, but I arrived close by shortly after lunch and have spent the last couple of hours sitting in the sun and swimming.'

'I am pleased you're here.'

'I hope so. I did rather invite myself and gave you little opportunity to refuse.'

She smiled. 'I found that flattering.'

'That's kind of you – I just felt…' But the sentence remained unfinished as she placed a finger across his lips.

'No, Peter, this is not the time to talk. I'm sure that occasions to do that will come later.'

'Perhaps you're right.'

When they had settled with their drinks she turned to him. 'Now, I've been planning. First, when we've finished our drinks, we'll go back to the house and then, just for tonight, we can go out to dinner. But before I tell you my plans, you must tell me what you want to do.'

'I'm intending to enjoy a holiday for a week or so before settling down to the business of writing.'

'And do you have plans to travel elsewhere in France?'

'No, in keeping with my newly liberated state, I have planned nothing for this first week and am open to any suggestions, but I don't want to impose on you or disrupt any plans that you have.'

'Well, I do have a suggestion but it's entirely up to you to decide if it appeals. In view of your arrival, I've decided to take a week's holiday myself, thinking that you would probably enjoy a week of rest and relaxation.'

'Holiday?'

'Yes, of course.' She smiled. 'I have to work while I'm here. I put in a regular number of hours each day and only take time off for particular occasions. It's really very similar to an office routine.'

'I had never really thought of writing as an occupation in that way.'

'I'm sorry if I'm disillusioning you but the image of the author dashing off several hundred words of sparkling prose between bouts of heavy drinking and fornication is purely fictitious for almost all of us!'

'Now you're disappointing me,' he said laughing.

'I do, as I said, take time off from my schedule for

particular occasions – I have decided that you are a particular occasion. Come on, you can follow me back to the house. My car is the small blue Renault parked over there.'

15

The room was still cool although the morning was well advanced when Peter awoke and slowly oriented himself in the soft light of the shuttered room. He had slept well after his journey and a relaxed dinner in a small restaurant in a lane in Sarlat, well away from the regular tourist haunts. He rose and, throwing back the shutters, leaned out to take in the view of meadows stretching down to the pines in the valley below. Lizards ran with small convulsive movements across the cream-washed, sun-warmed walls. The meadow grass was decorated with tall purple spikes of meadow clary interspersed with the soft blues, mauves and pinks of scabious, chive, orpine and ragged robin. He showered and dressed and stepped out onto the terrace. Sally was already sitting there reading – coffee and croissants on the table. She looked up. 'I take it that you slept well.'

'I did indeed. It's so peaceful here and the view from my bedroom is idyllic.'

'Well, this is the first day of R and R for both of us. There's no rush. I've been thinking of how we might spend the next few days but you must tell me if this doesn't appeal to you.'

'I'm a stranger here; my first impressions are that anything you suggest will seem magical.'

'I'm not sure I can promise magic, but I can offer you a view of an idyllic and in some ways an untouched part of rural France. There are many things to see and places to visit: châteaux, gardens, the caves, small villages and mediaeval towns. It's important that we do not try to do too much. It's all too easy to become over-châteauxed round here. I would suggest that the days might go something like this. We start with a leisurely breakfast as we're doing today and decide where we want to go; there's a lot to see without having to drive very far. As long as this weather holds then we should picnic at lunchtime: baguette, pâté, cheese and fruit and, of course, a glass of wine – after all this is France. Then we can simply relax or swim in the river or, if feeling enthusiastic or energetic, we could continue on our touristic way or take a walk. We can shop for provisions for the evening on the way back to the house. How does that sound?'

'It sounds wonderful.'

'It has the advantage that it's not too prescriptive and we can accelerate the pace or take our feet off the gas and slow down according to how we feel each day.'

* * *

The week that followed passed for Peter as if in a dream. The repeated pattern of the days provided a loose framework for their activities without imposing any constraints on their freedom to modify their plans at a moment's notice. Guided by Sally, he quickly became familiar with the mediaeval town of Sarlat which was just a mile away. They wandered through its narrow, crowded, guttered streets, exploring its hidden courtyards surrounded by ochre buildings with windows shuttered against the sun. They drove up to the proud, self-consciously picturesque bastide of Domme, perched on its promontory high above the valley, the houses bleached by the sun. They looked down through the summer haze at the river far below as it wound its way through the green landscape offering a view like some half-forgotten impressionist painting. They visited the immense castles of Beynac and Castelnaud facing each other across the river, implacable rivals through much of their history, the great gardens at Eyrignac and the caves at Lascaux in the valley of the Vézère.

The week of freedom reached its final day. Sally and Peter lay on the small beach by the river which he had visited on the day of his arrival. A lunch of wine and bread and brie had engendered a feeling of contentment and ease. They lay looking at the trees growing from the cliff and clinging to the rock-face like lichens. The shadows from their sun-dappled leaves creating a pointillistic pattern on the river below.

'I have much enjoyed a pretext for a week away from work and I have enjoyed your company,' said Sally, 'but tomorrow my holiday must be over. We have allowed the simple sensuous pleasures of this week to flow over us but we have not talked about you. What are your plans now?'

'I too have enjoyed this week. It has created a clear space between the life I've left behind and the one I hope to lead. It has also given me the chance to see recent personal events in perspective, to a certain extent, although I still have some unease and perhaps a sense of guilt over Ann.'

'I don't think you should use words like blame and guilt or right and wrong. Events and interactions occur and people are people. But what now?'

'I must leave and head back to England. I thought I'd find a remote place to stay, away from the distractions of person and place at my flat and settle to writing.'

Sally hesitated. 'I have a suggestion to make, but it comes with strings attached. It has been a good week and, after a week of your company, I should be happy for you to stay and write here, if you would like to do so. The strings are these. I shall work to my normal routine which is writing from nine to twelve-thirty and again from four-thirty until seven in the evening. I set myself a target of fifteen hundred words a day and I take Saturdays and Sundays off each week. Occasionally I go into Bergerac to visit the library there.' She smiled. 'You see, it's not so very different from being a solicitor in London. The main difference is that the surroundings are more pleasant and I don't spend time commuting into central London from a flat in Barnes, as you've been doing, or a semi-detached house in Gerrards Cross. I am quite strict about my schedule and I will not be interrupted.'

Peter was about to protest that he had to get back to England but then thought for a few minutes. There was no compelling reason why he should return the following week and he had been captivated by the environment. 'I should very much like to do that, if it would really not inconvenience you.'

'I think we should be quite business-like about this and I suggest we try it for a month and if it doesn't work out then we can call a halt with no hard feelings on either side. I also suggest that we should retain our independence. As I said, I sometimes go to the municipal library in Bergerac and I also make use of archives in some of the smaller towns and local museums. You must also feel free to come and go. Naturally, at weekends, we will be free to choose to do things together as we've been doing so companionably this week but that shouldn't inhibit either of us from doing things independently. I think it's important that we don't intrude on one another by enquiring about progress on a daily or weekly basis. I'm happy to be a sounding board if you would find that helpful and I'm sure there will be times when I shall want to bounce ideas off you but it should be on our own initiatives.'

'That sounds very fair. This is probably the first time in my life that I've been at liberty to make such spontaneous decisions without considering my responsibilities to others.'

'There are two practical issues which we should perhaps discuss. First, do you have the necessary materials here for writing?'

Peter laughed. 'As it happens, I do have two reams of paper in my car and I have several pens. I also came with a dictionary. I'd thought that if I was touring around and was on my own in the evenings I would try and transfer some thoughts to paper but I've been enjoying myself too much this last week and have achieved absolutely nothing so far. I shall try and adopt your disciplined approach. I shall write longhand initially and then later try and transfer my efforts using a typewriter, slowly and painfully with two fingers, revising as I go.'

'Sounds good. The second question is, what are your culinary skills like? I suggest that we each take responsibility for the catering on alternate weeks – doing the shopping and cooking dinner. I should be happy to take the first week.'

'I can cook though my culinary skills are limited but I should be happy to accept the challenge if you will accept the risk.'

She laughed. 'I can live with that – or at least I hope I shall!'

* * *

The rest of the day passed in the sun. In the evening they walked the mile through the rich rose of the sunset to a restaurant in the town. It lay in a courtyard behind a low sandstone arch, brightly illuminated, the lights casting widening shadows across the cobbles. The interior and the courtyard were alive with noise from family groups. The red and white checked table cloths covered wooden tables and the meals were served by the children of the patron with shy smiles. The evening darkened as they dined until the sky became a smooth deep indigo and when they came out to walk back to the house they were caressed by the soft warm air. The atmosphere remained balmy as the stone of the houses slowly and reluctantly yielded the heat gathered from the oppressive sun of the day. The tall narrow buildings illuminated by hidden floodlights threw grotesque shadows up to the night sky. Lovers walked languorously hand in hand from deep shadow to pools of light. Sally took Peter's hand as they wandered comfortably through the market place and streets, surrounded by the contented sounds of people at ease flowing out from the restaurants and bars. This was a night to savour. Slowly they walked along the track up the hill towards the pine woods which led to the house.

They stopped on the edge of the woods and looked down on the small encapsulated and brightly lit town below. They walked round a bend and were embraced by the darkness of the wood – a darkness which was dense and mysterious to the city dweller. The perpetual glow of the city sky at night was absent and the night shades enclosed and confined them. The soft smell of the pines and the rattle of the cicadas seemed to emanate from outside their private universe. The ground was soft and yielding under their feet, a bed of pine needles over the moss-embedded grass. The call of a forsaken owl emphasized their solitude.

They stopped once more and Sally turned to face Peter. She stood for a moment face upturned and then slowly pulled him close to her, kissing his eyes, his lips, his neck and then his chest as she loosened the buttons on his shirt. He returned the kisses and moved to free the buttons on the front of her dress and enclosed her breasts with his hands. He paused, gently caressing her nipples and then kneeling kissed them, holding his head close to her. 'Oh Sally, you are so wonderful.'

'No, Peter,' she laid a finger across his lips. 'Don't talk.' She knelt facing him and slipped the shirt off his shoulders. They lay back together facing one another as they softly probed and explored.

'Sally, you're beautiful and I think I'm falling in love.'

'Shh,' she said covering his lips with a kiss. 'I think we're still a little overdressed for this sort of thing,' and with two quick movements her dress and underwear were cast aside and slowly and deliberately she undressed Peter, kissing his face, neck and chest as she did so and then softly with the tips of her fingers she stroked the inside of his thighs as he gently caressed her until neither could contain the intensity of the emotion any longer and he entered her.

They lay back resting, comfortable and fulfilled, with Sally curled in his embrace gazing at the dark sky above. They stayed there for some minutes gently caressing each other.

'I'm sorry to sound so mundane,' said Sally after a pause, 'but I think we should put at least some of our clothes on to walk back to the house.'

They entered the living room and Peter embraced her again. 'You are wonderful, Sally.'

'It's kind of you to say that but not entirely true.'

They prepared for sleep.

'Can I … shall I push the other bed into your room?'

'No, Peter. I have to say gently, it's not like that – something has changed but not everything has changed.' She paused and looked across at him. 'Don't look so crestfallen and hurt.'

'But it was wonderful. Didn't it mean anything to you?'

'Yes, Peter, it did,' she smiled, 'but possibly not quite the same thing that it meant to you. The whole world has not been inverted because we've fucked.'

'That seems a very cold view.'

She went over and laid her hands on Peter's shoulders. 'No, anything but cold. We have had a very good week – a

162

week of indolence and pleasure. For me this holiday week has been magical. We have talked together and remained silent together. We have taken great pleasure in each other's company. The week has now ended and out there in that warm sensuous atmosphere we have shown our appreciation of what we have shared by enjoying each other's body. It seemed the most natural thing in the world to do. It was neither cold nor casual. I don't do casual sex – but I do look upon you as a particularly special and loving friend. Our chance meeting in Northumberland has proved to be a special and significant event for me.'

'But I think I love you.'

'No, Peter, you and I are free people and to be in love can imply possession. We can be involved and love without being in love, which too often implies exclusivity.'

'But I'm more than happy to relinquish some of that freedom.'

'Peter, I don't believe you should think of diminishing the freedom which you have so newly acquired. Let us be loving friends. We have come together as independent free spirits. We should cherish and revel in that independence and the freedom which it grants us to share as we've been doing for the last week, without entering into a compact which would place obligations and commitments on one or both of us. Now it's time that we went to our beds.'

'Perhaps you're right,' he said a little ruefully, 'but it might take me some time to acquire the necessary flexibility of thought and attitude to manage my emotions.'

'I'm sure you'll achieve that. Now I'm going to give you one more long and loving kiss before we retreat to our beds.'

16

The morning started early. They met on the terrace for breakfast. The strong light of the day filtered through the trees. Peter had slept well and was able to recover some of the ease which had been the hallmark of the previous week.

'Well, I shall clear these things away and then it will be time to retreat. What are you planning to do?'

'I shall have to start sometime, so I guess this is where I catch my breath, take my imagination in both hands, pick up my pen, start writing and see if I have what it takes.' Sally kissed Peter saying, 'Good luck – we've had a wonderful week, my loving friend, and I am happy that you are here.'

Peter sat on the part of the terrace that was shaded from the sun and looked at the daunting supply of white paper in front of him. He leaned back in the chair and his thoughts carried him back to the previous evening. He found the prospect of the relationship offered to him appealing and exciting in abstract, although it was difficult to think dispassionately of Sally as the arousing memory of the contact between their bodies in the woods intruded upon and finally filled his consciousness. Recollection of each stage of the preceding day leading to its final consummation drove all the partly formulated ideas from his mind. Restlessly, as the rattle of a typewriter filtered through to the terrace, he rose to his feet and paced up and down. He finally decided to walk back down the track to the town but stopped where he and Sally had lain the evening before. He turned into the clearing and, shielding his eyes from the sun, looked up through the canopy of the trees as the memories of the previous night returned with an erotic urgency.

He strolled back to the house but was unable to settle to writing. The emptiness of the paper and the poverty of his imagination seemed to mock him. Finally, he took his car and, having bought some beer and fruit, drove to the shingle by the river where he lay in the sun. He soon fell asleep only to find when he wakened that the heat of the day had passed and that he was almost alone. He drove back to the house, anxious at his failure to consign even a single thought to paper.

The following days passed. He remained unable to compose himself sufficiently to write. The challenge of generating a compelling story line, creating characters and elaborating these to create a novel seemed too momentous and the inventions of his mind too prosaic. When he did occasionally consign words to paper, he became dispirited and downcast as he examined his efforts, dismissing them as banal and pedestrian. He started to take the car out during the day and pass the time in solitude in an attempt to escape from his inadequacy. That first period of freedom had been lost and although he explored further he was unable to recapture the joy of seeing, smelling and touching places which had so excited him the previous week. He became resigned to being a lone tourist, sitting in cafés with a coffee or a tisane. The hours of these days dragged slowly until he felt he could return and re-join Sally, freed from her self-imposed discipline in the evenings. They talked little and only about trivial matters as he felt constrained by his failures, all the more brought into focus when he was daily able to hear the persistent clatter of the keys of her typewriter which marked her steady progress. Her routine and apparent productivity drove him to wonder if he might have been wiser to have returned to England and gone into a solitary self-imposed exile, distancing himself from the allure of this environment and the ever-enticing presence of Sally. He knew he could not be certain that he would be any more successful elsewhere and progressively a mood of defeatism pervaded his thinking.

The week merged into the weekend. 'Do you know what day it will be on Monday?' asked Sally over breakfast on the Saturday. 'It will be "une fête nationale", the fourteenth of July which celebrates the storming of the Bastille. I'm planning to work this Saturday but take Monday off as it will be a public holiday. Why don't you think of doing the same? Towns and villages will go crazy with celebrations and fireworks. Why don't we join them and give ourselves the opportunity to go a little crazy too? But that's for Monday evening. What would you think of a quiet day on the beach by the river beforehand? We could go back to where we spent last Sunday for lunch and a swim.'

Peter fell silent at the implicit suggestion that he might rearrange his work schedule to fall in with Sally's suggestion. He was ashamed to admit that his efforts had amounted to absolutely nothing. The first week had indeed been magical but now it was becoming an increasingly distant memory, an enchanted interlude. They set off on the Monday having bought the obligatory baguette, cheese, fruit and wine for their lunch and headed for the shingle beach. They lay back after their picnic and Peter said quietly, 'Sally, I think it was a mistake for me to stay and probably an error to think that my literary talents might extend beyond the drafting of wills.'

She raised herself on one elbow and laughed. 'Peter, this is nothing. It will come to you if you set yourself a schedule to write. You don't need to feel that you have to sit and write "A novel by Peter Bowman, Chapter 1, Page 1".'

'Now you're teasing.'

'No, this is a topic on which I would never tease you. You've done a remarkable thing by leaving your established life behind you. Few others would have done this.'

'What do you mean then?'

'Perhaps, just for once, I'll break my self-imposed ordinance and offer some advice. Write something. It doesn't matter if it's not and never becomes part of some major literary work. You won't write something to challenge "War and Peace" in the literary canon straight off. Describe people, scenes and events. Spin stories around them, fantasy stories if you like, and the rest will follow.'

'I have tried to do that but when I read it back it seems either pretentious or trite.'

'That will often be the case until you've established a flow. You told me about your encounter with those two young people in Bloomsbury and you recounted the events of the day with wit and fluency. There is a story there and certainly one that could be spun around it, particularly after your further chance meeting with them.' She laughed. 'You seem to have a talent for chance encounters! Or go and sit in the market place in the town and observe people and their mundane daily activities. There is plenty to see there, the local people, the tourists, the puce-faced English on holiday struggling to comprehend and be comprehended, the superior sounding expatriates still often speaking inadequate French and sometimes with atrocious accents. Let your imagination run freely. If you feel more comfortable, write a short story or two, although practitioners of that art claim that it's a greater challenge than writing a full-length novel.'

'I shall persist. I know I haven't totally burnt my bridges behind me but I have dismantled them sufficiently to ensure that I shan't have the face to go back without producing something, however mediocre.'

Sally leant across and kissed him. 'You're being too hard on yourself. You're welcome to continue to stay here, as I said a week ago, but if you feel it would be better to establish an eremitic existence back home then you should do that. I'm not suggesting that you should – you should simply do what you feel is likely to work best for you.'

'No, I should like to stay. Perhaps my mistake was to expect that this bewitchingly beautiful environment would somehow diminish the harsh realities of attempting to write.'

'Peter, I should be very happy if you do stay but remember the choice is yours and you are free to decide otherwise at any time.'

They lay back and basked in the sun for a little longer

before swimming across the river and back again, arriving many yards downstream due to the strength of the current.

* * *

They drove back to the house and left as the sun was setting to spend the evening in Domme. They parked on the edge of the village and walked to the centre where they sat in the square enjoying a glass of wine and observed the scene. The market place filled progressively with revellers as a band played in the background. Just before seven they joined a throng moving along the cliff top walk towards the Jubilee Garden for the firework display. They stood at the back of the crowd and watched as the display erupted, throwing multi-coloured stars into the air in the shapes of exotic flowers of chromatic brilliance, glittering multi-hued rain and luminescent waterfalls, all of which hung over the river and slowly died in the valley below. Each fresh manifestation was greeted with rounds of applause. Finally the spectacle was over and they re-joined the crowd to walk back to the village, enlivened by a group of lads who threw firecrackers amongst the walkers.

They decided to drive down from the promontory to one of the quieter villages by the riverside and installed themselves on the terrace of a restaurant in Beynac, overlooking the river.

'Peter, I had a call yesterday and I have to go back to London on Wednesday. There is some problem with the contract for my last series of articles and my agent feels that it's imperative that I should be there to sort it out.'

'Is it really necessary?'

'Unfortunately, it is but since I have to go I shall catch up on one or two other things while I'm there. He also hinted there might be another project in the offing which would interest me. I should be grateful if you could drive me into Brive to catch a train to Paris. I'll fly from there. There's absolutely no reason why you shouldn't stay on at the house. Since it would be your week to be responsible for the catering, you're getting off lightly!'

'Probably more to your advantage than to mine!'

'I'm not sure how long I shall be gone but I'll call and let you know. Is there anything which I can do for you in London?'

'I don't think so, although I might get you to post a letter to my parents. They know I'm in France but they don't know where, nor did they know I would be away for more than a week or ten days. I'll write tomorrow. I might perhaps write to one or two others too. There's also one other thing. I never expected to be away this long. Would you have time to go over to my flat and see if there is any post and also give a key to Sue Hepscott who lives below? I can give you a letter for her and perhaps you could post the others for me.'

'Consider it done. Now let's enjoy the remainder of the day.'

They lingered after dinner on the lighted terrace looking out into the night, enjoying a coffee and a brandy. They sat at ease, lightly clad and relaxing in the warm evening but as they sat there quietly in each other's company, an urgency developed between them and the conversation lapsed. 'We must go,' said Peter.

'Yes, it's time to go.'

Peter drove back in silence with Sally's hand resting lightly on his knee. The still night air fanned their faces through the open roof of the car. He opened the passenger door for Sally when they reached the house and they walked through to the terrace. She came directly into his arms as he kissed her and held her tightly to him. Through her light summer dress he could feel her breasts and the firm points of her nipples against his chest. Their thighs touched and she swayed slowly from side to side against him. Eagerness and anticipation flared and she led him across the terrace to where the airbeds and rugs still lay on the ground. Slowly and gently they removed each other's clothing and then with pleasure, enhanced and prolonged by previous knowledge, they explored each other's bodies sensuously and lingeringly with their hands, their lips and their tongues. She gently moved on top and encased him and they reached their climax together. They remained for some time in that position and then Sally whispered in his ear with a smile, 'I think we've got the hang of this.' She slowly rolled off and they lay back embracing. Peter leant across and whispered, 'I'm beginning to understand that being a loving friend could be quite habit-forming.'

She kissed him and whispered back, 'Yes, and it's a habit I would not want to kick any time soon – and it need not be restricted to weekends.' She got up for a moment saying, 'Stay there', and went into the house for some more rugs. They slept under the stars until awakened by the sunlight of another day.

17

Peter turned away shortly before the train was lost to sight. He stayed in the town just long enough to buy some provisions for lunch before driving back along the river to the beach which he now regarded proprietorially as their beach. He suddenly felt the isolation of the solitary foreigner abroad, largely cut off by language, customs and culture from those around him. Alone, he was drawn back into the uncertain vortex of his own thoughts. He sat on the beach for a short time and then, ashamed of his own lack of resolve, gathered up his lunch and drove back to the house.

He carried the small desk from his room out onto the terrace, made himself a coffee, and settled down to write. Mindful of Sally's suggestions he wrote three vignettes, the first recalling the scene in Domme on Bastille Day, the second describing the market in Sarlat and the third an account of his two chance encounters with Cass and Stefan. He stopped and read these through as he took a late lunch. Although not wholly satisfied with the prose, he felt they had an immediacy and appeal. He reflected on the need to imbue anything that he wrote with authenticity and it was clear this could only be achieved if based on his own knowledge and experiences. He thought back over the last year and felt that he could create moving pictures, in words, of many of the events which had finally led him to this quiet sun-stippled terrace in the Dordogne.

It was late afternoon by the time he had revised the three vignettes and he drove back to the river in a more relaxed frame of mind. As he enjoyed the late afternoon sun, an idea started to evolve in his mind. The personal stories of many of his clients frequently contained dramatic elements ranging from tragedy to comedy to high melodrama. He could construct a tale around what the tabloid newspapers were inclined to refer to as a "tug of love" over a child but with a twist. The twist he envisaged was that the husband would be an English potter domiciled in France while the wife would be French but holding a senior and secure job in the financial sector in England. This would draw together his knowledge of the law and the opportunity to create scenes and episodes in both countries. He drove back to the house and then walked into Sarlat for the evening. He bought himself a reporter's notebook and sat outside at a restaurant in the balmy night air. He leant back to enjoy the scene as he drank a kir before ordering his meal, observing the promenaders and making notes, his senses more alert after composing the three vignettes earlier in the day.

His newly found focus made it possible to establish a routine and, although he did not always achieve quite the same level of discipline as Sally, he was determined to reach a target of fifteen hundred words a day. The completion of each day's task was at times a burden and at others a pleasure. On some days it was gratifying to note how quickly the pages of script accumulated and on such days he would often continue writing until late in the day, more than filling his self-imposed quota. He spent little time re-reading the product of his day's labours. It seemed more important to construct the story and then return to re-shape and embellish the narrative as necessary.

He took time each day either to swim in the early afternoon or to walk in the early evening after the heat of the sun had diminished. He remained in the house most evenings, taking a solitary meal and reading before retiring. Some evenings seemed interminably long and it was difficult to suppress thoughts of Sally. Her company and her encouragement had been essential but the precise nature of his relationship with her remained an enigma. He recognised and envied her sense of detachment and autonomy and her wish to retain her independence. He released himself from his introspection on two evenings by eating in Sarlat and in one of the nearby villages, occasionally exchanging trivia with English or Dutch tourists.

* * *

It was in the middle of the week after her departure that Sally called to say she would be concluding her business that week and had found a flight to Bordeaux which would arrive early on the Saturday evening. Peter consulted the map and saw that it was over one hundred and fifty kilometres to Bordeaux with the airport on the far side of the city. He decided to drive there on the Friday afternoon and stay overnight before meeting her the following day. It was a slow journey alongside the ever-widening river as it made its way to the great funnel of the Gironde. The holiday traffic was heavy but he reckoned that it would have taken much longer the following morning. He reached Bordeaux shortly after four in the afternoon but circled the city and drove the additional fifty kilometres to the coast through the maritime pines of the regional park of the Landes de Gascogne. He arrived late at Cap Ferret and found a room for the night close to the Bassin d'Arcachon.

The following morning he checked out of the hotel and drove to the broad beaches of the silver, shimmering Atlantic coast. With six hours in hand before he was due at the airport, he strolled across the beach and watched the long breakers rolling in. As the sun rose to its height, he had little hesitation in stripping to his trunks and entering the water. After a few paces he dived through a breaker and swam effortlessly out from the shore. He watched the sparkling reflections of the sun on the spray flying off his arms as they drew him through the water. Finally he reached an area of flatter water well beyond the breakers and, rolling onto his back, he floated on the swell. The shore seemed remote, and beyond the waves he could see the sand, hard and white in the sun. The occupants of the beach moved remotely, shouting soundlessly, locked in their own worlds. Behind the beach was a row of tall, gabled villas with ornate, baroque balconies; the summer haunts of wealthy Parisians he assumed. The largest of these at the extreme northern end of the village stood a little apart from the others. Here it was clear that the summer season was in full swing. The windows and doors facing the beach were all open. Figures moved purposefully in and out carrying undistinguishable articles while a group of workmen were erecting a marquee in the grounds to one side of the house. He lay for some minutes absorbing the sun and cooled by the water until disturbed by a small cloud crossing the face of the sun. Turning, he saw that the outgoing tide had taken him some distance from the beach. Initially unconcerned, he started to swim towards the shore but it was apparent after a few minutes that he was making little progress against the tide and the current. Stopping to tread water he found that he was being carried southwards and further out. He decided to swim obliquely across the current, aiming to reach the beach nearer the mouth of the bay and then walk back to his clothing. He was beginning to make slow progress towards the shoreline when the distant drone of a motor yacht disturbed the soft sound of the swell and increased as it approached. He wondered if he should hail the boat and was about to dismiss the idea when the motor was cut and it drifted towards to him. There were four people aboard, young, tanned and relaxed. The helmsman stood holding the wheel.

'Monsieur,' he shouted and Peter waved. 'Monsieur, il me semble que vous avez peut-être un petit problème.'

Peter hesitated. His limited French was certainly sufficient to understand this but his knowledge of conversational French was not adequate for him to say that although he was confident he would reach the shore he would nevertheless appreciate being picked up. He swallowed his pride and a great deal of sea water. 'Oui, monsieur, c'est vrai, s'il vous plaît.'

He swam across and two pairs of arms pulled him aboard. As they did so, he slipped and fell into the well of the boat. He lay there gasping as the throttle was opened, the engine accelerated and with the wake flowing out astern the boat circled and headed towards the solitary house at the far end of the beach.

'Gee, that is something we have landed,' drawled a female American accent from somewhere above his head.

Peter looked round at the various ankles which were at his eye level and selected a slim pair which he hoped would match the appealing quality of those tones. He pushed himself up with his arms, looking up as he did so, and it was with a shock as his eyes travelled up her legs and on towards her face that he saw she was not only very beautiful and evenly tanned but also that she was totally naked.

'Oh, my God, I'm sorry,' he said involuntarily as he quickly averted his eyes and sat on the thwart. He then saw that the other two, apart from the helmsman, were also unclothed.

The other occupants of the boat laughed at his obvious discomfiture. 'You're a long way out of UK territorial waters. It was a firm bet you were English,' said the young American woman at the stern. 'Even with a mouthful of sea water no Frenchman could speak with such an appalling accent!'

'Ah, yes.' He looked up momentarily and then, driven by some involuntary compulsion, he glanced down at her firm and evenly tanned breasts.

'Hey!' She took his chin and lifted his face so that he was looking directly into her eyes. 'Monsieur l'Anglais, my name is Julie Christie – what's yours?'

He recovered quickly and looking at her said, 'Oh yes, and mine's Gypsy Rose Lee.'

She laughed. 'That's better, but that really is my name. Nobody had heard of the other one when my parents were selecting a name for me.'

'I'm sorry, you must have more than enough jokes of that nature. I'm Peter Bowman.'

'Well, that's cleared that up. That's Marie,' she indicated the other young woman, 'and the guy with his arm around her is Danny. The helmsman is Pierre. He's Marie's brother.' The others waved greetings and, as the boat approached the shore, they slipped into their bathing costumes which made Peter feel able to look around with less overt embarrassment. 'I guess we would have dressed earlier if we had known we'd be receiving guests.' They docked at a small landing stage by the house which had been the focus of all the earlier activity.

The marquee which Peter had seen while swimming was now fully in place and, as they approached, he observed staff erecting tables, arranging chairs and setting out glasses and cutlery on linen cloths. Others were rigging ornamental lights in the trees and along the terrace. A figure ran down from the house to the jetty to hold the bow steady as they disembarked.

'This is Pierre and Marie's house – or more correctly their father's.' The house looked even larger close at hand and architecturally more disproportionate than it had from a distance. The balcony overhung the wide open French windows, the dark wood was extravagantly decorated and the eaves projected over the terrace with exuberant carving in a style more suited to the Tyrol than the Atlantic coast.

Marie shouted something across the lawn in French and Peter was embarrassed when a man appeared carrying a large towel and a beach robe which, after some protest, he put on. 'You'll stay for a coffee, of course,' she added in almost accentless English. It was more of a command that an invitation.

'I must go and retrieve my clothes and see that my car's alright.'

'Of course, but have some coffee first.'

Fifteen minutes later he insisted that he should set off to retrieve his clothes and thanked his rescuers profusely for their help. 'I'll take a walk with you,' said Julie.

It was a stroll of about a kilometre up the beach to where he had left his clothes. Julie explained that this was a summer property belonging to Marie and Pierre's family. Their father was a wealthy businessman from Lyon. The Carnot family was well-known for throwing extravagant parties two or three times each summer season. The house had been taken over by caterers for the last couple of days so they had decided to take the boat out and swim offshore. These evenings were well-known and invitations were freely and widely distributed among the influential, the beautiful and their followers. Julie explained that she had become a friend of the family since she had worked in New York for a number of years with Marie where they had shared an apartment. She had been coming to France regularly for many years but was now working in Lyon, dealing in commercial property and thus she now saw more of Marie and her family. 'You must come to tonight's party,' she said.

'I couldn't possibly, you hardly know me.'

She laughed. 'You have at least met two members of the family which is more than can be said for some of those who show up at Chez Carnot. You've also seen rather a lot of them!' she added with a smile.

'No, I won't know anyone and I should be quite out of place in that company.'

'You would fit in just fine and you would help decrease the average age of the guests a bit, which would be no bad thing.'

'Well, it would have been good but I have to meet a friend at the airport just after six this evening. I shall have to leave in a couple of hours or so, but it would have been interesting,' he added, thinking that this might have provided another experience which he could translate into words.

'You could bring her too – I'm assuming it's a her.'

'Yes, it is.'

'Well, bring her along.'

'Oh no, we have to drive back to Sarlat.'

'You could stay the night.'

'Well, I'll have to see. I should speak to Sally about it.'

'I sense I'm progressively dismantling the barriers which you keep erecting. Some do stay after these parties and the villa has innumerable rooms.' She looked at him enquiringly. 'Would it be one room or two?'

Peter hesitated. Could he make this sort of commitment on Sally's behalf? Finally he said, 'I'm not sure.'

'Good, that's settled then, but one room or two or should we leave that as an open question?' she asked mischievously.

'I think it should be two.'

They gathered Peter's clothes and drove back to the villa in his car. The four of them had a light lunch together on the lawns, accompanied by a very dry and aromatic Sancerre. The time came for Peter to drive to the airport to meet Sally. Marie and Julie insisted on accompanying him to forestall and override any objections that might be raised about the arrangements for the evening. With the inevitable delay in the arrival of the flight, they passed the time on the observation balcony looking to the west as the sun, glowing richly, fell towards the pine forests on the horizon. As the light was starting to fade they saw the plane approaching from the north. Twenty minutes later, Peter was greeting Sally as she came through the barrier. He introduced his companions and described the events of the day and the plans that had been made for the evening. These were accepted with little comment and no surprise and he felt a little hurt that she had not protested that she wanted a quiet evening and, by implication, to be alone with him.

It was almost dark when they arrived back at the house. The garden was brilliantly illuminated by the lights in the trees and those blazing out of every window. A growing throng ebbed and flowed ceaselessly between house and terrace, terrace and garden, garden and marquee. Overloud voices and stridently insincere laughter betrayed the social uncertainty of some of the guests. Peter observed the variable geometry of groups, endlessly disaggregating and re-aggregating. Some small, secluded groups stood resolutely apart, seemingly defying others to break into their private caucuses and challenge the security they had found with their peers. Others moved ceaselessly around greeting real and imagined acquaintances with a shout, a wave or brief physical contact. He moved away and sat on a small wall beyond the lawns and, from the security of the semi-darkness, looked in on the party watching the guests as they moved erratically and randomly like moths held in a ring of light. Sally had been swept away from his company, with a shrug of her shoulders and a look of amused resignation, by a tall, elegantly dressed man talking volubly in French. Peter swung his legs over the wall and looked out to sea with his back to the party. Separated from Sally and his newly found companions, he began to feel isolated and regretted that he had been persuaded to stay for the party. The memory of the evening with Sally in the pine woods overwhelmed him with a strength which heightened his perceptions, to the extent that he could feel the firm, dry support of the pine needles and the characteristic resinous smell. Suddenly feeling very solitary, he got to his feet and went towards the house to look for Sally but failed to see her amongst the throng. Disconsolately, he walked out to the small landing stage with a large glass of wine and sat on the edge, overlooking the sea. The noise of the revellers behind him and the surf in front concealed the soft steps approaching from behind.

He looked up as the melodious American voice interrupted his reverie. 'Not thinking of swimming again, are you?'

'Oh, hello, Julie,' he said distractedly.

She sat down beside him laughing. 'That was not a greeting which could be expected to enhance Anglo-American relations.'

'No, I'm sorry. I was thinking.'

'Your girlfriend – she's great.'

'She's not really my girlfriend. She's no-one's girlfriend;

merely her own person and a friend.' He could not find adequate or appropriate words to describe his relationship with Sally.

'I guess you know what you mean but I'm damned if I do.' She grinned. 'Are you regretting that you stayed?'

'No, of course not,' he said with unnecessary emphasis, 'but I don't know any people here and my French, as I've already demonstrated to you, is grossly inadequate for social repartee. Sally speaks the language fluently as her mother was French.'

'Well, I can think of better things to do than discuss our various linguistic shortcomings. Perhaps you can dance, or even just sway, holding onto me better than you can speak French.' She took his hand, pulling him gently to his feet and they moved back to the centre of the stage.

The evening slowly, languorously resolved into a series of soft-focus images as Peter succumbed to the gentle seductions of the wine and the warm, sinuous pressure of Julie's body as they danced into the night. As the party waned they sat down and Peter was suddenly overtaken by a huge tiredness. His head fell gently onto Julie's shoulder. She shook him gently awake. 'You've had a busy day, water baby. It's time you went to your allotted bed.'

18

Peter awoke uncertainly the next morning and took some time to re-orient himself. The silence of the rambling villa was only broken by the soft chink of cups and saucers and occasional murmured words emanating from the terrace below. He threw back the shutters and looked out to the sea. Glancing at his watch, he was surprised to see that it was almost ten. He quickly showered and dressed and made his way through the empty villa to the scene of the revelry of the night before. Looking round, it was difficult to envisage that there had been a party for fifty or sixty guests the previous evening. The marquee was still in place but the tables and chairs were neatly stacked and the detritus left by the guests had been cleared away. Julie, Marie and her parents were just finishing their breakfasts but drew a chair up for him and called for fresh coffee.

Peter introduced himself and François Carnot stood and shook his hand. 'Good morning, we never really met properly yesterday but I am François and this is Madeleine, my wife. I hope that you slept comfortably.'

'I certainly did and I must apologise for my late appearance this morning. I hope I've not held you up in any way.'

'Not at all, we are having a quiet day after the revelries of last night.'

'It's a spectacular and amazing location for a party. The villa and garden are a wonderful setting and, of course, your weather helps.'

'Yes, but if you were here in the autumn and winter you might not think that the weather was so wonderful then, with the wind and rain driving in from the Atlantic. But I'm glad that you enjoyed the party. I hear that you had an adventurous day yesterday.'

Peter smiled and glanced at Julie and Marie as he spoke. 'I did but the knights who rescued me were not clad in shining armour!'

Julie laughed. 'I have to admit that we were a touch déshabillée.'

François looked at Madeleine and raised his eyebrows. He turned to Peter. 'I spent a long time talking to your friend, Sally, yesterday. She speaks immaculate French, much superior to my English. She tells me you're a lawyer-turned-writer and that you're staying in her house near Sarlat.'

'The first part is correct – as for the writing, that's a work in progress, as we would say in England.'

'She said she thought that it was bold of you to leave your work for a year to try something so entirely different.'

'Possibly foolhardy.'

'Would it be proper to ask what the book will be about?' asked Madeleine.

'It's often said that all first novels are autobiographical. This is not but I felt that I had to base it on my own knowledge and experience. It's about a custody battle between a French mother and an English father. I learnt something of French family law while dealing with a case a year or so ago. Of course, there is much more to the story than the law. There are major emotional and cultural dimensions. I need to know more about the law in this country to ensure that I get the details right. I know there's nothing more infuriating to a reader who has expertise if an author fails to get some of the fundamentals right.'

'We may be able to help a little there, if you were to come over to Lyon. We know two lawyers who speak good English, who are "sympa" as we would say, and who, I'm sure, would be happy to talk to you informally. You must give us your address and we'll give you ours.'

'That's a very generous offer.'

'Well, we are always happy to receive guests and Lyon is a very interesting city. Have you ever been there?'

'No.'

'You should.' Peter looked around. 'Are you looking for your friend Sally? She had breakfast early and went for a walk up the beach. She said that she needed some fresh air after her time in London.'

'You should take up the invitation to visit Lyon,' added Julie. 'It is a lovely city and authentically French.'

Sally returned, kissed Peter on the top of his head and sat down to join them for coffee. 'That was wonderful, I not only walked, I took off my shoes and ran barefoot on the firm sand along the water's edge.' She looked across at Peter. 'I don't know what other plans you have for me for today but we should head back to the house sometime.'

'I didn't really have any plans for you yesterday. I

was simply swept along by the flow of events and the persuasiveness of my saviours, Marie and Julie!'

Julie grinned. 'It was not too difficult to storm your ramparts.'

'No, it rarely is. It was an interesting evening and thank you for rescuing me, not once but twice.'

Sally looked across quizzically at Peter and then turned to Julie. 'Peter has a proclivity for chance encounters!' She turned back to Peter. 'If you don't mind, we should say our farewells to the Carnots and Julie and be off.'

* * *

Peter drove silently, closing his mind to all but the mechanical, semi-reflex process of manipulating the car as they ran into a summer storm. The converging limits of the road, the repetitive beat of the rain and the mesmeric effect of the unceasing movement of the wipers fixed his attention.

'How about stopping for a coffee and a sandwich?' Sally's mundane question after almost two hours on the road interrupted his reverie.

They stopped at a small roadside café. A faded advertisement painted on the wall enjoined them to "Buvez Byrrh". The brightly striped plastic awning dripped rainwater continuously and advertisements for Suze and Dubonnet swung creakingly in the wind. They ran in, crouching to minimise the effect of the rain, and made their way between metal tables and wooden-slatted aluminium chairs into the dark interior. The juke-box was playing persistently and stridently in one corner, controlled by a self-appointed disc jockey in a leather jacket. They sat at one side of the café and, after a further prolonged silence, he leant forward and asked, 'What happened to you last night?' He was unable to avoid an edge creeping into his voice. 'I was looking for you,' he added, concerned that he was sounding disappointed and betrayed. The concept of being an independent, loving friend appealed to him but adjusting to the reality was proving to be a slow process. Sally laughed. 'I don't know what you're laughing about,' he said grumpily.

'About you or, more accurately, about last night.'

'I don't see that that explains anything.'

'Possibly, possibly not.' She shrugged her shoulders.

'Well, where were you then?'

'I don't know quite what you are asking me,' she looked at him enquiringly 'or perhaps I do. But you're not really expecting me to answer that question, are you, particularly when it is phrased in that way?'

'Well, I spent some time looking for you without success.'

'So, are you asking me to apologise for dissipating your time so carelessly and thoughtlessly?'

'I missed you,' he said abjectly. 'I had hoped and expected that we might have some time together.'

'Well, we have all the time in the world now,' she said gently.

'Hell, yes, I know,' he said apologetically. 'It was just that I missed you and wanted to spend time with you. Then I bumped into that lot and thought it might be amusing and even useful to go to the party.'

'And so it was, but what did you expect? An opportunity

to watch the decadent haute bourgeoisie disporting themselves?'

'Something like that, I suppose.'

'It must have been something of a disappointment to you then. No orgiastic behaviour, no public fornication.'

He laughed. 'I really don't quite know what I expected but whatever it was, it didn't meet my expectations.'

'Perhaps you shouldn't have gone into it with any expectations – well-defined or otherwise. To do so tends to lead to disappointment more often than not.'

'That seems unduly pessimistic.'

'No, not pessimistic. It's possible to learn some truths from observation but that's the first stage and, in my view, it must be approached with an open mind. The processes of analysis and interpretation come later. I know this is not the approach adopted by many in my trade but it's my lodestar. Those who are determined to identify some pattern in events based on their preconceived views may well do so, at least to their own satisfaction, but they must expect to be challenged by those who operate with a different mindset. Those comments are not intended as advice. They're simply a personal view shaped by my own journalistic experience.'

'I know, you've said this before but I still find it difficult to accept fully.'

'That's fine. It's not part of my approach to life to try and influence and advise others. You're your own man. My observations suggest that all our lives are influenced by random external events and we react to them in ways which are influenced by our backgrounds and culture to a greater or a lesser extent. I'm inclined to see life as encapsulating a series of events which are then interpreted by people who frequently search for underlying explanations, sometimes within the framework of an overall plan. I regard the search for a rational basis for everything as self-defeating.'

'I'm not sure I fully accept that and it seems very dispassionate. It also suggests to me that we have little control over our destinies.'

'No, my earlier comments were not for one moment intended to imply that we don't also have the opportunity to shape our lives. Of course we do and that's exactly what you're doing. The extent to which we fashion our futures depends upon our innate abilities and drive but it is also determined by our capacity to turn random external events to our advantage and prevent them becoming barriers to what we wish to do. But that's probably enough of my pseudo-philosophy.' She looked directly into his eyes. 'Let me just add one thing. Our first meeting on a cliff top was one random event which has led to us sitting in a café by the Dordogne in the pouring rain nearly a year later. The intervening events which have made that happen have included a second chance meeting, the rupture of your marriage (which whilst not random was wholly unexpected from your point of view), the death of a friend, your search for me and your decision to follow your instincts to write. These chance events and conscious decisions and probably many other factors finally led you here,' she paused, 'and I'm pleased that they did.' She squeezed his hand.

'So am I and I'm delighted that you are back.'

'Me too, you have the gift of serendipity. You should make the most of it, as you've done so far.'

Peter smiled. 'Yes, I am sorry to have been such a grouch.'

'Let's be off. I have several things to tell you when we get back to the house.'

* * *

They arrived back in the early evening as the rain was abating. Sally had been to Peter's flat but not until the day before she flew back to France. She had seen Sue Hepscott who had agreed to keep an eye on the flat, and collected some mail which had been lying there. Peter glanced at it casually. Most was of little importance but it included two bills which needed to be paid and there were two personal letters. He recognized his mother's handwriting on one but, although the writing seemed vaguely familiar, he could not immediately identify the source of the other. He put them aside to read later. He had planned for Sally's return and was ready to continue his duties as chef. He prepared a coq au vin and opened a bottle of St Joseph which he had bought for the occasion.

'How have you been while I've been away?' Sally asked as they sat back feeling mellow as they finished the Côtes du Rhone.

'Well, I think. I've started to write. I know you said that you didn't do advice but the suggestion that I should try writing some descriptive pieces based on my observations of events was good and I have written three. I might add the events of yesterday to the list. I have also created an embryo of a novel. Your non-advice was very helpful.' He grinned. 'I shall be entirely happy to receive further instalments. I've

191

decided to base the novel on a tug of love over custody of a child with the parents being split between England and France and bitterly divided over the care and education of the child.'

'That sounds good and how have you found living in France?'

'I am revelling in the freedom from everyday preoccupations – and, yes, I'm adapting although I wish that I knew more of the language.'

'I have something to tell you. I normally stay here until late September or early October. I then close the house up for the winter and go back to London. I had originally intended to stay a little later this year as my writing has fallen behind schedule but that plan has been thrown up into the air. I shall have to go away again and for some time. Quite out of the blue, I have been asked to write a series of articles about developments in the European Economic Community with a particular focus on Germany and France. These will be for a weekly journal called Europe Watch. The initiative appears to have been prompted by two factors: the first is that De Gaulle's veto on Britain's entry has been lifted by Pompidou and work on reactivating our application for membership has started. The other is that it's probable that Willy Brandt, who has been Vice-Chancellor in the coalition, will be elected as German Chancellor in a few weeks' time. It's inevitable that his policy of rapprochement with the east will become a major element of policy. This worries the French who fear a resurgent Germany. The focus will be on attitudes to British membership and the impact that improved West-East relations might have on these. I shall need to travel widely in both countries and speak to as many people as possible. This will put my other projects onto the back burner for a while as they don't have the same immediacy.'

'But why ever did they select you?'

She laughed. 'You might have phrased that a bit more delicately! You know that, amongst other things, I write on travel and produce features on aspects of European life. What you probably don't know is that I speak German as well as French. I've told you that my father was a diplomat. We lived in Bonn for three years when I was just entering my teens and I went to an international school there. The principal language of tuition was English but there was also a strong emphasis on speaking German. This was enhanced through playing with local school friends. The advantage for the journal is that I'm fluent in both languages. The intention is that I shall start this project early in September and be on the road continuously for about two months. It has been largely left to me to plan my own schedule. I shall have to fly back to London for a weekend to consult the commissioning editor just before and it's unlikely that I shall have time to come back to Sarlat after that before I get on the road. I also need to be in Germany at the time of the elections at the end of September.'

'I'm sorry. I can see that you were an obvious choice – congratulations. It sounds like a fascinating project.'

'It will also be interesting to build on my childhood memories. I lived there from 1949 until 1952, but I know childhood memories can be fragile and unreliable. I shall also try and interview non-Germans who have been living in the country over the last few years. You told me your brother lived in Frankfurt, didn't you? Perhaps you could ask him if he would be prepared to talk to me on an attributable or non-attributable basis. Peter, I'm very excited by the prospect. It's a fascinating challenge and much more substantial than any I've faced previously. I've been given a very free hand to develop the themes as I see fit, although I shall have to cross-check with my editor from time to time.'

'I can easily ask Matt. He works in the financial sector for a German bank and I'm sure he would be happy to talk.'

'Thank you. That brings me on to the practicalities. I shall be here through most of August and then I shall leave for Germany by way of London. That's why I'm in something of a dilemma about the house here. There seem to be two options: either we can close the house up in a month's time and you can return to England while I head for Germany or I should be happy if you wanted to stay here for a further couple of months. Then I would come back at the end of October and close the house in November. That would give you the chance to experience another fête nationale, All Saints Day, which is on a Saturday this year. I know this second option would limit your freedom so you are under no obligation to do so. The choice is yours.'

'My immediate reaction is that I should very much like to stay if you are really happy for me to do so – I think my month's probation is just about up! Thank you for the stamp of approval, even though you've been away for half of the last month. I'll need to go back briefly to England just to make sure I've set in place arrangements for settling domestic bills and to ask Sue to forward my post. I should probably do that during August.'

'There's no rush. If you have second thoughts, the plan can always be modified.'

Peter decided to open his mail. The letter from his mother updated him on minor family matters and hoped that he would be home at Christmas. He then opened the other letter addressed in the handwriting that had puzzled him. It was from Jenny, asking how he was getting on but also saying that she, together with Cass and Stefan, would be hiring a motor caravan and were planning to holiday in France in September. She suggested that they might stay at a campsite nearby for a day or two, in which case it would be good to meet up if he would still be in France. He turned back to Sally to say that this letter had given him a further reason to stay in the Dordogne until the end of October. He added that the Carnot family had offered to put him in touch with a French lawyer in Lyon and that he might travel there for a few days after the summer holiday period was over.

19

Peter was surprised at how speedily they established a modus vivendi as July turned to August. Sally's schedule remained as disciplined as ever and he was approaching his writing in a more methodical manner. The days acquired a comfortable routine. They would meet for breakfast and share a light lunch before swimming or walking in the afternoon. Much of Sally's time in the first week after her return was occupied with planning a schedule for the Franco-German project. She spent long hours on the telephone to her editor. She suggested that her person-to-person pieces should be set against the background of a formal poll, soliciting opinion from people in both countries. This was agreed and she then set out a possible schedule for her time and listed the contacts she would like to make. She planned to divide her time between pre-arranged interviews with politicians, academics, journalists and businessmen while building in some time for opportunistic additional discussions with others to whom she might be signposted by her primary contacts. The magazine group would take responsibility for setting up the interviews with relevant senior people. The remainder of her time would be allocated to random interviews on the hoof in the streets, cafés, bistros and bierstubes.

As they were sitting on the terrace one evening later in the week, comfortable and mellow after dinner, Sally showed Peter the outline schedule for her two months in Germany and France. He looked at the draft itinerary and gasped, 'God, I feel exhausted simply reading that! It's a pity that you can't do some of the interviewing here but I guess that "la France profonde" would not be regarded as being representative of the country as a whole!'

'This is going to require some organisation but the magazine staff will take responsibility for the detailed arrangements – appointments, travel and accommodation. It's an international magazine group so I'll be able to call on local offices in the two countries for some support. I've been thinking about timing. The first of September is a Monday so what I'd like to do is to travel to Bonn as my first port of call over the last weekend in August, having spent the previous week in London with the editorial team. I thought I'd probably travel back to London at the end of the previous week giving me a full week to finalise my schedule. What are your plans?'

'I also thought that I'd go back late next month. I should try and see my family and sort out the arrangements for the care of my flat. I also feel the need to bring back a better dictionary and a thesaurus. I would then return to Sarlat on the Thursday or Friday of the last week of the month. Perhaps we could travel back to London together?'

'Sounds like a good idea. The addition of a dictionary and a thesaurus gives the impression that you're becoming a serious writer.'

'Serious, yes, but how good remains to be seen!'

She smiled, 'I suspect you're being too self-effacing. I'm hoping, now I've agreed a framework for my time, that much of the administration will be carried out by the team back in London and I can spend some time on my longer-term projects. August can be an interesting time in this part of France. The French holidaymakers will leave in droves from the middle of the month, after the Feast of the Assumption, in preparation for "la rentrée" – the start of the new school year. The English holiday-makers will leave in large numbers a little later but they won't be replaced by any significant new arrivals as the English holiday period winds down. After that we see more of the expatriate residents who regard themselves as superior to the holidaymakers. They emerge with their questionable French and cluster in exclusive groups in the cafés and restaurants!'

'Surely they can't all be like that?'

'No, some speak excellent French and a small number do involve themselves in local activities.'

'Do you have local friends?'

'One or two – I'll introduce you to them before I go. They may be useful if you have any practical problems.'

'That would be helpful, but I was thinking that if I'm to be here on my own for two months I should take steps to improve my French.'

'I know a French teacher here in Sarlat. Would you like me to put you in touch with her?'

'Yes, that would be good.'

It was getting late. Sally leaned across and whispered in his ear, 'I have a quite outrageous question to put to you. Do you think that we could be loving friends indoors as well as al fresco?'

Peter laughed. 'Sally, that would be wonderful. I would be your loving friend anywhere.'

She laughed. 'I'm not sure that I'd be prepared to go quite that far – but anywhere within the bounds of public decency!'

＊ ＊ ＊

They agreed that they would return to England on the Thursday of the penultimate week in August, leaving Peter's car at the airport. They spent one evening during the week before leaving in the company of Sally's local friends. Jonathan and Tilly Browning lived in a small château in the valley of the Vézère near Les Eyzies. He was an architect and they had simply fallen in love with the area. They had bought the château on impulse and restored it, creating a small hotel with eight bedrooms. They could not have been more different from the other couple. Dermot and Jean Joyce were both potters based in Domme where they worked and also sold their wares from a small shop, in addition to fulfilling the demands of a limited number of upmarket retail outlets in England. This was a mixed marriage in Ulster terms and, although neither were believers, they had emigrated to escape from the religiously and politically divided community of Northern Ireland. Peter was amused to have the opportunity to meet a potter, having decided that the male protagonist in his book would be an English potter living in France. All were entertaining conversationalists and after a convivial evening both couples insisted that Peter should visit them while Sally was away.

They flew back to a gloomy London and parted at the airport, agreeing to meet for dinner the evening before Peter's return to France the following Thursday. He called his parents and arranged to go to Wimbledon the following day and stay overnight. He then telephoned Jenny to arrange to meet her over the weekend. She was apologetic but said she had already arranged to go to Newcastle on the Saturday to see her mother and would not be back until the Tuesday. Peter was about to say that it might be difficult to find another time before his return when she suddenly said, 'Why don't you come too? Mum would love to see you and so would I.' They arranged to meet just before midday at King's Cross and travel together.

He spent the next morning setting up arrangements to pay for the utilities for the flat and then visited Sue. She was still very quiet and subdued nearly a year after Andrew's death. She had returned to working full-time but was continuing to help in the local hospice shop at weekends. 'I simply don't seem to have the energy or initiative to do things other than those which I am expected to do,' she said sadly. 'I have no family close by and although friends have uttered stock phrases about time being a great healer, it still doesn't seem to get much better. The other popular nostrums I've been offered also do little to help.'

'Don't you have friends amongst your colleagues at the school or at the hospice shop?'

'I get on well enough with them but most have families and are preoccupied with their own commitments. I doubt that they would want a single misery like me around the place.'

He leant forward and held her hands. 'I understand that people juggling work and family life are heavily committed or even over-committed but perhaps you're being a bit too hard on yourself. I shall be away again for September and October but will be home over the winter. We should have a meal together from time to time then or perhaps go to the cinema or theatre.'

She smiled wanly. 'Yes, I should like that. Perhaps we could go with your girlfriend as well. She's lovely.'

He dodged the implied question of the nature of his relationship with Sally and simply said, 'Yes, she is lovely. Why don't we implement my suggestion straightaway and go round the corner to the pub for a sandwich lunch?'

Sue agreed to keep an eye on the flat and forward any mail for the next two months. They parted after lunch and he made his way to Wimbledon.

* * *

Peter was greeted effusively by his mother and with a restrained shake of the hand by his father. 'There's so much we want to hear. You simply must tell us everything that you've been doing over the last two months. We thought you were only going to France for ten days!' An extensive array of sandwiches and cakes had been prepared for afternoon tea. 'We knew you'd want a full tea. It's a meal that they don't do properly in France.'

Peter smiled. 'Perhaps, but they do the other meals extremely well.'

'No, that simply isn't true,' said Molly. 'They only provide a very skimpy breakfast. It's often served without plates and you see people dipping croissants in their coffee. It's a disgusting habit! It ruins both the coffee and the croissant. As for the other meals, the dishes are either saturated in garlic or covered with very rich sauces or both and they eat horsemeat!'

Peter laughed. 'You seem to have damned French cuisine pretty comprehensively.'

'Give the guy a chance to relax before you air the remainder of your prejudices about the French and start on the relentless interrogation,' said Geoffrey. Peter looked at his father. He had aged visibly over the previous year.

'Very well – where do you want me to start?'

'First of all, tell us where you are living. Who is this friend whose house you're staying in and have we met him? Are you there on your own or is he living there as well?'

He laughed at the assumption that the friend was male. 'That's at least three questions but I'll take them in sequence. The house is in the Dordogne in south-west France, very close to a beautiful small mediaeval town called Sarlat. The friend is not a he, the friend is a she and, no, you haven't met her. I only met her by chance a year ago. She's a journalist and she's living there as well. She spends the summer months there writing feature articles and the winter months in London. Her name is Sally Dunham.'

'But why have we never heard of her? Were you involved with her before you and Ann parted?'

'No, I was not involved with her as you put it and to forestall your next question we have separate bedrooms in her house.' He knew that this satisfied the criteria of being the truth and nothing but the truth whilst being not quite the whole truth.

'But how old is she?'

'I've never asked her that question, but I would guess very similar in age to me.'

'Have you met her parents?'

'What a very middle-class question but no, her parents are both dead.'

'So what are you going to do now?'

'I'm going back to France next week and will be there until early November. I shall be house-sitting. Sally will be travelling round France and Germany for the next two months, preparing a series of articles on attitudes to the possible accession of Britain to the European Community. She will then return to Sarlat and I will help her shut the house up for the winter before we both come back to England.'

'Is she a political journalist then? Anyhow, I'm not sure that we should join Europe, particularly as we were snubbed by de Gaulle and after all we did for him and France during the war. And don't start me off about the Germans!'

'No, she's not a political journalist but she writes general features, some travel pieces and some items of a more academic nature. She has a number of longer-term projects in hand, for example, writing about the impact of British expatriates living in France. She speaks both French and German fluently.'

'But what will happen to your flat while you're away?'

'Sue, Andrew's wife – now widow – has agreed to look

in and forward post. But if I could give her your number if there were a major crisis, that would be helpful. But I'm sure there won't be.'

'Yes, of course, but how is that poor woman? What happened was so terrible. I know he was difficult but even so.'

'She is still very down – I spent some time talking to her this morning and took her out for lunch in the pub.'

Geoffrey broke in, 'I did warn you that you were going to be grilled!'

'We just want to know how he's getting on. Now tell us how the writing is going.'

'I can't say much at present. It's going but I can't judge how good or bad it is. I've written between eight and ten thousand words.'

'What does that mean in terms of the length of a novel – how many pages would that be?'

'Somewhere around twenty to twenty-five pages, perhaps an eighth or a tenth of a novel of average length.'

'What does your journalist friend say about it?'

'I haven't shown her anything that I've written so far. I've been trying to maintain the flow and I shall then go back and revise.'

'And are you happy living in France?'

'Yes, it's very different, but in one sense I'm not really living there since I don't speak much French. I feel somewhat isolated at times. I'm planning to take some French lessons when I get back.'

'But you have O level French.'

'Frankly it's not much use for day-to-day living in rural France and even less so for social conversation. The pen of my aunt might be in the gardener's pocket but I've not yet come across an occasion where the phrases in my school books have been of any practical value! So I'll be going to a teacher in Sarlat.'

'What's it about – the book I mean?'

'It is based on a custody battle between separated parents, one living in France and one in England.'

Peter excused himself from his mother's forensic examination to have a shower and put his feet up before they reconvened for an evening meal. Molly returned re-invigorated to catechise him further as they seated themselves for dinner.

'I do hope that you'll join us for Christmas again and what will your friend be doing?'

'I really haven't made any plans for Christmas. It is, after all, only August and I have absolutely no idea what Sally might be doing or even what she normally does for Christmases. I shall certainly make sure that I do see you all over the holiday period. Do you know if Matt and family will be over?'

'I don't think they've made plans yet.'

'It would be good to see them if they are here – or, if not, I might travel to Germany to see them.'

'And what are you doing over this holiday weekend?'

'Tomorrow I'm going to Newcastle with Jenny to see her Mum, coming back on Monday or Tuesday.'

'But why ever are you doing that?'

'Jenny asked me to go with her and I'm fond of Peggy Robson. I regret that I never got to know her earlier. As you know, Ann had rather detached herself from her family.'

'Will she be there?'

'Not as far as I know.'

'Have you heard from her?'

'No, but I did bump into Jenny back in June. She had seen her and said that she was well. I sense that neither she nor her mother are too enthusiastic about her new partner. I suspect that much of the burden of keeping family contact with Peggy has fallen onto Jenny's shoulders.'

'Will we see you again before you go back to France?'

'I'll call you. I'll try and get down during the day on Wednesday, the day before I go back.' The discussion drifted into more general family matters and issues of local interest. Peter left after breakfast the following day and went directly to King's Cross to meet Jenny.

20

Jenny and Peter sat facing each other across a table in the train, looking out at the rain descending steadily on an already damp countryside. For a long time they sat in silence. Finally Peter said, 'I have a sense of déjà vu. It was an even wetter Saturday last year when I sat with your sister on a train to the north-east, the day after your telephone call to say that Graham was seriously ill. So much has changed for you, for Ann, your Mum and me over the last twelve months.'

'Most of it for me has been for the better. I miss Dad a lot, he was a good guy. I'm sorry that you never really knew him but I'm very appreciative of you making this trip with me. You were under no obligation to do so.'

'No, I wanted to do it. I'm just so sorry that I didn't know your parents earlier and that I didn't get to know Newcastle, but I've got to know you better. The only times I ever really got to talk to you were during that week when you stayed, I think during the first year of our marriage, and then again when you were in London for your interviews. I have a feeling that we got up Ann's nostrils a bit the first time with our joking!'

Jenny giggled. 'Yes, she often put on the wiser and older sister act. She felt that I was not sufficiently serious or focused. And, yes, my life has changed, no longer a student. I'm earning money and footloose and fancy-free in London. I'm enjoying the job and making friends – not just Cass and Stefan but others as well. Cass and Stefan may be a bit wacky but they are intelligent, know their way around London and are very caring. You've already discovered that. I must talk to you about our planned motor home holiday in France next month. Could we hook up while we are there?'

'For sure. We can work out a plan over the weekend and it doesn't matter if you decide to change it. I'll give you the telephone number and you can always call.'

'That would be great.'

'Let me ask you before we get to your Mum's. How is Ann – have you seen her?'

'Yes, I've seen her once since we last met. She seemed fine, but you know Ann as well as I do. She always has her emotions well under control. I'm really not at all keen on Francis, as I said before you went to France. He's definitely a bit flash and to me he doesn't seem to be wholly sincere or genuine. I'm pretty sure Mum thinks as I do, although she probably wouldn't say so. I'm a little unhappy that Ann sees her only very rarely although she does ring regularly.'

'Well, thank you. I genuinely hope she's happy. I think in view of the weather that we should take a taxi when we get to Newcastle. I saw a year ago that there was a small hotel on the road out to Cowgate and I've booked myself in there.' He smiled. 'It's more in keeping with my current unsalaried state than the Station Hotel. I can quickly check

in on the way out and then we can go on to your Mum –
unless you would like me to hang back so that you have
some time with her on your own.'

'No, you come on with me. She wants to see you.'

They were greeted very warmly by Peggy Robson as she
hugged her daughter and then Peter. 'I was so pleased when
Jenny said that she'd persuaded you to come with her this
weekend. I'd hoped that I might still see you sometimes,
even though Ann has left you. Jenny has been so good at
keeping in touch although she's so busy in London.'

'Not only busy,' she laughed 'but also enjoying London.'

'Well, you're only young once. I'm sorry I never saw
more of London when I was younger, but the time there last
Christmas with you and your family was wonderful. I was
so grateful.'

'Well, you and Jenny could show me the sights of
Newcastle.'

'There are more than you might think and Jenny can do
that. They are best seen on foot.'

'We could do that tomorrow,' said Jenny, 'and we could
also wander through the Sunday market on the Quayside.'

'Sounds good.'

They spent a quiet evening together in the flat. Peter
sorted out one or two minor domestic items of paperwork
although it was quite clear that Peg was managing well.
She reassured Jenny that she was getting out and met with
friends at the nearby social club for a pensioners' lunch once
a week. 'I'm not that old,' she insisted, 'I'm only 66 and
feeling good.'

The Sunday was still showery but Jenny and Peter set

off for the city centre on the bus and wandered through the streets of classical Dobson and Grainger Georgian buildings. They walked from the Grey Monument, erected to mark the work of the architect of the Great Reform Bill, along the elegant curve of Grey Street and then made their way down the sharp incline of Dean Street to the quayside, dominated by the Tyne Bridge high overhead. They wandered through the market stalls towards the swing bridge and the Stephenson double-decked High Level Bridge beyond, with the trains passing over the upper level to and from the central station. They then turned and climbed up past the Castle Keep and the cathedral before finally catching a bus back to the flat.

'That was fascinating,' said Peter. 'I've seen so little of this city. It's sad that some of those beautiful buildings are not as well cared for as they might be.'

'There's a big debate in the city at the moment between those who want to demolish many and those who are campaigning to have them preserved. There's been a furious argument about an area called Eldon Square, not far from the monument, and part is to be torn down.'

'My vote, if I had one, would be for restoration.'

'Mine too.'

'By the way, I heard the forecast in my hotel room before I joined you this morning. The weather should be better tomorrow although we may have to dodge some showers. Do you think your mother would like a day out? I could arrange to hire a car and we could drive up the coast.'

'That sounds like a great idea.' They put it to Peggy and she agreed enthusiastically.

* * *

They left Newcastle on the Bank Holiday Monday and drove northwards, heading out to the coast by Druridge Bay, driving past Warkworth Castle and then inland to Alnwick. 'We might drive on up to Beadnell,' suggested Jenny. 'We rented a small house there for several summer holidays.' They continued up the coast and finally turned into Beadnell village. 'We rented one of those small bungalows over there – do you remember, Mum?'

'Of course, I remember,' she said sharply. 'I'm not gaga yet.'

They cruised up the lane and identified the bungalow by the huge pampas dominating the miniscule front garden. 'It was so small,' said Jenny, 'really more like a brick built caravan than a house. Mum and Dad would sleep on let-down beds in the lounge and Ann and I would be on bunk beds in the tiny bedroom. We used to fight over who should be on the top level. She nearly always won because she would play the big sister card. Those days were fun. Let's go on down to the beach.'

They parked near the lime kilns which overlooked the sheltered small harbour. 'They say that this is the only west facing harbour on the east coast of England and just look at that beach!' said Jenny excitedly. She pointed southwards to the open expanse of golden sand backed by dunes with the upraised craggy fingers of the ruins of Dunstanburgh Castle in the distance. They stopped to take in the view. A number of sailing dinghies were criss-crossing the bay in the intermittent sunshine. Many more had been beached on the sand, together with small rowing boats, tenders for the yachts moored out in the bay, and bilge-keel sailing boats standing erect on their twin keels. Children of all ages were playing beach games or running gleefully in and out of the water. Others were running up and down the sand dunes or hiding behind them.

'Come on, Peter,' Jenny grabbed his hand. 'I'll show you where we used to play. There were always people we knew here, either on days out from Newcastle or renting small houses for their summer holidays like us. We used to persuade Mum and Dad to give us our sandwiches and drinks and then we'd go into the dunes. Look, there are the rows of dunes. It's like the surface of the moon with humps and hollows. We could always find places to hide. Sometimes Ann would tell me to go and play with other kids of my own age and then she'd disappear into a hollow with one of the boys. We would spend whole days here and only come out when we heard the chimes of the ice-cream van.'

Peter stood on top of one of the dunes and looked south again to Dunstanburgh. It had been the starting point for his odyssey.

Jenny came up to him. 'A penny for your thoughts. You appeared to be lost in contemplation with an expression on your face that I cannot read. Come back to me, Peter.'

He turned and smiled gently. 'I should like to walk up to the castle.'

'Alone or with me?'

'It would be good to walk with you.'

'We should get back to Mum but I have a suggestion. It's quite a long walk from here to the castle and it's getting on for lunchtime. We could have a sandwich and a drink in the pub at Embleton. That's not so far from the castle and if Mum's happy to sit in the pub for a while, or outside if it's warm enough, we could then walk up there and back again. We could leave her the key of the car if she preferred to sit under cover.'

They walked back to where Peggy was sitting by the harbour wall. She looked up as they approached. 'I have enjoyed sitting here. It has brought back so many memories of when you and Ann were young. They were good days.'

'Yes, this was Peter's idea to come up the coast. It's made me quite nostalgic too. We had good times here. There were always friends from Newcastle to muck about with. We have a suggestion to make. How about going to Greys Inn at Embleton and having a sandwich there? Peter has said that he would like to walk to Dunstanburgh. It wouldn't take too long from there. Would you mind if we left you in the pub? We can give you the key to the car as well if you would prefer to sit there?'

'That would be fine.'

The sun came out again after lunch and they left Peggy sitting outside the pub as they headed off for the castle. They walked mainly in silence, partly on the track and partly along the sands of Embleton Bay. The shoreline was teeming with coastal birds: oystercatchers, sanderling, shovellers and little grebes with a variety of gulls out over the sea, wheeling with their characteristic strident shriek.

'Dad was a keen birdwatcher and there are colonies of terns just the other side of Newton going back towards Beadnell. They breed around a burn called the Long Nanny.

God knows why it's called that. Dad would often walk us along from Beadnell, making sure we could identify the birds we saw. It's a magical part of the coastline.'

It took them a little over twenty minutes to reach the castle. They walked up to the vantage point near the old gatehouse and then down to the promontory where they looked over the sea. Peter stopped, memories of the previous visit invading his brain. He looked round to his left half-expecting Sally to materialise. The sense of place assailed him with overwhelming force.

Jenny was standing a pace or two away from him. After a few minutes, she said very quietly, 'You have that unfathomable look on your face again. Does this place have some special meaning for you?'

He said nothing for some seconds. 'Yes, it has a number of special meanings for me.'

'Are you prepared to share them?'

'Yes, I am but what I'm going to say may not be very coherent.'

'I should like to hear nevertheless.'

'Perhaps we should talk as we walk back. We mustn't keep your Mum waiting too long.'

They set off to retrace their steps. Peter stated tentatively, 'I'm not quite sure how to begin but I think I should start here. It was, after all, my idea that we should come up here but I was not prepared for the extent to which the sights, sounds and smells would arouse such a mixture of interwoven thoughts and emotions in me.' Jenny took his arm but said nothing and waited for him to continue. 'You've not asked me much about my recent time in France.

The best place, perhaps the only place, to start is here at Dunstanburgh. It was just a year ago and that year has had a fantastical and unreal quality to it. All life is continuous but there are events and interactions which either at the time or seen in retrospect could be regarded as tipping points,' he paused, 'and, looking back, I know that this is where the present chapter of my story really started.'

'I should love it if you'd go on but if you would prefer not to then that's fine also. I'm in listening mode and am happy that anything you say should be subject to the observances of the confessional.'

'It's alright. I want to talk. There is a prologue to this chapter. Ann and I had had a discussion three days earlier with friends at home about ambitions and aspirations. It went nowhere very much and we all finally concluded that our various fantasies had as much substance as dreams of castles in Spain, although I did mention subsequently to Ann that I had an ambition to write. It all would have amounted to nothing if it hadn't been for subsequent events. It was that same evening just before the bank holiday that you telephoned to tell us that your Dad was so ill. You may remember, when we then came north, that Ann wanted to spend a day alone with your Mum and Graham. I decided to make myself scarce and explore the coast which I had visited once before. I walked out to the castle and then rested on the grass near the cliff edge where we were a few moments ago. There was a woman standing very close to the edge and I had an instinct, quite mistakenly, that she might be contemplating suicide. We got talking and I discovered that she was, is, a journalist. I also discovered that she had published a novel although it had not been a great success. We then had lunch together in the Craster Arms and I questioned her about her career and the challenges facing a writer. We spent the afternoon talking and exploring the coast and then parted company. That was my first meeting with Sally. It was what followed which put that afternoon into perspective.

'The next event was that evening with Andrew with its tragic coda. I had never expected to see Sally again but quite by chance I did. It was on the day that Andrew died. Ann and I had gone to see him in the hospital earlier that evening and as we were leaving I bumped into Sally, quite literally, in the doorway as she was visiting another patient. Seeing her triggered memories of the bank holiday last year and again, almost certainly, nothing further might have occurred, but the ambition to write continued to haunt the recesses of my mind and you were with me when we talked with Michael that evening. A few weeks after Ann had left me, I was feeling very low and I sought Sally out. There was something about her that had intrigued me. She is coolly self-possessed, highly independent, dispassionate, humorous, challenging and highly intelligent but she also has depths which seem to me to be quite inaccessible. There is a hidden Sally that I just don't know. I saw her again at around the time I spent that evening with you, Cass and Stefan when I told you I was bailing out from the office for a year to write but I was going to start that year by taking a week's holiday. I decided I would spend that week well away from my familiar surroundings and go to France. Sally has a house in France which she uses as her base for working through the summer months. She is very disciplined in her approach to her writing. I wrote asking if I might call and she invited me to stay for that week. At the end of it, she said I could stay on if I liked and use the house as a base to write, first laying down some very clear ground rules, and I have only just come back. She has been very encouraging and gently guided me without giving me any direct advice, so that I am now starting to write. She's in England at the moment but will soon be travelling all round Germany and France, preparing a major series of articles on attitudes to Britain in the light of the probability that we shall join the European Community. I shall be house-sitting and writing while she's away.'

'That's quite a tale. She sounds an interesting woman. Will we meet her when we come to France? But first, can I ask how the writing is going? Are we going to see a magnum opus?'

'No, you won't see her in France as she'll be away for the next two months. I simply cannot judge how the writing is going at the moment but I'm finding the process of placing words on paper much more straightforward than I did at the outset and I'm much enjoying it, but that's no guarantee of quality.'

'Has Sally seen and commented on any of your writings?'

'No, I haven't shown her anything yet. I feel disinclined to until after I've revised and polished my streams of consciousness to the best of my ability, but I shall do so at a later date.'

'I really have no business to ask this but are you and she what the tabloids would call "an item"? You can perfectly reasonably tell me to bugger off and that it's no business of mine.'

'No, it's a natural question and I think that the honest answer is "no", although it's more complicated than that. She is, as I said, highly independent.'

'Peter, you've been so open with me. It seems that your life has not just become more complicated but also much more interesting and much more fun. I feel flattered that you should trust me so completely. Now I'm going to do something quite improper that no sister-in-law or even ex-sister-in-law should do.' She stopped him and, putting her arms around him, kissed him fully and generously on the lips. She drew back for a moment, 'and I won't promise not to do that again.'

Peter smiled and held her for several moments before gently disengaging. They walked the short remaining distance back to Embleton holding hands. Peggy was sitting in the sun outside the inn. 'I'm sorry, we've been gone for longer than we expected,' said Jenny.

'Not to worry. I've been very happy here and have chatted to one or two others while you've been walking. It has been a wonderful day. Thank you for bringing me here. It has brought back so many special memories.'

Peter looked across at Jenny. 'It has brought back some special memories for all of us, and maybe generated some new ones.'

Jenny winked at him. Peggy looked at them enquiringly but said nothing.

* * *

Jenny and Peter took the train back to London the following day. 'Tell me what plans you have made for your holiday in France.'

'Stefan and Cass have arranged to hire a motor home for two weeks from the weekend after next. We don't have any clear plans and originally thought we would just wander where the wind blew. We've agreed that we should travel south and have all started to have ideas. Stefan has discovered that there's a jazz festival near St Etienne towards the end of our little break and he wants to take that in. It looks as though it's only a couple of hundred miles from the Dordogne and I've persuaded the others that we should visit you. They didn't need too much persuasion. Would that be alright with you?'

'Yes, of course. There are a number of campsites in the area which won't be crowded in September but I'm sure Sally wouldn't mind you camping next to the house. I'll ask her. I'll give you the number and you can call when details of your travel plans become clearer. You could even call en route but in any event I'll expect you for a day or two around the weekend of 12th September.' They parted with a kiss and a hug at King's Cross. 'À bientôt, Jenny.'

21

Peter called Sally during the evening of his return from the north-east and suggested meeting up near his flat the following evening as he would be flying back to France the next day. They met for a drink at the Sun Inn overlooking the village green and pond in Barnes and sat outside, glasses of wine in hand, watching the setting sun glance off the mellow red bricks of the lion houses across the green.

'I've so much to tell you,' said Sally. 'I tried to call you over the weekend but couldn't get hold of you. Perhaps you were with your parents.'

'No, I went to Newcastle for the weekend.'

'I didn't know that was on your schedule.'

'It wasn't. I'll tell you all, but first tell me what you've been up to.'

'I've spent three days at the office and need to be there for the next two. They've been very helpful but it's taken a long time and multiple telephone calls to arrange my planned schedule. You saw the list of places I'd like to visit but I'm sure I'll have to amend it on the hoof as the availability of people may change – you know how it is with busy people. The plan is that it will all be framed, so to speak, around the time of the Federal German elections on the last Sunday in September. My itinerary has layers of complexity as I need to factor in the availability of different people in different locations, all with busy schedules and many travel as part of their work. Then I must incorporate time for random interviews as well. It's a nightmare. I spent much of the weekend with maps of Germany and France trying to sort out the best and most time-effective itinerary. But tell me, what have you been doing while you've been here?'

'I went to see my parents as promised and spent a night there. Inevitably, I was grilled relentlessly by my mother. They still think I've taken leave of my senses and wonder at the extent to which I have allowed my emotions and events to shape my life since Ann and I parted. But it was good to see them. I called Jenny, my ex-sister-in-law. You may remember, I told you that she and her friends are planning to holiday in France next month. I wanted to meet and find out what their plans and timings actually were. She was off to Newcastle the day I left my parents' house and suggested out of the blue that I went too. She was also somewhat irritated that Ann had not been to visit her Mum for some time.'

'Did you hear how your ex-wife is doing?'

'Jenny has seen very little of her. She's not sure how happy her sister is. She doesn't warm to Francis and neither, I think, does her mother. Anyhow, I agreed to go. Although I have only met her Mum a few times, I am rather fond of her and I didn't have anything particularly planned for what was forecast to be quite a wet weekend.'

'And how was she?'

'On remarkably good form. I understand that it was a very secure marriage so she misses Graham very much. I also think the effort of looking after him had been considerable and she is now more at ease but somewhat lonely at times. She and Jenny are very close but she's much more uncertain about her elder daughter. I think, in part, she's surprised that Ann, who is the more conventional of the two, should have abandoned a marriage to someone as pedestrian and boring as me. Jenny, who's much more of a free spirit, has a strong bond with her mother. I sense that if Peggy had been born a generation later she would have been much less bound by the fetters of Geordie convention and would have been very much like Jenny.'

'So how did you spend this wet weekend?'

'I stayed in a hotel as her Mum's flat is so small but I spent the days with the two of them. On the Sunday, Jenny walked me round the historic areas of Newcastle and in the afternoon all three of us went and laid flowers on her Dad's grave. I wasn't sure what we might do to occupy ourselves on the Monday but, with the forecast predicting better weather, I suggested hiring a car and driving up the coast. Jenny and her Mum agreed with alacrity and directed us to a little village called Beadnell on the coast a little south of Bamburgh where we went last year. It was where they spent their holidays when Ann and Jenny were kids so it was a nostalgic trip for them which revived many fond memories. The bay at Beadnell is amazing – a long expanse of flat sand backed by dunes with an amazing array of bird life and Dunstanburgh Castle can be seen in the distance. Jenny was as excited as a small girl and really relived her childhood, running barefoot up and down the dunes! There seems to be something uniquely female about wanting to run barefoot on the beach!'

Sally laughed. 'It conveys a sense of freedom. You should try it as the next step in your emancipation!'

'Perhaps I should. Anyhow, we then went and had lunch in a pub in a small village between Beadnell and Dunstanburgh. I think it was where you parked your car last year. Then Jenny and I walked along the path and the beach to the castle.'

She smiled, 'I begin to sense where this narrative is leading – and?'

'I saw it as a sort of anniversary and the start of a journey. As Mao said at the start of the Long March, a journey of a thousand miles starts with a single step and, looking back, I saw that this had been the start of a long journey for me, an odyssey which is still not complete. I looked up the exact definition of an odyssey today. My dictionary defines it as a long, wandering voyage usually marked by many changes of fortune. That seems to describe my last year with great exactitude and it reminded me of our meeting.'

She laughed. 'You're just a romantic at heart.'

'Only when I have good reason to be.'

She squeezed his hand. 'What you've just said brings back happy memories for me as well. But what are the next steps on your journey?'

'Purely practical. I need to gather a better dictionary, a thesaurus, some reams of paper and rather more clothing than I took to France for my week which turned into two months, particularly as autumn will be well established by the time you get back to Sarlat. I shall then live the life of a hermit until you return!'

She smiled. 'I predict that you might not live an entirely cloistered life.'

'Perhaps not, but now let's walk along to the restaurant and have something to eat.'

'Good idea. The planning of my trip has been interesting but frustrating at times. I've been following the press. There's been a certain amount of coverage about our possible future relationship with Europe, and political figures as diverse as Enoch Powell and Tony Benn seem to be leading the forces against our joining. Incidentally, why do we keep referring to it as Europe when we're already geographically part of the continent and, from my point of view, culturally as well? The more I look at the ground I have to cover and the significance of the event, the more apprehensive and irresolute I become.'

'But you generally seem so unfazed.'

She laughed. 'Sadly no, Peter. You don't know what mass of uncertainties and insecurities lie deep beneath my carapace!'

'Would you allow a loving friend to lift it gently or penetrate it sometime?'

'Possibly. You're a good companion, Peter. You listen and you don't probe – well, not too much or too often!'

'Not from lack of interest or sheer curiosity. Some of it derives from my professional background but probably mostly it comes from the middle-class view that it's not quite the done thing to breach someone's privacy and innermost thoughts, although the urge to do so is often overwhelming.'

'Well, I'm grateful to you for house-sitting for me for the next two months. You'll find Sarlat a very different place once the summer visitors have all migrated.'

'On quite a different subject, would there be any problem when Jenny and her wacky friends come if they were to sleep in their motor home beside the house?'

'Not at all – and, from what you've told me, they're your wacky friends as well! It will also prevent you from following an undisturbed eremitic existence.'

'Touché, and I shall try and ensure that my French vocabulary is a little more extensive than that by the time you come back. Will you let me know how the project is progressing from time to time, when you have the odd free moment?'

'Yes, of course, and I'll let you have my itinerary when it's been finalised.'

The evening passed in easy conversation and comfortable silences. Finally, it was time to part. Sally held him close and whispered in his ear, 'I have a confession to make. I have a toothbrush and a pair of clean knickers in my bag.'

He kissed her. 'That's a coincidence as I have the ideal place nearby where you can brush your teeth and change your knickers.'

* * *

Peter arrived back at the house in France late on the Thursday and started preparing himself for a bachelor existence. He found a note addressed to him from Jonathan and Tilly Browning, inviting him to dinner on the Friday of the following week and offering him a bed overnight. He called and accepted with alacrity. He spent the following morning shopping and planning his work.

He found, unlike the first time he settled at a desk, that he was eager to put pen to paper. It no longer required determination and fixity of purpose to drive his pen forward in these remote and ideal surroundings. The words flowed at times without effort or strain and at others after lengthy periods of hesitation and contemplation. For the first few days he abandoned the work schedule that he had set himself and wrote steadily throughout the day. The occasional visits to the town for provisions were necessary but unwelcome intrusions. The narrative was taking shape.

The following Friday he drove to the Browning's château overlooking the Vézère. His breath was taken away by the eye-catching silhouette of the castle as he approached. The walls of the pale golden stone of the Périgord shone radiantly in the lambent light of the late afternoon sun. It had features of a defensive castle, with crenellated turrets and machicolations but it was also recognisable as a small Renaissance château. A long terrace facing the river fronted the castle, where a few of the hotel guests were taking a glass of wine. He entered and was taken aback by the great staircase which faced him and the massive chimneypiece dominating the side of the hall. The reception area was deserted. He rang a small bell and Tilly descended the stairway.

'Welcome to our little abode! It's good to see you again. I'm so glad you could come. I'll show you where you're going to sleep and when you've sorted your things out, you must come and join Jonny and me for a drink.'

'I have brought some night things but would be very happy to drive back to Sally's house. I know you're running a business here.'

'We wouldn't dream of it. We're entering the quieter time of year and will close for the winter at the beginning of November.' She led him to a room in one of the turrets overlooking the valley and the river. 'Come down in a few minutes. Part way down the great staircase there is a door marked "Privé". Ignore that and come straight into our own rooms in the castle.'

Peter took some time to adapt to the magnificence of his room and the view before making his way down to join his hosts. A glass of wine in his hand, he turned to Jonny and said, 'I can see why you fell in love with this place and why you might have bought on impulse. How much did you have to do to it?'

'A great deal. It took us a year, dealing with so many different trades and professions. Sally was very helpful once or twice with her immaculate French, overlain by her feminine charm.'

'But what a change in life!'

'Yes, but you've also done that.'

'Not with quite the same degree of finality. I've taken leave of absence from my firm for a year, at least in the first instance.' The last phrase slipped out inadvertently. This was the first occasion on which he had openly admitted the possibility that he might not return to his profession the following year.

'Nevertheless, I think it might have been more straightforward for me. I'm somewhat older. I'd just had my fiftieth birthday – two and a half years ago – when we saw this place. My practice had done well with renovations work and new builds in the twenty or so years after the war. We were fortunate enough to be comfortable financially and I felt I wanted a lifestyle change. I had always hoped to retire shortly before I was sixty. The chance finding of this place while we were on holiday seemed serendipitous. We jumped at the opportunity. This is the first season for the hotel and it seems to be doing well.' He looked at Tilly. 'And we have no regrets.'

'Absolutely not. We have retained a toehold in the property market back home with a small flat in London in the same block where our one and only son lives. The plan is that we spend our summers here and part of the winter in London. The winters in this part of France can be very cold.'

'How did you get to know Sally?'

'Ah, we knew her before we came here. Much of my personal architectural practice was focused on the care and restoration of historic buildings. I also designed a number of buildings in a classical style – or pastiches as my critics would have it. But they were popular with many people. I met Will and Colette Dunham many years ago when I was supervising some work on the British Embassy in Vienna. We got on well and when they returned to London between postings we would see them socially from time to time. We got to know them quite well. Sadly both died relatively young but Sally inherited Colette's house here near Sarlat.'

He poured Peter a second glass of wine. 'Now, you will have to excuse us for ten or fifteen minutes as we must go and glad-hand the guests. After all, the success of this place depends on them coming back and recommending it to their friends! We shall eat here in our part of the castle but the food will come from the hotel kitchen.' He handed Peter a menu. 'Browse through that and decide what you would like this evening. If it helps, I have put out a bottle of Gigondas for us to have with the meal.' By the time Tilly and Jonny returned, he had chosen an escabèche of mackerel to be followed by a fillet of beef with foie gras and a pepper sauce.

'That is an excellent choice but what about dessert?'

'I'm not sure I shall be up to a dessert after all that.'

'We can always add that later or offer you some cheese. We only offer a small number of choices and all that we serve is fresh. Now tell us how you got to know Sally.'

He explained that he had met her quite by chance and offered an abridged account of the previous year.

'And how well do you know her?'

'In some ways I feel that I know her well and in others scarcely at all. She can be a very private person, but you have obviously known her for some time.'

'Yes, for much of her teenage years and all her adult life, but what do you know of her family?'

'Only that her parents died relatively young and that she has no close family. She doesn't talk of them much.'

'You're right, she is a very private person despite her easy manner socially. You are, we believe, the one person who seems to have got close to her in the last few years. You are certainly the only one who has been invited for an extended stay here.' He paused before continuing. 'I hope that I'm not speaking out of turn and I hope you'll treat what I say in confidence. I only say it so that you may perhaps understand her better. She has had a difficult time. As you know, her father was a diplomat. She spent part of her childhood abroad in various places. Will retired slightly early, two or three years before he was sixty, after the death of their son, but then he himself died very suddenly. He committed suicide. It was devastating for the family. Colette had this house near Sarlat which I believe she inherited from her parents. She decided to cut herself off from all her links in London and move back here after his death. We saw her once or twice in the year after Will's death but then she developed an invasive cancer and died within two years of her husband. Sally was left on her own through her years at university and as she made her way in her career. She was well enough provided for financially and we would include her in some of our family celebrations but she's always been very independent and determined to chart her own course through life and has always avoided situations where she has been reliant on others.'

'She has never said more to me than that her parents were no longer alive. I've never felt that it would be proper to probe and I didn't know that she had had a brother.'

'That is the other major sadness in Sally's life. Her brother George was a twin and he died when he was fifteen. Sally and her parents were in Bonn when he died. He was at boarding school in England and contracted meningitis, as did two other pupils in the school. It was not long after that Will decided to retire early and that was followed by his suicide a year later. It's difficult to believe that George's death was not a factor in Will's suicide. Sally was very close to her brother, as twins frequently are, even non-identical twins.'

'Does she have more distant relatives?'

'Her father had a younger brother and she has some cousins. We met them briefly at Will's funeral but I don't think they were close. I believe the brother was a good number of years younger. As far as we know, there are no close relatives on Colette's side. Her family, of course, lived through the German occupation, although she was married and living in England by that time. She was always very reluctant to speak of it. You will understand why we sometimes feel protective towards Sally – although she is well able to look after herself. We sensed that you were becoming very close to her which is why I thought I would tell you this.'

'I like to think I am – and I value her friendship very highly. Thank you. I shall, of course, not break your confidence.'

'Tell us, what are her plans now and what are yours?'

'As you know, she has this project which will involve a great deal of travelling in this country and Germany and this will continue until the end of October when she will come back here. She then plans to shut the house up sometime after All Saints and go back to London for the winter. I shall be here until that time, writing. It's a wonderful haven.'

'Good, we shall certainly invite you over again and the two of you when she is back at the beginning of November. Now we should talk about less serious things and enjoy our dinner. We've been fortunate enough to find an excellent chef, an absolute prerequisite for success in this business in France. And you must tell us frankly if there is anything which you spot which might improve the environment for the hotel guests.'

'From what I have seen so far, that is unlikely.'

The evening passed quickly and congenially and Peter retired to bed, sated and mellow. He left his hosts the following morning and was pressed to return for an evening during October.

* * *

The following evening Jenny called to say that they would be arriving in Sarlat two days later and would probably stay for two nights before moving on to St Etienne. They arranged to meet at noon in Sarlat so that Peter could guide them back to the house. After dinner on the evening of their arrival, they relaxed to music which they had brought with them. They had driven south in a leisurely manner and stayed for several days exploring the valley of the Loire before heading for the Dordogne. Some evenings they had created their own music as Stefan had brought his violin along, in the expectation that there would be some informal music-making on the margins of the jazz festival in St Etienne. His musical career had developed over the previous few months. He had landed a job with the BBC Symphony Orchestra and was in the process of forming a string quartet with former students at the Academy and one of his new colleagues in the orchestra.

'I thought that your ambitions were to play Gypsy Jazz,' said Peter.

'Yes, they are but I also have other ambitions. I'm classically trained and love many types of music. Who knows where my career will take me! I'm happy to be labelled a crossover artist, despite the negative connotations that has for some. I just love playing, that's why I have my instrument with me.'

'Perhaps you might play tomorrow evening? I had some vague ideas for tomorrow, but it's up to you as it's the only full day that you have in this area. I was going to suggest that we drive up the valley of the Vézère and visit the prehistoric sites around Les Eyzies. There are also many châteaux we could visit but I suspect that after the Loire you may well feel that you have seen enough castles for this year. There are also some wonderful walks close to the village. I would also suggest that we go up to the bastide of Domme in the evening and watch the sun setting over the valley. It's a wonderful sight. Alternatively, if that all sounds too much, we could just chill out locally in Sarlat or by the river. Either way, I would suggest that we still go to Domme at the end of the day.'

They looked at each other and agreed on a compromise: a visit to Les Eyzies and a relaxed afternoon to be followed by the evening in Domme. At the end of the day they drove up to the village and walked along to the Belvédère de Barre, carrying a bottle of wine and glasses, to watch the evening sun slowly fall away in the west over the village of Beynac. The rays caressed the surface of the river, creating a phosphorescent golden ribbon which slowly faded to a deep blue as night fell. The sky dissolved from vivid azure to inky black and as it did so myriad points of light emerged from the houses along the river, casting threads of light over the darkening water. As the night encompassed them, they dropped back to the benches on the edge of the square and opened the wine. Stefan disappeared briefly and returned from the car with his violin. He played the jazz standard Dark Eyes, looking at Cass as he did so. She then walked across and kissed him, whispering in his ear. With an abrupt change of style and mood, he moved on to the light and lilting refrain of Dvořák's Humoresque and then slowed the tempo as he played the Meditation from Thaïs. He lingered over the sensuous phrases, the slow vibrato creating a sense of romance tinged with melancholy. He paused for a few moments; a small crowd had gathered drawn by the music and he received a round of applause. Stefan had been lost in his music-making and was unaware that he had attracted an audience so was surprised by the sound of the clapping behind him. He turned back to Cass, Jenny and Peter and raised his violin once more. The strains of Elgar's Salut d'Amour flowed over them and, as the final plaintive note faded into the dark of the night, they sat for a few lingering moments. Jenny leaned across to Peter and whispered, 'That was magical, it's all magical. Will you ever be able to leave this?'

'I don't know,' he smiled. 'Uncertainty seems to be the leitmotiv of my life at present but I'm surprisingly content with that.'

They ambled back to the centre of the village. Peter turned to them. 'It would break the spell that Stefan has cast if we were all simply to go our separate ways. Why don't we stay and eat here in the square?' There was little hesitation as they looked at one another and agreed. They finally drove back slowly to the house, reluctant to bring the evening to an end. Jenny came close to Peter at the door of the house and put her arms round him. 'I was just wondering if Cass and Stefan might have preferred a little more privacy for one night than is possible with three of us in the motor home.'

Peter looked at her and after some moments of hesitation he said, 'Jenny, I love you dearly but my life is complicated just now. I don't think that I am able to add to that complexity just at the moment.'

She looked a little rueful. 'I understand, but that proposition was not simply the effect of the mood of this magical evening nor a whim of the moment.'

'I'm flattered. I've got to know you better during the last few months than I ever did in the years when I was married to Ann. You are very special.'

'I did say when we were last together that I wouldn't promise not to do this again,' and she kissed him firmly on the lips and he responded warmly. 'Good night, you complicated man.'

He headed back to his bed uncertain of his feelings. A longing for Jenny pervaded his thinking and his body, and twice he was tempted to knock on the door of the motor caravan and bring her back to his bed. There was a straightforwardness and directness about her words and affections which encircled him with an opulent warmth. Her sincerity and lack of inhibition were so strikingly different from her sister and perhaps from Sally too. Yet here he was, in Sally's house and beholden to her for so much that had been exhilarating in his life over the last few months. She had provided him with a lifetime of experiences which he could never have envisaged when his original, poorly formulated ambition to free himself from the cage of conventionality had first surfaced with any force only a year earlier. It was difficult to analyse with any precision what she meant to him and impossible to foresee if he had a longer term future with her. Even if this were to be, it was not clear what the nature of the longer term future might be. Her alluring presence had bewitched him. Was she his lover or was he simply her loving friend? Was there a difference and could such a relationship ever be simple? He had been enamoured by her gently humorous and sardonic observations on life and circumstances and he had learned at least some reasons why this might be. But beneath the composed exterior he knew there was an immense capacity for kindness and generosity and almost certainly many other facets of her personality which he had yet to discover but which he might never unveil. He was not wholly sure that Jenny's final remark had been entirely right. Possibly it was circumstances which were complicated rather than that he was intrinsically a complex man; but maybe this distinction was simply sophistry on his part. Yet as he turned in his bed he reflected that he was happier than he had ever been during his adult life. Happiness and fulfilment, if not equanimity and tranquillity, could derive from ambiguity and perplexity. He wondered if his uncertainties would be resolved by the time of the self-ordained deadline when his leave of absence would come to an end, or might he, in footballing terms, require extra time or even injury time? He was quietly amused at the thought.

Cass, Stefan and Jenny left the following morning. As they were going, Jenny hugged Peter and said, 'Let's get together when you're back in the winter. I want to know how your complicated life is developing.'

22

Sally telephoned shortly after Jenny and the others had left. 'How are you? I'd been hoping to call you earlier than this but my time has been so taken up between travelling, pre-arranged interviews with a very tight schedule and trying to find time to talk to people informally.'

'I'd been wondering how you were getting on. Where are you?'

'I'm in Munich. This is the most challenging and interesting journalistic assignment that I've ever taken on. I'm accumulating so much material, some of it has an immediacy about it which needs to be reported promptly. I'm already feeding this back to London. At times I almost feel like a news reporter! But much of what I'm hearing and seeing will need detailed analysis and reflection if I'm to transmit properly the wide range of opinions which abound and the more subtle nuances which are fine-tuning those opinions. But tell me how you've been.'

'Well, since I've been back I've reached a point when I'm eager to start writing each morning and I quite often continue to write well outside the fixed times that I've set for myself. It remains a challenge but it is not a chore.'

'That's good news.'

'I hope so but I won't fall into the trap of assuming that quantity necessarily equates with quality! I'm currently scoring highly for effort but it will be a matter for others to judge to what extent my exertions have any literary impact.'

'I hope you've not felt too isolated.'

'No, not at all. I was invited to join Tilly and Jonny for a night at the end of last week. The castle is magnificent and the setting is amazing. The evening with them was very relaxed. I gather that you knew them long before they settled in the region.'

'Yes, they probably told you a little about the circumstances in which they first met my parents and that they used to socialise when we were back in London. But what about the evening with your ex-sister-in-law and her friends?'

'They came and stayed a couple of nights and left this morning. We had a magical evening yesterday in Domme. We watched the sun set over the river and as it grew dark Stefan played his violin – beautifully – gathering quite an audience of appreciative locals and visitors. It was a magical and, in some ways, a mystical evening. It was one of those occasions which one could wish to replicate weekly for the rest of one's days. It has left me with a picture which I have already tried to describe in words.'

'Peter, that sounds wonderful.' She laughed. 'It also sounds as if you could be seduced by the possibility of the life of a lotus-eater! You did after all refer to your journey as an odyssey! Perhaps you might need to be dragged back to reality at some stage.'

'I hadn't thought of it in that way and I certainly don't want to be dragged back to the reality of my former life just yet. But I have not totally succumbed to a life of languor and forgetfulness – at least not yet.'

'No, I suspect your middle-class protestant work ethic would never quite permit that. More seriously, there is one thing that I did want to ask you. I have recorded many of my interviews and have managed to find people to make copies of the tapes. I'm planning to have three copies made of each – one for London, one for me and I should like to send the third one to you by post every few days. I don't want to run the risk of any of this going astray.'

'Good idea and that's fine. But what are your plans after the end of next month?'

'I thought I'd return to Sarlat by way of London and spend my time writing there well away from the distractions of the city. What do you want or plan to do?'

'I've promised to go back to London to see the family over the winter and Christmas, but I have no fixed dates in mind. Would it be a hindrance to you if I stayed on until sometime around the middle of November?'

'No, the occasional distractions you offer would be more than welcome from time to time!'

'I'm more than happy to be a distraction, and maybe something more than that.'

'You are, but can we stop the conversation there? It's important not to say words that cannot then be unsaid.'

They spoke for a further few minutes and then rang off, leaving Peter with a deep-seated sense of unease.

* * *

Summer in the Périgord was turning to autumn. The pale ochre of the leaves in the previous week had become a mellow gold. The departure of the summer visitors had left the indigenous community to its own private domestic ways and the town now seemed quiet and introspective. The house felt emptier as each day passed. Peter found that the impenetrable quietude of the French countryside generated a sense of aloneness which was profoundly unsettling. He needed the opportunity to think clearly about his immediate future. Only three months of his leave of absence had elapsed but this had exposed him to many new environments, experiences and emotions which he was finding exciting and intellectually challenging but also disturbing. He had moved so far out of his comfort zone and was not sure he was adequately equipped to see his way forward. Much of his life in the last year had been shaped by extrinsic events and interactions. Sally's earlier words had found their target. He had embarked on an exhilarating but perplexing journey through a mysterious land and was travelling hesitantly to an unknown and unknowable destination. The writing was proceeding well, at least in terms of quantity. He had generated approximately thirty-five thousand words. The emotional tumult he had experienced at the end of Jenny's visit continued to perturb him at times. Sally remained intriguing, inscrutable and elusive. He relished her company as a mentor, as a friend and as a lover but a barrier remained between them which he had been unable to cross and which, perhaps, was insurmountable. He remained uncertain of his status in her mind but felt he was becoming increasingly able to view the evolution of their relationship with a degree of detachment. That evening, he selected some music to match his melancholy mood and was assailed by the plangent tones of the first Bruch violin concerto. He cooked himself a simple meal and opened a bottle of wine which he consumed slowly to assuage his sense of isolation before falling into a dreamless sleep.

The following Saturday, Peter decided to take a walk to try and clear his mind. This took him close to the Vézère and he realised he was not far from the Browning's castle. On an impulse, he walked into the reception and rang the bell. Tilly appeared after a few moments. She kissed him on both cheeks. 'Hello, what brings you here?'

'I was taking a walk along the valley when I saw your castle in the distance and walked over on an impulse, hoping to find you in and, perhaps, invite myself in for a cup of coffee.'

'Of course, it's lovely to see you. It's good to see regular visitors. Most of our guests are delightful but they are transient; you are rather less transient. Come in and have a coffee. Jonny has gone to pay a visit to his favourite caviste and will be back within the next half hour.' She scrutinised his face closely for a moment. 'You look tired. Come up to our lounge and tell me all that you've been doing over the last three weeks.' She looked out and saw a car drawing up. 'That was speedy. It's Jonny. He has either been very successful or profoundly disappointed! We shall discover which very quickly.' She glanced up as he walked in. 'Look who's just strolled in! We were just about to have a coffee and he was going to tell me what he's been up to since we last saw him. Have you had a successful trip to the caviste?'

He shook Peter's hand. 'Yes, very successful. I've bought some Mercurey and Givry. But let's go and have that coffee. I could do with a cup!'

'How is Sally?'

'She's well. Enjoying the challenge of the project and probing the reactions of local people – both the politicians and officials and also the man and woman in the street. She says it's very clear that Britain acceding to the European Community is not seen as an unalloyed good by many of the French. There appears to be rather more enthusiasm for it in Germany. She'll be back here at the end of next month when I'm sure she'll tell you more.'

'What about your plans?'

'I'm undecided at present. I shall certainly stay on here as a house-sitter until Sally returns and then I have promised my family that I'll be home for Christmas, but I'm not sure just now precisely when I shall leave. What about you?'

'We've reached the point in the year when the number of guests is dropping off sharply. We shall remain open for All Saints, which falls on a weekend this year, and then close for the winter. If Sally is back, you should both come over for dinner one evening that weekend.'

'And after that?'

'We're planning to establish a routine of going round the building and drawing up a schedule of works to be carried out over the winter. It should be fairly short as we've only recently renovated the place. We'll certainly go back to London for Christmas but probably not until early

December. Our son has a young boy who is coming up to two years old and we want to see him. He and the family came out here early in the summer and that was great. Why don't you stay the night and have dinner with us? Only four of the rooms are occupied tonight.'

'I came here on foot.'

'That's no problem. One of us will drive you back to your car and you can go and collect a toothbrush and then come back and stay the night.'

'That sounds like quite an imposition.'

'Not at all, we should enjoy the company. Where did you park?'

'A few miles up the river at Tursac.'

'Then it will only take a few minutes to re-unite you with your car. Why don't you come back at around seven, say? We should like to hear more about Sally's commission and also more of the reasons that induced you to leave your secure profession and take a year out.'

It did not take much persuasion for Peter to assent and he returned in time to join his hosts for a glass of wine while having the luxury once again of being able to choose from their menu for dinner.

'We're having an evening celebrating Lyonnais dishes tonight,' explained Jonny. 'They tend to be somewhat substantial but you should try them.'

He looked at the menu. 'You'll have to guide me here. I simply don't recognise the names of these dishes.'

'Very well – how about some suggestions? The soup is a pumpkin soup or you could try the quenelles de brochet. They are traditionally described as dumplings but that does not do them justice. They are much lighter than that, more like a mousse, traditionally made with pike and served with a Nantua sauce which is made from crayfish, celery, carrots and Cognac. Then I would suggest poularde demi-deuil, a chicken dish prepared with truffles thus giving rise to the alternate black and white appearance of the flesh, hence a chicken half in mourning. Finally, my preference would be for some cheese and we have bought in Saint Marcellin for the occasion.'

'It sounds wonderful. I'm happy to be guided by you.'

'We have avoided some other Lyonnais dishes which we felt might be less appealing, like tablier de sapeur. This literally means a fireman's apron but it's a tripe dish.'

'I should have been happy to pass on that!'

'Good – now let's see how good the recommendations of my caviste have been.'

'That was excellent,' Peter said as they relaxed with coffee and a brandy after dinner. 'The food was amazing.'

'We were talking about your decision to abandon your profession, at least for a year. What induced you to do so?' asked Tilly.

'I've been trying to analyse that myself and, like so many major decisions which we make about our personal lives, there are so many factors involved. Some originate from our own personalities but they are also shaped by experience. I've always enjoyed the physical process of writing and I've always enjoyed reading. I've noticed since I started putting pen to paper that I have become much more aware in my reading of fiction of the plot structure, the imagery which authors use and the ways in which they handle dialogue, either in the form of direct or reported speech. I've also become aware of my own limitations. My practical experience of writing until a few months ago didn't stretch beyond occasional stories written while at school to satisfy the demands of teachers. I suspect that my latent wish to write might well have remained unfulfilled if it hadn't been for recent personal circumstances which have given me a degree of freedom that I've never had before. The influence of others has also had an impact, particularly Sally, and an old friend from my student days who is also a lawyer. But you've done a similar thing in leaving and setting up here.'

'But I think you've been much bolder in a way.'

'I'm not so sure. I have the equivalent of a return ticket in my pocket.'

'Maybe, but as we said when you were last here, we were sufficiently secure financially to be able to leave and comprehensively burn our bridges behind us. We also have the opportunity to offer professional advice to other expatriates. Do you feel that you can see your destiny in the longer term?'

'No, I'm not even sure I can predict what the next month holds for me and 1970 seems like a distant country. I hope not to return home abjectly, with nothing of substance to show for my absence.'

'And if you're successful?'

'I scarcely dare consider that possibility.'

'We really have no right to ask this but what about your future at a personal level?'

'I wish I knew,' he hesitated, 'or perhaps I don't. The only thing I can say with assurance is that for the first time in my life I'm learning to co-exist with a state of incertitude. Slowly I'm adapting to this state and even starting to relish the lack of inevitability as to what the next day might bring. I know that sounds as if I'm evading the question but I simply don't know where I might be next year emotionally. I have benefitted from and at the same time been disadvantaged by a very conventional middle-class upbringing. I don't know what your backgrounds were but I might hazard a guess that they were similar to my own.'

'You're correct, but we should release you from this cross-examination. We're much enjoying your company and hope that you'll come back again at the beginning of November when Sally has returned. Equally, you are more than welcome to come again before that.'

'I think it would be appropriate to have a return match before that. I can't possibly match the quality of the cuisine provided by your chef but I can produce a meal which is edible and I can ensure that it's accompanied by some good wine. I'll call you to fix a date. There is, however, one thing that I need to arrange first. I received an invitation to visit Lyon to talk to a lawyer there. This would be valuable for my book. I need to see when that might be convenient for my hosts. The introduction to Lyonnais dishes was wonderful so it seems it would be worth going there simply to eat!'

'It is. Lyon regards itself as the gastronomic headquarters of France and you can scarcely walk along a street without tripping over a Michelin star. It's also very French and a remarkably beautiful and historic city. You'll enjoy it. Make sure that you take the time to be a tourist as well.'

23

The following day Peter wrote to François and Madeleine Carnot to ask if he might take up their invitation to visit and talk to one of their lawyer friends. He received a response later in the week with a warm invitation which offered a number of options. They pointed out that there would be two major civic events in Lyon before Christmas which might be of interest to him. The first would be the arrival of the Beaujolais Nouveau on the fifteenth of November and the second the Fête des Lumières on the eighth of December. If neither of these dates were possible, they suggested that he stay for three nights from Thursday 16th to Sunday 19th of October. This would give him half a day to speak to their lawyer friend and a day and a half to see Lyon. He accepted for the last of these dates with alacrity.

He drove to Lyon and located the Carnot's apartment in a late nineteenth century building in the sixth arondissement, close to the Rhône and overlooking the Parc de la Tête d'Or. He was warmly greeted by François and Madeleine and shown to a spacious room with a view of the park. After he had abandoned his bag he joined them for a coffee. 'I hope you will be happy about what we have done but we have made various arrangements for your stay. Marie, Pierre and Julie will be joining us for dinner this evening. Tomorrow our friend, Armand Delacroix, will meet you for lunch so that you can talk about your project and discover how we deal with divorce and its consequences here in France, and then we plan to eat out tomorrow evening. You cannot visit Lyon and not visit one of our more renowned restaurants. On Saturday, sadly, we have to abandon you as we must visit Madeleine's mother in Beaune who has had a fall and broken her hip but Julie lives quite close by and she has offered to look after you and show you the city and then provide you with a bed for the night. I hope you will not mind that we have had to change the arrangements slightly.'

'Not at all. I'm just grateful to you for offering me your hospitality and making these arrangements. Can I offer you dinner tomorrow?'

'Absolutely not. You are a guest and a first time visitor. Maybe if you come again then we should consider you to be an honorary Lyonnais. And if you do come again, you should certainly try to time your visit to coincide with one of the major local events which we mentioned in our letter.'

The following day Peter made his way to the chambers of Armand, close to the Palais de Justice and they went to a small restaurant nearby. It became clear from the discussion that the system in France was in many ways similar to that in England, the jurisdiction under which the divorce would be granted being determined in most instances in France, as in England, by the country of the habitual residence of the parents. In the majority of cases in England, sole custody would be awarded to the mother with access arrangements for the father; in the remainder of cases sole custody might be awarded to the father or joint arrangements agreed. In France, on the other hand, the Family Courts generally tended to favour joint custody arrangements unless there were exceptional circumstances. The issues Peter was hoping to explore in his novel were those where one parent would not accept the ruling of the court and would obstruct access to or, more seriously, abduct the child. Enforcing a judgement in a civil matter, which was delivered in one jurisdiction when the child was living in another, was particularly difficult, challenging and time-consuming, and often impossible. The difficulties of the situation were often aggravated by partial media reporting in the two countries concerned.

Peter left after lunch and decided to walk for a time before returning to the Carnot's apartment. He wandered over the Rhône and turned left along the bank of the river. He cut in towards the heart of the city and the vast red gravelled expanse of the Place Bellecour, surrounded by monolithic nineteenth century buildings with the great equestrian statue of Louis XIV at its heart. He collected a street map from the tourist office and then walked slowly up the Rue de la République to the Hôtel de Ville on the Place des Terreaux. He stopped for a coffee and then took a bus back to the apartment. The rest of the day proved to be one of pure indulgence. His hosts took him to La Mère Brazier, one of many starred restaurants in the city and one which epitomised the leading role of female chefs in the development of Lyonnaise cuisine.

Saturday was clear and mild and the Carnots guided

Peter to Julie's apartment in the third arondissement before departing for Beaune. 'I hope you're feeling fit,' she said. 'This is a city best explored on foot but I would suggest that first we take the bus and then the funicular to Fourvière. That's the hill with the basilica which you can see from the central square and many other points in the city. I love this city and showing it off to visitors.'

Half an hour later they had reached the summit of the hill. They explored the Roman amphitheatres and then entered the great white basilica with a tower at each corner which dominated the skyline. 'This is sometimes known irreverently as the upside down white elephant,' she said. 'It was built as a tribute to the Virgin Mary for saving the city from the plague, cholera and various other threats, such as Prussians. It's also the focus for the Fête des Lumières in December. The centre of Lyon is closed to traffic then and people place candles in their windows throughout the city.' Peter was not ready for the elaborate gold-encrusted and marble interior with its massive mosaic scenes depicting episodes in church and French history. It was overwhelming and contrasted strikingly with the vast but much simpler crypt below. They exited and wandered across to the promenade from where they had a spectacular view of Lyon and beyond before descending to the mediaeval city immediately below on the banks of the Saône. Here they explored the old cobbled streets and the twelfth century Gothic cathedral of Saint Jean with its ancient stained glass depicting the redemption and its elaborate astronomical clock.

'We should pause for lunch,' said Julie. 'Where did you eat last night?'

'At La Mère Brazier.'

'Then we shall do something very different. You cannot come to Lyon and not visit a bouchon.'

'With my limited but improving French I thought that was a cork or a traffic jam!'

'And so it is, but here in Lyon it's also a designation for a simple restaurant serving traditional Lyonnais dishes. The portions are robust rather than nouvelle cuisine and we should treat ourselves to a Pot Lyonnais.'

'Whatever's that?'

'It's a uniquely Lyonnais quantity of wine which comes in an open-topped bottle with a thick glass base containing 46 centilitres. The best bouchons are over the Saône on the Presqu'île which is the heart of the city. It will be a late lunch but we can relax as we have all day. This was the area where you walked yesterday, wasn't it?'

'Yes, but I only scratched the surface. This is wonderful and you're a great guide. I can see you love Lyon. How long have you lived here?'

'A little more than two years.'

'Did you speak French before you came?'

'Reasonably well but I speak it much better now. I need to in my job.'

'You said you were in property.'

'Yes, I deal in commercial property for an international property and development company based in London. So I travel there from time to time.'

'If you don't mind me asking, how was it that you decided to leave New York and come here?'

'I worked in real estate back home. I was born in a small

town in Wisconsin. After college and getting married I lived in Seattle but when the marriage broke up after three years I decided to move to New York. It was a parting by mutual agreement. There was no cataclysmic event which precipitated it. We just were not well suited. Jake has remarried and now has two children. We exchange greetings at Thanksgiving and are on amicable terms. I spent just over two years in New York which is where I met Marie. I decided to leave after she came back to France.' She laughed. 'The journey to Europe completes the journey from small town girl to international sophisticate!'

'So did you specifically seek a job in Lyon?'

'No, but I did find a job with a British company which was expanding its operations in continental Europe and I was posted to France. Initially, I spent a year in Paris and then was sent here to open up an office for the region.'

'You seem to have quite a social life here. How did you manage that?'

'The Carnot family were very generous and are very inclusive but there are so many other things to do here. There's a wealth of opportunities for listening to music and in the winter the mountains are near enough to go skiing regularly at weekends. There's also an association which welcomes those new to Lyon and this includes people from overseas as well as French who have worked outside the country. It brings together an interesting bunch of people. Now you know almost everything about me! I shall have to turn the tables on you at dinner and interrogate you.'

'I've no problem with that but my life has been much less interesting and adventurous than yours.'

'I'm not so sure about that, based on our first encounter. Come on, we have more sightseeing to do. We should explore the Presqu'île.' They walked through the Place des Terreaux and the town hall and made their way slowly with many detours down to the Place Bellecour and then to rue Victor Hugo. They finally came to a halt by the station where they enjoyed a coffee and a pastry. They agreed that they had done Lyon comprehensively and returned to Julie's apartment as it was getting dark.

'I thought we should have something authentically Lyonnais this evening. It's time to start with a glass of kir before we eat. Try reading the newspaper and let's listen to some music while I get some food ready.' She handed him a copy of Le Figaro and put on a recording of La Bohème.

'This is considerably more comfortable that a garret in Paris,' Peter said as he relaxed with a glass in his hand listening to the music while Julie busied herself in the kitchen. He abandoned his attempt to read the paper after a few minutes and looked round the spacious living room, examining the books on the shelves and the collection of LPs and tapes. Three-quarters of an hour later dinner was ready, a meal commencing with cervelas, a pork sausage stuffed with pistachios served cold with a glass of a sweet white wine. This was followed by a coq au vin and a local cheese.

'Now tell me some more about yourself. I learned a little when we met at Cap Ferret but not very much.'

'Yes, I was very drunk and a little grumpy that evening or perhaps a little drunk and very grumpy. Today has been wonderful. The wine and kir has made me a little drunk this evening but far from grumpy – just mellow.'

'You look very comfortable. I know you're a lawyer and an author but tell me how you came to be in France.'

'I can scarcely claim to be an author. I think that is an appellation which should be reserved for a published writer. My coming here resulted from a convergence of my fantasies, changes in my personal life and a series of random occurrences.' He recounted the sequence of events of the previous fifteen months. 'I'm increasingly coming to believe that much of what shapes our lives is the consequence of random factors, I suppose, a little like the random genetic mutations which are the basis of natural selection.'

'Being carried a little too far offshore when swimming was, I imagine, an example of such a random event.'

'Yes, and still a source of some embarrassment when I think of it!'

'You shouldn't be embarrassed – we would not be here in my flat this evening if you had not swum out at that point and on that day at that time. Nor would we be here if the four of us had not gone out in the boat to escape the frenzy of activity as preparations for the party were being put in place.'

'Perhaps this is more representative of chaos theory where small changes in initial events can result in substantial and unpredictable consequences in dynamic systems.'

'And how is your girlfriend, or your lady companion who is not your girlfriend?'

'She is currently in Germany reporting on attitudes towards the British as they consider applying again for membership of the European Community.'

'And your status or her status now?'

'Still as indeterminate and nebulous as it was three months ago.'

'Does that unsettle you?'

Peter thought for a moment before answering. 'Sometimes, but less than it did. This last year has meant that I have become more ready to accept uncertainty. I've also learned to understand that there are aspects of all of us which are simply unfathomable and that I shouldn't necessarily attempt to interpret the thoughts and emotions of others through a lens which is uniquely my own. I guess our personal lenses are never made of plain glass and all will distort images and this can lead to tensions and misunderstandings. I'm learning to relax and accept people as they are and to avoid the temptation to frame my understanding of them to match my own perspectives or prejudices. My relationship with Sally is both challenging and stimulating but also relaxed and intimate. I'm not sure that I'm making a great deal of sense. I should help you clear the dishes.'

'Well, that is an effective way of changing the subject but the offer is willingly accepted. Let's do that and then have a coffee and perhaps a digestif.'

They headed back to the salon and at Julie's suggestion went to the shelves to select some music. 'What would you like?' she asked.

'Anything gentle at this time of the evening.'

She handed him a tape. 'How about this?' It was a collection of Chopin Nocturnes.

'That would be great. It has been just a wonderful day,' and on an impulse he leant across and kissed her on the lips.

She came closer. 'Yes, for me too.' She put her arms around him. 'I think that merits a response in kind.' They kissed for a few moments exploring with their tongues. She leaned back and whispered in his ear, 'If you go on like that I shall get seriously over-excited. Please don't stop.' After a few minutes she whispered in his ear again, 'Two bedrooms or one? I have a strong view as to which I would prefer.'

'I have learned some key French phrases – je suis en accord!'

* * *

Peter awoke the next morning to find himself alone in the bed. Two minutes later Julie returned still naked with a tray bearing coffee and croissants. 'This is the only civilized way to breakfast in France.'

'You will find I'm a willing student of all things French.'

'I've already discovered that – I would even go so far as to say that you've reached an advanced level very quickly. I know that you have to leave today but don't feel that you have to rush.'

'Nothing would induce me to rush today.'

They stayed in bed until lunchtime and then reluctantly got up and dressed. He whispered in her ear as they did so, 'If this weekend is a demonstration of chaos theory in the real world, then I'm all for it.'

She laughed. 'Me too. It has been a weekend to remember. It would be wonderful to see you again. I'm not applying pressure and I shall have no regrets if it turns out to have simply been a single weekend. If so, this has been one to store in the memory bank and retrieve from time to time and recall with pleasure. So what are your plans now? How much longer will you remain in France?'

'I'm not clear about that at present. I'll probably go back to London sometime next month. I have a commitment to be in Sarlat until Sally returns which will probably be next week.'

'I have two thoughts – no, I have many more than that but I have two proposals. The first is that you might like to come back to Lyon for the Beaujolias Nouveau on the fifteenth of November or we might perhaps meet in London or in fact do both. Not only do I have to visit two or three times a year but I've persuaded my parents to spend the Christmas holiday period in London this year. They will be there from the twentieth of December until the third of January, so I shall be staying in London over part of that period.'

'Either or both. I'll give you my address and telephone numbers and will call you when my plans are a little clearer.' He held her tightly. 'I shall not forget this weekend either.'

24

Night fell as Peter drove slowly and contentedly back to Sarlat. He was surprised that he had little sense of disquiet or feelings of angst. Had he been disloyal to Sally? He was not certain. He could not be sure of the nature of the tacit contract which he had with her or even if there was a contract. He was aware he owed much to her intellectually, emotionally and practically. Yet the impulse which had led him first to embrace Julie and then share her bed had seemed entirely natural. The overall impact of the experiences of the last few months had engendered a freedom of thought and action which suggested a number of possible scenarios for his future. The immediate future, however, would be influenced and shaped by events and the interactions between Sally and himself when she returned in two weeks' time.

Sally called from London the following week to say she was planning to return to Sarlat just before All Saints. Peter agreed to pick her up from the station. He booked a table for dinner in the restaurant in Beynac where they had eaten on Bastille Day. She arrived that evening and they left for dinner almost immediately, returning home to their separate rooms. Peter left the house early the following day to buy fresh croissants and Sally emerged just before ten to join him for breakfast. 'I know that I was quite uncommunicative last night but I was simply exhausted after two months on the road and then two days in London.'

'I know. How has it all come together?'

'Generally pretty well. I've filed four articles and have promised the editor another four. Three have already been published on a weekly basis. I've established a pattern so there are now weekly deadlines for the delivery of the other four. I've also got agreement, in principle, that I should go back at a later date as negotiations progress and see the same people again. Your brother's insights and those of other expatriates were very valuable.'

'What are your plans now?'

'I'm going to stay here probably until the end of November to get these further articles written and sent off. I don't want to interrupt my work schedule by moving everything back to London. I also want to start sketching out the framework for a book. I shall have to go back to London to access libraries and consult people for some of the historical and political background, which I'll do over the winter and the first few months of next year. But what have you been up to?'

'I've been over to the Brownings again for dinner. I owe them one. Perhaps we could invite them over at the end of next week when the hotel will be closed for the winter?'

'Good idea – will you organise it?'

'Yes, I'd be happy to. I also took up the Carnot's

invitation to visit Lyon and see their lawyer friend. That was helpful. I'm not sure if you know the city but I was very taken with it and the cuisine!'

'No, I've only been there once. And now?'

'I thought that I'd go back to London around the middle of the month and set to work there.'

'How has the writing been going?'

'It's progressing. I've now consigned between forty and fifty thousand words to paper. I want to go back and try and transcribe it, using a typewriter and revising as I do. I suspect that I'll have to resort to a professional typist at some stage but I'm not ready yet to show it to anyone else. What will you be doing when you get back to London?'

'I'll still have a lot of work to do and I'll also want to pick up the projects which I had to drop when this Franco-German assignment came up and develop my ideas for a book.'

'Would you prefer me to stay around until the end of November or would I be a distraction?'

'Peter, it might seem unkind to say so, but it's not important either way. I shall be very preoccupied for the next month. You should go ahead with your plans. I do, however, plan to take two days off now and would be grateful for your company.'

'What will you do over the holiday period in London?'

'I often join the family of a former colleague for Christmas and I shall probably do that again.'

'It would be good to see you in London.'

'Yes, I'll call you when I'm back and we can get together in London.'

'What would you like to do with your mini-break?'

'Almost anything that will not involve listening to taped interviews or sitting down at my typewriter.'

'It's a mild day – how about a walk? We also have an invitation to go over to the Brownings sometime this weekend. I'll give them a call.'

Peter sensed that there had been a subtle change in the nature of the exchanges between them. Their conversations had become more formal. He was unsure whether this was due to tiredness on Sally's part or to some reserve on his. He was also conscious that there might have been some change in his demeanour which she had detected. However, it was not the time to explore openly the precise nature of their relationship and it was more than probable that such an exploration would be incomplete, inconclusive and unsatisfactory.

The following fortnight passed companionably but it was clear that there was a zone between them which neither wished nor thought to enter. Each remained within their own domain, familiar strangers each drawing some comfort from the other. Peter was concerned by the lack of Sally's customary vitality and the flatness of her affect and general lassitude. Gentle probing was met by non-committal responses, and offers to assist in anything but the most mundane of tasks were courteously rebuffed. They came a little closer one night when each responded to a mutual need for intimacy but this was a union between longstanding friends, pleasurable but lacking passion or urgency.

* * *

Peter decided that he would leave by mid-November. He expressed some concern to Sally about leaving when she appeared to be under stress. She assured him that she would be fine and that it was very likely that if thrown back entirely on her own resources she would soon recover her characteristic vigour. He considered the possibility of driving back to London by way of Lyon to see the celebrations which mark the arrival of the Beaujolais Nouveau and after some hesitation he called Julie. 'Do come,' was the instant response, 'and you need to arrive the day before, on the Friday. The day begins at midnight and you'll miss most of the fun if you arrive on the Saturday.' He told Sally he would be returning by way of Lyon and that he would be back in London after the weekend. They agreed to keep in touch and Sally promised to call him when she had decided on a date to return to London.

He drove off with some misgivings about leaving Sally but with a sense of eagerness to see Julie once more. She was right. There was a buzz in the city and he received an enthusiastic greeting. 'The time for more of that will come a little later,' she said after they had embraced, 'but we need to organise ourselves. The day of the arrival of the Beaujolais Nouveau begins one minute after midnight tonight. The barrels will be unloaded from barges at the Quai de Pécherie and then rolled through to the Place des Terreaux outside the town hall where there will be banners announcing "Le Beaujolais est arrivé". There will be quite a party in the square. It may be a little wet but not too bad, so be prepared.'

They walked over the river and into the city through the throng. Undeterred by the weather, they joined the crowds outside the Hôtel de Ville. The party was already under way with a band playing on one side of the square. Many people already had glasses in their hands. As midnight approached, the assembly started to count down and prepared to welcome the men rolling the barrels into the square. A cheer erupted as they arrived and within minutes wine was being offered to the onlookers. Julie leaned across to him. 'This is ideal weather for drinking the Beaujolais – slightly chilled. It's at just the right temperature. The locals always quote Daudet who said that there were three rivers flowing through Lyon, the third being the Beaujolais!' She held a glass up so that Peter could inspect the pure garnet colour illuminated by the lights of the square. 'The advantage of this third river,' she added, 'is that it never becomes muddy.' After two glasses they left and strolled back to Julie's flat hand in hand.

Peter awoke late to find Julie bringing him a cup of coffee. 'You did say that you would be heading for England tomorrow. Can you be persuaded to stay through the rest of the weekend?'

He was about to say that he had to get back but reflected that there was no necessity for him to do so and that he had made no commitments to anyone. 'I don't see why not, if you can tolerate this intrusion into your private life.'

'Good, and I think that I'm sufficiently robust to manage the intrusion. I could scarcely do otherwise since I've encouraged it! I have a suggestion for today – how about going out of town for the day?' Julie drove him out to the mediaeval village of Perouges, a short way to the east, where they wandered along the cobbled streets and had a plat for lunch. He remained concerned about Sally, however, and in the evening he asked Julie if he might call her. She assented and diplomatically busied herself in the kitchen. Sally answered the phone and assured him that all was well and that she was now getting on top of the voluminous material which she had collected over the previous two months. 'It was kind of you to call – where are you now?'

'I'm still in Lyon and enjoying the city and the Beaujolais Nouveau celebrations were great fun. I went down there with Julie.'

'When are you heading back to England?'

'I'm leaving early tomorrow and will be back in London late on Tuesday. If I may, I'll call you again in a few days' time.'

'That would be good.'

They rang off and Julie came back into the room. She looked at him. 'It sounded as if you were concerned about her.'

'Yes, I am. She seemed very despondent when I left and quite unlike her usual composed and controlled self. But she sounded much better this evening.'

'It sounds as if you're very fond of her.'

'Yes, I am although I'm not sure that fond is the right adjective. Equally I'm not sure that I could find the right word, even if I collected my thesaurus from the car and thumbed through it – not that I'm planning to do that! It's an amalgam of fondness, affection and love. She has been a friend, a mentor and an intimate. My head asks me if I should be talking to you about Sally and hints to me that there might be something disloyal in doing so; nevertheless it seems quite natural to do so.'

'My head tells me that I probably should not be encouraging you to talk. It's up to you. I am receptive though.' She walked across and put her arms round him. 'Nothing you say will alter my feelings for you – but everything you say gives me further insights into the hidden Peter Bowman.'

Peter put his head on one side and looked quizzically at her. 'If I'm honest, I'm not sure that I could say with any precision what exactly my relationship is with you. All I do know is that I have enjoyed your company and that making love to you has been wonderful and seemed an entirely natural thing to do.'

'I'm happy with that. You're excellent company and I hope that despite the challenges of geography we shall continue to enjoy each other's company in all ways. Neither of us knows what the future might have in store for us separately or together. I am content with that and I appreciate your honesty and openness.'

'Sally has this phrase "loving friends".'

'I like the concept and I love the reality. I hope that I've acquired that status.'

'You have been shortlisted and appointed!'

'Then we should confirm that relationship in the immediate future.'

＊ ＊ ＊

Peter left Lyon on the Monday to return to England. He and Julie promised to keep in touch and arranged to meet again in London over the Christmas period.

25

Peter looked round his flat the morning after his arrival back in England. The time he had been in France had been invaluable and had effectively removed him from the trivia and concerns of everyday life in London. With Sally's encouragement and example, he had established a disciplined approach to writing which he was sure he could now continue in his own flat. He was about to leave to re-stock with the essentials of daily life when the doorbell rang. It was Sue investigating the noises which she had heard from her flat below. She had assumed that he had returned but wanted to reassure herself that this was the case. She was on her way to work but invited him to join her for a coffee that evening. It would be the first step towards picking up the threads of his social life in London and he determined to do so that day by calling family and friends.

Three days later he had been out and returned at the end of the afternoon. As he unlocked the door of the flat, he heard the sound of the kettle boiling in the kitchen. He opened the door slowly and was astonished to see Ann standing by the kettle looking very despondent, preparing to make a pot of tea. 'What are you doing here?' he asked in surprise.

She looked up. 'I persuaded Sue to let me in. I probably shouldn't have done but I didn't know where else to go.'

'What's happened?'

'I've left Francis.'

'Why – what's happened?'

'It's a long story,' she hesitated, 'or perhaps not such a long story. It had always been whispered around the building that he was a bit of a womaniser but he denied this and dismissed it as office gossip. It has become clear over the last nine months that it was not only office gossip but it was also true. There was an incident early in the summer and he promised that it had been a one-off and would not be repeated. I discovered at the start of this week that the affair had continued without interruption. I really couldn't take that so I've left him. I packed my bags early this morning and left. He didn't make a great deal of effort to dissuade me from going and oddly that also hurt.'

Peter sat down at the kitchen table and took the mug of tea which Ann offered him. 'I am so sorry. What are you planning to do now?'

She sat silently for several minutes before saying, 'I really have no right to ask this but I was hoping that you would let me come back.'

'Do you mean as my wife?'

'Yes.' After a moment she added, 'I do know it's unreasonable to ask this and entirely out of the blue. I'm sure you won't want to answer that immediately.'

There was a long pause before he did answer. 'Ann, a lot of water has flowed under innumerable bridges since Valentine's day. It will not flow back again. My life has changed immeasurably since then, maybe temporarily, possibly permanently. But whatever I might be doing and wherever I might be, my life will and can never be the same again.'

'I know from Jenny that you've been staying in France writing, although she doesn't say very much, but I am still your wife. Can you not try and look at things from my point of view, whatever you may have been doing?'

'I'm trying to do so but, be fair, I also have to look at it from my point of view and I cannot see that we can recreate the life which we had a year ago.'

'Why not? I'm sure that I can adapt or have you found another woman?' She looked across at Peter who was patently discomfited by this direct question. 'I can see that you have.'

Peter hesitated before answering, picking his words with some care. 'The answer is that I have made some new friends, some of whom are women but the answer to the implications of your question is "no".'

'I know you're still seeing Jenny and that you took her to Newcastle. That seems very disloyal.'

'Yes, I have seen Jenny on several occasions. And I didn't take her to Newcastle. I went with her to Newcastle at her suggestion when she had already planned to go and see your mother. I was, am, fond of your Mum, but I have not been and never have been "seeing" your sister in the sense that you insinuate.' Peter was getting angry at this interrogation. 'I'm fond of your sister too. She has become and remains a friend and the suggestion that I have been disloyal is inaccurate and ironic, considering the circumstances which led to our parting.' He hesitated once more before adding, 'Ann, I really do think we should stop this discussion. It has the potential to descend into a flaming row which I don't want and which will certainly not help you.'

There was a long silence before she said contritely, 'Yes, I'm sorry. You're right but what am I to do? I've nowhere to go.'

He hesitated again for some moments and then reluctantly said, 'You can stay here for a few days in the spare room while you find alternative accommodation. I assume you're still in your job.'

'Yes, but I can't continue working there now. I shall be looking for other opportunities.'

Later that night, after he had gone to bed, there was a knock on the door of the bedroom. 'Can I join you just for tonight? I feel so alone.'

'Ann, that's not a good idea. If you cannot sleep, I'll make some tea and we can sit and talk in the kitchen for a bit. I understand that you feel isolated and friendless just now and, if I can help, I will but we simply do not have a future together.'

'Yes, you have made that clear and you're probably right. It's not quite the right phrase but I guess I've made my bed and now I must lie on it – alone.' She gave a wan smile.

The following day Peter rang Sue's doorbell. 'I'm sorry that I let Ann into your flat,' she said when she answered. 'I probably shouldn't have done that but she looked so desolate. Is she still here?'

'Yes, she slept in the spare room. She really had nowhere else to go and I couldn't refuse her that. She hoped that we might have a future together but I cannot see that. But I can see it will difficult sharing the flat for an indefinite period until she finds somewhere else. She told me she will also be looking for a new job. I was wondering whether you would consider putting her up for a time?'

'Yes, with pleasure. She was very kind to me after Andrew's accident and death. It's the least I can do. There will then be less pressure on her to move on very quickly, which might avoid her making a hasty decision which she would later regret. I can see that it will ease what could be a very difficult situation for you.'

'That would be immensely kind of you. And how are you doing now? It's over a year since you lost Andrew and I know how much he meant to you.'

'I've started to come to terms with it although it will still be some time before I feel able to socialise fully and freely again.'

'If you're providing accommodation for Ann, I hope that you both might have an evening meal with me from time to time. I can reassure you that after more than four months in France my culinary skills have improved! Also, I've never thanked you properly for keeping an eye on the flat and for forwarding mail.'

'That was no problem. I hope your time away was productive and how is your lady friend who brought your keys round?'

'She's still in France as she has several articles to produce for her magazine group within the next week or so. She'll be coming back to London sometime next month. I think I would describe her as a friend who is a lady rather than my lady friend! She is a highly independent woman who has been very helpful to me.'

* * *

Peter invited Michael to join him in the flat on the Saturday following his return. He arrived shortly after seven. He looked at Peter. 'I've just bumped into Ann on the stairs – she was going into the flat below yours. Are you together again?'

'No, her liaison with her new partner didn't work out so she has left him. She showed up here quite unexpectedly a few days ago because she had nowhere else to go.'

'Are you likely to get together again?'

'No – she suggested it but it would not, could not, work now.'

'You say that very emphatically.'

'Yes, and it's right. She spent a night in the spare room here and then I asked Sue in the flat below if she might accommodate her. I've said I'd be happy to help her find other accommodation. She's in a bit of a mess. It's not just kindness on my part. There's also a certain amount of self-interest involved. So much has occurred since I left London at the end of June.'

'Are you going to tell me about it?'

'Sure and I hope you'll bring me up to date with your life.'

'So how is the magnum opus progressing?'

'I think that parvum opus would be a more satisfactory description at the moment. But I'm enjoying the physical process of writing and there are many days when I'm eager to complete my breakfast and get on with it. I've started with a topic which I know something about – a tug of love story with an English father domiciled in France and a French mother working in England. I've had a discussion with a French lawyer but most of the issues occur when one or both parents act in ways which are not in accord with the law in either jurisdiction.'

'And how is this going to turn out?'

'I really don't know. It seems curious to say but as I write the characters develop and take on lives of their own. I go over possible scenarios in my own mind and try and assess what each character would be likely to do next as they move forward in the narrative. I'm as curious to see what the outcome might be as you are!'

'That seems a rather anarchic way to proceed!'

'It probably is but I rationalise it on the basis that it mirrors life and I'm enjoying the uncertainty.'

'And is that true of your life in general?'

'I think it is. I don't know if at the end of my sabbatical I shall return to being a boring, jobbing solicitor or if I shall have found a new career. I have lived all my life until early this year travelling along predetermined tracks and I'm now finding the uncertainties of my present existence exhilarating. I've met people and been exposed to environments, events and emotions in a way which has never been the case before.'

'Give me some examples.'

'I suppose the experiences which mainly stand out are the ones which are uniquely French. I have experienced two particularly French celebrations – Bastille Day in rural France and the arrival of Beaujolais Nouveau in Lyon. This has been on top of living in "la France profonde" and starting to see it as local people do, rather than as a tourist, although my perceptions are still limited by my inadequate knowledge of the language.'

'That lists the events and that must have been fascinating, but tell me about the people, including the newly acquired friend or friends.'

'That has perhaps been the most intriguing and exciting element of the last year but, most of all, it's complicated.' Peter recounted his personal and emotional experiences over the previous six months.

Michael leant back in his chair with an amused smile on his face. 'Complicated appears to be the understatement of the year, if not the decade. Let me just run this past you to see if I've grasped the essentials. In five months you've abandoned your eminently respectable job and acquired two lovers: one an enigmatic English journalist with a periodic need for intimacy and the other an extrovert internationally-minded American with a healthy sexual appetite. At the same time, your ex-wife and your former sister-in-law are both bidding for entry rights to your bed, although not simultaneously, but admission to both has been denied to date. Complicated gets nowhere near being an adequate description and yet you seem to be entirely relaxed about it and even insouciant. Is that a reasonable summary of the present position?'

Peter laughed. 'Yes, stripped to its essentials, that's about right.'

'I said on an earlier occasion that I would not and should not offer you advice. I'm certainly not going to now. It would be a very brave man who would venture into this particular emotional minefield! It's clear you've shed all residual traces of your nonconformist upbringing, but I'm curious. Your year away from your partnership is less than half complete. On the basis of your experiences to date, I'd hesitate to predict what your personal situation might be after another six months. What do you see as your future after next summer – licensed libertine or salt of the earth family man?'

'I really don't know and I'm wholly unconcerned. Now tell me what you've been doing in the last few months and how your political aspirations are shaping up.'

'First, I cannot for one moment match your narrative for interest, but I have been shortlisted as a prospective parliamentary candidate for a seat in the north-west. It's difficult to judge my chances of being selected but if I am, there's a good chance of my being elected, as it's been held consistently by Labour for many years. More usually, a tyro would be selected for a safe Tory seat first time around. That's the standard approach and if the aspirant candidate were to cut the majority significantly, or at least do better than national trends, then he or she would stand a good chance of being selected in a more hopeful constituency later. It looks as though I might have by-passed that stage in the process. I have, however, discovered that it's helpful to have a wife, even in this day and age. That would obviously be straightforward if I had your allure but unfortunately I have no queue of beautiful women, or even any unprepossessing women, wishing to declare their undying love and devotion to me! Any tips you can give me would be invaluable. You must keep me in touch. I can scarcely wait to hear the next instalment!' He laughed. 'I might even be tempted to write a novel myself, based on your recent activities!'

'I shall be here for the next few months at least, and

probably permanently. Yes, it would be good to see more of each other, and possibly you might even meet some of the characters in the drama – but probably not all at the same time!'

'It would be good to see Jenny again and meet the others. I should be the soul of diplomacy.'

26

The telephone rang in the flat a few days later. Jenny said that she was planning to see Ann that afternoon and asked if he would be free to go for a drink afterwards. She arrived shortly after six and suggested they talked first and then went to the pub round the corner a little later. 'I heard Ann was staying with Sue in the flat below you,' she said. 'She told me that she'd wanted to come back to you but that you had refused to let her stay in your flat.'

'Jenny, that makes it sound more brutal than it was. It really was not like that. This will be quite difficult to explain but I should like to be open with you. What happened is this. I came back here about ten days ago to find Ann in the flat. Sue had let her in. It was obvious, as you have discovered, that she has had a very unhappy time. I'm genuinely sorry the relationship with Francis didn't work out, although from what she told me it might be better for her in the long run. She said she hoped that we might get together again permanently and asked me to think about it. She also suggested that we should share what had been our bedroom that night. I did say, as gently as I could, that I would find it difficult to reverse the clock and that too much had happened to her, and to me, since last February for that to happen. You know much of what has been happening to me. It's difficult, I know. I really don't want to be judgemental. I've seen this when handling divorces. Perfectly decent and reasonable people marry when young and over the years their personalities and ambitions develop and grow, sometimes in harmony but sometimes independently. It's not a question of fault; it's just the way people are. If I look back at us, I can see there had been a degree of divergence and that we had probably been growing apart for some time. It's just that it occurred over such a long time frame and so slowly that probably neither of us recognised it. Ann's decision to leave simply brought everything into sharp focus and forced me to take a more analytical view of my life than I'd done previously. It also, as you know, encouraged me to reappraise my future and, as a result, I've discovered additional dimensions to life which I had never previously envisaged. I couldn't go back now. I asked Sue if Ann could stay in her flat while she was looking for alternative accommodation. This was partly because I'm in the flat writing for much of the day. I could foresee tensions, however hard we tried to avoid the thin ice, particularly if we were both there in the evenings and over the weekends. We could, I suppose, by mutual agreement, have arranged that one or other of us was out at those times to minimise opportunities for confrontation. I also thought the independence of each of us might be compromised if we felt that courtesy demanded we discuss our daily activities in a companionable way as we would have done a year ago. That said, we have seen something of each other and, together with Sue, the three of us have had a meal together and I've no doubt we'll do so again.'

She looked at him. 'Thank you for being so frank. I suspected that the arrangements had been reached in a more sensitive manner than Ann had implied. She is feeling very fragile, hurt and rejected at the moment and is inevitably finding it difficult working so close to Francis and his latest conquest. I know she's actively looking for another job and I think it's quite likely she'll look for one outside London. She tells me that there are a number of television production companies in other cities. I naturally want to be supportive but equally I don't want to be regarded as her advocate or apologist.'

'Can I ask if you told Ann that we were going to have a drink together?'

'Rather shamefacedly, I have to admit that I didn't. I even went so far as to walk down the stairs from Sue's flat and then creep back up again quietly after the door closed! She was quite angry when I told her we had seen each other a few times since your split and she accused me of disloyalty.'

'I suspected as much – the same charge was laid at my door when she came here ten days ago. I really do hope that things work out well for her – one cannot expunge more than four years of sharing and marriage, and nor should one. Equally, I would not wish her views to disrupt our friendship'

'Neither do I. Although I'm not quite sure what I might have said, or she might have said, if she had caught me furtively climbing back up the stairs to your flat! I'm so glad that I've seen you and we've had this discussion. It puts things into perspective. Ann is my sister and I will do everything I can to support her but I cannot think why she threw you over for that two bit Casanova.'

He smiled, 'I guess that's a compliment.'

'Absolutely and it should not be taken any other way. Now tell me, how has your life been since I last saw you in September?'

'Let's go for that drink and I'll bring you up to date with my life and you can tell me what you've been up to.' He grinned. 'Perhaps we'd better make a stealthy exit down the stairs or we might be suspected of having a clandestine affair!'

'Well,' she said when they were settled, 'tell me all.'

'It has been, by my standards, quite adventurous.'

'I heard a little about your friend Sally's activities as her articles are being published by another magazine in the group that I work for. I've been reading them. They are a remarkable and insightful account of attitudes to this country overlain by a raft of longstanding prejudices. I understand that the high-ups in the group are very pleased with them. It would be good to meet her sometime.'

'You will, but how has your life been progressing?'

'The trip to France was a great success – not just the time in the Dordogne and that wonderful evening which will become a lifetime memory but also the jazz festival in St Etienne. Stefan was able to play informally on several occasions. There was an amazing party atmosphere there. I see him and Cass perhaps once every two or three weeks. They're great company. As for the rest, work is still good and I've been travelling up north once a month to see Mum. She's doing well.'

'And have you found anyone to make it a foursome with Stefan and Cass?'

'No.'

'Nothing in view?'

'Maybe a figure in the mist on the horizon but like all figures in the mist the image is evanescent!'

'Are you going to enlighten me further?'

'No, the likelihood is that it will come to nothing.'

'OK – but to change the subject, what are you doing for Christmas?'

'Ann and I are both going to Newcastle to be with Mum. We spent last Christmas at your parents but it will be the first time that we've both spent Christmas in Newcastle for many years.'

'Jenny – I think we should let Ann know that we have had a drink together. If we are to do so on other occasions, which I hope we shall, she'll undoubtedly find out and this might fuel suspicions on her part. I'm happy to tell her. I'm planning that once a week or so I'll have a coffee or a meal with her and Sue and it would be quite straightforward to tell her next time I do that.'

'You're right, but mischievously I should be quite happy to keep her guessing.'

'How about going somewhere for a pizza now?'

'Lovely idea, and you can tell me all about your complicated life since September.'

'I'll give you an edited version since it has become somewhat more complicated!'

'I should much prefer to hear the unexpurgated version!'

* * *

Peter called Sally the following morning. She told him she had completed the first series of articles and just managed to meet the deadlines for submission. She was feeling very much more relaxed and would probably be coming back to England the following weekend. He told her he had seen Jenny who had reported that the office gossip was that the first series of articles had been very well received. Sally promised to make contact after her return. He awoke the following day to a light covering of snow but saw on the television that this had been dense in some parts of the country. He called Sally again. The weather had been worse in central France. The snow had been particularly heavy in the valley of the Dordogne and she was without power. She assured him that she was managing and that she had an ample supply of logs for the fire. It was anticipated that power would be restored later that day. She was planning to batten down the hatches and leave once the roads were passable again.

Sally finally got back to London on the Sunday a fortnight before Christmas. They arranged to meet two days later at the Bodega, the restaurant where they had eaten previously. She was in good spirits. She confirmed that she had received very positive feedback on her series of articles and that the editor was happy with the suggestion that she return for a further visit the following year. This would generate further articles and probably provide the basis for a book. She planned to dedicate her time over the coming winter to doing the necessary research for a book on the impact and the extent of the integration of British expatriates in France, and also the possible project on the role which French culture had played in the works of English language writers who had lived in France.

He leant across the table and took her hand. He felt his instinct that a rift had developed between them had been incorrect. 'It is good to see you – no, it's lovely to see you. You were looking very tense and withdrawn when I left to go to Lyon. I was worried.'

'I was tense – but solitude proved to be a good companion and once I had set myself a work plan and settled down to type, it was hard work but I managed to keep up to schedule. The final few days in Sarlat were not much fun. I was without power for over twenty-four hours so I only had cold food to eat and I oscillated between my bed and the log burning stove. The Brownings were in the same position and we kept each other cheerful with multiple telephone calls. The roads were still not wonderful on Thursday but we left in convoy and stopped for the night near Orléans before driving on to the Channel.'

'What are your immediate plans?'

'I'm going to chill out, an appropriate expression seeing what the weather's like this December, and then get to work in the New Year. I shall go and spend two nights with an old colleague and his somewhat riotous family over Christmas in their very cold house but I shall get a very warm welcome. They live in Norfolk and it will be a very traditional family Christmas. By the way, the Brownings have invited both of us to dinner on the Saturday between Christmas and New Year. I hope that you can make it.'

'I can see no problem with that.'

'They live in North London – I can give you the address and we can drive up there together.'

'They've clearly known you and your family for a long time. They told me how they first met your parents. Would you tell me a little more about your family? I think you told me when we first met that you had no close family. You must have lost your parents at a very young age.'

She hesitated for some moments before saying, 'Yes, I was still in my late teens and I suspect you've sensed that those years have cast a long shadow over my life. I was particularly close to my father. I also had a twin brother who died in his teens of meningitis. I was also very close to him and this was perhaps reinforced by our peripatetic life. His death had a devastating effect on my parents but he was also very special to me and to many others. My father committed suicide six months later and the feelings of guilt which overwhelmed us were all-pervasive. We were in Bonn when George fell ill and we didn't have time to get back to see him before he died. Then after Dad's death, the sense of guilt was unimaginable and it must have been many times worse for Mum than for me. Our failure to recognise the level of despondency which had overtaken him left a permanent mark. It was a signal failure on our part not to have understood how desolate he felt. Mum moved back to France, to Sarlat. She could not bear to be close to things which revived instant memories of George and my Dad, nor did she want to see friends. She died shortly afterwards, having developed a highly invasive cancer. She was an extremely sad woman.'

'Perhaps I shouldn't probe.'

'No, it's alright. Two or three years ago I could not have had this conversation without becoming tearful and it's possible I might still do so.' She paused and looked directly at him. 'I have shared much with you, Peter, and I can and may well share more but I'm sure you'll understand the reasons why I am so protective of my independence. In one sense it's all I have. Maybe one day I might feel able to open up fully to someone but I've not reached that stage just yet. That's not a reflection on you. It's simply the way things are, the way I am. I suspect it's to my disadvantage and I'm happy to have you as a loving friend. I say this with difficulty but, because I feel I cannot be bound by or to anyone at the present stage of my journey through life, it's only fair that your friendships and loves should not be restricted by my gremlins. They are my gremlins and ultimately it is up to me to manage and finally, I hope, exterminate them. Having loving friends – no, I've got that wrong – having a loving friend is something that I value more highly than you might have thought at times over the last few months.' He held her hands and gently caressed her arm.

'Do you have other relatives?'

'No-one close. My father had a younger brother but he was eight years younger and he lives in Canada. They were never close. Now you know,' she said. 'I know that you've created new friendships and I am genuinely delighted for you, so tell me what has been happening to you since you left Sarlat.'

'Well, my life has not been entirely uneventful since mid-November. As you know, I went to Lyon for the celebration of the Beaujolais Nouveau. It was just great fun. I was intending to leave the following day but was persuaded to stay on for another day by Julie Christie and I left to come home after that weekend. Since I've been home I've been writing, but there have been a number of distractions. Ann's lover was two-timing her and she appeared unannounced in the flat a few days after I got back. She wanted to come back but I had to say that too much had changed. I suspect our marriage might not have worked out long term anyway, even if that Casanova had not intervened, although that may be no more than a judgement made with hindsight. I know it would be impossible now and doomed to failure. She had nowhere to go so I said she could stay the night in the spare room but then Sue downstairs offered her a bed while she's looking for other accommodation and that seemed like a much better option. She's also looking for another job, possibly out of London. I can see it would be impossible for her to continue to work alongside the man concerned and his current paramour. I've spoken at length to Jenny, with whom I get on very well, and she has been very supportive of her sister. I've also spent an evening with my oldest and closest friend, Michael Rattray, whom you would probably be interested to meet. Saying that, I shall arrange a dinner party to demonstrate my newly acquired culinary skills – will you come?'

'Of course. It is good to see you again.'

'How about New Year's Eve, if you have had no other offers?'

'Yes, that would be good.'

'I will see if Michael and Jenny are free for that evening.'

'One thing you haven't mentioned has been your writing.'

'Despite the distractions I've been quite productive. I calculate that I'm now between two-thirds and three-quarters of the way through the novel. The plan is to complete a draft by the end of January and then type it up, revising it as I go. I'm hoping that I shall progress from typing with two fingers to at least four in the process.'

They called for the bill and Peter leant across. 'Thank you for all you have done – you have taught me more than you might think.'

She took his hands. 'It has certainly not all been one way traffic.' She continued to hold his hands. 'I wonder if you might be prepared to extend your loving friendship until tomorrow morning?'

'I've come quite unprepared – I have neither a toothbrush nor a change of underwear with me but after the last few months I'm prepared to live that dangerously!'

27

There was less than a week to go until Christmas. Peter arranged to spend the nights of Christmas Eve and Christmas Day with his family and then called Jenny and Michael to say that he was planning a dinner party for New Year's Eve. Michael had been out when he called but rang back to say that he was free that evening and, even if he had not been, he would have cancelled almost anything to join the party. He added that, in the light of Peter's revelations when they had last met, it might also be of considerable ethological interest! Jenny told him that she and Ann would be staying in Newcastle for a week from Sunday 21st of December and that she also was free. She asked if he would be inviting Ann as well. He replied that, for a variety of different reasons, he felt it would be difficult for all of them if he did but he might invite Sue if she were on her own that evening. He decided to probe gently the next time he had a coffee with her and Ann.

He went down the stairs that evening and invited himself in for a cup of coffee. These occasions were frequently strained with often long silences punctuated by their sporadic conversational efforts. It was clear that there was little interaction between Sue and Ann. The one still had a degree of desolation and remained burdened by a sense of guilt following her husband's death while the other was rudderless and, without an anchor, uncertain about where her life might take her next. Ann's presence had revived painful memories and her wretchedness had not been good for Sue.

Peter broke one of the longer silences. 'You said you were planning to look for another job,' he began looking at Ann. 'Any irons in the fire as yet?'

'No, it's still early days and this is not the ideal time of year to be job-hunting. I think I might get out of London.'

'Are there not more opportunities in London?'

'Yes, but there's also a growing range of opportunities in the provinces in regional television and with an increasing number of independent production companies, including several start-ups. These often prefer to be in the provinces where rents are cheaper. I shall start looking seriously in the New Year. More independent companies are coming into play as more programme-making is contracted out. Accommodation will also be less expensive in the provinces.'

'What are your plans for Christmas? I understand that you'll be going to see your Mum in Newcastle.'

'How do you know that?' she said sharply. She then added, 'Have you seen Jenny again?'

'Yes, we had a drink and a pizza together last week.'

'That seems a strange thing to do.'

'Not at all – I'm fond of Jenny and she's good company.'

'It somehow doesn't seem appropriate.'

'I really don't understand why you should think that,

Ann. There was nothing inappropriate about it. There's no reason why we shouldn't be friends just because you and I have parted company.'

'I still feel it's not right. I'm not sure which of you is taking the lead in this but it just feels wrong.'

'Ann, neither of us is taking a lead, as you put it. You're reading into a simple friendship much more than is there. It does not and will not undermine Jenny's feelings for you in any way. She's going to come round to my flat with some other friends on New Year's Eve.' He realised that this was the first time he had used the possessive pronoun in the first person singular when referring to the flat which had been theirs. He saw that it had not gone unnoticed by Ann. She remained silent. He turned to Sue. 'I can assure you that it will not be a noisy or a riotous party and that you won't be disturbed. What plans do you have for Christmas?'

'I'm fortunate, I have a large family who have always been very supportive. You may remember I have two sisters and two brothers living in Lancashire and the West Midlands and what seems like dozens of nephews and nieces. I shall stay with two of them for the week that Ann is away and will be very well looked after indeed. I have even wondered whether I might go back to Lancashire to work.'

'You told me that you were still helping in the hospice shop. Are you still doing that?'

'Yes, and I'm beginning to do some other things as well. A colleague at school has persuaded me to join a choir and that's been good. We rehearse once a week and have three concerts a year. I sometimes join other members of the choir for a drink in the pub after rehearsals. I'm in a much better place than I was when we had lunch at the end of August.'

'You're probably better off here in London amongst colleagues you know and with the possibility of new friends through the choir.'

'Possibly, but I shan't rush into making any decisions and will see how things go over the next twelve months or so.'

'Maybe the next twelve months will bring good things for all three of us.'

* * *

The following morning the telephone rang and Julie's voice wished him good morning. 'My parents arrived in London yesterday,' she announced, 'and I shall be flying in tomorrow. Sadly, my stay will be shorter than I had anticipated. I shall only be in London for four days, flying back the day after Christmas. I'll explain when we meet. I expect you'll be staying with your family over Christmas but would you be free to join us for dinner in two days' time? We'll be staying at the White House Hotel,' she paused, 'after all, where else would Americans stay! Shall we say 7.30?'

'I shall be there.'

Forty-eight hours later Peter travelled to the White House close to Regent's Park. Julie met him in the foyer and introduced him to her parents, Bob and Marlene. This was their first visit to Europe. 'We Americans are not very adventurous,' Bob explained. 'A journey to the East Coast is normally about as exciting as it gets for us. We're planning to see something of London and then go on to Paris for a weekend in the New Year where Julie will meet up with us again and help us with the language. You Brits have so many countries and so many languages on your doorstep. I don't know how you cope with that!'

Peter laughed. 'By and large we don't or not very well. The British are disgracefully bad at languages. They often have little incentive to learn as English is almost always everyone's second language if it's not their mother tongue. But we largely hold you responsible for that as the most populous Anglophone country in the world.'

'Yes, not many of us learn and can speak another language and many Americans are deeply suspicious of those who can,' said Julie, 'especially if it's French! I can at least expose my parents to a little European culture while I'm here and in France.'

'We tend to think of the Brits as rather sophisticated – a bit like people from Boston but with superior accents.'

'I think that would be a serious mistake. This country, like all others, has all sorts and conditions of people. It would be wrong to think that those who speak standard English are necessarily cultured.'

'Well, we have a few days here. I know that some things will be closed part of the time but we shall go to the theatre and visit one or two museums before we fly to Paris. We shall make the most of it.'

'I'm sorry I'll not be in London for longer but there has been a change in my life,' said Julie. 'My company is posting me back to New York and I have to be there by the beginning of March. That's why I've had to truncate this trip. I shall be very occupied for the first two months of next year. I'm very sad to be leaving after only two and a half years but I'm afraid I'm not the master or mistress of my own destiny.'

'We shall be glad when she's back in the States,' said Marlene, 'even if it is on the East Coast.'

It was shortly after 9.30 when Bob said, 'We're going to leave you two to have coffee and a drink. We're still a bit jet-lagged having come from Seattle and with a seven-hour time difference. I know it's still early afternoon there but we need to catch up on some sleep. It's easy for Julie with just an hour to adjust to.' They said their goodnights and left.

'I'm glad that you've met them. I shall be busy over the next few days being a tourist guide even though many things will be closed between now and the twenty-sixth.'

'When did you hear that you were being sent back to New York?'

'Only last week. It seems that there's been a crisis in the office there and the manager has been fired. I don't know the details but I have to fly over there for a few days in the second week in January to meet staff and the interim manager. No doubt I'll hear all the grisly particulars then. I really am very sorry to be leaving Lyon. It's such an interesting city and I have made good friends there as well as some from a little further away. I'm going to get each of us a brandy and then you can tell me what your plans are.' They waited for the drinks to arrive.

'I intend to have the first draft of my book complete by the end of January and then revise it and seek literary advice on how best to proceed. I have no illusions – it might bomb, but even if that happens I'll console myself with the thought that it's better to have tried and failed than not to have tried at all. I have gained so much from this year – and I'm only half way through it.'

'How is Sally and would she be able to help?'

'She is much better and more relaxed. She finally got back to England after the appalling snow storms which must have affected you as well.'

'Yes, the city was almost isolated and some of the major roads were impassable. But going back to your writing. Would Sally be able to help?'

'I think she might be prepared to offer an opinion. If she does, I hope she'll feel able to deliver uncomfortable messages without any concessions to my sensitivities.'

'Do you have any doubt that she'll be able to do that?'

'No, but it's important that I should be realistic, particularly at the end of a year which has oscillated between the unreal and the surreal.'

'It would be good to keep in touch – I should love to hear how you get on.'

'Will you come back to France?'

'Possibly for a vacation but I think it's unlikely I'll come back to work there. I simply don't know what life's got in store for me professionally or personally back in New York. I think this is the end of a short-lived but never-to-be-forgotten idyll.' She looked across at him. 'Or perhaps not quite the end, if you would be prepared to be an English gentleman and see me to my room.' Peter smiled as she took his hand and led him to the lifts.

They lay back relaxed in the bed. 'C'était pour la mémoire,' she whispered in his ear.

'Elle était une mémoire très précieuse,' he whispered back.

Julie laughed. 'Something has just occurred to me. When my marriage broke up, my mother hoped that I would remarry although there was no-one in sight and it was certainly not a high priority for me at that stage. But there was one saying that she repeated constantly. It was that "there are more good fish in the sea than ever came out of it". I suddenly thought that you were a remarkably good fish to have caught, albeit temporarily, and now sadly I have to let you go but I'm sure you'll be caught again, even if it doesn't happen quite so serendipitously. Take care and be happy, my loving friend.' Then as an afterthought she added, 'And you should safeguard your other loving friend. I can see that she is very special to you,' she grinned mischievously, 'or should it be loving friends in the plural?'

28

Peter's family arrived in Wimbledon to re-enact the well-rehearsed rituals of Christmas. After the traditional visit to church, they gathered for drinks in the lounge and the ceremonial unwrapping of presents while Matt and Jilly tried, and largely failed, to keep a note of the donors of gifts to their two sons. It was not long before the boys decamped to other parts of the house to test their new acquisitions and the men relaxed as Molly and Jilly retired to the kitchen to complete the final preparations for Christmas lunch.

'This is very different from last year,' said Geoffrey. 'Peter's life has changed so dramatically since then.' He looked across at Peter. 'Did you have any inkling that Ann would be leaving you when you were here last Christmas?'

'None at all. I guess in times past I'd have been considered a cuckold. Maybe there were signs that I should have detected but I didn't.'

'Are you being a little hard on yourself?'

'Possibly. Perhaps, even if she hadn't fallen for one of her colleagues, it might not have worked out longer term anyway. Marriage or any relationship is such an uncontrolled experiment.'

'That suggests a lack of commitment.'

'No, not really. We can never really know how relationships are going to evolve in the longer term.'

'I'm not sure that I would agree with that. Marriages need to be worked on to be kept in good repair.'

'Yes, but even then, they cannot necessarily be expected to work in every case.'

'Have you heard from Ann recently?'

'Yes, she came to the flat earlier this month just after I got back from France. Her relationship had just broken up. It seems that he was, and is, a serial womaniser. She's very bitter about it.'

'Are you likely to get together again?'

'She did suggest it but I have said no firmly. I do feel very sorry for her. She has been devastated by the experience.'

'Is that a final no?'

'It has to be – my life has changed hugely since the summer.'

'So the Robson family is no longer a part of your life.'

'Not entirely. I've seen Jenny on a few occasions and she'll be coming to a dinner party I've organised for New Year's Eve.'

'Is that entirely proper?'

'Ann thinks it isn't but I was always fond of Jenny. She's a good friend. I went with her to see her mother during the summer and, to answer your direct question, it has been entirely proper.'

'Anyhow, Peter has an amazing girlfriend,' chipped in Matt. 'I met her in the autumn. She's a very smart cookie and speaks excellent German – much better than mine.'

'How did you come to meet her?'

'Through Peter. She's a journalist and is writing a series of articles on German and French attitudes to the possibility of Britain joining the European Community. They're based on interviews with people in both countries as well as with some expatriates. They're being published in a journal called Europe Watch which I've been buying as I was interested to read them. It's a serious magazine and I thought the articles were excellent; her insights were very sharp and her descriptive powers outstanding. Such a development could have a major impact on the financial sector and would open up all sorts of career opportunities.'

Molly and Jilly had come back into the room during this exchange. 'So who is this girlfriend?' asked Molly. 'We've not heard of her.'

'Yes, you have. She's the owner of the house in France where I've been staying, although she's been away for most of the autumn in Germany and elsewhere in France. I told you about her in the summer when I was here.'

'So is it serious and when are we going to meet her?'

'I'm sure you will sometime, but girlfriend is not quite the correct designation – she is both rather more and rather less than that.'

'Now you're talking in riddles. Lunch is ready and I suspect the riddles in the crackers will be less opaque than yours.' Molly however continued the cross-examination of her son. 'What do you plan to do when this year is over?'

'I really don't know at present. It all depends how things work out. I've written more than two-thirds of a first draft of my book which I shall complete in January and then spend a month or so revising. After that, I shall have to approach a literary agent and see if it is publishable. Beyond that, who knows? But I've always had a plan B – I can go back to the law.'

'Will you be going back to France?'

'I don't know at this stage – I should like to but it depends when Sally goes back there and if she's prepared to offer me accommodation again. I think I'd accept if she did but it's a matter for her.'

'It sounds like a very semi-detached relationship. I hope you know what you're doing.'

'So do I, but I'm not necessarily sure that I do and if I've got it wrong then it will be for me to sort it out. Either way, I'm entirely relaxed about it.'

'Well, it is good to have all the family here again for Christmas.' Molly looked across at Matt. 'And will you be staying in Germany for the foreseeable future?'

'Yes. As I said, so much is changing now and there are innumerable opportunities in the financial sector.'

'This is far too serious a discussion for Christmas Day – let's go for lunch. Geoffrey is already attacking the bird. He calls it carving but it is more like butchery when he gets under way. He justifies his approach on the grounds that it's better to get the job done quickly and have the meal hot rather than do it elegantly but slowly.'

Matt and Peter looked across at one another. This was a perennial comment reviving memories of past Christmases.

* * *

The torpid and languorous days between Christmas and New Year stretched ahead, dedicated by some to frenzied spasms of shopping interspersed with periods of unrestrained consumption of alcohol. Peter felt no compulsion to engage in either of these activities and retreated to his flat to occupy himself with writing. He was well provisioned, having been persuaded by his mother to carry away large quantities of cold turkey and mince pies. The day after Boxing Day he collected Sally and they drove to the Brownings' flat in Highgate. They drew up at a tall white tower block and ascended to the fourth floor. The curtains had not been drawn in the reception room and Peter was drawn over to the windows to look at the immense, brightly-lit panorama of the city to the south.

Jonny came over to join him. 'Often we don't draw these curtains. We just enjoy the view winter and summer, night and day. Do you know this building?'

'No, I don't know this part of London at all.'

'It's called Highpoint and is well known in architectural circles. It was designed by Lubetkin who also designed the penguin pool at London Zoo, which I'm sure you must know.'

Peter smiled inwardly, recalling his visit with Cass and Stefan more than a year earlier. 'Yes, I have been to the zoo, relatively recently in fact,' he said as he winked at Sally.

'Do I detect that it has some particular significance for you?'

'Yes – but it's a complicated story.'

'Well, the form of the building is known as international style. This developed between the wars and is characterised by rectilinear forms, little decoration, open interior spaces and light. I mustn't lecture you on architectural history but we love it.'

Tilly came into the room and embraced them both. She looked at Sally. 'How are you now after our experiences of being snowbound? That was a pretty dreadful journey back to Calais, wasn't it? Have you thawed out fully?'

'Yes – but at least we had a very convivial dinner at that hotel en route to cheer ourselves up, and thank you for arranging for your caretaker to go and check on my house. It's good to know that all is well.'

'So what are you up to now?'

'I've a lot of work to do on those projects which I put on hold for my Franco-German project. I'm planning to return to France and Germany, but quite when depends on how the political initiatives develop. It all might change after the general election, which I imagine will probably be next year.'

'Have you decided when you'll be going back to France?'

'Not yet. I need access to libraries here for much of what I'm planning to do.'

'And will you go back to France, Peter?'

'That all depends if there is an invitation forthcoming from the landlady.'

Sally looked across. 'I think that's a real possibility.'

'Then I think there's a real probability that it will be accepted.'

'Well, you must let us know when that will be. Now that we have a key, we can open it up for you and get some basic provisions in for your arrival.'

'That would be very kind.'

* * *

Tilly turned to them over dinner. 'May I ask indelicately how things stand between you two? We have known you, Sally, for a long time and have seen a fair amount of you, Peter, in the last six months.'

Sally and Peter looked at one another.

'Tilly, I think you've been, as you said, very indelicate and put them on the spot and it may be a spot they would prefer not to inhabit,' said Jonny. He turned to Sally and Peter, 'I think you can, as the Americans might do in these circumstances, plead the Fifth Amendment.'

'To do so,' said Sally, 'would probably be an answer in itself, but one which could then be interpreted in a number of different ways.'

Peter looked across at her. 'We can, of course, prevaricate, equivocate, dissemble, obfuscate and generally be economical with the truth.' He laughed, 'And you can see that I have learned to use a thesaurus in the last six months.'

They all joined in the laughter. 'That was one of the most superior examples of prevarication that I've ever come across,' Sally responded. She turned to Tilly and Jonny. 'You are longstanding and very dear friends so I'll answer for myself and leave Peter to speak for himself which, as you have heard, he is well able to do. I think you know we met by chance, twice, and then subsequently by design. We have got to know each other well, very well, and have many things in common. I have felt very comfortable in Peter's company although I'm not sure that he has always done so in mine. I have shared things with Peter which I have shared with almost no-one else. I have no wish to change anything at the moment. As for the future, I'm happy in the knowledge that it simply comes one day at a time.'

'That's very frank of you,' said Jonny, 'and, considering that you've been ambushed by my dear wife, I can understand that you might have some reservations about being fully open, particularly when you and Peter have not had a chance to collude beforehand. Peter, do you have anything to say – silence under these circumstances is perfectly acceptable?'

'I have little to add.' He smiled. 'Sally is right that I have not always felt comfortable in her company. She can be very challenging but I've found that exciting and motivating as well as discomfiting. I wouldn't wish that to change. She has had a liberating influence on me. I've had a richer experience of places, events and emotions in the last nine months or so than I've had at any time in my life. I suspect that such experiences cannot continue at this high level indefinitely, although I'm sure they may well do so for a time. But there have been quieter and more introspective moments and these have also been ones to treasure.'

Tilly walked round the table and kissed each of them. 'Thank you. It was, I know, an undiplomatic question but I have no regrets in asking it and I hope neither of you do. I'm sure you'll conduct a post-mortem on the evening after you've left. It was a question born out of love and affection for both of you.'

As they drove back, Peter asked, 'Did you mind being asked that question by Tilly?'

'I might have done three months ago but Jonny's comments and your intervention gave me a few moments to think and, no, I was happy to respond. I only hope that I didn't say anything that was problematic for you.'

'No, you didn't. Perhaps there'll come a time when we shall have such a discussion à deux but I'm sure you would say, and I would agree, that now is not that time.'

Sally smiled. 'You have changed so much in the last year.'

'Several people have said that, with varying degrees of approbation or, in the case of my mother, mild disapproval!'

'And I also have changed.'

29

Jenny called Peter from Newcastle to say that Ann had been invited out for dinner on New Year's Eve by colleagues and that Sue would be on her own. He went down to Sue's flat to ask her to join them for dinner but she protested she was now so unused to social occasions that she might dampen the spirits of the others. He insisted that, if she were to join them, there would only be the five of them and she could always retreat to her flat if she wanted to withdraw. She finally agreed to accept.

As midnight on New Year's Eve approached, Michael looked questioningly at the others. 'We have talked of many things this evening. I was thinking, before I joined you all, that in some ways I'm the odd one out here. There have been changes in all your lives over the last year or so – some major and some minor (mainly major) while my life has been proceeding along well established and apparently immutable lines. It led me to wonder what 1970 might have in store for all of us and the future in general. I was reminded of something that I had read when in my teens. I searched it out on my bookshelves earlier today. It was this: "the past is but the beginning of a beginning, and that all that is and has been is but the twilight of the dawn". It always seemed to me that this encouraged a positive view of the future without denying the past. I wonder what each of us might see for our futures and I think it would be very interesting to share hopes and ambitions, although each of us, of course, has the right to retain our innermost thoughts within our own private domain.'

'I think I recognise your quotation,' said Sue. 'It's H G Wells writing on the future.'

'Yes, you're right. I'm conscious that my own wishes for next year and the years beyond are limited to one but it is a substantial wish and one which I have a capacity to influence, although the final decision will not be in my hands. Jenny and Peter know that I've had an ambition for some time to enter parliament and I've been shortlisted as prospective parliamentary candidate for a constituency in the north-west so it would be close to my home turf. It will be very interesting since it's a seat that Labour has held for many years, so selection is likely to be followed by election as long as the candidate doesn't do anything totally disastrous. The interviews will be held next month as there's likely to be an election this coming year. More commonly, new candidates are expected to win their spurs in an unwinnable seat before getting a run in more propitious circumstances.'

'That would be great,' said Sue. 'I would vote for you – I'm a Lancastrian born and bred.'

'Do you have wishes for the coming year, Sue?'

'Yes, but they are quite modest ones. I'm beginning to see the possibilities of new beginnings and new friends. I've already told Peter, and was saying to Michael when we were talking quietly together a moment ago, that I've joined a choir and I'm also putting in more time at the hospice shop. I feel these possibilities are being reinforced by occasions such as our dinner here tonight. This evening has been wonderful. It's the first party of any sort that I've been to since – well you know when. Thank you, Peter, for persuading me to join you. You pointed out I had an easy escape route if it was too overwhelming but it hasn't been, and I certainly shan't leave until next year is under way. I just hope that my temporary house guest is starting to look positively to her future.'

'I too,' added Jenny, 'although after spending a week with her in Newcastle I don't think there's much chance of that happening soon.'

'And what would you like the New Year to hold for you, Jenny?'

'I don't know but I suppose the honest answer is uncertainty. That has been the dominant characteristic of the last year and I have found it exhilarating and motivating. Much of that has come from new or changed relationships, suggesting the possibility of further new relationships and developments.'

'That's a very positive but also a very general view; it almost qualifies as a politician's response! Do you have any more specific ambitions?'

'Not that I can articulate at the moment. I'd only add that I'm very open to new opportunities, both professional and social.'

'That's fair but how about you, Peter? You've absented yourself from the routine of everyday life to pursue a dream.

Maybe more significantly you've released yourself from your inhibitions and developed and grown relationships with the result that, without wishing to sound patronising, you've changed incalculably.'

'I'm not sure I can add much to that or to what Jenny has said. I do, however, have some very concrete ambitions, as you know, and have set myself various targets for the completion of my novel.'

'Would you, could you, ever return to your previous incarnation?'

'That's not a straightforward question and I really don't know the answer. It will depend at least in part upon the success or failure of my literary efforts. Perhaps, like Jenny, I too am prepared to revel in a state of uncertainty.'

Michael looked at Sally. 'I seem to have slipped into the role of inquisitor. Perhaps it just comes naturally to lawyers! We haven't met before this evening so I feel hesitant to ask you to expose your wishes and ambitions.'

She smiled. 'This is the second inquisition I have been exposed to within the last few days. The previous one was by old family friends. I feel I should respond as I have happily absorbed the aspirations of others and it would seem churlish not to, but I shall pick my words with care. It's now very nearly midnight and what I have to say will conveniently fill that period while Peter ensures that we all have a full glass in our hands. I have some very concrete ambitions as you do. I've learned much from the last year and have undertaken a commission quite unlike anything that I've done previously. It has sharpened my analytical skills and enhanced my sensibilities and given me a new understanding of time, of place and, above all, of people. Those experiences will colour and shape all that I do in the coming year and beyond. I've also acquired new friends, including some remarkably good ones, hence my presence here tonight. I too, like Jenny, look forward to experiencing further the unpredictability and indeterminacy of events and the ambiguities of people. Now it's only one minute to midnight and I shall clamber off the hook upon which you have so neatly tried to impale us! I would only add that if I were ever to be arraigned for some serious offence, I should prefer to have you acting for the defence rather than for the prosecution!'

'Thank you for the compliment. It would be interesting to meet up again in a year's time but now let's welcome 1970!'

* * *

Sally and Peter were having coffee in the kitchen the following morning when Jenny came in at about ten in a nightgown. 'I'm sorry I've not dressed yet but I was dead to the world after last night. Michael was amazing but, as far as I can remember, I think we all managed to avoid any major indiscretions.'

'Probably, but one can never be quite sure what Michael picks up; his perspicacity is remarkable and, of course, he has the advantage of having known me for well over fifteen years.'

'So what indiscretions do you have to conceal?' asked Jenny with a smile as she poured herself some coffee. The doorbell rang before he had a chance to answer.

'Literally saved by the bell! Now I have the chance to dodge that question,' said Peter as he got up to answer it. He was surprised to find Ann at the door. He started to say 'Happy New Year – I hope you had a good evening …' but was cut short.

'Has Jenny been here all night?' she demanded loudly.

'Yes.'

'Why is she still here?'

'Because I suggested she should stay the night.'

'Why? That was quite improper.'

'I asked her so that she wouldn't have to travel across London at a time when there was almost no public transport. We had a very good time last night.'

'You bastard!' she shouted. 'I don't want to hear you revelling in it!'

Jenny came out of the kitchen before Peter could respond, having heard her sister's raised voice. 'What the hell do you think you're doing here?' Ann demanded.

'I think I heard Peter say that he invited me to stay the night and that is what I did,' she said coolly.

'You're no better than a tart,' Ann shouted.

'Hold it,' said Peter harshly. 'You should stop right now before you say anything further which you will certainly regret. Your sister is certainly not a tart and you should apologise straightaway.'

'Certainly not.' She looked back at Jenny. 'And what is that gown you're wearing? It looks like mine!'

'It was in the cupboard in the bedroom and I put it on while I had a coffee. Here,' she said angrily, 'you can have the bloody thing. I certainly don't want to go around in your cast-offs!' She undid the belt and threw it on the floor and stood there absolutely naked, staring defiantly at her sister. Peter laughed.

'This is far from funny – put it on again at once! I won't have you stripping off in front of all and sundry.'

Jenny was incandescent with rage by this time and almost on the verge of tears. Very slowly, her voice shaking with emotion, she said, 'I'm an adult and I will choose when and where I strip off and it has absolutely nothing to do with you.' Very slowly, and still looking defiantly at her sister, she picked up the gown and put it on again.

Sally had come to the kitchen door during this angry exchange and was looking quizzically at the three of them.

'And who the hell's that with that supercilious expression on her face? What's she doing here?' Ann continued to rage.

Peter said very quietly, 'She's a very good friend and again the reason that she is here has absolutely nothing to do with you. Now you've caused enough upset for one morning and you're making a fool of yourself, so just go.'

Sue had heard the noise and had come up the stairs and she took Ann's arm. 'Peter's right, Ann. Come back down to my flat.' She led her away, shaking and tearful.

Peter put his arm round Jenny. 'Come back to the kitchen and have some more coffee.'

She sat silently for some time, angry and unhappy. Eventually she said, 'I'm so sorry. I shouldn't have taken the gown off but I was so angry at what she said and her insults.'

'It was a wonderfully impactful and dramatic gesture,' said Sally. 'I think in retrospect we'll be able to laugh at the episode. It provided quite a tableau. When I came into sight she obviously imagined that we had been up to all sorts of orgiastic behaviour to mark the New Year!'

Jenny looked at her and smiled. 'Thank you, yes, you're right and at some stage I shall put things right with Ann. She is after all my sister, even if at the moment I feel that I never want to see her again.'

Peter hugged her. 'I'll talk to Ann later. She and I do need to sort things out. She's not only upsetting and alienating family and friends but she's at risk of becoming a woman whose life will be dominated by resentment at the way the cards have fallen for her. And that will make it increasingly difficult for her to move forward.' The doorbell rang again. 'Oh God, I hope that this is not round two.' He answered the door to find Sue standing there alone. She joined them for coffee.

'Peter, Jenny, I'm so sorry about what happened. I didn't know that Ann had come up to your flat until I heard raised voices. I'd been telling her about our party yesterday and hadn't realised that she was misinterpreting my account of the evening in such a way. It must have been very difficult and what she said to you, Jenny, must have been very hurtful. I'm so sorry that I was unable to stop her coming up here. In her present state her imagination is working overtime.'

'Sue, you really can't be held responsible in any way. You've already been very good to Ann, and to me, by accommodating her.'

'It was the least I could do as she was so kind and supportive to me after Andrew died. I've been talking to her and putting her straight. She has calmed down for now and I think would like to apologise. I wouldn't dream, of course, of turning her out but I think it would be good for all of us if she were to move on fairly soon. She still carries a torch for you, Peter, but I can see that your life has moved on. I understand that and I'm happy for you. I just hope that Ann can find a future for herself.'

'I too,' said Jenny.

'May I suggest that you leave it for a day or so before you talk to Ann? She needs time to reflect and I'm certain she's doing just that. I also wanted to say thank you to all three of you, and I'd say the same to Michael if he were here. Last night was the best evening I've had for a very long time. I'm just so grateful that you persuaded me to join you. It took me a long time to go to sleep last night because Michael's questions and all our answers led me to think much more positively about the future. So thank you and you all get a hug and a kiss.'

'She's a lovely woman,' said Jenny after Sue had left. 'I should go and get showered and dressed and,' she laughed, 'I apologise again for being such a brazen hussy!'

'Ann may still carry a torch for you,' said Sally after Jenny had left, 'but Jenny is carrying armfuls of them.'

'I'm not sure about that. I've never been, or rather I've never seen myself as, a source of attraction to the other sex.'

'That in many ways is why you are. Many women avoid vain and self-regarding men like the plague. Now I've embarrassed you,' she said laughing. 'What are we going to do on this wet and windy day? How about a walk when the rain lets up, and with Jenny too if she'd like to join us?'

When Jenny returned she turned down the suggestion to join them for a walk. She had agreed to join Cass and Stefan in going to a concert that evening. 'I agree with Sue. It was a wonderful evening and I am so happy to meet you, Sally. Peter, thank you for your support. I'm still embarrassed by my behaviour but,' she giggled, 'only a little. Although I was so angry, I rather enjoyed making the gesture – probably more than I should have done! Sally's right. It will be a story to share with selected friends and I shall share it with Cass and Stefan this evening. You must join us sometime for some music, Sally. I will make it up with Ann, but perhaps not today.'

* * *

'Well, what are your immediate plans for 1970?'

'I am going to be spending a lot of time in libraries mugging up on the background of writers who have lived in France. I want to increase my knowledge of the literature and review any critical analyses I can find. Then there is the other project which I have in mind, to explore the extent to which British expatriates are integrating or failing to integrate with local communities. I sense that quite a number of the more linguistically confident who live permanently in France are starting to get involved in local issues. I also need to acquire a better background in French and German history before I return to follow up my visits in the autumn. But what about you?'

'That's one hell of an agenda. I feel exhausted just hearing you spell it out! Mine is much simpler. I have set myself a target of finishing a first draft of the novel by the end of January. I shall spend two months revising it and then, with considerable trepidation, I shall open it up for comment and criticism.'

'That may sound more focused but I don't underestimate the challenges involved.'

'Do you have an idea when you might go back to Sarlat?'

'None at all; it all depends upon how long it takes me to do what I need to do drawing on library resources in this country. I can't see that I shall get back there until the end of April at the earliest. But how about you?'

'I've learned from you how serious a business writing is. Now that I've established a rhythm, I find it totally compulsive and there are times that I resent external distractions and time away from my desk. I find myself thinking continuously about the narrative and dialogue.' He looked across at Sally, 'But there are also times when diversions and distractions outweigh all that.'

'I'm pleased at that. I should like to suggest that after tomorrow we lock ourselves away in our own flats and perhaps get together at weekends. After our walk, I'm sure there will be some suitably sentimental film which has been revived for New Year's Day on the television. I should like to snuggle up to you on the settee and watch. There's just a risk that such a film might stimulate lustful thoughts so I should like to stay for another night, if I may?'

'That's extraordinarily forward of you, but what a good idea!'

* * *

Peter walked down to Sue's flat the following day after Sally had left. Sue let him in. 'Ann is in the lounge,' she said. 'She's very down and full of remorse. I think your timing is right.

I'll leave you alone with her and then perhaps we should all have coffee together.'

He walked into the lounge. Ann was sitting with her head in her hands but when she saw Peter she got up and went across, put her arms round him and held him very tightly. 'I'm so sorry. You were right. I've been a fool and I behaved appallingly. Sue has been so good to me. When I had calmed down she spoke to me very bluntly and I realised that my behaviour has done nothing but upset the people I care about. I know what's happened has left me simply feeling bitter and dejected and I must get over that. She told me what a good evening it was and how much she had enjoyed the company. In my shrewish mind I misread the scene in a totally unjustifiable way and, even if I hadn't, it was no business of mine. It's just difficult sometimes to relinquish the role of the bossy older sister. I know I must move from here and find another job and I shall steer well clear of office Romeos in the future. I won't make that mistake again. I must also go and see Jenny and hold out an olive branch or even a whole tree. What I said was unforgivable.'

'Sally and I sat down with Jenny after you'd gone. She was very upset but she's not one to bear grudges. She would welcome an approach and, if I may give advice, the sooner the better.'

'I know, you're right. I didn't get to meet your other friend but Sue said that she was lovely and, although I say it with some reluctance, from what Sue says, a very good fit for you.'

'Thank you, that's generous. I don't know if this is for

the long term or not but I'm happy at present and can live with that. I have brought your nightgown down for you.'

'Thank you, but I'll never be able to wear it again without feeling a deep sense of shame. I'll give it to Jenny partly as a peace offering. Anyhow, it looked better on her than it ever it did on me. I'd like to give you another hug and just say that I hope we'll be happy. I've learnt several very painful lessons in the last day or so but I'm pleased I have. I'm also happy that New Year's Eve has given Sue such a lift. She's more alive than she's been at any time since that awful evening when Andrew had that accident.'

30

The first three months of the year were cold and snowy. Peter and Sally went to earth in their own flats determined to meet their self-imposed targets, each living and working in their own circumscribed worlds. The rapprochement between Ann and Jenny and Ann's departure for a new job in Birmingham were noted with approbation but failed to distract them from their undertakings. News of the world outside scarcely encroached on their consciousness. External events seemed to be happenings on a distant planet. They only came together occasionally as their determination to meet their specified objectives led to a reduction in the frequency of their weekend trysts, and increasingly these became more formal and distant than before. Sally called him in mid-March and suggested that they might go away for two or three days over the Easter Bank Holiday weekend.

They met on Good Friday and drove to the Cotswolds. They checked into a country hotel which offered log fires amongst its other attractions. Peter was able to relate that his novel had finally been revised to the point where he felt he could not make many more significant improvements and it was now in typed form. 'Would you like me to read it or would you prefer me not to?' asked Sally.

'I'm sure it could be polished further but a week ago I felt I'd reached the point of diminishing returns. I should love you to do so, but only on two conditions. The first is that it should not interrupt your own work and the second is that you must be brutally frank in delivering an opinion. I'm aware of the comment that everyone has a book in them and in most cases that is where it should stay. I'm ready to be told that.'

'OK, I'm happy to read it and in fact would very much like to. I've witnessed the period of its gestation. At the same time I should issue a health warning. I'm not a professional reader and I certainly should not be the sole arbiter. I do have a friend who is an agent who specialises in literary fiction and, if it seems appropriate, I could approach her but that would be up to you. Do you have a typescript with you?'

'Unsurprisingly, I do.'

'Would you be happy if I were to read it on my own after the weekend? It would be easier to read it when I'm alone and I would rather it didn't intrude on our time here. There are things which I need to talk about with you.'

* * *

It was dry the following day and they set out to walk to Chipping Camden for a pub lunch. They walked in silence for a time until Sally turned to Peter. 'I'll be going back to Sarlat towards the end of April. I need a prolonged period of solitude to work through all the notes I've made in the last three months and to read all the books I've bought for my project on expatriate authors.' She paused and took his hand. 'I also have to think through certain personal issues of which the most prominent in my mind is you. Before I say any more, I do want you to understand a number of things. I suspect some of what I'm about to say might upset you which is the last thing I want to do but it might be unavoidable if I'm to reveal everything that's on my mind. I shall also say some things which won't upset you but they may, knowing you, make you blush. Please, will you let me just talk and hear me out? I've been rehearsing what I need to say for days and it's going to be difficult enough and I may not say it very coherently.'

'I don't think there's anything I can say in response to that.'

She hesitated. 'Although I've been rehearsing what I want to say, it's still difficult to start. Perhaps I should start with our first chance meeting. There was something about that first meeting in Northumberland, which generated a spark despite my defensive efforts to disconcert you. I know that you must have felt something too as you sought me out last March. It was the same instinct that led me to invite you to France when you wrote in June and even more strongly when I suggested that you stay on. So much has flowed from those first few weeks in Sarlat. I achieved a feeling of contentment last summer which I have rarely experienced before. Life has also been very fulfilling for me professionally over the last nine months, maybe more so than ever before, and you have been a constant in my life over that time. At the same time, your life has expanded and you're far from being the man you were when we first met. During the course of New Year's Eve, at one stage I was talking quietly with Jenny and Sue, and we all felt that your decision to break free from the chains of your conventional life had been life-changing in the most positive of ways. I think this was only indirectly the consequence of your parting from Ann. It has been, in my judgement, mainly the result of your courage in taking your life into your own hands and following your own personal star. It has been a privilege to have been an observer – and a very close one at that. You've been a steadfast friend and I've shared more with you than I think I have ever done with anyone else. We were catechised by the Brownings and interrogated by Michael at Christmas time and their questionings have compelled me to examine myself in a way that I haven't done for many years and in a way which I have found both difficult and disquieting.

'From the way I teased you when we first met and on many occasions since, you've been aware that however close we have become there has always been a degree of reserve on my part and, I hasten to say, that has nothing to do specifically with you. It comes from a defensive instinct which resides somewhere deep inside my psyche. I want to try and explain the origins of that reserve and that will involve my sharing emotions with you which I have never shared with another soul and ones which I generally prefer to keep concealed.

'You know something of my childhood. The loss of my brother George followed by Dad's suicide and Mum's cancer, all over a short period of time, has left a permanent mark. I think most of all it was Dad's death which cast the longest and deepest shadow over my adult life. I've already told you that it left me and Mum with an ineradicable sense of guilt because we had failed to recognise the level of his depression and despair, and thus we both felt we had failed as human beings. It destroyed Mum psychologically, and then the cancer destroyed her physically and cruelly in less than a year. I spent some time with her and nursed her at the end but it was difficult to get close because she was so damaged emotionally. I think at times she even resented me as the one healthy survivor and soon to be the only survivor from what had once been a united family.

'The reasons for my reserve are, I suppose, twofold. The first is that, having lost so much, I'm very wary of deep emotional entanglements and concerned that they too may turn out to be transitory and even searing emotionally, so I hide within a carapace which has largely protected me until now. I've devised an approach to all contacts which allows me to engage easily with people with a mixture of light banter and intelligent conversation but also permits me to deflect any moves towards developing closer relationships. The result is that my relationships with others, particularly men, have been ephemeral, again until now. Don't misunderstand me. I'm not pleading that I've had an unhappy life – in most ways it is, and has been, an interesting and fulfilling one. The other reason relates to Dad's suicide. Circumstances accounted for this to a large extent, but I've always been conscious that there's a substantial genetic element in depression. Since then it has always been at the back of my mind that this might also be my fate at some unspecified time in the future. I once said to you that I didn't want your life to be afflicted by my demons and that remains true.

'And this brings me back to you. I said I needed to discuss something with you and I know this has not been a discussion but more of a monologue. At the end of our first week together in France, I felt something that I've rarely felt in my adult life and the smell of pine needles still evokes powerful and pleasurable memories. You felt that the act of sex would mark the start of a commitment and were initially upset that I seemed to treat our making love with a degree of coolness which you found difficult to reconcile with your experience. I've never really said to you that your adaptation to and acceptance of the role of a loving friend has been of inestimable importance to me, but I do so now. Your tolerance of my sensitivities has allowed me to enjoy your company and this has greatly enriched my life. You've been loving, gentle, intimate and above all fun to be with. I believe and hope that our relationship has also bestowed on you a degree of freedom which has expanded your experiences and emotions. It has brought me to a point where I'm uncertain about my future and our future, and I need time and solitude to examine my innermost feelings. This is a new and unique experience for me and, although it may seem a somewhat negative compliment, I hope you'll accept that it's also a tribute to you.

'I also need to say something else. I cannot predict the outcome of my soul-searching but it's important that you don't feel constrained in your activities by thoughts of what might be. I feel like a stranger in an uncharted land, a land like those plotted at the margins of the known world on mediaeval maps where the cartographer simply stated "Here be dragons". But the dragons here are within me; they are not ones which threaten me from without. I'm not a believer but I see an analogy with Christian clambering up the Hill of Difficulty. I too am seeking the correct path but know that there may not be a correct path, simply a choice of acceptable paths. You've already demonstrated your individuality by following your star. There may be other stars which will transit your firmament which you might wish to follow and, if that's the case, you must do so. I suspect you too feel that you're wandering through an alien and exotic land but you have entered by a different border point and are exploring it with wonderment and pleasure. You're free in the Delectable Mountains.

'I'm being fanciful now and I should stop, but I wanted you to understand my dilemmas and not think ill of me. I would like to see you before I leave for France and there is also some unfinished business which we need to conclude with your book before I go.'

They walked on in silence for many minutes before Peter said, 'That cannot have been easy and I appreciate your openness. I too have been wondering about the nature and future of our relationship.' He smiled. 'I'm not certain that I've ever been entirely sure about its exact nature. And no, I would not, and could not, think ill of you. I think, if I'm honest, that the general thrust of what you've said doesn't come as a great surprise although the details tell me so much more about you. I'd always known there were depths which were off limits to me – and I'm sure that there'll always be some which will remain permanently closed to me and that is right. None of us can ever know another human fully and completely, and maybe it's good that that's the case. I think I need time to reflect too.'

'Yes, and now it's close to time for lunch. Why don't we walk back to the hotel after lunch and make ourselves comfortable in front of the blazing log fire and simply enjoy each other's company for the rest of the day, as we've done so many times in the past nine months. When I say that, it seems a remarkably short time but in other ways I feel I've known you for a lifetime, and if you were wondering about the possible implications of that last statement, they are all positive'. She stepped in front of him and held him very tightly and then whispered in his ear, 'I'm not going to seduce you out here, it's too bloody cold for that sort of thing outdoors at the end of March – but later?' She took his arm and steered him into the pub.

* * *

Peter looked at Sally as she awakened the following morning. 'I've been awake for some time just watching you. Come close, I have been reflecting.' He propped himself up on one elbow and looked down. 'I was tempted to say some things, many things, following on from what you said yesterday. One thing which does occur to me now was your analogy that I was happily exploring the Delectable Mountains!' He caressed and then kissed her breasts gently. 'That seems to be a very apt and entirely accurate analogy.'

Sally laughed. 'Now you're over-interpreting what I said! Nothing of the sort was in my mind when I drew that analogy yesterday but I'm more than happy to allow your over-fertile imagination to take control of your hands.'

'I take no responsibility for this; the words Delectable Mountains will always come to mind now when I hold you and, if I remember rightly, it's from Mount Clear in the Mountains that one can see the Celestial City.' He paused and held her for a few minutes before saying more seriously, 'Like you, I've been rehearsing my words and I want to be sure that I don't say anything inept. Sally, you mean so much to me now and, in many ways, have become an integral part of my life. You have played a major role in freeing me from fetters of which I was scarcely aware and guiding me to a place where I can envision a life in which I feel enfranchised to exercise a wider range of choices over my future. Much of this I have gained through observing and interacting with you. The stratagems which you have adopted for defensive purposes have been challenging but at the same time liberating for me, and have led to my emancipation. I understand your need to reflect on things and know that you'll need time to do that. I also understand that you can't realistically forecast how long that process will take and it could be some time. I've learnt that it would not be helpful for me to pressurise you and what I am about to say is not a subtle, or even an unsubtle, attempt to do that. I have mapped out a course for myself which has now developed its own momentum. That course is not, however, predestined and I know there'll be opportunities to change direction and divert my energies into new endeavours. I'm not saying this very clearly but I shall be living a life dominated by a certain ambiguity until I know the outcome of your period of reflection. At the very least, until that time, my life is partially intertwined with yours.'

'I do follow and your lack of certainty parallels my own, but don't forget that you are enfranchised and thoughts of me must not be seen as a fresh set of shackles which limit your freedoms.'

'No, I've learned from you that one can (and I'm thinking of myself when I say this) have close relationships without necessarily making long-term commitments and this is one of the reasons I've felt so relaxed during the last few months. I've had choices and degrees of freedom which I have never previously had, though I now know that this is not entirely correct. The freedoms were there but I was not sufficiently percipient to recognise them and, if I had, I would probably have lacked the good sense and the confidence to take advantage of them. I'm also conscious that personal relationships must always be handled with sensitivity. As I said earlier, we can never read fully the thoughts and emotions of others and I'm quite accepting of that. The element of mystery and the unpredictability of the future which results from getting close to someone add to the pleasure of relationships, and that has been especially true with you. I didn't understand your designation of "loving friend" when you first used it but I believe I do now. It embraces everything we've shared, and our light-hearted enjoyment of each other's bodies has been a natural consequence and component of that. Now I think I should stop rambling! I'm sure you'll only welcome interruptions of your own choosing during your time in France, but I wonder if you would accept an occasional letter from me which I would send without imposing any obligation to reply?'

'Yes, that would be good and news about you and those whom I've come to know through you would be more than welcome. I'd anticipated that the two part discussion which I felt that we, or maybe just I, needed to have would be much more emotionally difficult than it has been and I'm grateful. We have shared deeply felt emotions and are still loving friends and, whatever emerges from my reflections and convoluted thinking, that will always remain a treasured memory.'

'That sounds like a valediction.'

'No, simply an au revoir'.

31

The long and tedious journey back to London on the Bank Holiday Monday was not improved by delays caused by an accident on the dual carriageway. The slow, intermittent forward movements of the traffic were further impeded by futile exercises in lane-changing by impatient drivers. They duly parted and Sally promised to have read the draft of his novel within the week. There would be a chance to meet and discuss it before she returned to France.

The following day Peter languished in bed until after nine and eventually rose. For the first time for many months he lingered over his coffee and wondered how he might fill his time now that he was temporarily freed from his self-imposed routine. Almost three months of his sabbatical year remained. He wandered listlessly around the flat and then went out to buy a newspaper. He skimmed through it but there was little that held his attention or stimulated his curiosity. The sense of resolution and purpose which had driven him to embark on his personal odyssey and the vigour and zeal with which he had pursued his vision had evaporated. They had been replaced by irresolution and doubt. All elements of his life were in a state of uncertainty and disarray. Some of the factors which would enable him to reset his compass were wholly outside his control. Questions circulated endlessly in his mind. Would his literary efforts pass muster when judged by professionals? If they did, would they have sufficient commercial impact to enable him to be a full-time author? If so, did he have a second or third or subsequent book in him? Had he simply poured everything he had into his first manuscript? Did he have a clear view of his personal future? Would it be with Sally? Could it be with Sally? Had his dalliance with Julie been of any lasting or symbolic significance? Would his current doubts in relation to his emotional life ever be replaced by the certitude which had been its hallmark previously? Might he develop an attachment to someone else or might he remain unattached, at least for the foreseeable future? If the last of these, would or could it lead to contentment? Was he prepared to return to work and settle into the often monotonous and painstaking routine of family law after this sabbatical year? Did he wish to continue living in suburban Barnes when a life in France had so many potential attractions?

It was evident that he needed to make some decisions about his future before the month was out. He felt it would be helpful to rehearse these quandaries with Michael who had invited him for supper on the Saturday. He telephoned the senior partner in his practice and made an appointment to meet him a week later to discuss his return to work. This minor administrative task completed, he continued to sit at his desk contemplatively as he moved one or two items around haphazardly on the surface. It occurred to him that it was often said that first novels were autobiographical or based on real life experience. He started to entertain the notion that a fictionalised account of his intellectual and emotional peregrinations in pursuit of his goal might provide the basis for a further novel, even if this would require him to expose his own thoughts and innermost feelings. He reflected that the events of the last year had made it possible for him to think of doing so to an extent that would have been inconceivable previously. Some of the vignettes he had composed could be incorporated into such a narrative. Stimulated by the idea, he began to draft an outline for a further work and the action of transmitting his ideas to paper rapidly developed its own momentum. It took no more than a day for his work routine to re-establish itself.

* * *

Michael opened the door to Peter as he arrived for supper. 'I know you said you'd like to use me as a sounding board this evening, as you wrestle with the self-imposed complexities of your life,' he said with a smile, 'but I hope you won't mind that I have another guest here tonight.'

Peter looked a little disappointed. 'I had been hoping for a discussion à deux.'

'I'm sure we could still do that and you may not feel too uncomfortable to have a second sounding board, particularly one who is already fairly familiar with the intricacies of your life.'

He looked puzzled. 'Have you been briefing someone about me?'

'No, I'm not the source of her information. You may have been floating through the last year on cloud nine but, she is as aware as I am, that everywhere your cloud has rested there have been considerable atmospheric disturbances. Come on through.'

He followed Michael into the flat and found Sue sitting with a glass of wine in her hand. She got up and kissed Peter. 'You may be surprised to see me here.'

'I'm responsible,' said Michael, 'and I should explain. We met on New Year's Eve, as you know, in your flat. I was very taken with Sue and the two of us talked a lot quietly that evening. Amongst other things, she told me that she was singing in a choir. I wanted to see her again so, as I used to be a chorister in the cathedral as a kid, I showed up, was auditioned and accepted. It was devious, I know, but then I am a lawyer. That sort of thing comes naturally to me and it was a means to an end. Over the last few months we've seen a lot of each other – and I'm enjoying the singing as well! You've been so preoccupied that you've clearly been unaware of the trysts taking place in the flat beneath yours!' He sat on the settee next to Sue and put his arm around her. 'I cannot remember when I was last as content as I am at present.'

'It has been wonderful for me too,' said Sue. 'This is the first time that I've felt able to be close to someone since Andrew died and it simply feels right. We both have a lot to thank you for.'

'I am surprised and was obviously blind not to have spotted Michael's, probably rather furtive, comings and goings. I'm very happy and, he's right, you probably do know as much as anyone about the intricacies of my life. His crack about my presence being associated with atmospheric disturbances has a grain of truth in it, but only a grain. I have on a number of occasions felt that I've been at the eye of a series of storms but I would point out, as scientists do, that association is not necessarily evidence of causation!'

'I'm not sure that's not simply a specious evasion.'

'You're being too hard on me. But tell me about your plans and all the developments in your lives to which I've been so blind.'

'Well, you've picked up on the most important development. You know I was short-listed for a safe seat in the north-west. Well, I missed out on that but I was contacted subsequently. They told me that I had been regarded as a strong second and would be high on the list if the candidate was ultimately unable to stand, or for another suitable seat. Realistically, that will not happen now the date of the election has been announced and is only weeks away. The best hope would be if there were to be a bye-election in the next year or two. I hope it would still be in the north-west. Sue travelled with me for the interviews and was an invaluable asset – but she is much more than that. Now, tell us what you plan to do, as your leave of absence must be nearly up.'

'I would if I could but I simply don't know at present. I'm not in a position to resolve some of my uncertainties. I've completed a draft of a novel and Sally is having a preliminary look at it with instructions to be brutally frank. It will then need to be reviewed by an agent and that all takes time. If it clears these hurdles, then there will be a question of getting it published and publicised. There are still several mountains to climb. The challenges are daunting. There are occasions when I feel I've been instructed to travel to the moon and only provided with a bicycle for the journey! I'm hoping matters will become clearer over the next few months. Of course, my sabbatical is up in ten weeks or so and I must talk seriously to my partners about returning to work. In the meantime, I've started to write another book – the process of writing is becoming a bit of an obsession. Clearly, I shall have to go back to work, even if I decide to leave permanently at a later date.'

'It sounds as if you would prefer to carve out a new career for yourself away from the partnership.'

'Yes, I think it does but I shall have to have a means of earning a crust. The judgement might be that my book is crap and that I have no real literary talent.'

'Have you thought of working part-time? The centre is always looking for lawyers and there are several who work part-time. In this day and age, there are a number of opportunities for part-time working.'

'No, but that's a good suggestion.'

'Now tell us about Sally.'

'She has been working away at her projects and we have met up most weekends. She'll be returning to France in two or three weeks' time. She says she needs a long period of solitude to work through the projects she has in hand and to resolve a number of personal issues and, to forestall your question, she tells me that I am the foremost of those.'

'And how do you feel about it?' asked Sue.

'I understand and respect her requirement to think. She is an independent woman.'

'She's certainly that but that was a very neutral response and strictly not an answer to the question I was asking.'

Peter smiled. 'I thought I wouldn't get away with that! My response was simply a lawyerly side-step. I guess my real answer to your question is that I simply don't know. She has been my lover, my friend and my mentor and the last of those has not only been in relation to my writing. She has enabled me to see the world not just through a new lens but through many different lenses. She has, I believe, made me more perceptive, more tolerant, more empathic and more analytical, and less critical of others. She herself has had a challenging life. Her twin brother died in his teens and she lost both her parents over the course of the next two or three years. She is determinedly independent and, yes, I love her dearly but am I in love? I simply don't know and I'm not sure that I have a yardstick by which to calibrate such emotions.'

'So, what next?'

'Sally must have the time she needs. She's not scared, but she is wary of involvement and commitment. She has this deep-seated concern that any relationship might also prove fragile and transient. This is a dilemma for me, as I guess it would be for any potential suitor. An excess of fervour on my part would probably raise concerns about the durability and sincerity of the underlying emotions, while too laid back an approach might imply a lack of seriousness and commitment. To answer the other part of your question, I shall probably return to work, at least for a time, but without enthusiasm. Whatever the future holds for me, this year has changed me irrevocably and, whether successful or otherwise as a writer, I can see that I shall have to re-shape my life.'

'And if Sally returns, having overcome her gremlins?'

'I guess there are several possible scenarios which may or may not involve a closer relationship. I really don't know what the outcome might be. But bring me up to date with what has been happening with Ann.'

'As you know, she left my flat late in January and is now renting one in Birmingham. She calls from time to time and sounds more at ease than she was, perhaps more than at any time that I've known her. She told me that she had wanted to come back to you but that you felt it would not work out well for either of you. I think you are right and I suspect she would agree now. I believe that the spectacle on the morning of New Year's Day, with that amazing scene of Jenny naked and wearing no more than a challenging look, had a deep impact on her.' She paused, 'But I believe she would like to keep in contact with you as a friend.'

The evening ended and as Peter rose to leave, he looked at Sue. 'I suspect that I'm wasting my time in offering you a lift home.'

She looked at him. 'Yes, I'm happy to say it would be a waste of your time!'

* * *

Sally called on the Monday morning to say that she had finished reading his draft and asked him to her flat for lunch. He arrived and greeted her with some anxiety. 'Sit down and have a glass of wine.'

'Is it that bad?'

'No, Peter, I enjoyed it. You write well, but I knew that from the vignettes you wrote when we were in France. That's not to say that it couldn't be improved, but that's true of all manuscripts. The tale you tell is a touching one and the narrative is quite compelling. I was drawn along always wanting to know what would happen next. Some of the twists in the storyline had the capacity to surprise while I felt that others didn't work quite so well. I said to you earlier I'm not a professional assessor of manuscripts nor am I a literary agent but I think it's certainly good enough to get an opinion from one. I've made some suggestions in pencil and I think it would be worth a further revision before submitting it for evaluation. I should be happy to recommend a former colleague who is an agent and that at least will ensure that it is read. Please don't take the view that my measured comments mean that I'm lukewarm about it. I enjoyed the script and do hope that you'll be successful but you know it's not easy to get published. I hope nonetheless you'll feel that your year out has yielded its own rewards even if it is never published.'

'Thank you for doing that. I'm happy to give it a try after a further revision and, in answer to your last comment, this year has indeed been a revelation. Even if ultimately I spend my days as a jobbing solicitor, I shall never regret what it has offered me and what you have offered me.'

'So how are you occupying your time before returning to the law, although I suspect that you have no great eagerness to do that?'

'No, you're right. I've been doing a number of practical

things, attempting to resolve some of the uncertainties in my life although some are outside my control. I've taken up writing again and discovered that it's habit-forming. I have also seen Michael. He has fallen for Sue in a big way and vice versa. She's a different woman now. I was just so happy to see them both together. I think this is likely to be the real thing for both of them. I've also heard from Jenny. She has asked me to join her, Stefan and Cass for a musical evening in Camden this Friday. She particularly asked that I should invite you to join us.'

'Let's do that. It fits in perfectly as I shall be going back to France on Sunday.'

32

Peter saw his senior partner and arranged to return to work on the first of July. 'You've started something now,' he was told. 'Others are indicating that they too would like to have a sabbatical. One good thing has come from it though. Grace, the locum you found, is excellent. She's looking around for other openings so I've been looking to see if we could afford to keep her on. The workload has risen and if others are planning to take leave of absence then there are good reasons for extending her appointment as an associate. Ultimately, it will all be a matter of what we can afford. I shall take that thought to the partners meeting next week and it might be helpful if you were to come along as well.' Peter agreed to do so but, prompted by what he had just heard, the idea that he might negotiate a return on a part-time basis was starting to develop in his mind.

The partners meeting went well for Peter. The discussion focused on the affordability of another solicitor and whether this could be justified on the basis of the increased workload and the enhanced fee income which it would generate. It became increasingly clear that the arguments were finely balanced and at this point Peter proposed that he work three days a week while retaining his position as a partner, with a commensurate reduction in his share of the profits. He left the room while his colleagues considered this possibility and was recalled to be informed that his proposition was accepted, subject to certain restrictions on his freedom to practise independently. He was happy to agree.

* * *

'Don't think about the future tonight – simply enjoy the present,' Sally whispered in his ear when they met to join Jenny, Stefan and Cass for the evening.

'This will be an evening of farewells,' he said sadly. 'You will be back in France in two days' time and in a few weeks, reluctantly, I shall have to abandon my sabbatical year. I've taken so much more than leave of absence from my profession. I've said farewell to many of the inhibitions and limitations that my imperfect vision allowed everyday life to impose on me. I hope I can return to the Elysian Fields I've inhabited this last year, but I'm not sure I shall be able to do so. Nor do I know whether such a path is open to a traveller on a part-time basis! I'm also not sure that I've the talent or the courage to burn my bridges comprehensively behind me. But I shall certainly continue to make nostalgic visits to the places that have been the waymarks on my journey.'

Jenny introduced Sally to Cass and Stefan. 'We have news,' said Cass. 'Stefan is about to go on tour so we have decided, very amicably, to spend some time apart. It has worked well and we have had fun, especially in France when we camped by your house, Sally, but neither of us is ready yet to make a long-term commitment.'

'Sally and I were saying just before you arrived that this was, for us, an evening of farewells. It sounds as though that may have been more prophetic than either of us imagined.'

'But why are you saying farewell? Are you parting company?'

'Yes and no. Sally needs some time alone to work and to think through her future and I'm ending a journey which has meant so much to me, as I return to the law, at least part-time. It was in many ways, most ways, more of a pilgrimage that a journey. I'm not really sure if the journey has ended or if it has only just begun. It's possible it will continue, or I might be on the threshold of another voyage or I might be going nowhere! I said to myself more than a year ago that I didn't want my life to be haunted by thoughts of what might have been. My mind is now dominated by innumerable "what ifs".'

'But does that mean that you and Sally are parting company?' asked Jenny.

'Yes, no, perhaps,' said Peter after a long pause as he looked at Sally, 'but you must ask Sally as well.'

'I think Peter's opaque and ambiguous but succinct answer sums it up. I'm sure that whatever our futures hold for us we have fashioned a bond and will continue to meet.' She slipped her hand into his. 'That is the least of my aspirations and,' she nudged Peter, 'knowing Peter's talent for accidental meetings, both coincidental and contrived, I'm sure this will continue to be the case. We were saying just before you arrived that we should enjoy the present tonight, and that is what we intend to do.'

Jenny looked from one to the other uncertainly and eventually said, 'I'm not sure what to say and I'm not sure I understand what you are saying exactly.'

'I suspect we are no clearer in our own minds than you are,' said Sally ruefully.

Jenny put her arms round both of them. 'I too have had an amazing year but the most important element of it has been new friendships. I can only say that I love you both and would be upset to lose either of you as friends. This occasion would have been complete if Sue and Michael had been here. Their presence would have been a counterbalance to the partings and farewells.'

The theme of the evening was swing and big band music. The dimly-lit room behind the pub had a raised stage and a small floor for dancing, surrounded by tables. The background music was at a volume that made conversation difficult. Sally pulled Peter close to her and locked her hands behind his neck, whispering, 'Dance with me.' She held him very tightly as they swayed to the music and he became aware she was crying soundlessly.

'What is it?' he whispered.

'I said that we should enjoy this evening and so I am, although that may not be apparent just now. I know I need my period of seclusion and quietude but I'm also fearful. Is this the beginning of the end or the end of the beginning or simply a way-station on a shared journey? I tried to explain my dilemmas to you – they remain unresolved. What I dread most is that I'll lack the courage to resolve them, that I'll be overcome by timidity. But you should dance with the others and I should compose myself. I don't want my melancholy to be transmitted to them.'

Peter led Cass to the floor. 'You seem very relaxed about your impending parting from Stefan.'

'I think it had run its course – at least for now. It was good but it never had an air of permanency. You were there at the start. It was real fun and spontaneous, but throughout it was a liaison between two free-living and independently-minded individuals.'

'And do you see your future in the longer term as a wholly independent woman?'

'I really don't know. All human relationships add to our lives and shape our progress and this one has certainly done so for me – as has knowing Jenny and you. As the poet said, "I learn by going where I have to go". Maybe one day I'll take a more programmed course through life, or maybe not and certainly not yet! I expect you think that this is simply capricious on my part!'

'Not at all now. That bewildered and unhappy man whom you first met on the bench might have done so, but not now. He has grown older and hopefully wiser.'

'Sally doesn't look like a happy lady.'

He looked over Cass's shoulder to their table and saw that Sally was being hugged by Jenny. 'No, she isn't tonight. She has some private demons to confront.'

'And are you one of those demons?'

'I don't believe so but my relationship with her may have awakened some dormant ones.'

'She needs support.'

'Yes – but she also needs to be confident that her decisions are hers and hers alone.'

They returned to the table and had a further drink before Jenny looked across at Peter. 'It's my turn now – I don't want to miss out on the dancing. Your gigolo duties are not through until you have danced with me. I'm not so sure my suggestion that we should all come together this evening was necessarily such a good one. I reckon Cass and Stefan will be fine and despite their protestations I suspect they may well link up again.'

'That sounds like an unfinished sentence.'

'It is, but that's because I simply don't know the rest of the sentence. Your Sally is a very complex person.'

'That's true but she is not my Sally – she is Sally's Sally and she always will be. That's a major part of her attraction. That's her charm but it's also a cross she has to bear. Whatever the future holds in store for her or for me or for us, she has given me so much that she will always be a part of me.'

'In a way that Ann was not?'

He paused. 'I wasn't drawing comparisons and in fact that didn't even cross my mind, but if I'm honest I have to agree you're right.'

'Peter, it's that honesty and openness, together with your willingness to venture into the unknown, which appeals to Sally and others. What you don't know is that Sally and I have met on several occasions since New Year's Eve. We have become good friends and shared many confidences. Whatever the outcome of her period of reflection, she hopes, and I hope, that we shall all remain close. I see no reason why that shouldn't be so, and I hope it's also true for you.'

'Do I have a choice?'

'No, absolutely not, and if I feel that you're backsliding, I shall speak to you very severely! I think you should take Sally home.'

* * *

They drove slowly back to Sally's flat. 'Will you stay for just one more night?'

'Again that's sound like a valediction, an adieu.'

'No,' she said sadly. 'The words just came out wrongly – I just need the comfort that only you can give me just now. I simply want to forget for tonight that I shall have to live the rest of my life in the future.'

'That sounds very melancholy.'

'No, just uncertain and perhaps somewhat fearful. Oh, those words didn't come out right either. My anxieties are simply that I cannot see clearly what that future holds nor can I specify what I would like it to hold. You've been amazingly patient and sympathetic and I've not treated you well.'

'My patience largely results from what I have learnt from you and I've been more than happy to enjoy the freedom that you have granted me.'

'Peter, I never granted you that freedom – it was yours and yours alone to take. I want you to know that whatever conclusions I reach about my future, I shall come back and talk. It's more important to me than almost anything that you should understand those conclusions. This level of vacillation on my part is most uncharacteristic and that is one of the reasons why I'm having difficulty in handling it. Jenny has been a sensitive sounding board and her non-directive and non-judgemental comments have been invaluable in helping me to focus. I'm talked out now, come to bed and just hold me close.'

* * *

Jenny called Peter during the following week and they agreed to meet for a pizza one evening. 'I was wondering how you were and whether you were pining for Sally. Have you heard from her since she left?'

'No, but then I didn't expect to – have you?'

'Yes, she wrote when she arrived in France to apologise for her tearfulness that last evening but otherwise it was a pretty non-committal letter. She also said if I saw you that I should pass the Brownings' best wishes on to you. I'm not quite sure who they are.'

'Very long-standing friends of her family who have been very kind to both of us.'

'She suggested that I might go out for a few days later this month but I don't think that I can do that.'

'Why is that?'

'Both practical and personal reasons. It would not be straightforward for me to take time away from work just now and I'm not sure that I'm in a position to offer wholly unbiased advice. Tell me what you're doing with your time now.'

'I'm putting in some time writing, which has become something of a compulsion. I'll carry on doing so even when I return to work at the beginning of July, whatever the judgement is on my first offering, but I have already had enough time to sketch out the framework of another book.'

'Would you be prepared to tell me what it will be about?'

'This time it will have elements of autobiography, and will be the tale of a middle-class man approaching middle-age who has a brainstorm and cuts loose for a year.'

'And how does this saga end?'

'I wish I knew – but at present it's a mystery!'

'Will you let me in on the mystery at some stage?'

'Of course, but I'm sure that all will become clear to all in due course!'

33

The telephone rang in the middle of May. It was the literary agent inviting Peter to meet her on Friday afternoon a couple of days later. 'I'm Connie Freedman. I was previously a journalist who worked with Sally. This has been, in a way, a poacher turned gamekeeper conversion, although I should prefer the term gatekeeper.' She offered him a coffee and looked across her desk. 'I have accelerated your script through the appraisal process – Sally can be very persuasive. I should say, first of all, that no single agent can be the sole repository of wisdom and that all judgements in this game are to an extent subjective. That said, I have, as I usually do, shared this with a colleague.'

'That sounds like the prelude to a courteous rejection.'

'No, not entirely. There is much which I found appealing in the tale you've written. It's generally well-written, it's a human story, it's touching and it has an air of authenticity about it. Sally told me that you're a solicitor by profession.' He nodded. 'I'm sure that you want me to get on with what I have to say. This has real merit although there are areas which could be improved which would require you to work with an editor but that can and should be straightforward.

Before I go on, can I ask what your future plans might be?'

He explained that he had taken leave of absence for a year and was due to return to work at the start of July but on a part-time basis. 'Are you planning to continue writing? Do you feel driven to do so?'

'Yes, and I've already started on another book. In the remaining weeks before I go back to work, I hope to have sketched out a framework and written the first few chapters.'

'Good, I was hoping you would say that and can you briefly give me an idea of the theme of the narrative?' He did so. 'That's helpful. I do have an offer to make. It may well be less than you hoped for but it's the best I can do at present. My recommendation is that we should not look for a publisher just now, but if you can provide another book and if, and it's a challenging if, that also reaches or even exceeds the literary merit of your first script, then I think there would be a reasonable chance that a publisher might offer you a two-book deal. I can, of course, make no promises and what I say is simply advisory. You're free to approach others who may view this differently. The world is a difficult place for debut authors. I add that not to discourage you or deter you from speaking to others but simply so that you go into this with your eyes fully open. But if you have the drive and ambition to go ahead then I would urge you to go for it – and I hope that you will.'

He laughed. 'This is such an alien environment for me that I am amazed. I thought the most likely outcome would be failure and probably abject failure, so what you say is extraordinarily encouraging. I'm happy to trust your judgement.'

'In that case, it would be helpful to me if you could keep me in touch with progress periodically – say every three or four months – and perhaps we could meet again early in 1971. I shall summarise my advice to you in writing.'

* * *

Peter made his way back to the flat elated that his efforts had met with a modest level of approbation. He felt the need to share his pleasure and stopped at Sue's flat on the way up to his own to see if she and Michael might be free for dinner that evening. She said that they would but added cryptically that it might be better if he were to return to his own flat before making any firm commitments for the evening. Puzzled by this enigmatic piece of advice, he climbed the stairs to the floor above. He was immediately aware that there was someone in the flat, evoking memories of the occasion six months earlier when Ann had returned after the break-up of her relationship with Francis. Once again noises were emanating from the kitchen. He went through to find Sally making tea.

'What are you doing here?' he said in surprise and then hastily added, 'It's good to see you.'

'I asked Sue to let me in. We both thought that you wouldn't object.'

'Not at all, but when did you get back from France?'

'Earlier today. I came straight here from the airport as I wanted to see you.'

He walked over and kissed her. 'Let's go into the lounge and have our tea. I have something to tell you.'

'I know. Connie called me to say that she was seeing you today although, very properly and professionally, she did not tell me what she was going to say. I just wanted to be here to celebrate or commiserate with you as appropriate. So which is it?'

He recounted the content of his discussion with Connie and concluded, 'The message was neither one of gloom and despondency nor was it one which evoked unrestrained ecstasy but it was closer to the latter than the former. Even if nothing comes of it, ultimately I have learned something of myself in the last year.'

'That is impressive and don't underplay the achievement. It's a tough world out there for a debut author, as I've already discovered for myself. I'm absolutely delighted.' She hugged him. 'I really could not be more pleased.'

'I spoke to Sue on the way up, before I knew that you were here, to ask if she and Michael were free for dinner this evening and they are, but it should also include you. I suspect she has already made the assumption that it would be the four of us.'

'Can we decide that a little later? I wanted to talk to you and this will be much more difficult.'

'I suspect I can sense what is coming.'

'Probably, but you have been, and are, so important to me that I want you to understand. I have been in a state of ferment for the last few weeks and all the questions and uncertainties that I revealed to you over Easter have been at the forefront of my mind. I have been over and over all aspects of our relationship. I have relentlessly sought comfort from Jonny and Tilly who have been the most understanding and stalwart of friends.' She took his hand and turned to look directly at him before continuing. 'Peter, you have come closer to me than any man has ever done but I am still unable wholly to suppress my demons. When I shall or whether I ever will remains to be seen. I hope that at some stage I do succeed; this state of turmoil is painful. The next thing I'm going to say is entirely selfish but I'm going to say it. It would be wonderful for me if we could continue to be loving and intimate friends. I'm simply scared that if I offer more I shall disappoint you and myself. I even wonder at times if I'm intrinsically incapable of making an unconditional commitment to anyone. I hope that's not the case and it may simply be a matter of time before I'm able to do so. But I believe you're capable of doing so and thus I am absolutely emphatic that you should not feel what I have said places any obligation on you. As I hear my own voice, I know that what I say sounds appallingly manipulative and self-centred. It takes no account of your feelings or how these might have evolved over the last year or even the last month.'

He sat forward on the settee, with his head in his hands. She knelt on the floor in front of him, taking both his hands in hers and nothing was said for several minutes. 'Peter, I have monopolised you and the discussion and have taken very little account of your feelings. It would be helpful to me if you were to talk and react, but in saying that it sounds as if I'm seeking a particular response from you and, implicitly, I'm asking you to meet my needs and accept my conditions but I know that these may not chime with your own. If you want me to go, you must say so and if you want to spend the evening on your own or on your own with Sue and Michael, you should do that.'

'I don't quite know what to say and anything that I do say now is likely to be confused and incomprehensible.' He thought for a few minutes. 'When I was dancing with Cass last month, she was talking about her parting from Stefan. She quoted a line of poetry to me saying, "I learn by going where I have to go". It struck a chord with me and has haunted me ever since. It has in many ways been my leitmotiv for much of the last year but it has also made me recognise that there are circumstances when the route which one identifies and wishes to follow is barred.' He paused. 'No, maybe that's too strong. Possibly it's just littered with obstacles. The only courses open then are to change course and circumvent the obstructions or readjust the compass and head off on another bearing entirely. I'm not sure which is the right route for me and, deep down, I continue to feel that I must continue to "learn by going where I have to go". One question I need to address is whether there's an intrinsic deep-seated need in me to make an unconditional commitment to another and if not now, when. It seems curious. When we first met on that cliff top you appeared to me to be so carefree and independent and I saw myself as the one constrained by convention and middle-class angst and expectations. At the end of that first week in France, when we first made love, I knew with absolute clarity exactly what I wanted but now I cannot be so sure. I have accepted the role of loving friend and have absolutely no wish to resign from that position. But it seems that whilst I have been adjusting to a new and liberating situation, your comportment has changed and elements of a previously concealed persona are emerging from behind a mask. I seem to be, in part, responsible for unmasking and resuscitating some dormant demons, which has been a painful process for you. At the same time, I've shed many of my inhibitions but whether this is simply a temporary emergence from my shadows or whether it's permanent, I cannot say.'

'Peter, I can't judge the last but your analysis of my position is uncomfortably perceptive and, irrespective of where our futures might lead us, this year will always remain a treasured memory for me. I think I should go now.'

'That's not necessary and I should be sad if you were to leave now.'

'Maybe – but it would be better and it would be good for you to be with friends. I shall be going back to France in a week or so and have various things to do while I'm here – but please remember that you are a free agent and I have no right to make any claims on you.'

'Sally, Michael and Sue are not simply my friends; they are our friends and remember, I have a modest triumph to celebrate to which you have made a significant contribution. If you were to leave now I should be very sorry and very aware that there is a great void in my life, even if the exact dimensions of that void are not known to me at present.'

* * *

At the end of the evening, she kissed Peter and said, 'I don't know when or if we shall meet again but you know very well how to find me. I think it would be right to say "sayonara".

As I understand it, it has a sense of destiny about it, meaning "it must be thus". It doesn't presage a return, like au revoir, but neither does it overtly deny such a possibility. It doesn't offer a benediction, like farewell, nor does it have the finality of goodbye or adieu. We must just pause for a time to see what our destinies might reveal to us.'

* * *

Peter found it difficult to settle to anything over the next week and filled his time in trivial displacement activities. He called Sally's flat several times but there was no reply. The May Bank Holiday weekend was approaching and he felt a pressing need to escape from the confines of his flat and London.

Following a restless night, and on a whim, on the Sunday he drove to Newcastle and checked into the hotel where he had stayed the previous year. The compulsion to return to Dunstanburgh and recall the start of his odyssey was overwhelming. He drove slowly to Craster the following day, as he had done nearly two years before. The warm, cloudy and oppressive weather matched his mood as he walked along the coast to the castle. Sitting in a secluded corner of the ruins, he was quickly lost in thought. The repetitive thunder of the waves striking the base of the cliff sheltered him from the ambient sounds generated by those walking through the site. This was where it had started – this had been his gateway to a future which was still uncertain, a future which was now unalterably different from the life he had foregone.

Would reflection on this spot help him to identify the next faltering steps into this future? Had he learned by going where he had to go? The learning process, initiated and driven forward by events over the previous two years, was far from complete. Would it ever be complete? Would he want it to be complete? Would he even wish to reach an endpoint, a final destination, a terminus? Had this period in his life reshaped his mindset and liberated his thinking irrevocably and, if so, where might this take him? He reflected that, if this was the case, this particular question was unanswerable. Incertitude was an immanent element of learning by going. His writing might or might not flourish. It would be judged by others but it had become a major component of his being. But this was only one component of his emancipation. There remained a void, a vital element missing, a sense of partnership which he had experienced and sampled freely but had never been able to imbibe to the full. It had been a unique and distinctive relationship which he had enjoyed and revelled in with Sally. But there had always been a barrier, literally a no-man's-land, a zone of exclusion to which he had been denied entry. He longed to see her again and once more enjoy her company, her challenges, her humour, her intellect and her body. Was this enough? His instinctual reaction was that it would not be sufficient. Would or could the relationship develop and deepen further? If not, would a freedom to establish other friendships be adequate compensation for an inability to diminish the distance between them? He could not be sure that this was so. Did he also lack the ability to make unconditional commitments? It was not clear in retrospect that he had ever done so with Ann. Was this simply a question of time, maturity and person? Would a freedom to develop other relationships diminish his ability to commit himself wholly to one in the near or more distant future? There was also Jenny, who had walked here with him a year earlier. She had become a warm, uncomplicated and understanding friend – or was she destined to become more than a friend? He thought back to the evening in France when she had suggested joining him in his bed and the memory evoked a sharp pang of desire.

He had arrived back where the odyssey had started. He was revisiting the place yet sensed he was also seeing it for the first time. It was also a different place. It was not simply a location and an environment but it was an amalgam of a physical environment imbued with actual and virtual human presences, emotions, memories and future aspirations and fears. This place was, and would forever be, full of memories and each of those in turn would generate flashbacks and remembrances of times past and possibly glimpses of times to come. Too many of these memories reflected a sense of loss or hopes and aspirations as yet unfulfilled.

He was startled out of his reverie by a voice from behind:

'We shall not cease from exploration

And the end of all our exploring

Will be to arrive where we started

And know the place for the first time'.

He turned to see Jenny standing close behind him. 'T S Eliot,' she said. 'It seemed so apt seeing you sitting in this place meditating.'

'You were in my thoughts and you have materialised

from my daydreams and, more than that, you have read my mind. How did that occur?'

'I came up to the North-East to see Mum. I tried to call you in your flat this morning as I needed to talk to you and see you. I then called Sue as there was no reply. She said that you had left early yesterday, simply saying that you would be away for a day or two. As it's a bank holiday, on a hunch I called the hotel where you stayed last year and discovered that you were indeed in Newcastle. It wasn't difficult to deduce after that that you would come here. It was clear to me last year that this place has acquired an iconic significance for you and I know you have a sentimental streak.'

'Yes, and as last year and the year before, I've been reflecting on the uncertainties in my life. The only difference is that one cohort of doubts has simply been replaced by another!' Peter looked closely at Jenny. 'I sense that this is more than simply a cliff top reunion – you said you needed to see me. You sought me out for a reason?'

'Yes, let's sit. A lot has happened since Sally left you ten days or so ago, which you should know about. She didn't go back to France as soon as she had planned. I so much wanted to contact you but it will become clear from what I am about to say why I haven't done so. I think you know that Sally and I have become close. She called me after leaving you and was in a hell of a state. I would have called you then but she expressly forbade me to do so. She needed support and I went over to her flat and stayed there until I had to leave to come north. She was cursing herself for what she had said to you and for what she described as her intellectual and emotional detachment. She worries about her inability to express her deeper feelings and it's clear to me that her passions run deep, deeper than you might ever imagine, and they are intensely felt. I didn't know where to turn for help or advice. Eventually I persuaded her to see my doctor who put her on some medication and she became considerably calmer.'

'You should have called me.'

'I wanted to but she got so upset when I suggested it that I didn't feel that I could. She wouldn't even pick up the phone when it rang as she felt unable to talk to you in the state she was in. I guess you were probably one of the more persistent callers.'

He nodded. 'Where is she now?'

'She returned to France yesterday. She asked me to give you this which she wrote just before she left.' She handed over a sealed envelope. 'I think you should read it now.'

He opened the letter.

'Dearest Peter,

This is the most difficult letter that I have ever had to write but writing seems the most straightforward way of communicating with you after our many lengthy and difficult conversations over the last few months. They have been painful and challenging for me and also, I suspect, for you. I felt so rotten after I left you the other day that I delayed my return to France and rang Jenny. She is an amazing friend. She came to stay with me. I needed both her shoulders to cry on and she generously made them available. I felt that I had been a fool and that I might never see you again. Saying sayonara implied that I saw my destiny as being determined *by the lottery of life rather than by choice. I have cursed myself again and again for my blindness and my feigned intellectual and emotional detachment. We have shared so much joyfully, companionably and lovingly and I have not treated you well. It is for you to choose if you wish to see me again, as a friend or a loving friend, but I find I cannot just walk out of your life unless that is your express wish and I hope that you will not decide to walk out of mine. Ultimately, the next steps are a matter for you to decide – or even whether there are to be any further steps. I might wish it otherwise but I know that any plans for your future must now be left in your hands.*

I shall be back in France by the time Jenny is able to pass this on to you. You know you are welcome here at any time.

With my love as always, my loving friend
Sally'

Peter sat with the letter in his hand for many moments and then looked up at Jenny.

'You look bewildered,' she said.

'I think that's because I am.' He hesitated. 'Do you know what Sally wrote in that letter?'

'No, of course not. All I do know is that she's one hell of a confused lady and that her feelings for you run very, very deep. It looks as if it has disturbed you. Do I have one hell of a confused man on my hands as well? Do you wish to share whatever it is with me?'

'I think you should read the letter for yourself.'

She sat on the stones and read and then re-read the letter. Finally she looked up and asked, 'What do you plan to do?'

'I'm not sure what to read into that letter – reading

between the lines has never been my strongest suit. Whatever my response and whatever I do, it places a heavy responsibility on me. I certainly have no wish to walk out of Sally's life but I just can't foresee if and how my relationship with her will or should develop.'

'Peter, I can only repeat that Sally's feelings for you run very, very deep. I cannot determine what you should do – that has to be down to you. As she says, how your relationship develops is largely in your hands. I sense that there is still a disturbed and confused lady behind the words in that letter. She has bestowed many gifts on you – I don't say that to place a burden or an obligation on you – and you also should not underestimate what you have given her. She has made as strong a commitment to you as her history and her emotions will permit. Sally's right; any further steps, or at least the next steps, must be down to you.'

'Jenny, I'm very confused and anxious. My first instinct is to leap into my car and drive to the Dordogne. But I'm also fearful – will I cause more confusion and distress in her mind, and, perhaps also in mine, although that is far less important? If I were to re-enter her life or if I were to exit her world, would I simply reinforce her presumptions that relationships which touch her are doomed to be transitory and evanescent?'

'Peter, I really can't answer those questions, pertinent though they may be. I simply don't know the answers to them. In fact, they are unanswerable.'

'My instincts tell me, urge me, to go to France. Five weeks of my sabbatical year still remain. I cannot simply walk out of Sally's life – I need to see her.' He thought for a moment and looked across at Jenny. 'Would you be able to come with me? It's clear that she trusts you as a friend and confidante,' he paused and added, 'as do I.'

'Sally suggested before she left that I might go out for a few days in June but I said I wasn't sure I'd be able to do so. It would not be straightforward to take time away from work just now and I'm not sure I'm necessarily the best person to dispense advice. I feel that I would just be in the way.'

'I have no ambitions to offer advice to Sally – I simply want to provide support and, without wishing to put you under pressure, I am sure your support would be invaluable to both of us.'

After a few moments Jenny said cautiously and hesitantly, 'Alright, I'll see if I can arrange to have some time off. I too am worried. Do you think we should let her know we're coming and run the risk of rejection or should we just arrive unannounced?'

'I think we should let her know – I'll drop her a note as soon as you've been able to fix a date when you can have some time off work.'

34

Peter posted a card to Sally simply saying that he and Jenny would be coming to Sarlat and planned to arrive late in the afternoon of 12 June.

The drive south evoked vivid memories of the journey which he had made the previous year. On that occasion, he had been exhilarated by a sense of release and adventure but now he was more reflective, more uncertain and more anxious. So much had occurred since then and during the preceding twelve months. They spoke little during the journey, each preoccupied with their own thoughts. They reached Souillac and turned westwards along the well-remembered road by the river, the late afternoon sun irradiating the houses and throwing their reflections onto the luminous water. They left the river and headed towards Sarlat and Sally's house. The house was locked and her car was not in the driveway. It was evident she was not at home.

Jenny looked at Peter and asked, 'Did you tell her when we would be arriving?'

'I didn't give an exact time, I only said we would arrive late in the afternoon. I didn't receive a reply, but I only wrote a few days ago when we knew that you'd be able to take time away from work. She'll have just gone into Sarlat and will be back soon, I expect. Let's sit on the terrace and enjoy the sun.' They sat there for an hour or so, relaxing and dozing in the early evening sun. Finally Peter said, 'I guess it's possible that she has gone away for a day or two and not received my card. We should go and see the Brownings. They'll know if she is away and they also have a key to the house.'

They drove the few miles to the Brownings' hotel and rang the bell at reception. Tilly came down a few minutes later. She put her arms around him. 'Peter, thank God you're here. We've been trying to reach you at your flat in London. You've obviously heard the news – I am so sorry.'

Peter looked at her, his heart sinking. 'Tilly, what are you saying? I've heard no news of Sally for a fortnight or so.'

Tilly stood back and looked directly at him with her hands on his shoulders. 'Oh God, Peter – come up to our lounge.' She looked across at Jenny, 'And you too, please come up. Did you come with Peter?'

Tilly led them up to their private quarters. Peter introduced Jenny and explained that they had both come to see Sally as they had been concerned about her. 'Oh God, I'm so sorry – you don't know.' She went across and put her arms around him again. 'There's no easy way to say this. Sally's car left the road two days ago and struck a tree full on. Peter, she's dead. No-one knows exactly what happened.'

Peter looked at her silently, uncomprehendingly. Eventually he said, 'How could this have happened?'

'We really don't know. Nobody knows. It was early in the morning, very early, and it was a clear dry day. She was on a fairly straight stretch of road and nobody saw it happen.

There were no other cars around. As we understand it, there was no mechanical problem with the car but it is still being examined.' Peter fell back into a chair, his head in his hands. Tilly crouched and put her arms round him. Jenny, also in tears, knelt beside the chair and put her head on Peter's arms.

They remained like that for some minutes. Eventually Peter said haltingly, 'Where is she now? I should like to see her.'

'The police came to us as they found our names in the address section in her diary. Jonny went to identify her formally – he said she looked very peaceful.' She paused. 'I'm sure they will allow you to see her, if that is what you want to do. It would probably be a good idea for one of us to go with you. It will help with the language and access. We could perhaps do that on Monday after the weekend is over.'

'What do you think, what do they think might have happened?' asked Peter apprehensively.

'We really don't know – she might have been distracted by an animal running out or I suppose she might have fallen asleep at the wheel or it may be there was something wrong with the car – even something as commonplace as a sudden blow-out of a tyre. It does happen.'

'The alternative is too awful to contemplate. But had you seen her since she came back to France two or three weeks ago?'

'Yes, several times. She came over for a meal about a week ago. She seemed to be more relaxed than when she was here in May but, as you know, Sally can, oh God, could be very reserved.'

'I stayed in her flat for a week just before she came back to France,' said Jenny. 'At the end of that week she was in a considerably better place than she had been earlier but she was still quite disturbed.'

'She told us you'd been staying with her and what a wonderful friend you'd been. Peter, we just didn't know what to do – we knew that we had to contact you – she didn't have any close family, as you know. She was not in touch with her father's younger brother and it's quite possible that he's no longer alive. There was no-one with the name Dunham in her address book. We simply weren't sure whom else we should contact – all the other names were unfamiliar to us. Many were clearly professional contacts from the addresses and then there were a number of names with private addresses but none of them meant anything to us. Will you look at it as well, Peter?'

'I will but I'm not sure I'll be able to add anything much. Sally's life was very compartmentalised. The only other people I can think of might be the family in Norfolk with whom she used to spend Christmas. I'm not sure of their name but it might be possible to identify them from their address. They've known Sally for some years. Could we talk more about this tomorrow? I just need to go outside for a while to try to take this in.'

'Would you like me to come with you?' asked Jenny tentatively.

'I'm not sure – yes, it might be helpful but I'm not sure how much I want to talk – if at all.'

'That's alright.'

Peter looked over at Tilly. 'Do you mind if we just go and walk quietly somewhere in the grounds?'

'No, of course not. I'm just desperately sorry to be the

bearer of such awful news. Take as much time as you want. We have two spare rooms here in our flat – I think it might be best for you to stay here for the moment. We can go over to Sally's tomorrow as we have a key and you can decide what you want to do, and what we need to do, after that. You are more than welcome to stay here.'

Jenny put her arm round Peter as he walked slowly and silently to the edge of the pines which lay behind the château. He sat on a bench with his head in his hands – mute and uncomprehending. Eventually he turned and said, 'Jenny, what have I done? I can't believe this – I don't want to believe it. But it's true. I've failed her and it has all followed from my immature wish to follow my fantasy and become a writer. I've killed her.'

'Peter, don't say that. You can't be held responsible – we don't even know what happened for sure and quite possibly never shall. Remember, I spent a week in Sally's flat at the end of last month and we talked endlessly. I know that she had worried in the past that her fate might be the same as her father's but that did not arise while we were together. Her main concerns were that she should make things right with you and that the two of you should remain close, very close. They were very positive thoughts.'

'I should have come out here straightaway after we met in Northumberland. I should not have delayed. Everything would have been different had I done so.'

Jenny shifted uncomfortably, aware that the delay in Peter's departure for France was due to the time it had taken for her to arrange leave from work. Eventually she said, 'No-one could have known that this would happen.'

'But I should have called – I should not simply have sent her a card. I only did that because I had a postcard of Dunstanburgh Castle and I knew that would strike a chord with her. Even if I couldn't let her know immediately after the bank holiday when we would be coming, I should have rung to let her know that we were planning to be with her in June.'

'Oh Peter, you could not have known what was to happen – nobody could have foreseen this.'

'Is that really true – can it be true? Would this have happened if our paths had not crossed?'

'Peter, I can't answer "what ifs". Nobody can. They are unanswerable.'

'There is so much more that I might have done. I should not have let her go last month.'

'I don't think you could have stopped her. It was Sally's decision that she needed time – it was her choice. I know that from the long evenings we spent together before the bank holiday weekend when we talked endlessly about her life and her hopes for the future. I know she was thinking positively when she left and that you were central to all her positive thoughts.'

'But I could have done more – phone calls or I could have written. I should have written.'

'Peter, I'm quite sure if Sally could communicate with you now, with us, she would say continue living, follow your stars and dreams. We may both have to live with a sense of inadequacy, even if it's not justified. And we'll never know if it's justified or not. Either way, we have to live through a time of intense sadness – we have lost a remarkable friend.' Jenny looked up to see someone coming towards them. 'Peter, someone's coming over – could this be Tilly's husband?'

Jonny came close. 'I don't want to intrude but I just came to say how sorry I am that Sally has gone and how terrible it must have been for you to learn of the accident in this way. Like you, we cannot come to terms with it. It's so final.' Peter nodded. 'She seemed somehow more content when we saw her last week than she had been a month or so earlier when she discussed her emotional turmoil with us. You must both stay here with us for the next few days. I'll take you over to see her on Monday if that is still what you want to do.'

'Yes, I do, but what happens after that?'

Jonny sat beside them. 'I understand there will be a post-mortem as it was an accidental death and I assume some sort of an inquest. We're not sure how these things are done in France.' He paused. 'This might not be the best time to discuss this but we need to think what to do after tomorrow. As far as we know, Sally had no close relatives. Someone needs to take steps towards finding out if she does and for organising her funeral. I think it will probably have to be the four of us.' Peter nodded. 'We should also go over to the house and make sure that all is well there. There is never going to be a good time to discuss these things but it might help us all if we were to have practical things to do.' Peter nodded again. 'We simply have no idea what Sally's wishes might have been.'

* * *

The following days passed almost as if detached from a reality that none of them wished to acknowledge. The sense of finality was too overwhelming to comprehend fully. Peter and Jenny went over to Sally's house. They collected the mail from the box. It included the card he had sent. She had not seen it. Peter cursed himself again and again for his failure to telephone. It was simply a whimsical and romantic act which had led him to post an image of Dunstanburgh to Sally. He could not free himself from the thought that possibly she had deliberately driven the car off the road. It was not possible to envisage what thoughts might have colonised and filled her mind, and what feelings of despair might have driven her to her death. Jenny, Tilly and Jonny reassured him endlessly that it was most likely to have been a tragic if inexplicable accident, but it was impossible to dispel the sense of melancholy and guilt which overcame him.

Jenny searched through Sally's address book and found the names of David and Jane Straker in Norfolk. Peter called them hesitantly, explaining who he was, and was surprised when they immediately responded by saying that they knew that he was Sally's lover. He choked and was unable to continue for a few moments before he could tell them of Sally's death. There was a stunned silence before they asked what they could do to help. Peter was relieved to receive the offer of help and they agreed to take steps towards organising the funeral once the legal formalities had been completed. They confirmed that Sally had no immediate relatives and they believed that the uncle in Canada had died a few years earlier. Peter then called Michael who agreed to arrange the repatriation of Sally's body to England, after the police investigation had been completed and the Procureur had issued the burial permit.

* * *

Peter reflected as he listened, once more, to the melancholy and dispiriting words of the Anglican funeral service that his odyssey had been framed by two accidental deaths. Andrew's challenges had provided the stimulus that had initiated his journey. Sally had been his companion, mentor and lover who had given him the assurance to pursue his aspirations and to reshape his life in so many ways. He was close to despair at the thought that this was a journey he would have to continue alone, yet it was not a journey he could or should abandon. Among Sally's innumerable gifts to him was this enduring legacy, a legacy more valuable than any tangible item, a legacy too valuable to squander. He knew that he had more to learn by going, with no certainty about a final destination, but go he must.

35

Nearly a year had passed since Sally's death. Jonny and Tilly had invited Peter and Jenny to the Dordogne to mark the anniversary. Jenny had suggested going to Dunstanburgh over the May Bank Holiday weekend beforehand, which they agreed would be a fitting prelude to their trip to France. They parked the car once more in Craster and the smell of kippers instantly triggered memories for Peter. They walked silently and slowly along the coastal path to the castle and then very slowly to the cliff edge. Jenny took his hand and said quietly, 'This place was so important for Sally and you, and it has also become so for me. I feel that today is a day of pilgrimage and that this, in a sense, is a shrine to her memory. She has given both of us so much.'

They stood looking down as the waves struck the base of the cliff, throwing diaphanous plumes of spray of infinite variety into the air. The thunderous noise as each successive wave cannoned into the rocks below sheltered and isolated them from their surroundings. Peter looked at Jenny. 'It was a good idea to come here. We're standing on almost the exact spot where I first saw Sally three years ago.' He pointed. 'I was resting on the grass just over there.

It's somewhat ironic that my first concern was that she was contemplating suicide, although it became clear that nothing could have been further from her mind at that time.'

Jenny looked at him and said gently, 'And we don't know that it was ever at the forefront of her mind. I know, as you do, that one of her demons was the thought that her father's fate might also be a portent of her own destiny. But during the week that I spent in her flat last year, she was certainly agitated and anxious but never once did it appear that she was in any way suicidal. Through her agitation, she had hopes for a positive future – and a positive future in which you would be not only a major part but the major part.'

'I still find it difficult to get the thought out of my mind that she might have ended her own life.'

'Peter, we can never know exactly what happened that morning but there is one thing of which I am absolutely certain. Sally would never have wanted to generate demons in your mind.' They walked up the slope and sat by the walls of the castle.

'You're right. I was struck by what you said just now that this journey is in a sense a pilgrimage. This place has been so important to us – perhaps we should come here every year. I've never been able to decide what should be done with Sally's ashes – perhaps we should scatter them here. So many key events seem to have happened during the last three years, since that first meeting.' He looked at Jenny. 'And you've been the most wonderful and supportive friend to me throughout, as you were to Sally. I'm so glad that you are coming with me to Sarlat next month.'

* * *

It was a long drive to Sarlat and Peter and Jenny arrived at the house late in the morning at the start of the second week in June. Tilly and Jonny had bought some basic provisions for them and left a note saying they hoped that they would join them for dinner at the château at the end of the week. Peter walked round the house opening the shutters and, as he did so, the bright midday sun flooded in. Wandering through the rooms, he recalled the last time he and Jenny had been here nearly a year ago when, with the help of Jonny and Tilly, they had performed the melancholy tasks of sorting Sally's possessions and arranging for them to be repatriated to England. He walked back into his room in the house and stood by the window. The view was as he remembered it with the meadow stretching down to the pines in the valley below, the mauves and pinks of the wild flowers amongst the meadow grass and the spasmodic movements of the lizards on the wall. He smiled as he recalled the mystical moment when he had awakened that first morning in this room. It had been and remained a scene of unparalleled beauty and serenity. He turned and walked out onto the terrace where Jenny had laid out the baguette, cheese, pâté and wine that they had bought for their lunch. He walked to the edge of the paved area and looked towards the woods which lay between the house and the town. Tears filled his eyes as the memories engulfed him. Jenny remained silent.

Finally, he walked across to the table and sat down, looking at Jenny as she silently handed him a glass of wine. He began to talk haltingly. 'You know, in some ways, many ways, I was dreading coming back to the house here. I was just not sure what memories it would evoke nor how I would feel. I thought that Sally's presence would overshadow every moment that I spend here and so it does, but not in the way that I had feared. I can certainly sense her presence but it's a benign presence, a caring presence, a benevolent presence. I can understand why this place provided her with such a degree of peace which she found difficult to find elsewhere, despite its memories for her. This place has retained its magic in a way I never thought would be possible. I think it also helps to allay some of the concerns I've had about the nature of her death. It has been one of the most important way-stations for me during the last three years. My times with Sally are too important to forget or suppress.' Jenny laid a hand on his arm. Peter continued, 'We're here for a week and I'd been wondering what we might do during that time. We should certainly accept the Brownings' invitation to dinner but I should also like to re-visit the local places which Sally and I used to frequent – Sarlat, "our" beach by the river, the walks we took, Beynac, Domme.'

'Would you prefer to do that on your own?'

'No, if you would like to, then I should very much like you to come with me. You too became close to her and were a good friend. I feel I want to share my memories of Sally with you and I know that you'll understand if at times I'm tearful, but I don't want to forget. I want to remember positively. Perhaps you'll share some of your memories with me? I guess you have some of this area too from the time you spent here with Stefan and Cass. There are not many emotions that I haven't shared with you over the last year –

and that goes back to our first visit to Dunstanburgh nearly two years ago now.'

* * *

'I think that we should drink to Sally,' said Jonny on the Saturday evening. 'She was a remarkable woman who not only touched but also changed all our lives.' They were sitting round the dinner table in the Brownings apartment in the château. 'It is one year ago today that she died. We'll never know exactly why or how it happened but it's much more important to cherish the memory of her and the times when we enjoyed her company.' They raised their glasses.

'Tell us what you've been up to this week,' said Tilly. 'We are so pleased that you've come back and that you're here with us this evening.'

'I have to admit that I was very apprehensive about coming back,' said Peter, 'but in many ways it has been a good week, although naturally tinged with sadness. I had thought that to return to a place which had become such a symbol of so much important change in my life would be unbearably painful after what happened, but it has not been so. It's true it has been painful at times but it has also been a good week. Sally and I shared so much while I was here. I, we, have visited places which I got to know so well, evoking memories of the times that Sally and I spent together, and these have been good memories – ones to treasure. Visiting them has helped lay some ghosts to rest.'

'We are so pleased about that,' said Jonny. 'We were wondering what you intended to do with the house.'

'I was totally taken aback, when Sally's will was found in the flat in London, to find that codicil leaving the house in France to me. I couldn't believe it. My first reaction, particularly remembering the sad time we had spent sorting out her effects, was to come back this summer and put it on the market but now I no longer want to do that. I want to keep it and to come here as frequently as possible. My times here have become an intrinsic part of my life. I don't want to lose that – this place is too precious to me now.'

Tilly looked at him. 'You have no idea how happy that makes us. We were so concerned for you when you left last summer to go back to England for Sally's funeral. We would have understood it if you had decided to sell the house, but you provide a link to Sally whom we looked on as a surrogate daughter and that would have been severed if you had decided to sell. Sally loved you dearly and I am quite certain that her death was a tragic, if unexplained, accident. She made her feelings for you very clear the last time we saw her. I cannot believe that she would have ended her own life – that love was simply too important to her. I'm sorry,' she added as Peter's eyes filled with tears. 'I didn't mean to upset you.'

'No, it's alright,' said Peter. 'I do want to be able to talk about her. She was so important to me. I don't wish to expunge memories nor do I wish to make it difficult for myself or for others to talk about her. And you and Jenny provide a tangible link to Sally – and that is one I never want to lose.'

'We are also happy that you're thinking of coming back here regularly,' added Jonny. 'Having got to know you well now, we're beginning to look on you as part of our extended family. But tell us – what are your plans and how's the writing going?'

'Quite well, I think. I've completed a second book. I seem to have struck a reasonable balance between working part-time and writing. The first two books are now with the agent and they're going to be published.'

'That's great news! Will you now become a full-time author?'

Peter laughed. 'It's not as straightforward as that. I need to have confidence that I have further books in me. Each time I've finished a book, I've been left with the feeling that I've shot my bolt and offered up everything I have in me. There's also a small question of income. Most novelists don't become seriously rich or even moderately rich! I shall continue as I am for at least a few more years. I should love to reach the stage where I could give up the law and spend half of each year here in France, but that is a bit of a pipe dream at present.'

Tilly looked enquiringly at Jenny. 'We know from the many hours we spent talking to Sally last spring how much she had relied on your friendship and support. What does the future hold for you?'

Jenny smiled. 'I wish I knew,' she hesitated, 'or perhaps I don't. These last two years have been momentous for me as well. I hope that regular time in France may be a feature of my future, but what will be will be!'

* * *

Peter drove slowly back to the house after dinner and as they entered the lounge, he said, 'I know it's late, but would you be prepared to sit and have a drink with me before we go to bed? I just feel the need to think and talk. This week has been so full of memories, which have been enhanced by our conversations at the Brownings. They are such generous and open-hearted friends. I wouldn't like to lose them,' he paused, 'and Tilly's gentle probings are always thought-provoking!'

'I'll get us both a brandy,' said Jenny. 'Talk, or sit silently if you prefer it – I'm equally happy either way. Like you, I feel this week has also reconciled me to the events of last year, to a much greater extent than I'd ever thought possible.' She smiled. 'And I shall mellow further with a brandy!'

They sat for many minutes in silence, cradling their drinks. Peter finally broke into their private reveries and said, 'I'm so glad we have visited the places that Sally and I felt were special to us, and it seemed absolutely right that you should share them as well. Then there was our visit to Domme, which brought back memories of that magical evening with you and Cass and Stefan, talking of whom, I think we need some music.' Peter got up from his chair and selected a record from the shelves and placed it on the turntable. The soft and alluring sounds of Elgar's Salut d'Amour filled the room. After a few moments, he turned and looked across at Jenny who had put her glass down and whose eyes were filling with tears. 'I'm so sorry,' he said. 'I should have realised that this might revive difficult emotions for you. It just seemed appropriate – I'll take it off.'

'No, don't do that,' she said, half tearfully and half smilingly. 'It certainly brings back memories but they are ones that I want to keep fresh in my mind.'

Peter walked over to the chair where she was sitting and

took both her hands, pulling her gently to her feet. He put his arms around her. 'Jenny, I don't quite know how to say this. We have shared so much over these last two years – it seems as if we've had a lifetime of experiences over that time. Some of those have been immensely happy and some extremely sad, but we've shared them, as well as our thoughts and emotions. You've been Sally's confidante and you've been my confidante. I feel we have become loving friends in all senses but one.' He paused. 'Do you remember that evening when you suggested you might join me to give Cass and Stefan some space and privacy? So many memories of the last three years have flooded back into my mind this week, including that magical evening in Domme. You have no idea how close I came to taking you into my bed that night!'

She giggled. 'I was rather presumptuous, wasn't I? But it just seemed that it would have been the most wonderful and natural way to end the evening.'

'Yes, and so it would have been, but I'm wondering now if that offer is still open? It would enable us to seal our loving friendship!'

'Yes, Peter, it is.'

He hugged her and continued, 'Our week here has helped to clarify my thinking and there's something else I need to ask you. Jenny, it has taken me a long time to recognise what an intrinsic part of my life you have become. I don't know where our loving friendship will take us but, if nothing else, these last few years have taught me to take risks with my life and I have this overwhelming desire to take a risk with you – would you be up for it?'

'Peter, you don't even have to ask.'

What might have been is an abstraction
Remaining a perpetual possibility
Only in a world of speculation.
What might have been and what has been
Point to one end, which is always present.

Literary References in the Text

Chapter 7

'Men make their own history, but they do not make it as they please; they do not make it under self-selected circumstances, but under circumstances existing already, given and transmitted from the past'.

18th Brumaire of Louis Bonaparte – Karl Marx

Chapter 29

'The past is but the beginning of a beginning, and that all that is and has been is but the twilight of the dawn'.

The Discovery of the Future - HG Wells

Chapter 30

References to Christian, the Hill of Difficulty, the Delectable Mountains and the Celestial City.

The Pilgrim's Progress – John Bunyan

Chapter 32

'I learn by going where I have to go'.

The Waking – Theodore Roethke

Chapter 33

We shall not cease from exploration
And the end of all our exploring
Will be to arrive where we started
And know the place for the first time

Little Gidding – Four Quartets –TS Eliot

Chapter 35

What might have been is an abstraction
Remaining a perpetual possibility
Only in a world of speculation.
What might have been and what has been
Point to one end, which is always present.

Burnt Norton – Four Quartets – TS Eliot